T0278380

Marta's Notebooks

Marta's Notebooks

Talila Kosh Wollner

CHERRY ORCHARD BOOKS

2024

Library of Congress Cataloging-in-Publication Data

Names: Kosh Wollner, Talila, 1949- author. | Meerschwam, Mirjam Hadar, translator.

Title: Marta's notebooks / Talila Kosh Wollner ; translated by Mirjam Meerschwam Hadar.

Other titles: Maḥbarot shel Martah. English

Description: Boston : Cherry Orchard Books, 2024.

Identifiers: LCCN 2024020757 (print) | LCCN 2024020758 (ebook) | ISBN 9798887195971 (hardback) | ISBN 9798887195988 (paperback) | ISBN 9798887195995 (adobe pdf) | ISBN 9798887196008 (epub)

Subjects: LCSH: Wollner, Martah. | Holocaust survivors--Psychology--Fiction. | Physician and patient--Fiction. | Holocaust, Jewish (1939–1945)--Hungary--Personal narratives. | Holocaust, Jewish (1939–1945)--Slovakia--Personal narratives. | LCGFT: Biographical fiction. | Novels.

Classification: LCC PJ5055.51.O3698 M3413 2024 (print) | LCC PJ5055.51.O3698 (ebook) | DDC 892.43/7--dc23/eng/20240525

LC record available at https://lccn.loc.gov/2024020757
LC ebook record available at https://lccn.loc.gov/2024020758

Copyright © 2024, Academic Studies Press
All rights reserved.

ISBN 9798887195971 (hardback)
ISBN 9798887195988 (paperback)
ISBN 9798887195995 (adobe pdf)
ISBN 9798887196008 (epub)

Book design by Kryon Publishing Services.
Cover design by Ivan Grave.

Published by Cherry Orchard Books, an imprint of Academic Studies Press
1577 Beacon Street
Brookline, MA 02446, USA
press@academicstudiespress.com
www.academicstudiespress.com

To Gal, to Alma

Contents

Note to Reader

This book combines fiction and non-fiction. The Notebooks section of this work is in its entirety a memoir written by Marta Wollner. The memoir and other fragments of Marta Wollner's writing in the book are in a different font.

Part One

MARTA

Winter

Though her Hungarian friends called her Martushkam her name was Marta. Marta Krauss. This was how she introduced herself at the first morning's meeting with the other patients in the mental health ward of the hospital in Haifa. She arrived that winter on account of what was diagnosed as severe depression and was released towards the end of summer. During these months of her stay at the hospital something changed, and when she left, she felt she was about to find back her life. The morning meetings were part of the therapeutic program conducted by Dr. Hermann Neuman, the psychiatrist in charge of the mental health department. His therapeutic approach was humanistic, as they called it at the time: it relied on conversations with patients, and it encouraged their creativity. He believed in the good influence of these group meetings in the morning, even when patients sat slumped and withdrawn in their chairs. Something about the moderator's voice, he assumed, would reach them and resonate. In addition, he thought that the meetings helped patients to adjust themselves to their stay in the hospital, something which would eventually stimulate the therapeutic process.

When Marta entered the room some of the patients were there already, sitting silent and heavy. She noticed feet tapping fast the floor, trembling knees, staring eyes—and a great fear took her breath away. Crazy, she said to herself, but immediately corrected: poor things, istenem,[1] how would she endure this? What would happen to her in this place, alone, a long way from Andy? Noticing a hand waving, beckoning her to approach, she walked reluctantly in the direction of one of the chairs. Recognizing Dina, her roommate, she smiled at her weakly. They had met the previous evening, her first in the hospital, and Marta had immediately felt that she was "all right," that she would manage with her. And that had reassured her. Dina returned her smile, still pointing at the empty seat next to her, and Marta felt warm. Not everything in her surroundings was alien and threatening. She passed the row of chairs and sat down next to her roommate, making herself small in the

---

1   Hungarian: my Lord!

seat. Again, Dina smiled, but when she looked around at all those unfamiliar people a sigh of despair escaped her. The room scared her.

In recent years, fears like this had attacked her from time to time. She was gradually less able to cope with the tension that went straight to her stomach when in the company of strangers, in unfamiliar places; sometimes it grew into a panic and shortness of breath. Looks cast in her direction, unknown faces observing her, they made her shrink, flooding her with feelings of inexplicable guilt and a terror that memories she had managed to bury were about to revisit her. There was nothing she could do about this except keep any outings away from home to a minimum. Home was a safe haven where she could protect herself from the danger that loomed, as she felt it, everywhere, anytime, continuously. The routines at home soothed her. She sewed, baked bread, made cheeses, grew herbs, cooked dainty dishes, and knitted sweaters from complicated patterns she found in a Swiss knitting journal. Later on, she decided to buy a knitting machine and started knitting sweaters for people, sometimes even selling them. Her knitwear was colorful, adorned by complex jacquard patterns which testified to her good taste, her talent to make original, unusual combinations of hues, colors, and patterns spoke to the passion inside her, her ability for joy. In her childhood her delight in life, her curiosity and courage had been unmistakable, though they went hand in hand with a hypersensitivity, vulnerability, and weakness. Her character was wild and took her up and down. She could be insolent, daring, recalcitrant, a fearless fighter, and at the same time lacking in self-confidence, easy to offend, hurt to the point of paralysis; full of joie de vivre yet miserable, introverted and defeated. When she was a child, the smallest trivialities could unsettle her. Being forbidden to wear a certain dress, or shoes she wanted to put on for the wrong occasion, would cause her to erupt into bitter tears—and it might go on a long, long time, until she was exhausted. But the depression that brought her to hospital was not about a triviality. After all that had happened, Marta, injured, feared more injury to come, even when she was happy.

At home she dedicated her entire self to Andy and their two children, Naomi and Michael, taking great care to toe the line, precisely, to protect them from what went on destroying her from within. And when the children grew up, the thought that they might leave home conjured up another intolerable threat. At dinner time, when the four of them had always assembled, she now increasingly found herself facing Andy on her own. Naomi and Michael were already living in another time zone. Andy and she had a shared history. They had been utterly in love, had married for love, but also as two people fated to cling to one another for dear life, if they were to continue. And that is what Andy did: he went on, he managed to start over, forget, put solid walls around himself. Not Marta. Always on that thin line, it was dangerous to move ahead, yet there was no going back either; one had to keep one's balance, stay put, and avoid a fall. Yet she fell. The rope snapped, and she fell.

It was sudden. She was sitting, waiting for her turn at the public health clinic, gazing at the woman opposite her. Her face looked familiar. She went on looking as slowly something about the woman clarified—and then it flashed, the memory, like lightning. She knew this woman, she remembered where they met and what happened there. She remembered this body, heavy, sagging now, on the bench, but young and strong and arrogant at that time. At that time this woman had worn a grey uniform that hugged her slim body tightly—unlike them, in their old, torn rags—her blond hair gathered into a large bun, exposing a slim, long neck. The woman's cold blue eyes had fixed on her as she stood, bald and shivering like all the others during the roll call, waiting to be checked and counted, waiting for the worst. It surfaced all at once, like a bubble rising, released from murky depths. Seeing Marta's horrified expression, she lowered her eyes, rose and left. Too late. Already, memory was piercing consciousness like a poisoned dart. Marta felt anxiety's slow progress from her feet to her heart, which missed a beat, and she collapsed. She did not remember how she was rushed into the nurse's office where they revived her. She did not remember the doctor's questions: "Marta, what happened? Marta!" She did not remember her own muttering: "That was her . . . I'm sure . . . that was her . . . " The doctor injected a tranquilizer and she fell into a profound slumber. No longer could she go on forgetting in order to live. The recollection stuck and she could not continue life's routines. Profound and dark grief now lay upon her, dragging her down, a sorrow that she had always known and feared lay in store.

The doctor at the public health clinic advised hospitalization in a mental health unit and referred her to the department of psychiatry in a Haifa hospital. Andy brought her there. It could not be helped. He borrowed a car from work and they drove there in silence. The sky was overcast and a thin rain came down like needles. Andy switched on the windscreen wipers. Marta stared into their rapid movements from side to side as they wiped the streaming water from the windscreen, again and again. I'm on my way to the madhouse, she thought. She was not a healthy woman; she had already visited hospitals several times after the war. The first time was in Budapest, soon after liberation. That is what they called it: liberation. Like many of those who had managed not to die in the camps, but did not know how to go on living when the gates opened, she ended up in hospital.

In the years that followed there were some more hospitalizations—for weakness, headaches, high blood pressure. These health problems forced her to send the children to her sister so she could recover; but a mental health ward—never. She was not crazy. She was sad, drowning in grief. It kept coming in on each and every breath, and all the cells of her body were soaked in it. The road turned and twisted, and though Andy slowed down on the bends, Marta felt more and more nauseated. She asked for Andy to stop, opened the car door, stuck her head out, and threw up her breakfast. The rain fell on her hair and face joining her tears.

The hospital's parking lot was full of large puddles, and Andy looked where he could park so they could get out of the car without soaking their shoes. A drizzle continued as they headed towards the department which was situated at the far end of the hospital grounds. Passing through the open area, she could smell the sea and hear the waves hitting the shore. Further out she observed the long necks of cranes and the sterns of ships. It was that port. She did not want to think of what happened there when they arrived and her man, her closest and most beloved man, who protected her, was taken away, vanished. She had stopped being able to make sense of what was going on, but Erika was with her then. Her little sister came to welcome her and looked after her. The tides had turned. It had been she who had taken care of young Erika and looked after her—looked after both of them. Andy held the umbrella in one hand and her suitcase in the other, while Marta shrank by his side. Being close to his body reminded her of a vague promise of safety, but as soon as they entered through the wide door she was, again, inundated by the same paralyzing fear of death. Her body remembered the terror and her breath stopped, just like then.

"Dušička,"[2] whispered Andy, "it will be fine. All will be fine. You'll see—they'll look after you well here, and you'll grow stronger and return home. Don't worry."

"Yes," she whispered back, and she thought she heard his voice trembling, "I hope so."

They approached the reception office. A nurse, who was busy, gestured for them to sit down, while she went on consulting the papers that were heaped on her desk.

---

2 Slovak: My little soul.

"Yes, who are you?" She looked at Marta.

"Marta Krauss," Andy answered, and Marta nodded.

"Krauss, Marta," said the nurse and skimmed through her list. "Ah, got it. So you are Marta Krauss."

"Yes," answered Andy.

"Who are you?" asked the nurse.

"Her husband," he replied. "I am accompanying her. We have a referral to the hospital. Here it is." He held out an envelope he had taken out of the pocket of his jacket.

The nurse opened the letter and read it at a glance.

"Yes, all right, I see," she raised her eyes to face Marta, "We will get you registered and then I will take you to your room. It will be a few minutes. That's the procedure, you see . . ."

The nurse began to fill out a form asking for details every so often: name, date of birth, address, family status, reason for hospitalization . . . Andy replied to all these questions; Marta sat at his side in silence. How efficient, this nurse, she thought to herself, unable to decide whether she liked her. She was doing her job. She would have liked her to smile a little. Yes, a little smile would have been good. She followed the pen's rapid progress on the form as it noted down all the details in big letters. She looked at the thick fingers' firm grip on the pen, the strong and full arm, the concentrated expression.

"Very well," said the nurse, "We're done. All there's left to do is go to the ward—which is also the point to say goodbye." She turned to Andy.

"But . . ." Marta shrank, turning her terrified gaze to him.

"Maybe . . . Can I come along with her?" asked Andy. "I think I'd better carry her suitcase to her room, it's a little heavy."

"We'd rather not," said the nurse, "This is the procedure for a first hospitalization. We'll manage the suitcase."

Taken aback, Marta wondered who they were, this "we," and why she spoke about a first hospitalization. Could this be just the first, to be followed by ever more hospitalizations? How many? What about the children? Pale, she looked Andy's way again. He had always been with her, and the thought of remaining here on her own, without him, bore her down with a crushing fear. Andy rose and put the suitcase on the chair. Marta too got up. Andy hugged her tight; her arms dangled by her sides. She stood motionless in his embrace, feeling the warmth of his body, his strength. What would happen next?

"Dušička, I'm going now," Andy said, "Please don't worry. It is going to be all right, you will see. This is a good place and they know what to do in cases like . . ."

"But Michael and Naomi . . . What about them?" Tears announced themselves in her voice.

"Dušička, remember we talked about that, everything is going to be all right. They're not babies, anyway—they're already halfway out of home,"

"No . . . not halfway . . ." she tried to protest, "they're . . ." She wanted to say something but gave up.

"Duši, everything will be all right, you'll see. I'll talk to the doctor on the phone and I'll come back and visit as soon as I can."

"Yes," Marta said obediently, lost, "all right, it will be all right."

Her arms stayed heavy, dangling at her sides when Andy kissed her forehead. He left the office, walking away slowly towards the exit. Watching him walking away from the office window, Marta, terrified, said to herself: "That's it. Now I am alone. Môj Bože,[3] now what? Drahá matka.[4] She stood motionless, as if waiting for a wave to come and drown her, for a catastrophe, but nothing happened. The sense of abandonment that sometimes took hold of her in the mornings, when she found herself alone after the early bustle, once Andy had left for work and Naomi and Michael for school, this desolation did not attack her now. Marta gave the nurse a worried look and she answered with her artificial smile.

"Sit down," she directed her. "You can sit down again. Really, your husband is right. It is a good place, and the people who come here get better . . . usually they do. Anyway, when you're sick you need a doctor, don't you? Here's a sheet with the unit's daily schedule. It isn't very complicated. Everybody here keeps to this schedule. You'll get the hang of it very quickly. You strike me as an intelligent woman, and anyway, this is a small ward. It doesn't take genius." She smiled in Marta's direction, but Marta was not amused. "Meals are served in our small dining room," she continued. "You'll see for yourself—it's all on this sheet."

Marta took the sheet and stared at the words, the lists. Breakfast at seven, lunch at one, and dinner at six thirty. The nurse observed her slow movements and took back the paper.

"And here, this is a list of the things to do. We have a rather nice choice of creative activities and people pick what they like. As they please," she explained. "And about your therapy, it's like this: tomorrow, after the morning meeting with all patients, which is how we start every day, you will get to meet

3   Slovak: My God.
4   Slovak: Dear mother.

the head of the department, Dr. Neuman. He'll have a chat with you and will decide about your treatment and who will treat you. Don't worry, he's excellent and knows exactly what he's doing. Now let's do some initial checks, just to see if everything is all right."

The nurse gently took Marta's arm and put three fingers on the inside of her wrist to check her pulse while keeping a steady eye on the wall clock. Then she noted down something on a sheet of paper. "That's good." She smiled faintly. "Now roll up your sleeve so we can measure your blood pressure."

Marta felt her heart beating faster. She stretched out her arm towards the the instrument. The nurse fastened the cloth cuff and pushed the cold metal disc of her stethoscope onto Marta's skin, making her shiver. The cuff grew tighter around her arm until it felt slightly unpleasant, and then the nurse let go of the black rubber ball. Marta let out a small sigh at the familiar sense of release. She looked at the nurse's intent expression as, this time without saying a word, she wrote on the sheet.

"I don't think you're running a temperature," she said as she put her hand on Marta's forehead. "No, no temperature." She put the sheet of paper into a brown binder which she left on the desk, scrutinized Marta, as though wondering what to do next, and then, abruptly, said: "Right. We're done. Let's go to your room. Come along, I'll show you where it is."

The nurse picked up the suitcase with an ease that surprised Marta, and opened the door of the office and invited Marta to follow her. Marta held on to her coat and went with the nurse towards the wing where the bedrooms were situated, through a long corridor whose walls were covered up to shoulder height with bright paint, and which were dotted with doors opening into the bedrooms.

"Here we are," said the nurse, pointing at one of the doors.

She knocked lightly, opened it, and gestured for Marta to enter. There were two beds in the room, each of them flanked by a bookcase. Against one of the walls stood an old wooden closet, whose two doors were kept shut by a metal hook, and facing it was an open window with a pale-yellow, cotton curtain, its hems embroidered. A colorful shawl lay on one of the beds, and there was a small pile of books on the top of its bookcase. Marta, having picked up the suitcase, walked to the other bed, put the suitcase down, and sat.

"Your roommate is Dina Yarkon," announced the nurse. "She went out today. She had visitors, and they all left together. You will meet her in the evening or tomorrow morning. For now, you can get yourself settled into the room, and organize your things. Take your time to get used to the place . . . Tomorrow you'll start becoming one of the ward." She smiled. "Anyway, dinner is at six thirty, you remember? You'll find your way to the dining room easily. Is there anything else you need? Would you like to know anything? Anything you didn't understand?" When Marta raised her eyes at the nurse it seemed to her that she was impatient. "All right. All right, yes. I understand. Thank you." Satisfied, the nurse smiled and left the room, and Marta stayed alone in the world. She sat herself down on the bed, then she got up, opened the suitcase, and began to put her things in order. She hung the clothes she had brought along on the hangers in the cabinet, and put shirts, underwear, and socks on an empty shelf. Next she entered the tiny space that served as a shower room, placed her washbag on the shelf, and sat down again on the bed. Arranging her things had a calming effect, these simple motions that sorted everything into place. But where was her place her own? She looked at the walls around her. What would happen to her now? What would become of her? Would she get better? Become well again? Go back to how she was, before? How was I, before? she wondered. A remote, blurry memory. "Môj Bože, have I already forgotten how it really was? Moja drahá mamička . . . otecko . . ."[5]

It was cold in the room and Marta put on a coat. She lay down on the bed, stared at the ceiling and slowly sank into a deep, troubled sleep. In her dream she and Erika, her sister, approach their home in Šurany. They reach the town tired after a long, exhausting walk. Dragging themselves through the empty streets, they know they are being watched from inside the houses, from behind shutters and curtains. The house looks just like she remembers, but around it everything is deserted. Deserted, silent, ominous. When they approach the steps leading to the front door they confront a huge, unfamiliar animal, its grey, sprawling bulk covering the stairs. It is a small-headed monster whose tiny eyes glare at the two of them, a huge body that ends in a broad fin which every so often lifts, then heavily and forcefully slaps the stone surface. The slapping sound resonates in the silence, the looming, ominous silence. Then they find themselves inside the house. Deep desolation, there too. The walls show where framed pictures, removed, once hung, vanished furniture. The floor is strewn with broken kitchen utensils, rags that once were clothes in their closet. In a daze they wander through their home, passing from room to room with a growing sense of alarm. Suddenly the slapping

---

5   Slovak: My dear Mommy . . . Daddy.

sound of the monster's fin becomes audible and its shrieking as it comes after them. They must save themselves. They run for the children's bedroom, shut the door, but the monster throws its enormous body against it and shatters the door. Bolting for the window, terror struck, they try to open it and escape into the garden, but the window doesn't give. They are trapped. They yell and bang their fists against the window; "Segítség!" but no one is there.[6]

Bathed in sweat and breathless she roused at the touch of a gentle hand on her arm and a soft voice that said: "Wake up! Wake up, it's a dream, just a dream." Marta went on shouting: "No, it isn't a dream! Help!" A freckly face and deep blue eyes looked at her with concern.

"Hello. I am your roommate. It looks like you were having a bad dream. Just so you know: that happens a lot here, at first. To me too. I still wake up from an occasional nightmare, but a lot less."

Marta listened to the voice, looked into the bright face, the clear eyes, and pushed herself up, her hands on the sides of the bed.

"I am sorry. Thank you," she said.

"Nonsense! No need to apologize. I am Dina," she said and held out her hand. "I'm from Kibbutz Degania, near the Lake of Tiberias. And you?"

"I am Marta, I am from the Upper Galilee," she replied, "near Tsfat, you know . . ."

"Sure, I know," said Dina smiling, "So we are like neighbors, a bit. Upper Galilee and Lower Galilee. I'm pleased to meet you. But what about dinner—have you eaten?"

Marta started. "Oh dear! What's the time?" She looked at her watch. "Well, I'm too late for dinner. Probably the nurse will be annoyed, but I'm not hungry."

"Nonsense! The nurse—who cares? You want a cup of tea? We have an electric kettle here, for the residents, and I have tea and coffee from the kibbutz. I'll go and boil water. Ah, and I even have some biscuits a friend from the kibbutz brought me."

"Thank you very much," said Marta, "That's so kind of you." Dina's lips pursed a little. She moved the one chair in the room midways between the two beds and on it she placed two cups of tea, leaves afloat, and a plate with cookies. Sitting down on her own bed, she looked at Marta, who was still

---

6   Hungarian: Help!

propped up on her elbows. "Here, take it," she said and held out the cup. "Take care, because it is very hot; take it, here."

Marta bent over and stretched out a hand to take it by its handle while still leaning on the other. Dina lifted the other cup, took a cautious sip, looked at Marta, and said:

"Welcome to the mental health department, welcome to the room."

"Ďakujem" Marta whispered back.

"What? What did you say?" smiled Dina.

"Thank you. It's Slovakian. Thank you."

***

Marta was a good-looking woman. Though not tall, her body was lovely, well proportioned—shapely legs, narrow hips, round breasts, and soft shoulders. Her feet and hands were delicate, her ankles and wrists slim and elegant; their gracefulness was brought out when she wore her best leather shoes with the low heels and put on her leather gloves. In spite of the scarcity of those times, the constant need to be frugal, resourceful, she would not compromise on quality. This had been passed onto her by her father who had been so knowledgeable about textiles and always made sure his children were dressed in clothes made from the choicest materials. "We aren't rich enough to afford cheap clothes," he would say. For years they had to wear these wonderful-quality winter coats made from wool that never wore down or grew tattered. Her face was pretty and quiet, concealing great agitation. Her skin was smooth and light, her nose, turned up a bit, high cheekbones, broad forehead, finely drawn eyebrows, and a dark, intense expression. Neither happy nor sad, her eyes, dark, seemed to be looking up from the depths. Her dark hair, thick and plentiful, gloriously framed the reserved beauty of her head.

She never used makeup. Its coarseness put it out of the question, even though she did look after herself. Once a month she took the bus to Haifa to have her hair done by Vera, an energetic, attractive woman her age, who was from Hungary too. She felt comfortable under Vera's hands; she liked how she handled her abundant hair while they chatted in Hungarian about this and that, while she was soaking her fingers in a basin with tepid water. Edith, the beautician, had a room right next to the hairdresser's, and on her regular visits, Marta always dropped in there as well. Edith also spoke to her in Hungarian, but she was older than Marta. Edith gave her a facial, which involved covering her face with a nourishing mask and warning her not to neglect her skin, "what with the climate up there in the Galilee." Edith prepared moisturizer and face cream and put them into two small plastic pink containers, which would last till Marta next treatment. Into a plastic vial, Edith poured a thick fluid, her own concoction, a cleanser and moisturizer.

The Hungarian language cradled Marta, warm and gentle. Though it was not her mother tongue she loved speaking it and she loved hearing it spoken. At home they all spoke Slovakian, and her parents spoke German between themselves. She loved the Slavic melodiousness. At school they spoke Slovakian too, until the Hungarians came and everything changed. After the war she continued in Slovakian with Erika, and later with Andy, but it pained her, that language, and she switched to Hungarian. She spoke Hungarian after the war, in Budapest, with her friends from the youth movement, her new family. Once they all reached the kibbutz they made a point of speaking Hebrew, but Hungarian slipped into their conversation and the accent stuck, a last remnant of what had been.

Hungarian became a window onto a lost garden, the life she once had. Hungarian did not smart. She felt alive in it, unfolding into a splash of colors, like a palette, like a fan. Though their Hebrew words were limited and alien, she and Andy insisted on speaking the language, using a dictionary. With the children they took care to speak Hebrew only, erasing the languages they had brought along from there, but Hungarian leaked into their conversations anyhow. They did not notice, or maybe they did not want to children to understand: Vigyázat, a gyerekek hallgatnak . . .[7]

Sometimes she and Andy had friends over, from the youth movement, from the kibbutz they had left, and in that company, Hungarian flowed: juicy, cheerful, and feeling free, she laughed out loud. In time, slowly, Slovakian faded from their speech, even between her and Andy, in the kitchen, in the living room, in bed. It was dangerous for them, Slovakian. The Hungarian she spoke with Edith and Vera at the hairdresser's, neither too close nor too remote, felt the most comfortable, allowing the sounds of her childhood to ring out without causing pain. Each time Marta returned to their small home from the hairdresser, the place devastated her a little less; for a bit she would feel she was gaining strength, in spite of everything, to cope with this grief, with life.

---

7   Careful, the children are listening.

When she arrived at the hospital with a referral from her doctor mentioning depression, nightmares and a nervous breakdown, Marta was in her early forties. Many years had gone by since they all been rounded up in the town where her family had lived for generations. In a tightly packed, silent procession they had marched to the train station. A train took them to a collection point from which they were made to take another train heading east, where they were doomed to die, though they did not know about that yet. Her parents and sisters arrived together. Her elder brothers were already gone, having been rounded up like all the young men and sent to do forced labor.

Marta and her sister Erika could have left town with false papers that Shosha, from the youth movement headquarters in Budapest, provided, but their father still believed that they would be taken to a place from which it was possible to return. He said the girls were to stay. "Whatever happens to us will also happen to them. Our family stays together." With the boys gone, Marta was the eldest, and she felt responsible. Anyway, she never meant to leave them in the first place. Later, Erika said she would not have survived in Budapest with the false documents, given her Jewish looks and her fearfulness. She survived Auschwitz because of Marta, who stuck close to her until the end.

It was hot in the train, unusually hot for June. Noticing the sweat on her mother's forehead, Marta tried to make her a little more comfortable by fanning her with a raggedy newspaper she found on the carriage floor. People had brought things to read on the journey.

So much had happened in the following years, good and bad, and things had changed; but nothing ever changed or affected what happened to Marta there. That wound and the fear of further wounds always ruled her life. On returning, she did not believe she would ever laugh again; when she heard others laugh it puzzled her—how was it possible? Then things completely changed. She was carried away on a dizzying, intoxicating desire to live, love, forget, and not to think. To get away from the wound. She built herself a new world without a past, a life without memories, knowing all the time, though, how shaky the foundations were. This was why she took care not to overload them. Not to remember, not to think, not to miss. To be here, now, with whatever was happening, to keep busy. The events around her happened fast and took her from her pain, yet still she heard the faint, remote rustle of a slow, persistent pulling-back. This noise had grown into an unbearable din, and now she found herself here, in the hospital.

She remembered how she had been struck down, as if by a bolt of lightning. The moment she identified the woman facing her, in line, like herself, waiting for the doctor, the everyday routines she had managed to create were ruined.

Everything stopped. The image flashed onto her consciousness from the depths of dark chaos, and there it stayed, stuck like a red flag. She and Erika had seen her on their first morning in Auschwitz after first being separated from their father and then from their mother and little Eva. They had robbed them of everything they had on them, including their hair, which was cut and collected into a tall heap, and they had thrown them something to wear, something that was not theirs and didn't fit. They had killed their mother and Eva before morning and turned Marta and Erika into beings from another planet.

That morning they did not recognize each other. The group of young women looked like a group of monkeys, Marta remembered. Shocked, they gazed at each other, bizarre shaven-headed creatures, their eyes raw, their faces warped with terror, dressed up like puppets in a carnival of horrors. There was another roll call to make sure anyone unfit for labor had not sneaked into the group, anyone not entitled to live even a short while more, anyone who had to die immediately—now. With her thick hair removed, Marta looked small and younger than her years. The woman who sat facing her waiting to be seen by the doctor, had been young, handsome, tall, and arrogant on that first morning. A kapo. Picking out Marta, she had yelled at her, asking how old she was, and immediately struck her hard, shouting: "Liar! You're not seventeen." The woman started yanking her out of the line, and little Erika started screaming, weeping, drawing her back into the line with a strength she did not have, but which, yes, it turned out she did have: "She is seventeen, she is, she's bigger than me." What saved them was the impatience of the Nazi officer, who shouted to the kapo from the other end of the line: "Go on! Why are you wasting your time there?" The kapo let go of Marta who fell back into Erika's arms. That is how it was there. Life or death; it was sheer coincidence.

Marta and Erika stayed in their line until someone barked the order to return to the barracks. In shock, side by side, exhausted, holding hands with a love neither had ever mentioned to the other. Neither before, when they were girls-sisters-rivals at home, nor later. When they did speak up, only tiny crumbs of words were came out. All they said was that they survived because they were together, because a core of nurturing power had remained, a loving, protective core of family, even when that family was already gone. It happened at such speed. In the blink of an eye, the family came undone. The fear.

She remembered. When the carriage doors were unbolted and they were taken off the train, exhausted by the journey, dazed by the chaos and shouting, paralyzed with fear, moments before their father was violently taken away from them, pushed roughly, and gone forever, he had managed to pour a fistful of nuts into their hands, final provisions for on their way. "Eat that"—a last memory of fatherly care which continued to protect them when it was just the two of them. "Eat that." Marta remembered the hard round shapes in the pocket of her coat. With her hands stuck deep into the pockets she held onto the nuts, hard, gathering their father from them. Soon the nuts went with the coat and all the other clothes that were taken away from them. Earlier, their mother and little Eva, too, had been taken away, torn from them with the same headlong and screaming brutality.

They had no idea how it came to be just the two of them at the nightmare's dead center, but that was how it was. They stuck to each other, looked after each other and managed not to die. Marta was the older sister, taking the place of their mother when Erika nearly lost her mind early on during the journey on which they were sent. From within the shock and helplessness that gripped them, Marta looked after Erika desperately, fearing what would come. In those terrible conditions, care of that kind saved lives. What saved Marta, gave her the ability to persist, was responsibility for Erika and the hope of eventually reuniting with everyone. They both clung tight to this hope. When everything was over and they realized the catastrophe's proportions, Marta broke down.

The flashing image of the morning roll call, that first day in Auschwitz, cut her breath. She remembered feeling suffocated, screaming, "I can't get air," just as she was passing out. She continued having trouble breathing afterwards, too, as though she could not get enough air into her lungs when they were begging for more, air which hurt, though, when she did at times manage to take a full draught. A tightness in her chest and an occasional stinging in her lungs interfered with her breath.

After the incident at the doctor's clinic, she lived as though she was afloat between two opposing streams, trying desperately to maneuver between these forces, opposing the movement, any movement. It was impossible to go with the stream, but just as impossible to resist it, to move away, back off. Gradually her power was eroded by other things; she had a feeling of falling behind, trailing behind Andy, behind Erika, like her desperate worry about Naomi and Michael. How would she save them from what had happened to her then and was destroying her now? The children were gradually moving away from her and into their own lives, and she saw the invisible burden they carried on their backs. That is how it was. They were born into it and nothing could alter that fact. She had read in a book once that we are not the future, we are the past. They did not know it yet, but this was what was awaiting them. Thoughts did not leave her in peace.

The distance from Erika was painful. She missed her. When it was all over, Erika announced she didn't want a family. She could not go through it all over again, and now she was slowly building up her life with Yehoshua. Though she too created a life with Andy, Naomi, and Michael, Marta felt abandoned. Maybe it was in her nature: this yearning. It was an unstoppable yearning for fullness. Something gnawed at her and came between them. How could it be that she, the strong one, opinionated, the star student who went to the gymnasium in the nearby town, she who was loved and courted, who had great dreams about leaving home, studying, living life to the full, and getting out of the small town, she who managed to pull through—how did she end up without strength, empty, so defeated? While Erika, the obedient girl, shy, who followed her like a shadow, admiring, Erika who depended on her to survive, managed better to forge herself a new life. Erika was not a dreamer like Marta. Erika was practical; she had her feet firmly on the ground. No exalted dreams for her—so she was not devastated when dreams shattered.

Yehoshua filled up the crack that had opened up between her and Marta and this enabled her to go on. Erika was not at fault, but Marta's offense ran deep. It might also have been in her nature, this taking offense, losing hope, being cautious. Andy's life was moving confidently ahead and this should have reassured her, filled her with confidence. But what about her own life? The exciting, amazing life she had dreamed of? The discrepancy was great and disheartening. She even felt guilt at times, but did not have the strength to do anything about it. That was how she arrived for a long stint in Haifa Hospital's mental health unit.

***

The unit was run according to a fixed daily schedule. After breakfast, patients assembled for a meeting with a member of the medical staff. Next, they would choose from the crafts activities in the group activities room, get immersed their work, talk a little with others, get to know them and make connections. Most of the time, an introverted, withdrawn silence prevailed in the room. Now and then this silence was interrupted by the hushed sounds of tools and work, the instructor's movements and comments. Disorder broke out only very rarely, and voices were not usually raised. Individual sessions with psychologists and doctors took up the second half of the morning routine. It was a small ward with about thirty beds and most patients suffered from symptoms of anxiety and depression. Though they were also given medicine, in addition to psychotherapy and creative activities, Dr. Neuman emphasized the centrality of the personal relation with the patients, and instructed his team to encourage dialogue.

Lunch was served at one o'clock, and after that most patients went to their rooms to take a rest. Their sessions with therapists, their medication, and their illness itself in the first place, took a great deal of energy and they needed some hours of rest or sleep during the day. In the later afternoon visitors were welcome, or outings, as it was not a closed unit. You could go out into the small garden which was visible from the department's windows. It consisted of a patch of meager grass with a sprinkling of poinciana trees, under which there were some dilapidated wooden benches, some broken by now. Another possibility was to leave the premises and take a stroll among the small houses surrounding the hospital on its one side or along the seaside promenade. This promenade ran close to the building's entrance, and you could walk down it until you reached a large, deserted building, The Casino, which had once buzzed with life, music, and parties. Dinner time was early, following which you could spend time in the so-called "culture room"— Marta called it the "ugly no-culture room"—to listen to the radio, drink tea, leaf through the papers. Finally night arrived which rarely gave solace, and was mostly visited by roaming predators who bared their teeth and struck out their claws.

Mornings, on waking, were always confusing, a slow swaying between hope and despair. Getting out of bed demanded time and strength: to raise the body, move toward the door, head to the dining room, into a new day. Though the therapists tried hard, the morning meeting was not easy. People sat hunched and silent in their chairs, bodies heavy and drooping, or else tense and trembling, and often the conversation did not really take off. While the composition of the group changed every so often, with new patients joining and others released back to their homes, the morning sessions seemed always to stay the same. The same heaviness, the same difficulty, the same silences. Speech was hard, and for some, like Marta, almost impossible. She thought that, in spite of the patients' frail mental health, the general mood in the unit was not awful. People did not run amok in the corridors, did not scream, and did not bother each other. Like planets, each moved in their private track, passing between the bedrooms, the consulting and activities rooms, the dining room, and garden. Each carried their grief and pain, their body wrenched at times by mental agony. Marta could not speak without having to explain. Her roommate, though awkwardly direct, accepted her with a reassuring ease. The paralyzing fear Marta had felt on that first day when she arrived, receded to its normal place, where it lay folded deep in the pit of her stomach.

Every new admission to the ward began with a long conversation with Dr. Neuman. An experienced psychiatrist, he took great care to maintain an empathic distance from both patients and staff. He listened with reserve, gently and patiently, as he tried to understand the person who was facing him and decide on the best way of treating them, and mainly, who would be the most suitable therapist to treat them. Therapy, he said, must aim at the patient rather than the malady. Again and again he reminded his team to pay close attention to the injured person rather than acting as experts on that person's illness. During their weekly staff meetings, he asked members to consider various possible approaches, leaving them plenty of room to move and choose. As for himself, he did not take patients for therapy, but rather supervised the other therapists and doctors. The staff trusted his management and, in spite of their heavy workload, never complained about Dr. Neuman referring yet another patient. Their surprise, therefore, can be guessed when they heard the new patient, Marta Krauss, was going to be his.

Marta first met Dr. Neuman the morning after her arrival. At the end of the group session that morning, the coordinator approached her and said that Dr. Neuman was waiting to receive her for a first meeting in his office, which was near the reception and the entrance door.

"Talk to me?"

"Don't worry," she assured her, "That's the way it's done here. He is in charge of the unit, and he has to get to know the patients. He meets every person who is admitted for a first assessment."

"Assessment?"

"Yes, to see what treatment is best. It's an illness, after all . . . you understand."

Marta nodded, but she knew, privately, that this wasn't a matter of understanding. How could it be treated? What was the point? Still, she rose slowly and said, "All right. I will go to his office."

When she walked into Dr. Neuman's office, Marta briefly closed her eyes, and then she opened them again. After the grey-walled corridors, the whitewashed bedrooms, the activities room whose large windows poured in light, she had now entered a secluded room. A different world. A large brown desk, with a massive wooden chair, occupied one side of the space. The wall behind these was covered with shelves densely filled with books which stood in a disorder that pleased her. The desk looked out over a large window covered by a long curtain which left just a chink showing one of the poincianas in the garden and a strip of cloudy winter sky. Opposite, on an old, frayed rug, stood a low table covered with a table cloth embroidered in earth colors and two brown reclining chairs with dark wooden armrests. The room's duskiness was just right and pleasant.

When she faced the older man behind the desk, he smiled at her. He got up, moved in her direction, stretched out his hand, and said, "Hello Mrs. Krauss, I am Dr. Neuman, the head of this department. I would like to have a chat with you. I mean, I would like us two to have a chat so I may get to know you a little. That's what I do with everyone who comes here, it's a way of getting acquainted . . ." His voice was soft with a Slavic sounding accent, music she was very familiar with.

"Pleased to meet you."

"Take a seat, won't you, it will be more comfortable to talk when sitting down," he said, touching her shoulder lightly and steering her toward the easy chairs. Marta sat down in one and he sat down in the other, crossed his legs, and leant back. Marta stayed on the edge of her seat, her body a little rigid.

"Maybe to begin, you should tell me what brought you here, what happened?"

Marta noticed the quietness of the room. The unit's noises and voices came to halt at the door of this office. In this room, silence, it seemed to her, took physical shape, turning into a soft, thick, and inviting wrap. She felt herself leaning back into the chair, her muscles relaxing. I'm at rest, rest is what I need, to plunge, to let go . . .

"Marta . . ." The slight Slavic lilt reached her and she looked his way. Dr. Neuman sat in his chair, placid, his attention focused on her.

"Tell me a little about where you're from? Where is it that are you joining us from?"

"I'm from the Galilee. We live near Tsfat."

"Who do you mean by 'we'?" his eyes smiled.

"We, that is, Andy and myself, and we have two children, Naomi and Michael."

"How old are they?"

"Naomi will turn eighteen soon and Michael is fourteen," she halted, and added quickly, "And me, they sent me here for further treatment."

"And what happened? Why did they decide you should be hospitalized? Can you tell me about that?"

"The doctor at the public health center decided. I mean, after I fainted. I don't remember very much, but I do remember that I fainted and that afterwards it was hard for me to recover."

"Do you feel sad?" asked Dr. Neuman.

"Yes, oh yes, I am very sad."

"And to Tsfat and the Galilee, you came from where?"

"From the kibbutz. We first arrived at the kibbutz, but we didn't want to stay there."

"And before the kibbutz?"

"Before the kibbutz?" Her voice trembled and she looked at Dr. Neuman, her eyes dark and obscured, flooding. She wept. Soundlessly at first, tears streaming down her cheeks, and then came her moans, her howls. She did not try to stop it, neither her weeping nor her howling which erupted from the depths of oblivion. Subterranean reservoirs of tears, mines of black salt poured their contents into the room, there was no way of stopping it. So she sat in the chair, hands covering her face, and wept until she reached the end of weeping.

Silence returned to the room and Marta remained with her eyes closed. She heard Dr. Neuman getting up and moving to his desk. When he pulled out his chair the sound reached her from a great distance, papers shifting, a book closing, drawers opening. She was cloaked by this silence, and the brown shades of the room sent their warmth into her. On waking she found she was covered down to her feet in a plaid blanket. It smelled slightly moldy, but not unpleasantly so. The sky, where it showed through the curtains, looked laundered, and on the low table by her side stood a flask and a glass. When she looked in the direction of the desk, she saw Dr. Neuman, who was writing.

"I am sorry. I fell asleep. I didn't notice." She straightened herself in the easy chair.

"That's all right, that shouldn't worry you. I brought you some tea from the dining room. Why don't you drink a little? We will continue our conversation tomorrow. Same time, is that all right?"

Pouring a little tea into the glass, Marta drank, enjoying the warmth of the liquid passing smoothly down her throat. She got up, folded the blanket painstakingly, and put it down gently on the seat. Quietly, as if trying to avoid taking up space, she stepped toward the door.

"Yes," she said before leaving. "Same time tomorrow. Thank you."

The walls of the corridor glared at her. She glanced at the unit's entrance door and then slowly walked in the opposite direction, heading for her room.

***

When was I ever alone like this? Far away from home? She could not remember. In her childhood years, a hidden power had drawn her out, and she tried to get out of the house whenever she could, feeling her wings were clipped there. For years now, an altogether different power kept her at home. Home became crucial to survive, keeping her out of the world. And look at her now, in the hospital, far from home, Andy and the children, she was sharing a room with a woman she did not know, and it was not intolerable.

This surprised her: she even felt a bit curious. What was going to happen here, in the psychiatric ward. I am ill. It's a hospital. We'll see what they can do. It might help, with all those doctors around. Maybe in the silence there, and all the space, she would manage to deal with the memories that attacked her, locked onto her, gave her no way out.

Marta had never discussed these things with anyone, not even Andy, even though their memories were of the same childhood. They observed a silent agreement not to talk about what had been, about what happened to their families. They had grown up in the same small town, their families knew each other, the children were friends. Zorka, his big sister, had been her good friend, while Andy had been the soulmate of Karol, her beloved brother. Andy's father had been principal and teacher at the local Jewish school, teaching all the Jewish children in town, her too. When Andy and Marta met again, after they returned, they did not mention all the others who had not come back—the parents, brothers and sisters, and scores of other relatives who had disappeared, traceless. No pictures remained, even, as though their families had had never existed. But the two of them knew. They and Erika were the only ones who knew that these people had once lived, that they themselves, too, had lived different lives, that there had once been family, home, child-hood. Like rare witnesses, they carried the secret of something indescribable, unmentionable. Sole witnesses who knew decidedly: it happened. It had.

As the years went by, the silence between them grew into a mine-strewn no man's land. Entry forbidden. Danger. A loud silence grew ever heavier, especially now that it was often just the two of them at home. When Andy returned from a day's work, she served his food silently and he ate in silence. And the evenings were long. The world enticed her children, same as it had with her when she was a girl, and all she could do was hope they did not feel their wings clipped by home. How could one know what they felt? Between them and the children, too, there were spans of silence. Silence that doggedly ate away at her resources, her ability to cope, to get up in the morning and go on until night. What was it? Depression? Madness? She would ask herself these questions with an indifference that troubled her.

Marta always knew that her memories were there, folded, murmuring in some corner of her body, abiding, and she did all she could to keep them there. In hospital, she let go a bit. There, her tangled memories came untied and floated up without rhyme or reason, like bubbles, like swifts cutting through the air inside her head. Memories from the year when she fought tooth and nail so that Erika would keep going, would not give up, and so that she, herself, would not give up and die. In their previous lives she had not been a particularly strong girl; they even considered her sickly. She was already suffering from stomach pains and headaches, and there was some-thing wrong with her spine, but her character was strong and energetic. She dared to do what Erika would never dream of. She had the guts to revolt, go against her parents' and teachers' authority. During that year, she drew on the strength throbbing in her. It drove her to struggle against the death to which they were doomed, to fight against collapsing under the senseless slav-ery into which they were forced. Erika was physically stronger than Marta, but Marta's spirit was sounder. She was the one who decided, made the small decisions thanks to which they managed to endure.

And other memories, too, of the life she began anew with Andy, came unbidden. The great love between them renewed her eagerness to live, repair the world. She found her strength once more; she was combative, opinion-ated, and dreamy again. She and Erika were part of a team of young people who ran a home for children in a Budapest suburb all by themselves. They called it a children's home, but it was an orphanage. Children who remained alone after the war, ripped away from their mothers and fathers, families, homes, were brought together in the home. Some of these children were only a few years younger than them, others were toddlers, all of them lost during the days and visited by nightmares at night, weeping bitterly, screaming, desperately calling out for their parents. Her wisdom, unusual ideas, courage, and gentleness made her loved and appreciated. Andy was the home's educational director. He radiated adult, thoughtful authority, which reassured everyone—the grieving children, who so badly needed comfort, and the counselors, too, who were grieving just as much.

Though hurt just like them, Andy's handsome and confident appearance, his broad perspective, the seriousness with which he took his role, and his insistence on making the home into a *home*, not just another branch of the youth movement, gave him an aura of leadership. When he and Marta decided to start sharing a room, their happiness knew no bounds. It was, for Marta, their wedding. She wanted no truck with a Jewish wedding and a rabbi. She would have nothing more to do with rabbis. Their love consecrated itself, taking its proud place in the world. It was a sublime love, forever, in a good new world. She was given to such romantic ideas. Their friends in the youth movement called Andy Krauss and Marta Weinrebová a couple of stars who were sure to shine.

In the kibbutz, to which they moved with the Budapest group, and to which they also moved their love, everyone continued to act busily and forget eagerly, convincing themselves it was possible to start a new life. At times she wondered whether it was their fear of memories that fired this powerful headlong drive to take hold of the future. Whatever the case, it allowed them to not think about what had been. Not to remember. She had some good years, years of oblivion, free of nightmares. The past seemed to have been erased and gone, and a new life took over. She knew, though, that it was still there, a dark pit waiting for her to stumble. Her face contracted when the thought crossed her mind. Everything, in the end, was so unlike what she had wanted, dreamt. Where had things gone wrong? Why? Had she expected too much? Wanted the impossible? One thing she knew: Andy had changed. He lived his life, moved forward, and forgot the things they had told each other. He drifted away from their star, and he went on to shine without her.

Years later, when the children were older, Marta found the courage to wonder what would have happened if she had acted differently. What if, for instance, she had stayed in Budapest, if both she and Erika had stayed there and tried to rebuild their lives? Or if they had gone to America, like so many others? What would have happened? What would have become of them?

Maybe she would have studied, as she had always hoped to do, and made something more of her life? Applied arts. That was something she would have liked to learn. Perhaps she would have become a writer. Questions one should not ask. What good were they now? And anyway, would she really have been able to learn anything and make herself a new life without Andy? Wasn't it exactly because they met Andy and the group of singing young people that Marta and Erika succeeded to return to life? The very possibility of life had struck her then. She had not believed in it until that moment.

She remembered the moment clearly. Like a revelation. It was the first time since their return that she had heard song, joyful singing—it was something she could not forget. She and Erika, "the girls," left Budapest with another two friends and Andy, heading for Balaton, to join a summer session of their organization. From the distance, the sound of singing reached them. She was amazed. The singing was happy and free—it was a group of young people celebrating life. As if nothing had happened, she thought in fear. How would she and her companions find their place in this joyful setting, still accompanied by the smell of those scenes?

Andy led them to this group of happy young people. Together with him, she saw life grow exciting, promising pleasures of body and mind. Andy held both past and present for the two of them. She felt secure with him. Only with him, she thought. Had she exaggerated? There was no way of knowing now, but there had not been much choice, it seemed to her; she would have collapsed without his protection. Maybe died. Yes, she might not even have lived. Perhaps the protection he gave her allowed her to be herself, even strong, obstinate, a mother of children for a while. It was during this joyful summer session that Yehoshua too entered their lives. "This is Yehoshua, my friend," said Andy. "We were together in the bunker, in Budapest."

She did not think, that morning, how their lives would become entwined, turning them into a family. "Szent Család" they called them in the Budapest youth movement and later the kibbutz: "the holy family." So full of ardor they were, so closely knit and apart from the group—a tight circle. Holy family. They all had a burning passion for the pure life. Driven by ideals, they wanted to touch truth, justice, goodness, and beauty. While hiding in the bunker, Andy and Yehoshua had become soulmates, brothers, and finally they became brothers-in-law. By their side, Marta and Erika could start their lives.

When Andy was recruited to the army and serving somewhere far away, and Marta stayed behind in the kibbutz with their baby girl, they wrote each other letters full of love and desire, yearning and happiness. Yes, she had been happy. Happy that Andy was hers, that he was just like he was, just as she wanted him. Duši, she called him, my Duši. She was in heaven, so happy with her little girl. The baby, she wrote to him, is like our love: pure, fresh, sweet, tender, and beautiful. Only when you have loved so much, can you have such a beautiful little girl, she thought then. She kept all the letters. They were in a square tin box. Now she did not dare to look at them.

Little Naomi. How pleasant it was to think of her, remember the baby she had been. Defiant even then. Just like Marta. In the kibbutz's baby home, Naomi cried constantly, and Marta did everything in her power—overturning their child-rearing ideology—so that she could breast feed more than the kibbutz caregivers allowed: once every four hours, no more. She needed permission? Permission to feed her own infant? The caregivers knew better what the infants needed than their young mothers. The caregivers gave them a good education: the tender newborns must not be spoiled by excessive parental love.

Marta was outspoken in her criticism of the collective's educational ideology, demanding its adjustment for her specific case, her baby. How much courage it took in those times! Run against the kibbutz collective! Her mother came to her help: "Your baby is hungry," she told her in a dream. "You're starving her. Killing her." For the first time since her return she dreamed about a member of her family. The distinct presence of her mother, who addressed Marta just like a mother does when her daughter has had her first baby, came like a blow, piercing the wound. She had let it be. Now it came back and smarted.

When they left the kibbutz, the holy family, they had nothing and were full of faith and hope that they would make themselves a life that was right and proper. Finally Marta would be able to get her small family away from searching, critical eyes; she would no longer have to control her feelings and adjust herself to the collective and its ideology. Different food would cook on her kitchen stove. Patiently and with curiosity she tried to recreate the flavors and smells she remembered from home. She mixed the vegetables that grew differently here with unfamiliar spices, yet every so often, when she served dinner, the light in Andy's eye showed that a forgotten taste had been retrieved. A powerful recollection of what had once been everyday life arose from their taste buds: mother's dishes, the lively, noisy kitchen, the constant women's chores of cooking, baking, preserving, drying, hanging, roasting, collecting, sorting. Memories of a cellar, its walls covered in shelves tightly packed with glass jars containing jams, salted summer vegetables, cherry preserve, chicken liver spread, pickled cucumbers, pickled cabbage, cooked plums. In one very dark corner stood bottles filled with the wine her father made. In serious lines they stood, these bottles. Strings of peeled dried apple rings hung between the shelves, bunches of dried garlic and onions, and a huge vat filled with potatoes occupied another dark corner. She remembered the smell, an intoxicating blend of dried fruits, onion and garlic, the smell of strong spices, food that had taken hours to prepare, and a light whiff of damp.

Marta had the strength, in those years, to restore those memories to life in her new routines. She remembered her mother, immersed in running the home and the kitchen, and now she learned everything she had refused to take in as a girl. In shorts and sturdy work boots, a kerchief tied around her neck, she tended the vegetable patch in the large garden, fed the chickens and geese, and made sure to water the fruit trees they planted instead of olive trees, the same trees whose flowering caught up with her again every spring; she washed the tiled floors in the house every day, mopping the water to the balcony, and from there to the rose patch they had planted; and hung out clean laundry to dry in the clear air. Also, she dried rings of peeled apple in the sun and hung them strung into long chains in the kitchen; she made jams from the fruit yielded plentifully by the trees.

The quantities of fruit the trees produced took them by surprise. So did the vine with its large bunches of grapes, which made her think that maybe one day they too might make their own wine. Meanwhile she patiently worked at her goulash, lecsó, cholent, rakott krumpli, and gombóc. She baked yeast cakes and dobos torta like those of her mother. Very slowly, unawares, she added her own imagination and creativity, her growing gift for cooking to what had been passed on. Now she began to write down in Hebrew recipes she collected from friends or from the radio. In the same little notebooks she also kept track of their little family's everyday expenses.

After Naomi, Michael was born. Now she had two children. Feeling responsible for whatever befell them, she made sure to keep out of sight what had befallen her. She never thought she was raising her children without a past, something that might affect them badly too. She did not consider that what she had been through was also, somehow, theirs, something their new Israeli names would not alter. They decided not to call the children after their dead. There were so many of them; how was one to choose whom to remember? Naomi and Michael made her feel that her life was divided between what had happened in the past, light-years away, and what was happening now. She managed, in those years, to avoid stumbling into the abyss of darkness between these two parts of her life. She was so very orderly and managed to do so much. When she thought about it now, in hospital, nearly drowning, hardly breathing, sinking ever deeper, she could not believe, could not understand how she did it. Dr. Neuman encouraged her to speak but much she could not tell. Not even about the good years of her childhood and about the good years when she succeeded not to remember and immerse herself completely in the new family, her young children, their bright, curly heads. Silence strangled her, and her neck would not relax.

***

Initially, Marta did not understand that she was Dr. Neuman's only patient. But she overheard some whispered comments, which sounded rather biting: "Ah, so you are the chosen one." And then she understood. Any gossip involving her put her off. She mentioned it in their room to Dina, who said: "Nonsense! Dr. Neuman knows what he's doing, for sure. They're simply envious, evil people. Loonies—what did you expect? All that matters is for you to get well, right? Return home. Forget about them." Dina's response reassured her. Marta was fond of Dina's rough and direct views; She lacked all arrogance or meanness. How far away her home was, Marta thought, without missing it now; it seemed to have sailed away—or was she the one who had departed?

Dr. Neuman's method was to create a temporary separation from patients' usual environment, forbid visits from relatives in the first weeks of hospitalization, to help them get used to their new life in the unit. Marta adjusted well and so she began the first phase of hospitalization without major upheavals. Settling in to the routine, she became a little calmer and plucked up the courage to be part of the place. Slowly she began to visit the activities room, responding to the choice of creative things to do, which suited her liking for craft work and her passion for colors. She picked out the boldest colors and combined them in unusual ways, and the small things she made were so colorful you might have thought them the work of a cheerful woman. She arranged small mosaic tiles into a naïve image of a house and tree and painted transparent bottles with intense blue wavy brushstrokes, deep green, and yellow flashes of light. She began to like her and Dina's small room, its simple furnishings, its ascetic modesty; Marta noticed that she herself was trying to make it nicer and she was pleased. And with Dina too she felt at ease, happy she was a painter. Dina's vivacious nature reminded Marta of herself. So long ago.

She looked forward to her daily meeting with Dr. Neuman in his office, when the door closed, leaving the world outside. Marta loved the gloom of that room, the window opening out on the grass, the old rug, and the brown upholstered chairs. She took the liberty of sitting in a different chair each time. Dr. Neuman, seating himself in the other chair, would say, "Hello Marta, shall we continue the conversation?" Even though she was silent most of the time. If it were up to her, she would have stayed in the room for a long time, sinking into her silence in an easy chair. For a very long time. The quiet of the room seemed to softly take over, consoling, a silence unlike its gnawing counterpart at home. What was she to talk about? What was there to say? She preferred silence, not to think, not to remember. Just to be there, close her eyes and feel she was all right for now. She was safe. Dr. Neuman was a doctor, he had chosen her, and she could let go, relax. Her need to be on guard constantly slackened because he was there. She took the medicine he prescribed, and the knots of tension and anxiety began to dissolve inside her. But speak about the catastrophe, the shock, the stubborn hope, this she could not yet do. Grief accumulated wall-like around her, and the conversations with Dr. Neuman proceeded haltingly. Her answers to his questions were sparing. Sometimes they talked about other things, like books she had read.

On one of their first meetings she noticed the doctor was familiar with quite a lot of literature, something that added points in his favor. A short conversation about books unfolded; she told him about *The Sun Also Rises*. Maybe she wanted to impress him, make him see she was not just sick. Maybe even then she already wanted to say something about the power of words. She told him, in that conversation, that she had loved reading from when she was little. In fact, they had been a family of avid readers. They had a weekly subscription to a children's paper, and the shelves at home were filled with all the Russian and German classics. All of them, except for father who only read the newspaper, were bookworms. She told him about how she admired Hemingway, his way of describing emptiness, the void, and existential despair following the war—the lost generation. That miracle of words, how it allowed one to express things. It mattered to her, to remember that words could do things, that they had power. A kind of possible redemption. Maybe one day she might write.

Dr. Neuman was a soul-doctor Marta was able to endure. She could not tell what it was about him, about his personality, that made her feel lighter.

Perhaps it was the cautious delicateness he had about him, in his attitude to her and to the world. She felt very good with it, even if she was silent. Dr. Neuman was a doctor she could respect and hold in regard. She could rely on him. That was not a small thing: to trust. She had always been resolutely critical, urgently demanding truth, even before the violation, and she had a sharply developed intuition for pretense, fakery. Now too, when she was hospitalized. The first buds of calm appeared inside her, bringing a tiny bit more air into the lump of anxiety in her lungs. It was all right to be silent; Dr. Neuman let her be. Sometimes it seemed as though he was letting himself be, joining her silence, understanding her deep grief. She so much wanted him to see the strength she had as well, her desire to live which was suffocating under the layers of sadness.

Dina's presence also helped her become used to the place. Marta saw her noble soul and sincerity underneath her rough exterior. Like Marta, Dina was ill, but she belonged to a different place and time. She was born and raised in the same Jordan valley kibbutz which she had never left, and yet here she was, because in her life too some string had suddenly snapped. She arrived at the hospital with her paint box and drawing books. It was the one thing she was willing to do, and she insisted on using the paints she had brought along from home, only them. She drew and painted most of the day, in their room too, she could not stop. Marta liked to sit and observe her, follow the movements of her brush—small, fast, nervous—and then to see the great whirlpools of color on the sheet. A merry-go-round of colors, sudden storms produced by Dina's small body. Marta thought they might be a little alike in their strong attraction to color, their commotions and their grey silences, their stubbornness. But Dina was painting!

Dina was the first Sabra with whom Marta had grown friendly. In the village in which she lived, local Sabras looked down on them, the immigrants. Andy, trying to approach them, sometimes attempted to reproduce their coarse way of speaking, but she was put off by their superiority, lack of subtlety, and ignorance. Dina was a different Sabra. A little like herself. Maybe that was why she was there, Marta thought. She was happy to have Dina as her roommate; it made the room feel a bit like home. It was warm and cozy, making up for the chill in the corridor and in the eyes of some nurses. In time they very cautiously began to talk about their pain, the silences, the torn threads. With Dina she could share her concern for the children, especially Michael who was at home with Andy, and her guilt about being a mother who was not doing her job.

"You are ill," Dina kept telling her. "You must take a step back, and in any case, it isn't so bad for the children's father having to be their mother for a little." Her eyes narrowed: "Maybe he will get to understand what it's like to be a mother."

"It isn't easy . . ." She found herself thinking of her own mother suddenly.

"Not at all easy." Dina's eyes narrowed again. "And it's about time men took note! Now you're a little free of all that."

"I don't think . . ." said Marta.

Marta noticed that in spite of her worries about home in her absence, she also felt somewhat relieved. Freedom from being the housewife she had not intended to become. That must have been what Dina meant. It was a good thing they were there together to speak about it. First they only talked in the room, cross-legged or with their knees folded to the side, each on her bed. Later, they also talked outside on one of the benches in the hospital's neglected garden. These were good conversations; they exposed their minds as they told each other things sincerely, heart-to-heart conversations of the kind Marta had been wanting so much. Dina tended to speak in a loud, sometimes blunt voice, Marta felt, but it did not trouble her. Dina did not overly insist on questioning her; it was Marta, actually, who asked Dina about her life because she was curious, it seemed, see into another world. Marta described her kibbutz, the village in the Galilee, Andy and the children, but she did not talk about what had been and was ruined. Sometimes Dr. Neuman looked out at them from the window of his office as he was working on patients' files. Marta noticed him from the bench where she and Dina sat, or maybe she was just imagining him observing them from his open window, looking into the garden.

During this first period in hospital, Marta's condition improved. She felt it herself, how her body moved more energetically, was supple, and how something inside her loosened up. She was happy find in the mirror that her face looked fresher, and she wondered whether Dr. Neuman also noticed it. Still, she needed a lot of rest, even an afternoon nap. Yes, she was growing stronger, even though the hospital food was nothing like what Dr. Netzah[8] the nutritionist recommended. He had saved her from the health issues that beset her after the war: Dr. Netzah taught her about vegetarianism and healthy eating habits. It suited her, such an approach, because she naturally

---

8   Hebrew: eternity/forever.

tended to avoid meat. It seemed somehow immoral, she argued, especially after the war. But vegetarianism, for her, was more than that: it constituted the essence of truth, a good and true tiding, pure, nearly spiritual. And Karol, her brother, had been a strict vegetarian from age fifteen, when hardly anyone knew what it was all about. So this made her feel closer to him. In addition, it was perhaps her way of being herself—antagonistic, wayward, reserved. While all around her industrial food was becoming popular, soup mixes rich with monosodium glutamate, she started her morning with a glass of tepid water and took care to eat healthy foods that had not been sprayed with pesticides. Each time Andy's work took him to the head office in Tel Aviv, she wrote him a shopping list for the health shop on Masaryk Square.

To Marta, it was very meaningful that the health store was situated on that square, called after Tomas Garrigue Masaryk, president of Czechoslovakia, whom she had greatly admired as a girl. "Masaryk square" rang a familiar note—it carried a greeting from the past. The shopping that reached her from there in brown paper bags was special to her. It also gave her a touch of solace when grief submerged her when Soviet tanks entered Prague, strangling the spring of that city and the entire republic. She was pained by the images of those tanks in Prague, and of Jan Palach, as well as by the fate of Alexander Dubček, who had been sent to Bratislava and put to work as a car mechanic or minor official. All this caused her sleepless nights. The few years she had lived in the republic had left their mark. In spite of the distance and the occupying regime she continued dreaming of the place where she was born.

On one of Andy's afternoon visits he found Marta lovely and charming again: she seemed to be getting better. She was happy to see him. Together they went to sit in the garden. Andy held her shoulders and told her how he missed her and how eagerly he and the children were waiting for her to return, though they were all right, there was nothing to worry about. They did not exactly know what was happening and nor did they ask: he was trying to keep them out of this story. Marta asked herself what he could mean by "this story" and whether her breakdown had put them in danger somehow? She was, after all, their mother. She felt her illness threatened the silence she and Andy believed would protect the children and themselves. They had an agreement, a tacit one, not to speak. They would not know, anyhow, how to tell the children, where to even start. Now she was not sure about it. Maybe it was not right to conceal her hospitalization from them. She actually wanted

Andy to speak to them, but she had to come clean about it with herself first. From when the children were born, she and Andy had been keeping an entire life hidden from them, so how were they to begin changing that now? She and Andy sat closely together on the bench in the garden for a long time, but Marta did not tell him about her conversations with Dr. Neuman. Andy walked her to her room and hugged her tight, telling her he had an appointment with Dr. Neuman so he could find out more.

On his way out of the hospital Andy knocked on the door of Dr. Neuman's office and walked in. Andy radiated charm. He was a tall, slim man, his hair black and full, his nose somewhat aquiline, his eyes green. His hands were strikingly beautiful—a pianist's hands. He had played the piano in the past, but now his fingers only drummed on the table. Dr. Neuman got up, moved towards him, and shook his hand.

"Pleased to meet you, Mr. Krauss. I am glad you could come in. I'm happy to meet you. Please take a seat."

"Thank you," said Andy and pulled the chair on the other side of the desk towards himself.

"Good thing you decided to drop in. I meant to ask you, that is, I wanted us to have a chat . . . You see, it's part of her treatment, Mar . . . Mrs. Krauss."

"Certainly. I would like to hear too. So what can you tell me? She is improving, isn't she?"

"As things are, I would like to continue her treatment the same way." The doctor ignored his question, for now. "In the future, I believe, close relations, her family, should be part of the treatment."

"I will do whatever it takes," said Andy and leaned back in his chair. "We will do everything needed for her to get better."

"Of course," said Dr. Neuman, "I will be in touch with you about that."

"But, still, doctor," Andy leaned toward Dr. Neuman, "what do you think? Could you just tell me a few things now? It seems to me that she is . . . better, that she's growing well again, right?"

"Yes. Definitely, there is some improvement, but she is still in quite a vulnerable condition. You see, contrary to appearances, she is not well yet. It's a serious depression, Mr. Krauss, clinical. That's what they call it. She's had a very bad blow, and it takes time to recover. Do you understand? I would not want . . . We might perhaps soon consider a short break, a weekend. I think that should be possible, but not right now, it will take more time."

"Just a short break?" Andy asked, frustrated.

"I know you are disappointed, but I think it is too soon to be talking about recovery. Her condition is improving, but this is just the start. It takes patience, Marta should not again . . ."

"No, of course not. I understand," Andy interrupted. "You are the doctor, and you decide. When will it be? Soon?"

"I hope so. Let's be in touch. But of course, I will have to discuss this with Marta too and see what she thinks."

"She wants to return," Andy answered quickly, "I'm sure of it. Everybody is missing her. She will be happy to return home."

"Yes. Did she discuss that with you?"

"Not exactly. But I know she'll be happy to go home. Home is her entire world, you know?"

"Yes, I am sure that will make her happy. But . . . We should really wait for a little longer. She must regain a bit more strength. We will get there. Please don't worry. Mr. Krauss, we're looking after her and she will recover."

"Yes, of course. Thank you very much, Dr. Neuman," Andy said and got up. "I am very grateful that you are treating my wife. You know that . . . it doesn't matter. Marta is sick now."

Dr. Neuman, too, rose from his chair and approached Andy, his hand stretched out. Andy took it in his two hands and then quickly left the room. Dr. Neuman went back to his chair, looked through his working diary, which lay open before him, and wrote down a few sentences, faster than usual. Then he closed the book and put his pen on top of it.

***

The next day, during their morning meeting, Marta was surprised when Dr. Neuman asked her to tell him about her time with Andy. She looked at him, as though taken aback. Why? she thought. How is that connected? I don't want to talk about it, she said to herself. It would be the first time she would talk a lot. The first time memories grew clear and organized, and she could tell them to Dr. Neuman.

"Yesterday?" she said. "Our meeting? It was good. Well, when I'm in a state like this, Andy may be like . . ." She halted.

"Like what?"

"How he knows to be, the way it was, in the past. In the beginning. The way we once were, in love, really."

"Can you tell a bit about how that was? What was Andy like?"

"We all adored him. He was a 'star,' you know, as they say."

"Who were 'we all'?"

"The whole team of counselors in the youth movement, me too of course, like everybody else . . . Not exactly like everybody else, because Andy was part of the family. Though he wasn't a brother, he was my brother's best friend. Andy was the only member of the family who came back . . . remained . . . I don't know how to put it."

"And why did you all admire him so much?"

"Because he was a natural leader. Our spiritual leader. He had what it takes to be a leader. You would feel secure when he was around . . . He was beautiful, very well educated, much more than us. We felt we would be safe with him. You see, we were all so uprooted, so hurt. All of us. We didn't even know yet how badly hurt we were. We could not think about it. And Andy too was injured, but he had drawn a line under it all. Put up high walls. Maybe his leadership qualities helped him do that."

"And between the two of you? Was he the leader between the two of you as well? How was that?" Dr. Neuman's face slightly contracted.

"Before anything, it was big love, love that saved me, and I believe it helped him a great deal too . . . Me it really saved, then . . ."

"Oh yes, love has such power. It can do miracles." Dr. Neuman leant back and his face relaxed somewhat.

"Now that I am here, at the clinic, I feel his love . . . like then. But that's not always how it is, you see."

"I see, and I know that your husband is very concerned about you. I met him yesterday and we had a little chat. He worries about you a great deal. But how shall I say it, Marta, dear? Relationships change. One cannot stay for how it once was, just wishing for what was."

"Oh, don't I know it! I know very well. Yes, maybe I'm being childish, but that's what I want."

"What would you want, Marta?"

"The impossible, it seems. I want us to be together, to be in love like we were before. I have not forgotten anything. It was so powerful . . . dizzying . . . it bore me up . . . and I want to stay up there." She sighed. "I would like it to be like that again. Sometimes I feel I am to blame, like something isn't right about me, sometimes I really feel that Andy . . ." She fell silent. "I feel that Andy did not stay true to our dream, that he's forgotten. He thinks about himself, not about the two of us. We no longer shine together the way we used to."

"You shone together? What do you mean by that?" Dr. Neuman smiled.

"That's what they said about us when we moved in together and we became an official couple. They said we were going to be a 'brilliant couple.'"

"'A brilliant couple'—why?" He went on smiling.

"Because each one of us, separately, shone" She smiled back. "So, yes, me too, I had my own way of shining, not like him, of course. He was very, very brilliant. So they said the two of us together would be something really special. That's what they said . . ."

"Who said?"

"Our friends in the youth movement. When we were in Budapest, the lot of us."

"Such a wonderful description."

"Yes." She sucked in some air. "It was wonderful. We were young and beautiful. But it's a long time since we stopped being brilliant. I don't shine at all. I am a star that's stopped shining, gone out."

"Marta," Dr. Neuman protested, "That's not . . ."

"Yes, that's how it is," she cut into his words. "And you know, even when a star shines, that doesn't mean at all it's alive. I read somewhere, I can't remember where, that the light of stars reaches us from such a huge distance, I don't even have the words for such a distance, that by the time the light reaches us from so far away, the star has long since stopped shining . . . The light comes to us after the star no longer exists . . . dead . . . it's inconceivable, don't you think? A sign of life arriving when that life has ended."

"But you are Marta, you are alive! You live and you cast your light! And you are not that hugely remote from here." He smiled at her. "Your light comes through."

"Where?"

"Here. To me and to everybody around, of course."

"But Andy and I no longer sparkle together," she insisted. "He shines alone—and that angers me and makes me sad. What can I do?"

"Yes," Dr. Neuman sighed, "I know about that. It is not easy."

"What is not easy?"

"How two people are supposed to go on living together, let alone go on shining together."

"Why is it that way? I find it insulting."

"I understand. But we already talked about how relationships between two people change. It's important to understand that. Maybe one should not take it as an insult . . ."

"So what do you think?" Now she was angry. "What should I do?"

"Marta," he said, his voice sounding sad to her, "we cannot expect one person to satisfy all of our need for love. You know that's impossible . . ."

"So, what is one to do?" she asked again, her boldness surprising Dr. Neuman. "You tell me what to do."

"There are things you can do. But for now we must not get distracted. We must focus on the reason you are here."

"My illness?"

"Yes, your illness. I believe as we deal with that we will also touch on other things, which might not seem connected right now; but things connect, tie in with each other. We humans are very complicated creatures." He looked at her, and again his voice sounded sad: "You understand, Marta?"

She nodded. It was the first time she had mentioned her relationship with Andy, her disappointment and anger. Now she looked at Dr. Neuman with embarrassment and saw he was embarrassed too. He shifted in his chair, his hands gripping the armrests. He removed his spectacles, took a handkerchief from the pocket of his jacket, wiped his face with it and next the lenses, and raised them to check the shining glass. Then he put his spectacles on the low table and put the handkerchief back into his pocket. His face was exposed and Marta could see his eyes. For a moment, there was great intimacy between them.

"Yes, dear Marta," Dr. Neuman continued, "it is very complicated. Complicated and human, you understand."

"But," she kept on, suddenly childish, "Andy and I, we had a great love. Not like everybody else. I must tell you. It was a promise! Even though when we were children," she laughed, " it was Erika, my sister, who was in love with him. Imagine, she was about three, or four!"

"And you?" he asked immediately.

"When I was a girl I had a lot of infatuations," she giggled. "I had suitors. Boys rather liked me, they said I had lovely legs. Interesting how they knew? Maybe when we went swimming in the river, in the summer." Her eyes smiled. "When I turned sixteen I decided it was time to fall in love. Ivan was the 'victim.' I fell head over heels in love, and the poor guy did not even know. And later . . ."

Later their lives had begun to change; there was danger in the air, though they did not know when and how it would reach them. As her child-like innocence waned, she fell in love with Erich. They were close, loving friends. Like her, Erich cherished grand ideals and she could discuss them with him. They went for long walks in the fields and talked. In the summer, he would take her along on his bike and they rode for a swim in the river. In the train wagon to Auschwitz, Erich had sat by her side and his presence steadied her. There too, they talked, whispering, sitting closely side by side. When they forced them off the train, with a lot of yelling, dividing men from women and children, she saw him standing among the men, trying to tell her something. She watched him detaching himself from the group, running towards her, shouting something, but she could not hear, she did not understand what he said . . . People were beating him with batons, his back folding in pain, and he was manhandled back into line. It was the last time she saw him. Nobody knew what had happened to him. He disappeared.

"Marta," Dr. Neuman said gently, "can we continue? Is it all right? You were saying that Andy . . ."

"Yes," she returned to the conversation. "In Šurany, our town, Andy was one of the family. He was my big brother Karol's best friend, I told you that, right?"

"Yes, yes, I remember. So you know each other from childhood?"

"All the way from childhood. But Öcsi—I mean Karol was . . ."

"Öcsi? Can you tell me about that name?"

"Öcsi?" She smiled. "That's a pet name, it means 'little brother' in Hungarian. He was called Karol after my father's brother who was killed in the First World War. Poor Öcsi, he got killed in a war too. Karol, that name, maybe he was fated." Marta grew quiet and briefly sank into herself. "Yes, Öcsi was how we called Karol, it was his pet name," she continued, "because he was Andy's little brother, Andy our eldest. Everybody called him Öcsi, even the teachers at the gymnasium. He was a brilliant student. He was really brilliant! He was admitted to the gymnasium when they only took in a lim-ited number of Jews. For me he was like my big brother, even though he was number two. Andy was quiet, modest, a gentle soul, and Öcsi was going to fix the world, he was a leader. Very charismatic."

"I thought your family was religious. The gymnasium . . . isn't that a sec-ular school, non-Jewish?"

"Yes, yes. Öcsi was not going to study at the yeshiva, no way. Our par-ents wanted him to. That was the way to go, especially when someone was considered a genius the way he was. But he refused. He was openly opposed to how the rabbi ruled the community. He thought it was close to being a dictatorship and he simply hated them, much like he hated anything that limited people's freedom to think and choose."

"And how did your parents take that? Weren't they observant?"

"They were religious, but not fanatical. They loved him and understood he was special, very clever, a rebel, but it wasn't easy. My father, Julius—I am not sure he was a great believer. He stuck to the religious rules because that was simply how it was, you know, but deep inside he was a modern man."

"Modern?"

"Yes. As a young man my father had spent some time living in Vienna, so that when he returned to his hometown, he was, as they said, kind of a man of the world. My father was not provincial. He read the Czech newspaper. A daily. *Prager Tagblatt*. He was interested in what was going on in the world, beyond the Jewish community. He would get excited by all kinds of innovations. I remember him buying a knitting machine for my mother, and we also had a radio . . . But our family were part of the town's Orthodox Jewish community, and the rabbis ruled with an iron fist. It was hard on us kids as well, but unlike our parents, we rebelled."

"What was it with the children?"

"We became involved with the Zionist youth movement. We learned some Hebrew. We sang songs, there were summer camps, we staged theater plays."

"Boys and girls, mixed?"

"Oh sure. We studied together in school too. They did not separate between us at all. And there were boyfriends and girlfriends. Both my brothers had girlfriends. Romantic ones." She looked at him, smiling.

"Yes, I already noticed—there was romance in Šurany!" he laughed.

"Oh, yes, there was."

"And your parents were all right with that?"

"You know, none of us went over the top. I don't remember any problems."

"And what did the other parents in town think about these youth movement activities?"

"Some parents were very much against it. Others were tolerant, they looked at it forgivingly, the way you do when children play. The rabbis actually vetoed it. But we weren't always impressed in the way our parents were."

"And in your family's home?"

"Andy and Öcsi, the boys, were doing things in the youth movement. Andy even moved to Budapest and continued there. Because of our brothers, Erika and me felt like joining in with the activities too. For me it was like touching God, or at least, coming close."

"And your parents? Did they agree with the activities?"

"I suppose they did. I don't remember discussions. Our parents were very busy, everyday hassles. My father worked hard in the shop. In addition to our family, he also supported some relatives who were desperately poor, and they relied on him for their livelihood. He simply transferred money to those poor relatives. It was easy for them, him looking after them, giving them money. And for him it was completely natural, though my mother was unhappy about it sometimes; she said he forgot that he had five children of his own to feed . . . His generosity sometimes angered her. He was an uncommonly generous man, our father . . ."

"It must have been very good to grow up with a father like that. And how well you remember. You remember a great deal, Marta. To have such a stockpile of memories, that's important. Very important."

"Yes, my father really was a wonderful person. When my mother complained, he'd say, 'I suffered so much when I was a boy. So now, as long as I can, I want to give and help.' That's what he used to say."

"And what about your mother? Can you also tell me a little about her?"

"My mother was very busy at home. Because women in those times did everything themselves, with their own hands. Even though she had help, she still worked from morning till night, and in addition she helped our father in the shop. We had nursemaids when we were little. There were tensions, upsets, because I did not really like helping with the chores, because I wasn't, as they say, a good girl. But now I appreciate everything she did." Her face showed pain. "Now I am sorry about . . ."

"You were a child, Marta, don't forget."

"My mother was religiously observant. I remember her, even at home, wearing either a wig or a head dress. She kept all the ritual laws, she took great pains."

"And your father? You were saying he wasn't like that."

"He wasn't so Orthodox, but he respected her. When they were married he promised her father that he would keep all the laws, that he would live an Orthodox Jewish life. He had grown less religious, before they married, as I told you, but for her sake he changed his ways. Though he kept his promise, he wasn't a faithful Jew."

She stopped, surprised herself by the flow of things she was telling. All of a sudden, images stood out clear, places, people. All of a sudden she wanted to tell these things to Dr. Neuman. She wanted him to know where she came from, what it was like, her life before.

"My father was a real human being," she went on, "a very decent man. All his clients knew that. He would never cheat! His non-Jewish customers even used to say he was so honest it was hard to believe he was a Jew . . . That was their way of complimenting him. "

Biting her bottom lip, she went on: "As children, we felt so safe with him. Our father was the head of the family, in every sense. He was a kind of example to us . . . He was strict with us, that's true, a little rigid even, but when he put his hand over each of us children's heads, we felt nothing bad could happen to us, we were safe and protected. I will not forget that moment, his hand on my head, and him whispering a blessing."

"Marta!" He was moved: "What a lovely memory! That's a very special moment."

"That's how it was. But when it came to the rabbis, my father's courage failed him. Such a pity . . . he should have ignored that rabbi. Maybe we would all have stayed . . ."

"Ignored the rabbi?" Dr. Neuman smiled. "What do you mean?"

"My father was thinking about Palestine. Some people from Šurany had emigrated by that time. We did not know much about what was going on there, but we knew it existed. In our youth movement they were talking about *Eretz Yisrael* too.[9] As our lives became more and more difficult, when more or less everything became forbidden, it was even forbidden to work and they took father's shop from him, he started mentioning the possibility of the family emigrating to Palestine."

"Really? Was he a Zionist?"

"Not at all. But it was so bad he was looking for ways to make things better for the family. He discussed it with us. He had a kind of plan. He considered buying a large car and we would all drive to Palestine."

"In a car?" he asked, amused. "All the way to Palestine? Did your father know how to drive?"

---

9   Before 1948, when Israel was founded, many Jews called what was generally known as Palestine, by the Biblical-historical name: Eretz Yisrael—the land of Israel.

"Yes, it was some kind of naïve dream. The entire family, all of us together. But it never got as far as practical planning."

"Why not? What happened?"

"He didn't dare. That's what happened. The rabbis were strongly against it. 'We do not settle in the Holy Land before the Messiah arrives.' My father stopped talking about it. They were very good at saving their own skins though, in the end. They did escape to Palestine and they abandoned their community. Miserable men . . . That's how it was." Her face lost color. "Our father did not know how to cope with the rabbis. I remember one Saturday, when father returned all pale from the synagogue, telling us about the rabbi's sermon about 'those who rather than sending their sons to the yeshiva, let them enroll at the Christians' gymnasium,' and as he was saying these words in front of the entire community he had looked intently at our father. Why did our father remain silent? Why didn't he respond?"

"It can't have been easy for him to fight the rabbis, I suppose. He was part of the community—you can't just break away like that. He must have wanted to protect his family's status in the community and his livelihood. And maybe it was also because your mother was so religious. Were there any nonreligious Jews in your town?"

"No, I don't think so. There were some who had become Christians. It didn't help them, poor people. They were driven out with the rest of us. Some went to Palestine. Yes, there were some. But you are right. My father respected my mother, but he was not Orthodox. We saw him breaking the laws, sometimes, when he thought nobody was watching."

"Really, like what?"

"On winter Saturdays, for instance, when it got really cold, he would sometimes add wood to the hearth, so it would stay hot. Once I even saw him switch on the light on a Saturday. Small transgressions like that. He did not think all these laws were important, but he was forced to observe them. But Öcsi, by contrast, was not willing to play along. He really did rebel."

"I'd like to hear more about Öcsi. Tell me about him. He seems to have been an unusual and brave fellow. He was the brother you loved best, right?"

"Yes, very much. I admired him so much. I could just go on and on telling you about him. He was an idealist and wanted to change the world. He was attracted to communism, but when he later joined the Yugoslav underground, he wrote he found himself forced to conceal he was a Jew. The Yugoslav communists turned out to be no less antisemitic than the Germans and the Hungarians. It was a huge blow for him. That was what made him become attracted to Zionism, I believe, but it was too late by then. He . . ." Marta fell silent.

"And he was a friend of Andy, wasn't he?" Dr. Neuman asked, continuing the conversation.

"Yes," said Marta, emerging from her thoughts. "They were like buddies, a team. Brilliant, both of them. They were so brainy and had already read a lot, but they were also up to boyish tricks, yes."

"What do you remember, for example?"

"I remember how they made a bet which of them would dare to get into the river in November . . . Can you imagine, the temperature of the water? Freezing. Our parents made a big deal out of that. They were so concerned for our health. Öcsi was punished, I can't remember what, but I clearly recollect how proud he was he had gone through with that bet. Punishments did not really impress him, he was so headstrong."

"And Andy? Did he go into the water too?" Dr. Neuman asked, curiously.

"Oh, he sure did. Of course he also went into that icy water and then caught pneumonia. He wasn't particularly robust. And in those days people died of pneumonia. He ran a high fever for some days, so that was a punishment in its own right. His mother went crazy with worry, she loved him so much, he was her only boy. Her eldest, and a boy with three sisters. You know . . ."

"Oh, I do, I understand. Of course. These two young fellows had character."

"Yes . . . Later Andy moved to Budapest. His parents enrolled him at the Jewish teacher college. Five years he spent there! Five years, he was a student in Budapest. We girls saw him as a man of the world. We were what you'd call provincial. We hardly ever left our small town. We would visit our grandad in Topolčany, a remote village, for the summer vacation, and once or twice we joined our father on a business trip to the big city, Brno, where he got supplies for his textiles shop. Once we traveled to a spa in the mountains. I envied Andy. I was dreaming about leaving, traveling, getting a taste of the wide world. I was so keen on having a different kind of life than ours in the small town. Andy would come back during vacations and tell us all about the wonders of Budapest. He found time, in spite of his studies, to walk around and get to know the city. We were enthralled by his stories. Andy had always been good at captivating an audience," she smiled. "Those stories of his about Budapest . . . some wonderful things, he told us."

"Yes. Budapest really is a splendid city," said Dr. Neuman with some longing. "What did he tell you about?"

"About how big the city was, the marvelous buildings, the streets, the Danube . . . The Opera! He spoke a lot about the Opera. Andy was very musical. He still is. He likes classical music. In those days he also played the piano. During his years in Budapest he went to a lot of concerts at the Opera. Budapest's Opera was really impressive, very beautiful, and obviously not affordable for a student. But he arranged something with an usher. A deal. So typical of him . . ."

"What was it?" asked Dr. Neuman, and smiled.

"I suppose you could say it was bribery," Marta said with a smile. "The usher got some money, and Andy was allowed in, as simple as that. He promised he would get us tickets, me and Erika, so we could go to the Opera together. We dreamt about it, but it never happened."

"Why?"

"Because the Germans invaded Hungary. Andy escaped Budapest. And then everything ended. Very soon. It all happened very quickly. They had to go about killing us in a rush before the war ended." Marta smiled wryly." And they managed to, those bastards . . . damn them."

"Yes. That was right at the end of the war."

"Our poor father"—now pain returned to her voice—"he was such an optimist, though perhaps he was trying to encourage us. He said it was a matter of time, that it was a passing phase. That it couldn't possibly go on. Look, the war is about to end, the Germans are losing. That's what he was hearing on BBC broadcasts. When they took away his shop and he had nothing to do, he helped my mother at home and taught himself some English."

Falling silent again, Marta sank into herself. She had a very sharp recollection of the morning when Andy, pale and distraught, wearing a creased grey suit, appeared at their home, pulled two tickets to the Opera from his pocket, and said, his voice shaky, "Look, I laid my hands on those tickets I promised. But now everything is lost. The Germans have entered Budapest. I got out at the last moment . . ."

***

After the war, everything changed. Their families were dead, strangers were now living in their homes from which all the old things had disappeared. Nothing remained. They were alone in the world. For Marta and Erika, Andy came closest to being a returned family member, and they were like family for him too. Marta and Erika had each other, but Andy was alone. Not one of his three sisters came back. For a long time he had hopes the eldest might return. Rumors were that she had been spotted, that she had survived. Marta and Erika had met her a few times during the year when they had all been dragged and dumped like mere things from one place to another. Terror-stricken, Zorka was sent to another camp and did not return. And so, the two families' remainders—Erika, Marta, and Andy—became one family. Many years later they understood that this was, for them, the only way to go on living. When Yehoshua joined them later they turned into a family of two couples, a "holy family." And when they left the kibbutz, they left as one family, insisting on the dream of a new, different life. In the end, they parted ways and set up homes in different, remote places. But they stayed a family of two couples and they did not mention what had happened to them.

Dr. Neuman, like Marta, was silent now. And the room was silent. Soft mumblings reached them from the garden through the window. It was the first time that Marta had spoken a lot about her father, her brother, Andy, what happened to them. She was aware of this. Though it hurt, she suddenly wanted to go on, explain more to Dr. Neuman, and maybe to herself as well.

"You were asking about Andy," she said.

"Yes, please continue. I am listening."

"You see, when we met him, my sister and I, in Budapest, and we knew that no one else from our family was going to return, it was a miracle for us, really. We were saved! We were no longer alone. We really felt like that. He was the person closest to our family, to the place and the life we had before . . . Like a ray of light cast, all of a sudden, into the endless darkness through which we were trying to make our way. We were lost until we met him . . . We did not know where to go, what to do with our lives now . . . now that it was just the two of us who'd survived. We were moving ahead with our arms stretched out, we couldn't see a thing, we did not know what direction to take, where. And then there was Andy, this meeting with him . . . and life became possible. It was clear to us that we would stay with him, go wherever he went. Our direction was Andy."

"I see," said Dr. Neuman quietly, "and then it was through him you got to the youth movement?"

"Yes. Well, we'd had some connection with the movement before . . . I told you my brothers were very involved, but when we came back it wasn't the movement we were looking for, we were looking for our family; we hoped and prayed to find them." Marta's voice trembled. "Yes, that's how it was when we arrived back home. Throughout our long way back, we thought, hoped, dreamed that everything would the same again . . . I cannot describe how much we wanted to find some member of our family. What kept us going was this hope to meet them again, just like it had given us strength in the camps. At least our brothers. We were convinced they would make it back, but no . . . neither them nor our father. We knew about our mother and Eva. We knew what happened to them. The next day we already knew we were not going to see them. But our brothers?" She winced. "When we returned to the town we saw Christians, strangers, in our house, we did not want to go in. Some woman was using mama's sewing machine . . . we stood and looked as if . . . It was another blow, taking you further down." Marta sighed and sank back into the chair. Looking at Dr. Neuman, she said, "Yes, that is how it was."

Much of what had befallen them on the way home she did not remember. Perhaps she did not want to remember. She recollected very well what had been going on around them. Europe was like an ant heap. An ant heap onto which someone had stepped, sending the ants running hither and tither in a panic. Thousands of people on the roads, heading everywhere. How did they find their way? She did not know, but she remembered they never stopped walking, machine-like, in one direction: home. They were given food and a place to sleep in the camps that were erected along the roads and teeming with refugees. But they never stayed. They walked. For months. They crossed countries, kilometer upon kilometer.

She had no memory of what they wore, what shoes they had on. It was like a great nightmare which they had to get through urgently and awake. To awake at home, with the family all around the Friday night table their mother had set. That was the one, single thing on their mind. What kept them going was a desperate hope to get their home back, the family; it pulled them onward to the place from which they'd begun. Already they were not talking about what had happened, what may have happened to their parents, brothers, little sister. They could not even think about it. Just move ahead. Yet the nearer they approached, the more they had to slow down, as though it had stopped being so urgent to get there, afraid of what might await them, of what they would not find at home. They played for time, dawdled, stopped for longer breaks on the way. They covered the final kilometers on the cart of a peasant who picked them up. They no longer wanted to arrive. They got off the cart and very slowly covered the last two kilometers, entered the town, and walked to the street in which they had lived. They stood in front of their house and looked. Through the windows they saw unfamiliar people, from the entrance to their father's shop they saw a stranger sitting behind the table. The world collapsed once again. This time without hope.

They did not want to ask or know what had happened with what was left behind in their home—the utensils, blankets, sheets, furniture, clothes, books, paintings on the wall. Everything that makes up a family's life. Their dresses, at least, no one would use! She had torn them to shreds. When they were rounded up and marched in one large, silent group through the town's streets heading for the train station, she'd managed to bolt back to their house which stood open and violated, into the children's room, and with the large scissors her father had used to cut into fabrics, she cut and tore up her dresses. Next, before leaving their yard, she removed the gold earrings with tiny sapphires from her ears and crushed them on the path, under the soles of her high shoes. When she returned she answered Erika's questioning look by making a scissor-like movement with her fingers.

"So then, where did you go? What did you do?" Dr. Neuman's voice roused her.

"There was a house there that belonged to some Jewish family, and it stood empty. I mean, nobody had taken it. The house had belonged to a friend of ours. She did not return. None of her family returned. That is where we went. It was organized for us by the municipality; this is where they sent people who managed to return. It is a bit ironical, how we put it: "managed to return." This person returned, others did not . . ."

"Why ironic?"

"I don't know"—a bitter smile appeared in the corners of her mouth. "One returns to a familiar place. One returns to a place where one might belong. That's what returns are all about, isn't it? We thought we were returning but there was nowhere to return to. No one to return to. All that had been—vanished. Swallowed up. Maybe the house was there, and the things that we had left inside it might have been there or somewhere else, and the shop too remained in place, with its bales of fabric . . . No, it was a mistake to have thought we were returning. That it was possible to return."

"And yet, this is where people went when the war ended."

"Of course, it was only natural. It's human, isn't it? One returns to the place that was home. The few who stayed alive, if we can call it life, because really a lot of them returned dead, you know . . . Anyway, people thought they were going back home, and they were hoping to meet their relatives there.

They hoped their family would return, or at least some of them. We all lived in hopes of reuniting as a family, going back to something normal."

"Yes, it's natural," Dr. Neuman said, nodding, "it's human . . ."

"What a mistake! How could we even have thought that it was possible to go back to how it had been, to normalcy? After all that we'd gone through. But we did not quite understand then what had happened. We did not know how terrible everything had been . . . We did not know it had been such a great catastrophe. That after it, nothing remained. And yet . . ." Marta paused for a moment and looked at Dr. Neuman. "You understand: People still had hopes . . . Yes, still, all those who managed to return, they returned to that house. That's where they all collected. I can't remember how we knew that was the place to go. Once we saw there was no home, no family, nothing actually, we were in shock, lost. We did not know what to do. People put up announcements there, in that house, asking for information about their families. The house for tracing relatives. Hardly any relatives survived. And yet, people kept looking and looking. Waiting and waiting. Maybe someone would turn up. That's where we spotted the note Andy had left. He'd written that he was back, in Budapest, with the Zionist youth movement, and he wrote his address. This is how we managed to find him. It was . . ." Tears welled up in her eyes and her voice broke. She leant back, covered her face with her hands, and wept. Her shoulders shook. Dr. Neuman leant towards her and offered her his handkerchief.

"Take it, Marta, don't worry, it's clean." Marta smiled through her tears, reached out to take the piece of cloth, wiped her wet face with it, and gave it back to him.

"Please, keep it," said Dr. Neuman. "Let's leave it at that, now, Marta. You spoke a great deal today. Let's leave it for now."

"All right." She folded the handkerchief and put it in her pocket, ready to get up.

He stopped her: "Before we say goodbye, there is something I want to talk about, and I think it will make you happy."

Marta looked at him questioningly.

"Yesterday I met Andy—you know that. He asked whether you could come home for a short break from hospital, for a weekend. I am asking you about the idea now."

Surprised, Marta shut her eyes. Dr. Neuman observed her.

"Would you like to spend the weekend at home?" he asked her again. "To meet the children? Do you feel you can?"

"Of course I want to," she responded immediately, and then hesitated. "I think I do. For a short vacation. What do you think? Do you think it is all right?"

"Andy very much wants it. He really made a point of it. He very much wants you to come home, see the children. But what matters more is how you feel and what you want."

"Yes, but what do you think?" she insisted.

"I think it would be good for you to spend time with your family, and I believe it will be all right."

Warmth flooded her. Michael and Naomi. She could not wait to hug them tight. What did they think? She had, after all, vanished, just like that. Perhaps they were angry, sad? How would she tell them about the hospital? Suddenly she remembered when little Naomi noticed the blue number on her arm. Does that hurt? she had asked her. Is that a wound? It is from the war, she had explained, and Naomi had never mentioned the number again. Michael never asked her about anything, he took things like that as they were. She had so much wanted them to grow up like everybody else. But, like everybody else. What was that? In their neighborhood, after all, almost the entire population were immigrants. On top of the hill lived the founders, the town's upper crust, as it were, and down below, it was people like them, the immigrants. All the families around them were scarred and wounded by the war about which the children knew nothing and did not ask. She missed Michael and Naomi. It was the first time she'd left them for such a stretch. Yes, she wanted to return home. Dr. Neuman said they would go on with therapy till the weekend and then decide. I must remember the good things I had, she told herself; I must remember all of it, otherwise I'll truly go mad.

***

She prepared her small suitcase the evening before. Dina gave her a drawing, which Marta liked. Airy watercolors sketched the shores of the Lake of Galilee, there were soft-outlined hills in the distance and a wild-fronded palm tree. Dina's gift moved Marta. "Nonsense! I'm happy to give a drawing to someone who knows how to appreciate it," said Dina, then wished her a good break and promised to stay put and wait for her here at the madhouse. Marta smiled, rolled up the drawing and promised, in return, that she would frame it. "I'll hang it in our room," she said, and saw it made Dina happy. Andy arrived late in the morning and the two of them walked down the corridor heading towards the door. He had the suitcase and Marta carried her small handbag and Dina's rolled-up watercolor. They went to the unit's office, and after some things were noted down in documents and diaries, the nurse wished them a nice weekend. "We are here," she said, "waiting for you."

No need, Marta said to herself. On the way home, she saw the villages through the car window, the wide-stretching valley with its ancient olive trees, the ploughed fields. She felt a rising nausea when the car took the steep and sharp bends towards the mountains. Andy drove confidently and smiled at her from time to time.

"Dušička, it is so good you're returning home," he said.

"Yes, I've been very homesick," she put her hand on his thigh, "I have been missing home."

"We have all been longing," he said and put his hand on hers. "Erika and Yehoshua too. Erika is so worried about you. They are very eager to come for a short visit tomorrow. Would that be all right? I said we'd see how you feel."

"I hope it will be all right," she replied, "I want to see them too. I have been missing Erika, but first the children. I must see them before anything."

After Andy parked the car and they got out, Marta stopped and looked at the house. She was returning home. They were here, waiting for her. The door opened, and a sigh escaped her. Michael and Naomi were coming her way. Her heart leapt. They seemed to have grown. She looked at them and then ran towards them, her arms stretched out. Her voice shook when she said their names: "Michki, my Nomchik." The two of them stood there, looking at her a little shyly. She hugged Michael tight, and then Naomi, and she sensed their bodies resisting, stiffening.

"Good you're back, Mommy," said Naomi, "good to see you."

"It's good to see you—finally," she said, trying to sound light-hearted but already aware of the heaviness.

Marta looked about her. The house was clean and orderly. Everything was in its place, and a jar holding red carnations stood on the table. She turned to Andy. He had remembered she loved carnations. It was so good to be home.

"Are you hungry?" Andy asked. "Naomi has prepared a light lunch."

"Thank you, Nomchik sweetheart."

They entered the kitchen and sat down at the table. "How lovely," she said, "How lovely and tasty."

"I hope it is tasty," said Naomi, "I hope . . ."

"Nomchik . . ."

As they had their meal, little was said. They took care not to ask too much, and she took care not to tell too much. She felt more relaxed when they finished the meal, but already she was overtaken by a great tiredness.

"I will go and have a little rest now," she said, smiling apologetically.

"Of course," said Andy, "let's take your bag to the room. It's just the right time for an afternoon nap. I'll lie down for a bit as well. But I'll clear up here first of all."

"You go, Daddy, go on," said Naomi, "you take a rest. I'll clear the dishes, clean the table, and do the washing up. Michael will help me."

Marta and Andy went to the bedroom, and Naomi and Michael stayed in the kitchen, silent, avoiding each other's eyes. It was that way between them too. Later, Michael went into his room and closed the door and Naomi lay down on the sofa in the sitting room, facing the ceiling, as she listened to the guitar sounds coming from Michael's room. Not long after, Andy came out of the bedroom.

"Mommy is asleep," he said, "we must let her sleep. The medicine she takes also makes her sleep."

"Sure, she should sleep as much as she needs." Naomi lifted a book from the low table, avoiding conversation.

Marta slept all through the afternoon and got up, her hair tousled, towards six.

"I've slept so long," she said, and added, smiling, "I'll go and take a shower now, wash off the hospital."

"Excellent," said Andy from the kitchen, "dinner will be ready by the time you come out. A Friday night meal."

"What are you making for us? It's so good to be back home. I am so happy."

"It's a surprise," said Andy, "a surprise."

When she came out of the bathroom, dinner was on the table, a challah bread in the middle and a two-armed candelabra with two candles. Andy served the lecsó he had cooked. Rice and fried vegetables. The hot food steamed, and the smell reminded her of forgotten meals. She tasted a little, and a smile covered her face.

"Dušička, it's just as it should be," she said, and Andy glowed with happiness. From the corner of her eye, Marta noticed that Naomi and Michael moved the fried vegetables to the edge of their plates. It was not food for Sabras. They spoke very little during the meal, but later, finally, the four of them felt more relaxed. Naomi had baked a chocolate cake for dessert, and

Andi served tea. Once they sat on the sofa, Marta told them about Dina and her drawings, and she showed them the one she had with her. She went on to tell them about all the activities the clinic offered, and about the garden; but about Dr. Neuman she said nothing. It wasn't the kind of thing one spoke about, she thought, and she didn't know what to tell them, anyway. That night, she felt strange in the shared bed, but she felt protected too, with the heat of Andy's body. He hugged her tight, her back turned to him, and he whispered:

"Martushkam, my dušička."

"Yes," she replied and fell asleep.

She stayed in bed until midday. On entering the kitchen, she saw the children's alarmed expressions. She passed her hand over Michael's head and sat at the table.

"Good morning, Mommy. How are you? Shall I make you a cup of tea?" Naomi asked.

"Yes darling, thanks."

"Would you like to eat anything? We're actually about to have lunch. Daddy made goulash, the way you like it, without meat."

"Where is Daddy?"

"I think he might have gone to the shed. He said he was going to make something for you."

"No, I won't eat now. Just tea. Thank you, Nomichka."

Marta hardly ate anything at lunch time, and later she went to lie down again. Towards the end of the afternoon, Michael went to a youth movement activity, and Naomi began packing her bag. She would be returning to Eilat the next morning, to the bird observatory, and before that she wanted to meet some friends. Andy went into the bedroom and lay down at Marta's side.

"Dušička, I am happy you came. And you?" he asked. "How do you feel?"

"I am tired," she said weakly, "I am so tired."

"Yes, I can see that. But still, are you happy you came?"

"Yes, but I am so tired. I think I have to go back there."

"Of course, Martushkam. We will return tomorrow morning. I noticed you don't have a bedside lamp in the room, so I prepared you one. I'll fix it when we get there, and then you'll be able to read in bed, before you go to sleep."

"Thank you, my Duši," said Marta and snuggled up, "tomorrow we will return."

***

On Sunday morning Marta and Andy drove back to the hospital. Andy's hands gripped the wheel hard and his eyes were fixed on the road. Marta, resting her head against the window, looked at the villages, the fields, the olive trees that were passing, like through a camera panning lazily. Andy drove confidently, slowed down at the sharp bends and the journey passed without her feeling her usual sickness. He parked the car in the large parking lot which was dry by now, and they crossed it, heading to the department. When they entered, Marta was not terror stricken as she had been the first time. She even felt the slightest bit of solace and she turned toward Andy with gratitude.

"Here we are," said Andy to the nurse in the office.

"Good morning, Marta." She aimed her words to Marta, beyond Andy's shoulder. "How was the weekend? Good, I hope. Your meeting with Dr. Neuman has been delayed because he's not coming in this morning," she said and cast a look at the clock that hung on the wall. "Well, the morning has already gone. We will shift the meeting to three in the afternoon. Now you can go to your room and put your things in order. You can rest till lunch time. Three o'clock, then, OK?"

"All right," said Marta. She looked at the clock, and then, questioningly, at the nurse.

"Well, yes. Dr. Neuman had to attend an unexpected meeting, but as you see, he has not forgotten about you." She laughed and said, "He made time for you in the afternoon, so that gives you an opportunity to rest."

Marta nodded. She and Andy entered the corridor heading towards her room. Andy carried the suitcase and her folded coat, and she had her small handbag on her arm.

"Is Dr. Neuman your therapist?" Andy asked, as they walked down the corridor. "I didn't know. You didn't tell me."

"Yes," Marta answered, "he is my therapist."

"But I understood he does not take on individual therapies. He has a lot to do, hasn't he, being the head of the unit?"

"Yes. No. I really don't know. I have not had meetings with anybody else. Do you think there's something wrong?"

"Of course I don't. On the contrary. I am happy the head of the unit is treating my wife. He is probably the best therapist they have here, so it's very good."

Reaching the room, Andy opened the door and Marta entered. It was empty and quiet. The two beds were made. Andy put the suitcase on Marta's bed and took a bag out of it.

"Now I'll connect that bed lamp I fixed, so you can use it."

Marta sat on Dina's bed, watching how he put the lamp on her bedside table and looked for the nearest wall plug. He moved the bed, bent over and plugged the lamp into the socket. Then he got up, shoved the bed back in position, and switched on the light. "Let there be light," he said, turning towards her, smiling. She smiled back, but he saw the tears.

"Dušička, everything will be all right, you will see. Dr. Neuman is a specialist, he will treat you as well as possible. You'll see it will be all right. Come on, get up, I am going now; I still have to put in at least half a day's work."

Marta rose and Andy wrapped his arms around her, again whispering: "You'll see, you'll be fine." Her arms dangled. They hurt.

"Look after them," she said, "look after Naomi and Michael—don't let them be sad."

When Andy was almost out of the room, Marta asking him what had happened to Erika and Yehoshua. Why hadn't they visited? Andy walked back into the room and hugged her again.

"They phoned on Saturday morning, and I told them you needed to rest."

Marta gently disengaged herself and thought she would have liked Erika to spend a little time with her. She was the only person in the world who knew; after all, they had gone through everything together. But things were not always easy with Erika either. The competition between them, from way back when they were girls at home—she could not shake it off. So here we are, she thought bitterly, in the end it's me, the one who was strong, popular, and determined, who is sick in hospital. I who looked after her throughout the nightmare we went through, and she doesn't visit.

It was three in the afternoon when Marta walked into Dr. Neuman's quiet and slightly dark office. It was good to be back. Through the window she saw the wooden bench on which she and Dina sometimes sat and chatted. The rain had returned, the bench was wet, and a puddle had formed near it.

"Marta," said Dr. Neuman, "it's good to see you again. How was your weekend home? "

"So-so . . . I found it a bit difficult."

"Yes, I understand. That happens, you know? Can you tell me what was difficult? Meeting the children? Andy?"

"I don't know what happened. Nothing happened. Suddenly it was hard, just like that. When I arrived home I was so happy, my heart jolted with joy. Andy tried so hard, and so did the children, but I couldn't tell them where I had been, where I had vanished, why I am in hospital, what had happened to me . . ."

"Did they ask you?"

"No. It's as though they knew they shouldn't ask, because if they did I . . . Something bad would happen."

"Something bad happen to whom?"

"Me . . . them . . ."

"What would have happened if you'd told them? Do you think you'll be able to, eventually?"

"Yes. But I don't want them to hear about those horrible things. I am afraid something bad will happen to them . . . I can't even think the past, so how will I be able to tell them?"

"Could you tell me what those things are?"

"Everything. That terrible wound which never heals. How they rounded us up and took us to that place where they were going to kill us. I cannot think about when they separated us. We couldn't grasp how it could have happened. We didn't understand what was happening. Yelling, dogs, beatings. All of a sudden we had become two groups, women and men. And later, again, we couldn't understand. They separated me and Erika from Mama and little Eva. It was all so fast that we didn't see that it had happened. All I remember is that Mama spoke to some Nazi officer who addressed her coarsely, telling him she was fifty-seven. I remember looking at her and wondering why she was adding ten years to her age. That's it, and then I did not see them again. Later I understood what had made her do that. Our mother understood that that was it, the end, death, and she wouldn't leave little Eva alone. It was a split second, and our family simply fell apart and vanished. They didn't even allow us to die together. I still don't know what happened to my father, my brothers. How can I even begin to describe this? . . . And then the camps, Erika and I . . . The lowest place. You think . . ."

A heavy silence filled the room, hung motionless in the air, and then like a thunder clap exploded into dire weeping. From her bag, Marta took the handkerchief Dr. Neuman had given her. He saw that the handkerchief had been washed and ironed. She wiped her face and then held it out to him, smiling a little through her tears.

"Thank you. I am sorry it . . ."

"No need, Marta," said Dr. Neuman, "You can keep it with you for now. There's no rush."

"I am tired," she said, "so tired. It's killing me."

***

The visit home turned out not to have done Marta any good. On the contrary, when she returned to the ward it became clear she was on a downward slope. Again, she closed in on herself, detaching herself from the ward's routines. She refused to join the morning assembly, stopped visiting the activities room, and no longer went into the garden with Dina. The only thing that went continued as before were the meetings with Dr. Neuman. The rest of the day, Marta mostly spent in her room, huddled in her bed. Conversation with Dina stopped almost completely. And when she did leave the room, she would pass through the corridor keeping close to the wall, her body drawn in, her expression even darker than usual, silent. Only rarely did she go into the garden, to sit alone on her and Dina's bench. Sometimes Dr. Neuman saw her, through the window of his office, sitting all bunched up on the edge of the bench.

During the weekly staff meetings, Dr. Neuman said that Marta should be left alone for now to allow her to have her own daily routine. No staff member expressed an opinion, even if they had different ideas about Mrs. Kraus's clinical condition. They understood that the responsibility for this particular case was that of the head of the department. He did not share his decisions about how he approached Marta's therapy and limited himself to short briefings about her condition. As for himself, he documented each meeting at length, devoting whatever time it took, and even more, to her therapy, in spite of his heavy workload. The professional team was not unaware of Dr. Neuman's special treatment, and sometimes they mentioned it to one another, but they never doubted his decisions and intentions.

Again, the meetings with Dr. Neuman became hard for Marta. Even though she felt his great sympathy for her, his sincere wish to help; and she really wanted, somehow, to oblige him and talk, but it was too difficult, almost impossible. The black, dense screen came down again, behind which memories could be heard whispering, breathing with difficulty, both alive and dead, detached from her. While Dr. Neuman tried to make her feel more at ease, Marta cowered in the chair, speechless.

"Marta," Dr. Neuman tried to get her to communicate during one of these meetings, "I made some small adjustments in your medication, and I believe it will soon start making a difference. You do take your medicine, don't you?"

"Yes." She nodded.

"That's important. The pills will help you, they will make you mentally stronger. But it is also important to talk."

"Yes . . . I . . ."

"I understand." Dr. Neuman hesitated. "We will wait. It will come."

"No. Nobody can understand," said Marta, "and I am not sure it will come."

"You are right, of course. But maybe we can say that I understand that it cannot be understood." He smiled.

"It cannot. It cannot," Marta said, smiling sadly.

"I agree. It sounds a bit strange, but that's how it is. Even though it's incomprehensible, I would still like to explain how I see it. Would you like to hear?"

"Hear?" Marta wondered aloud. "What?"

"How I see things. I would like to explain what I think."

"All right," she sighed, sinking back in the chair.

"In our meetings, I see you, I listen to you, even when you don't talk. Silence, too, is a kind of talking, isn't it?"

Marta nodded.

"Well, then. I can see how difficult it is for you. I understand. I don't know what it was exactly that happened, but I know it was terrible."

Marta nodded again.

"And then there is something else I see—that maybe you don't notice."

"What?"

"I see the possibility of getting well. And what's more important, I notice you have the will to get well, to get out of this situation."

"Yes?"

"Certainly! And I really want to tell you this. Sometimes when things are so this hard, you lose sight of it. I can definitely see the possibility of change. I believe you will succeed. That we will succeed together."

"Together?" She looked at him.

"You and I. As your doctor, I will do all I can for you to get well. But you, Marta . . . you have to do all you can, too."

"That is not much," she said.

"Right. That's exactly what this illness is all about. But it's something, nevertheless. Your power to get well will keep growing."

"I must find my strength. In the past, you know, I had it, but now . . ."

Suddenly she wanted him to know she had not always been this weak and defeated. She wanted him to know that she had had the strength, that she had been able to go on living even though everything that had happened was killing her slowly, all the time, more and more. Now this seemed so remote that she wondered whether she had not dreamt it up. Now she had no strength, she was lost. This sense of being lost scared and upset her. What would happen? She was afraid of what she had experienced in the past and she was afraid of what was happening to her now, of madness. Would she ever be able to approach the life she wanted, could she rid herself from the nightmare, her nightly terrors and horrors, the bog into which she was sinking ever deeper during her waking hours, every day? Her strength was running out. Though she did not want to go under, a huge weight was pulling at her, taking her down, and she could not find a hold and free herself.

These things also affected her relationship with Dina. After her return, Marta kept conversation to a minimum, and the words Dina directed at her remained suspended in the air, unanswered. They were not so close anymore. Dina was about to be released, and the approaching separation threatened Marta who became even more deeply immersed in her own grief. They did not often meet, not even in the evenings when both of them were in the room.

Marta lay on her bed while Dina got ready to return home in the Jordan Valley. She pulled her suitcase from under her bed and every so often packed a few things. Watching her, Marta remembered her family's suitcases, how they had packed them in a hurry, one for each. No more. What to take along? And why, what use would it be? Everything, after all, was taken away from them in the end. Where were all those suitcases now? From time to time, Dina noticed Marta was looking and would turn her face to her, letting her shoulders drop with a sigh.

"Oh, Marta, you will leave too. You won't spend the rest of your life here, right? You're not crazy."

Marta looked at her with dread. She was familiar with stories about people who had returned crazy, people who stayed in mental institutions. She wondered about the boundary beyond which there is madness and whether she was coming close. There were days when she felt at risk, when madness approached, surrounding her, too close, and there were other days when she felt nothing, to the point that she was not sure whether she still existed.

Marta wanted the intimacy between her and Dina to last, but grief got in the way. She worried that her low, intolerable mood would oppress Dina. She knew about this very well from back in their village in the Galilee. People did not want to know; they looked at her with distrust. It cannot be, they said. But she knew it did happen. People don't imagine that everything is possible, even the impossible. The few connections she made were with women like herself, who had themselves experienced these things, and who like her did not talk, could not talk. In the very same way that Erika and she could not talk when they were together. Dina promised she would write, stay in touch. She said that maybe they could meet once Marta was well and back home, but Marta could not imagine this possibility. Goodbyes were final. She had hoped for so many years that at least someone, still, had survived and was trying to find their way to her. For years and years she had listened intently to the woman on the radio reading out lists of names of people looking for relatives, names of places. Perhaps she would hear one of the names she was waiting for. She remembered little Naomi at play nearby in the room, watching her, puzzled. What could she tell the little girl?

In her medical file, Dr. Neuman noted down that he had observed a regression, back to deep depression. The medication is insufficient, he wrote, we must find another way. Marta must try to talk. He wrote that he should review her medical treatment and look for alternative therapeutic methods. He believed in the healing power of talk, in the therapist's listening presence, as well as in a personal, direct approach. Conversations, for him, were a valuable part of the treatment because, he believed, they enabled the doctor to get to know his patient better and even to identify with them. And in addition, things said in conversation were likely to help a therapist understand a patient's symptoms. And yet he was fully aware that patients often were unable to talk about what had happened to them. Words were dangerous, too explicit. In those cases, a therapist had to find creative ways around the problem.

Outwardly, Dr. Neuman did not appear a creative person. He tended to wear clothes in conservative greys and browns, meticulously pressed and ironed, though they looked well used and comfortable. He had never been seen wearing new or brightly colored clothes. Through summer and winter he wore the same grey socks, and his shoes and sandals came in shades of brown. The only sign of imagination was the colorful old scarf he wore in the winter. Nor was Dr. Neuman particularly inspired in his relations with his team. He usually stuck to formal address and made sure to keep a distance. He rarely had a casual interaction at work. He would have his coffee in his office and only join the others when they drank a toast to celebrate some personal occasion. His staff had grown used to the discrepancy between his grey appearance and his creative, unconventional therapeutic ideas.

Dr. Neuman had experience with patients like Marta. At the time, many people like her, who had survived and started a new life, were collapsing. The past came to settle its account: grief and pain attacked and demanded to be heard. Like a slow, relentless process of erosion, memories kept gnawing at the soul. Ever more victims, in a delayed response to trauma, found themselves in psychiatric wards. Dr. Neuman did not feel at ease with how these people were usually labeled: "the saved." Terminology matters, he argued, and these people were not saved from anything. They experienced trauma which they could not recollect, which they were forbidden to recollect, but nor could they forget. These people may have survived, but they were not saved. They went on being tortured and were suffering.

Dr. Neuman had followed many such cases over the years. In his experience, treatment of "the saved" demanded a great deal of compassion, recognition of the great suffering caused by reopened wounds and the difficulty patients had in getting better. Recovery was fragile, temporary, and it required, he argued, the therapist to take an interest in what patients said, to empathize, be present, listen. The mental wounds these patients carried were like unexploded landmines left in a warzone. They stayed in the injured soul and would explode upon the slightest careless movement. They could not be dismantled without care, without identification. Medicine brought some help, but, Dr. Neuman repeated again and again, it was talk—the patient's and the therapist's—that was at the center of the healing process. This was his position, though the hospital management did not always like it.

For Marta, her return from her visit home marked the beginning of a difficult period. But even though her condition grew worse, Dr. Neuman decided not to increase her medication. Medication always has side effects, and he hoped that they would be able to return to talk in order for something to open up. Their meetings continued as before, and Marta spoke very little. On one occasion, she mentioned the poetry of Jiří Wolker, a Czech poet she loved, a poet who had borne the sadness of the world. She identified with his short and tragic life and with his poetry about the soul's anguish. She read aloud to Dr. Neuman, in her own free translation, a poem about the poet's certain death from tuberculosis: "When I die, nothing in the world will happen or change, Only a few hearts will tremble like roses under morning dew . . ." She quoted the words he asked to be written on his headstone:

> Here lies Jiří Wolker, a poet who loved the world
> and fought for its justice.
> Before he could get his heart to fight,
> he died—a young man of twenty-four.

Wolker's poetry turned out to be the faltering start of exchanges about literature and poetry, conversations that removed both reality and Marta's illness from the room and gave her confidence.

It was during this phase, when Marta was saying so little, that a closeness between them emerged which was to develop over time. Of course, Dr. Neuman remained the therapist and she his patient, but there was something else too. It was hard to put a finger on what it was, but something now occurred the room. Following some changes of schedule, the their meetings moved to the early afternoon. This was when Dr. Neuman was less taken up by his other responsibilities. For Marta, the time was also more convenient. She could take a little rest after lunch and then go to his office. When she entered, he would receive her with a smile and ask her to sit down. She would feel his eyes on her, following her as she sat down in the easy chair with a soft sigh. She took note of these brief moments, how their eyes met, and she realized that he wasn't limiting the length of their meetings. She sensed he wanted to be in her presence, to talk with her, and she was aware of her own wish to be with him.

Marta observed some small changes in the room. A vase containing flowers now stood on the low table, and an electric kettle had appeared in a small corner created on a bookshelf. There were two cups and three small tin boxes carrying white labels on which someone had written "coffee," "tea," "sugar." Dr. Neuman would offer her something to drink, and usually she would answer, "Tea, please." Once he asked her whether she would like her tea with lemon, and she replied that she actually preferred hers with some milk. At the next meeting, when he gave her the tea, he apologized, "I am sorry, there's no fridge in this room, but here's concentrated milk," and squeezed the white tube. Thanking him, Marta stirred the thick, sweet paste into the cup of tea with a light movement of her wrist. She was very depressed, but not abstracted.

***

On the day Dina left to go back to her kibbutz, Marta stayed in the room. After breakfast, she returned to the room, lay on her bed, missed lunch, and failed to show up for her afternoon meeting with Dr. Neuman. A nurse found her lying in bed, covered up to her head. Marta said she was not feeling well and turned towards the wall. The nurse did not interfere, returned to her office, and reported back to Dr. Neuman. He asked her to make sure Marta took her medicine.

Throughout the day, Marta stayed in bed. In the late afternoon, Dr. Neuman gently knocked on her door, and when no answer came, he walked in quietly. Marta lay in bed, her arms lifeless on the blanket, her eyes staring at the ceiling. Moving a chair closer to the bed, he sat down. "Marta," he whispered and took her hand in his, "Marta . . ." She faced him, pulled her hand away, and put both her arms under the blanket.

"I am cold," she said, "I am so cold."

"It is quite cold in here, actually," he answered. "The winter isn't really over yet, even though . . . I think there must be more blankets in the cupboard." He looked around, got up, and went to the wooden cupboard. He took out one of the woolen blankets that lay folded on the floor of the cupboard, spread it over Mata, and sat by her side. "Is that better? You'll feel warmer soon. Would you like a hot drink?"

"No. I want to sleep," she said and moved her head. "Yes, I', getting warmer. Thank you—really."

"Excellent. I hope you can sleep well."

He bent over her and lightly touched her covered shoulder.

"Good night, Marta, we will meet tomorrow. I'll be waiting for you at the usual time."

Marta nodded from under the blanket. On leaving, he closed the door very carefully and then rushed to his room where he sat for a long time, Marta's file open before him. He made some notes, but soon stopped writing, leant back in his chair, and looked out the window into the descending dark.

Marta came for their meeting the next day. She looked paler and weaker than usual; her black eyes shone. Dr. Neuman got up and accompanied her to the corner where they sat.

"Hello. Sit down. I am happy you are here. I hope you slept well."

"Yes," Marta nodded, "I slept well, but . . ."

"Did you have dreams?"

"No, no, I don't remember any dreams. But I awoke with a strange feeling."

"Can you describe the feeling?"

"It was the air around me. As though something was stuck to me, stuck all around me, and going with me everywhere. A kind of suit wrapping me and sticking to me wherever I go . . . I cannot get rid of it."

"Is that a good feeling? A protective cover?"

"Not at all. It is something sad . . . dense . . . something that is stuck to me, I cannot get out of it."

"Something you haven't felt before?"

"Not in this way. When I first arrived, I felt a lot of sadness and pain inside, and now it seems to enclose me from the outside . . . Now it is from inside and outside at once. I . . ."

"Do you feel imprisoned?"

"Yes, that's what I feel."

"Is that somehow related to Dina?"

"Saying goodbye to Dina is so hard. It's a terrible thing, to lose a friendship."

"I understand it's hard to say goodbye, but you can keep in touch. It's not . . . I understand . . . And yet it is not what you think."

"No, I don't think."

"You developed a close friendship. That's very unusual here, you know. You are saying farewell to a friend, but that grief that envelops you, that's not just Dina. It is grief about many more farewells. Farewells that were forced on you. Farewells that were final and harsh. I hope we will be able to talk about them."

Back in her room, Marta tried to remember how the idea of writing had come up between them. Had it been Dr. Neuman? Was it she who had this image of herself sitting at his desk and writing? The idea was mentioned in Dr. Neuman's brown office, and it made her shiver. Many years ago, when everything that happened was still alive and burning inside her, she had thought about being a poet, being able to write it down. She always thought artists were the happiest people. Artists were able to express their feelings, and this allowed them to protect their souls. Again and again, she'd had this thought: not clear, not formulated, and she knew this was dangerous territory. Intense feelings burning her from inside. Grief, guilt, misery dragged her down in one rolling landslide after another. It was as though she were locked up in prison, yearning, but in vain, to get out. She was in a whirlpool of happiness and sadness, thrown from one state into another. Would she ever be able to write this?

Some years ago she had written. That was when Andy was away for work, and she stayed alone with the children for one entire week. The space of Andy's absence gave her a strange feeling of freedom and autonomy. She took an empty brown exercise book from the children, turned it back to front, and began to write. She wrote without any order, releasing the words into the world and onto the paper. She felt that writing was setting her free, making her feel good, but when Andy returned, she hid the notebook in the kitchen drawer, under the tablecloths and towels, and never went back to it.

When she told this to Dr. Neuman she saw his surprise. Yes, she wrote in Hebrew, she said. With mistakes, though. She smiled; she would probably always confuse some of its letters.

"*Alef* and *ayin* sound the same, how can you tell the difference?"

"I agree," Dr. Neuman replied and smiled.

"And then there are *tav* and *tet,* and *kaf* and *khaf.* I don't think I'll ever get them right."

"Yes, it's not easy."

"Really? So, yes, you could say I wrote in Hebrew, but with mistakes."

"Would you like to write again?"

"Maybe . . . I would like to go on writing in the exercise book with which I started."

Marta thought she would try and find the notebook next time she visited home and bring it back to the hospital. But she did not go out for another break. Dr. Neuman thought it was too early; it would not do her good, so she did not insist. During another meeting he again mentioned the idea that she begin writing again, and in a new notebook. Marta looked at the room and thought how happy she would be writing in Dr. Neuman's office. She felt protected there. A generous wooden table, walls lined with books, a light curtain in the window that opened onto the dull garden, brown upholstered chairs, and an enveloping gloom. She would like to sit down and write in a place like that.

Noticing her longing look at his office, Dr. Neuman said he would talk with the people responsible for maintenance and ask them to bring a table and an additional chair to her room. She could write whenever she wanted; he felt it was the right time. She looked at him in surprise, and then a smile formed on her lips. This is what Dr. Neuman wrote in his work notes: "Marta responds positively to the idea of writing! Continue!"

Some days later, on returning from a meeting with Dr. Neuman, Marta saw, by the side of her door, resting against the wall, an old desk with three drawers on its right side and a chair of the type they had in the activities room. She looked at them and then, with a decisiveness that surprised her, she dragged the furniture into her room, and arranged it near the window. This will be good—to sit at the table facing out, to turn my back to the room. Her window faced a small inner courtyard with a tall concrete wall at the end. Near her window was a messy pile of old furniture, some of it twisted and broken, and from some weeds and poppy flowers grew out of the cracks in the concrete pavement.

Marta sat at the table and looked out into the yard. How poor and ugly, she thought, and focused on the red of the poppies shining against the grey. Her hand went to the upper drawer, which opened with surprising ease. When she bent over it, she found a brown copybook and a pen. She picked up the book, glided her fingers over its rough cover, leafed through its empty pages, and then closed it again. On the cover, she wrote in hesitant letters: "Winter, Haifa." She looked at the words and they appeared detached from any context, almost alien. Winter, Haifa. The strangeness of the words, and between them, fascinated her, and she observed them as if they were graphic signs on brown paper, radiant. Then she read aloud: Winter; Haifa. The letters *het* and *het* in the Hebrew words *horef*, *Haifa* were harsh and grating. Marta returned the copybook and pen into the drawer and closed it.

Spring

Dr. Neuman did not ask Marta about the desk, but he was told it wasn't in the corridor anymore. That was enough. Sometimes, when Marta lay in bed, she looked at the desk and touched it lightly in pasing. The table made her happy. Sometimes she sat down at it, the notebook open in front of her, empty pages, words afloat in the air. She did not write, not just yet, but the wish to write began to emerge, a yearning to hold the pen, feel it moving on the blank paper, leaving marks. Words. She loved the act of writing, the movement of the hand making its marks. Her handwriting was pleasant, regular, a little stylized.

She had always strongly disliked any kind of excess. As an adolescent she had kept a diary. In the kibbutz, over a period of months, she had written daily letters to Andy. Love letters. In the first years, after the families no longer lived close by each other, she also had written to Erika. She had told her about their home in the new place, about the children, and about herself. There were years when she wrote to all kinds of remote addresses in an attempt to find out about her disappeared brothers. But this was something else. Her Hebrew characters showed that she had first learned to write in Slovakian, Hungarian, and German, from left to right. "How come you're writing like this?" Michael asked her once, looking on as she copied a recipe from the radio. "You write the wrong way around." Now, at times, her thoughts about writing were unclear. A kind of writing that would save the life she'd had—and maybe herself. It was not the first time that she'd thought about writing in this way. She knew that in spite of the time that had passed, and the silences, underneath layers that were darker than dark, she also harbored good memories, a whole family life, a happy childhood. It remained—how good. How difficult.

A whole life she'd had. A family. She could not put into words how she missed them, how full of pain this void was. At times her thoughts would stray to dangerous places. Oh, how happy her parents would have been with her small family—with Andy, Naomi, and Michael. How proud her mother would have been seeing her doing well as a housewife; how much, in spite of everything, Marta had learned from her. How good Öcsi's visits could have been, with he and Andy picking up their long conversations. How much calm would Andy bring along on his visits; what a beautiful aunt would little Eva have become . . . She must not let herself be carried away, because once they began there was no way of stopping her thoughts, and these thoughts would take her to their deaths—which remained blurry and beyond her imagination. Their last moments—how had they been? What were their thoughts . . . Each time she was assaulted by these thoughts she felt she was close to dying herself.

Dr. Neuman began to observe a tiny change after Marta got the desk and chair. She spoke a little more during their meetings. Slivers of childhood memories. Happy years. So much grief. "The grief, it does not go away. On the contrary, it grows," she told him during one of their meetings. "The passing of time blunts the memory of physical pain, the humiliations and fear we experienced. Those things can be overcome, I think. But my pain about the family, about them and me, us, only grows. It will be so big, at some point, that I won't be able to hold it. Could that be what is happening to me now?" An ongoing threat, suspended. Maybe if I wrote, she thought, maybe writing . . . She wanted to write after all. A writer whose name she did not recall had said that she wrote in order not to die, or something like that. Maybe that's how it is with me too, Marta thought. Maybe I need to write too.

She, too, noticed changes. The merest sensation: the density of air around her, the light. Sometimes, walking along the corridor, she stopped near the activities room, looking in as if she remembered something, observing the men and women working in quiet concentration. How deceptive, that calm. She remembered the huge gap between the silent action of her hands and the stormy thoughts inside her head. It was exactly when the body engaged in silent, familiar, and repetitive activity, when the hands dug into the clump of clay, used the paintbrush, or passed wool through the weaving loom, that thoughts were released to travel freely, like birds in the sky. She remembered herself in the room, how memories and images from the life she'd once had appeared out of nowhere. The colors made her yearn for the past; now she wanted to write.

On her shelf in the room, there were some letters Andy had written her, dutifully, once a week, a postcard from Dina, and a postcard from Naomi who was in Eilat studying the migration of birds. Marta's daughter wrote about the observation point, about the birds that arrived from the freezing north to spend the winter, about how pleasant the weather was during this season, before the great heat, and she asked how her mother was, hoping she was getting better. Kisses. Marta would answer all Naomi's questions, but first she would write Erika. Too much time had passed since they'd last met. She wanted to tell her what was happening to her and why she was in hospital. Erika was very familiar with her health problems, and she had often helped by taking Naomi and Michael off her hands. No, it was not something new, but a mental health ward was something else. And after all, Marta thought, she was here because of the image that had assaulted her, of the two of them and that kapo. Her memory was coming back. How would she tell Erika? Would she even want to hear?

Marta was saddened by the gulf that had opened between them, the awkwardness. They had after all been together all the way to death and back, slept huddled close for a whole year, worn the same filthy rags. Together they had endured forced labor, and together they had made the long journey back home. After that return, they had been together too. Clinging to each other, they went on, defending themselves against what was ahead and what was not. All this soldered a bond that would never be undone, they believed; but over the years, the bond was covered over by life, the life each of them built for herself, layer upon layer covering their closeness. The physical distance between them grew too. It took no more than a bus ride, but now it was no longer just the two of them: each with their own little family, each in her way trying to resume life. She did not remember when they were last together, just the two of them, alone.

But that was not all. She remembered what happened when the four of them left the kibbutz, Erika and Yehoshua, she and Andy, with a dream about a joint family, two couples and two little children. Life in a commune of their own, a commune of their authorship, their invention, the "holy family." They had left the kibbutz without anything, disappointed by the way it had lost its ideals, as they saw it, in the pursuit of the pragmatic and uninspired. They left convinced they could make the ideals they were dreaming of work, lead a spiritually meaningful life, a life of justice and equality, to move towards the "light," as they put it. They managed to find themselves an old, partly destroyed house in Tsfat, and there they lived together. A bubble of ideals within another town in ruins, among more houses that were also empty of former inhabitants, desperate and eager to fix the world, to fix their lives. But there had been disagreements, not so much about those ideals, more like irritations between her and Yehoshua about order.

Sometimes it occurred to her that it was not really about order, but was jealousy. She was aware of Yehoshua's admiration of Andy. He had beguiled

Yehoshua, during their time in the bunker, with his knowledge and broad education: he knew how to cite at length, in Hungarian, from Poe and Baudelaire, and from the Hungarian poet Endre Ady, and introduced him to the stories of Čapek the Czech. For Yehoshua, who had been educated in a yeshiva, a new, amazing world opened and carried him away. Most wonderful of all was music. Andy sang motifs from Beethoven's and Schubert's symphonies for him, from their piano sonatas, moving his fingers over imaginary keys. Andy nurtured Yehoshua and Yehoshua was captivated. Erika, it seemed, was not troubled by this, but Marta was. Yehoshua did not only come between her and Erika, but also between her and Andy, and because of this she bore him a grudge. Sometimes these thoughts troubled her mood. But the crisis eventually was about how to manage the household.

When they first met during that joyful summer after the war, she even appreciated Yehoshua's orderliness, and not less his ability to organize the work force which the movement decided to train in one of the mountain areas. They stayed in a vacation home surrounded by a peach orchard. The trees were full of fruit and the forest-covered mountains were burning in the colors of fall. They felt as though the gates of paradise had opened, were drunk on the beauty of nature, which seemed to have been left untouched by the recently ended war, and were giddy with their physical work in the woods, in the open air. The young men and women would go out into the woods in the morning to fell trees marked by the forester, a big bodily effort that brought them closer together; they were dizzy, feeding their dream about the new beautiful world they would build. Marta noticed that Yehoshua was one of the few who kept his feet on the ground. He did the boring, most crucial, routine work, providing the food supplies for their group of romantics. They had no idea how to go about organizing food supplies, about how food actually reached their table. They did not know anything about the dangers, in those days, of transporting food in areas plagued by hunger, how exhausting the negotiations with functionaries. What a drab, wearying, and responsible job he had taken on . . . And yet, you never heard him boast or complain.

She respected him, but had a hard time with his perfectionist way of running the household. She had her head in the clouds, was dreamy, rebellious, and the things around her were not placed perfectly; Yehoshua, on the other hand, had to have everything exactly where it should be. Irritations escalated into a crisis and from then on, they could no longer live together. She vividly remembered how it happened: it was about a letter from Šurany addressed to Marta and Erika. Someone who knew them sent them a letter, which took a long time to arrive, and it contained a photograph. This person had found this photograph thrown away in the yard of the town's synagogue. It was an old picture of the five of them facing the camera, with their father's cloth shop in their back: Andy, Öcsi, Erika, little Eva, and she, dressed in their holiday best. It was the wedding day of their aunt. She remembered that day well and the clothes, especially sewn for the occasion, that they were wearing. Eva was a toddler with golden curls, holding her toy rabbit by its long ear. They looked so real, so alive, not remotely aware of what was soon to unfold... Her heart broke. She took a long look at the picture, read the letter several times and put everything on the table.

In the evening, when she wanted to show the letter and the picture to Andy and Erika, they were gone. She searched and muttered anxiously: "Where could I have put them? I could have sworn I put them on the table." It took some time until Yehoshua came up with the envelope and its contents.

"All right. Now you can take it," he said angrily. "That will teach you to put things where they belong! The photograph is inside."

"You hid the envelope? Let me understand." She was amazed, pale with anger.

"No, I didn't hide it," came Yehoshua's rebuke, "I put it in its place. It's time you started putting things in their place, too."

She flushed and her eyes sparked. She faced him, enraged, pulled the envelope out of his hand, tore it to pieces, and threw the shreds on the floor. "That's it! I won't stay in this place!" she shouted and left the room, slamming the door, leaving Yehoshua, Erika, and Andy stupefied.

Late that evening she cast about under the table for the torn pieces of photograph, tried to glue them back together, but the damage could not be undone. Though she knew it would be no use, Erika nevertheless tried to reconcile Marta and Yehoshua. He apologized, Erika and Andy begged her to relent, forgive, but she wouldn't speak to Yehoshua at all. Nothing availed, not even Andy's explanations about the economic advantages of a shared household. She had never been pragmatic. They went their separate ways after a few weeks during which you could cut the air with a knife whenever Marta and Yehoshua were in the same space. Some months later she could be persuaded to visit Erika and Yehoshua in their new home and put the row behind her. Something had happened to the "holy family." What was hardest was the distance between her and Erika, in spite of the family get-togethers, mutual visits, the children who played together, the joint trips in the car Andy had from work. They all laughed together in Hungarian, but between them, Marta and Erika had stopped speaking Slovakian, their mother tongue.

Marta sat down at the desk and wrote Erika a long letter. She described the hospital, the thoughts that passed through her mind, and she told her that she missed her. She wrote she knew that it was difficult to get there by bus, but that she would be happy if Erika made a visit, so they could be together again, just the two of them, without Andy or Yehoshua. She so much wanted to feel that closeness between them, in her very body, to feel the force that bound them together, and be the old family again, not the "holy" one. She wanted to talk about it with Dr. Neuman. She might ask him to read the letter, that would be easier. She was not sure why but something inside her wanted for him to read, know what she wrote. That day she took the letter with her to their meeting and found herself offering it to him, right at the start of their conversation.

"This is what I wrote to my sister, yesterday," she said quickly.

"To Erika?"

"Would you read it? Please?"

Dr. Neuman took the envelope, looked at the address she had written on it, took out the letter, and looked at the sheets covered on both sides with her regular handwriting. He counted the pages and looked at her again.

"A long letter, Marta. It's very good you wrote. I promise to read it and return it tomorrow."

"No, please, read it now."

"Now?" Again he looked at her. "Hadn't we better use this meeting to talk about Erika, for instance. She has not been for a vis—"

"No, no, I'm asking you to read it now," she said, surprised at her own determination. "I'll sit and wait."

Dr. Neuman settled in his chair with a light sigh and looked at her with a serious expression, a little severe. "Marta, I cannot refuse you. All right, I will read."

He picked up the sheets and his eyes started moving along the lines. Marta too made herself easy in her chair and watched him reading her words, as though she was whispering them to him, making them pass straight from her to him, she thought, from one head into another, without any contact with the air. She looked at his face with concentration, trying to decipher the smallest movement; she watched his lips, the tension concentrated around his eyes and on his forehead. When he finished reading, he held onto the letter and briefly closed his eyes.

"Marta!" he said emotionally, "thank you for showing me this letter. You write so beautifully. It's written so . . . I don't know what to say . . . It's exact, yes, it's exact." He paused. "I am sure Erika will be happy with this letter. She must be missing you."

"We miss each other. I would say."

"Yes. I really hope Erika will visit. Even if it's just for a few hours. How do you feel now that you've written her?"

Marta blushed a little, glad that Dr. Neuman had read the letter, but especially because of his compliment about her writing. He thought she wrote beautifully, he liked what she had written. That was not at all on her mind when she asked him to read it, yet it moved her more than anything.

"Marta, how do you feel now that you've written to your sister?"

"Good. Very good, even, I think, yes!"

"Your bond is so strong I don't think anything can harm it. I can feel it in the things you wrote."

"That's right," whispered Marta, "and yet we have grown more distant. You understand. She continues without me."

"And you without her, Marta. That's how it is. But your relationship now is made of different stuff, the physical distance did not harm it, not significantly, I mean. If I may put it in rather strong words—your connection is carved in your souls, forever, if that doesn't sound too poetic." He smiled at her. "Do you agree?"

Of course she agreed. She liked his words: "carved in their souls," "forever." It felt comforting.

"Do send her the letter, Marta. I am sure she will come."

"That's what I feel too," she said. "Erika will come."

She had no doubt, but saying it herself and hearing it from Dr. Neuman was almost like feeling Erika's love physically, on her skin. It was an archaic love without which Marta would be unable to love anyone else, including Andy and the children. How she loved them! Suddenly it struck her. The love between her and Erika was unlike any other love in her life. This was what enabled her to keep the gate of love inside her open to the world.

***

Marta felt calmer now she had sent the letter to Erika. It was a first step. Perhaps now it would be easier to speak to Dr. Neuman. Both of them were awaiting Erika's visit, but things unfolded in such a way that Naomi was the first to visit. Marta brought Naomi's postcard to her meeting with Dr. Neuman and he suggested she tell him a little about her.

"About Naomi?" she asked, happy and worried at the same time.

"Yes, if you're willing."

"What do you want to know?"

"Whatever you wish to tell."

"Ah, Naomi," sighed Marta, "I don't have an easy time with her."

"Why?"

"She's rebellious. Same as I was."

"You were rebellious?"

"Oh yes. I told you before, rebellious and headstrong." Marta smiled. "You wouldn't believe it looking at me now."

"One can definitely believe it," he said, returning her smile. "You are still that way. I mean, they are features I can recognize in you . . ."

"That's not how I feel. In any case, Naomi is very rebellious. Poor thing," she sighed. "It's not easy at all with her father. Andy is a demanding father, he expects the children to obey. He is very exacting with them. Of course he loves them, but things have to be done the way he thinks right, the way he decides. That's not easy, you understand?" She stopped briefly. "It worries me, what is happening back there now."

"At home?"

"Yes, now that Andy is alone with them. Especially with Michael because he is quiet and sensitive, and Andy is not always sensitive enough."

"I am sure everything at home is fine, you should not worry on that account. You yourself told me what a fine youth leader he was over there, in Budapest."

"That's not at all the same. And he is no longer the same . . . Don't be so sure that everything is all right, Dr. Neuman. It definitely can't be easy for Michael."

"And for you? I mean . . ." He hesitated for a moment. "How does it work between you? Is Andy the one who decides?"

"In many cases, yes. You see, I'm no longer a rebel. I am a retired rebel." She smiled, and added, "Michael navigates somehow between the drops, but Naomi puts her foot down. There's a lot of tension between them; often she is forced to give up, take things on. She gives up, she has no choice."

"How do you take that? Do you interfere?"

"Sometimes I try, but only when we're alone, Andy and I. I tell him he's too hard on the children, sometimes, impatient."

"And does Naomi also oppose you?"

Marta fell silent. Naomi was restless, kept her distance. Yes, she also opposed Marta, but between mother and daughter it was something else. Marta wanted to talk about that relationship, about an unrealized intimacy, painful distance. She always looked in amazement at Naomi's ability to be and conduct herself, to find her own way. Even as a baby, her strength was surprising. In the shared playpen in the kibbutz children's home, Naomi, who was the smallest, struggled for her own space. At times she even attacked other babies, so that the caregivers had to remove her from the others. It pleased Marta that she would not give in and fought. Yes, even then she had a strong will to lead her own life—and she still did. When she grew up a little, Naomi began to draw circles around herself, boundaries, to keep people at bay and be in her own safety zone. Michael was more gentle-natured. He looked for closeness, cuddled up against her body, was easy. He remained close to her, but he was introverted and quiet, too quiet. Maybe that was how it went with second-born children.

How unlike each other they were, these two children! How each of them went their own way . . . and yet each was vulnerable too. We all are. Something might unexpectedly surface in Marta, or in them, there was no way of knowing. One must be cautious, hold the reins, keep steady and secure control over one's emotions. She knew all too well how exposed she was, as sensitive as a seismograph's needle to the slightest stir, any threat below the surface.

She made sure not to interfere with or upset Naomi's and Michael's lives. She was particularly cautious when it came to her relationship with Naomi. The two of them were careful. One day she found a sheet of paper on Naomi's shelf with a drawing of a red heart pierced by an arrow. "I also used to draw such hearts when I was a girl," she said to Naomi, put in mind of her many childhood infatuations. She was tempted to ask her about it, move closer, But Naomi grabbed the sheet and tore it to pieces. An absolute refusal of any possible intimacy. I understand her, she thought, she senses the danger and withdraws. With Michael it was easier, or maybe I simply didn't understand him at all.

"It's not easy to grow up with a mother like me. I get too immersed, sad. A lot of sadness. It's like an illness from which I don't manage to recover. Sometimes I worry Naomi and Michael will catch it too. A sad mother— that's not good for children. Not good. I do try to keep them out of my sadness, but before I do that, I must first move away from this grief myself, and that, I believe, is impossible. Which makes me sink even deeper. And then they . . . you understand? It's a kind of circle."

"That's very true, Marta. When a person who's very close and dear to us suffers, we identify with their pain and then it sticks to us too. Between parents and children it's even more intense. Without it one cannot think of moving towards recovery."

"What do you mean—recovery?"

"It's a good thing your children are sensitive to your pain. Had they been indifferent, insensitive to your state, it would have been difficult, it would have been hard to make progress with our therapy. But I always say that what really matters is what we do with that pain."

Dr. Neuman fell silent and looked at Marta. She returned his look as though waiting for him to continue. What does one do with the pain? What is possible? Something about his expression touched her.

"There's another important thing, Marta," he resumed, "and I ask you to remember it whenever you start feeling guilty . . . Guilt is what interferes most with healing."

"And say that is how it is—how, I wonder, dear Dr. Neuman, does one get rid of guilt?

"That, dear Marta, is part of the big problem." He laughed and went on: "A parent's suffering is very hard to take for a child, but that's not all there is to it. The question is, again, what does one do with the pain? Does this pain puts an end to love? That's the important question. When a parent does not feel love for their child, it's the most destructive thing. Love and care are the groundwork for relationships, for the child's ability to develop and grow. You don't need me to tell you that. When a child feels love and can trust it, he or she can cope with many difficulties." Dr. Neuman stopped, leaned back, and stared. Marta wondered what he was thinking. "I am sorry, Marta, if that sounded like a short lecture in psychology," he apologized a little, "but I am asking you not to forget."

"Of course I love them, it's . . ."

"That isn't always obvious, Marta. Not all parents know how to love their children. Sometimes they are unable because of what they themselves went through. That is very sad because children need love. They cannot do without it."

"Yes, I know . . ."

"The love you feel for them makes up for their difficulties and protects them. By loving them you enable them to live with your sadness without being badly hurt. That's a very crucial thing. We might say that you allow your children to live in spite of the sadness you are passing onto them, even if they are not quite aware. They are being loved, and that cannot be faked. They can build themselves in spite of what happened to you. Do you understand? It's important."

"I understand what you are saying . . . it's true," she said, surprised how he could know how much she loved her children. She did not remember talking about it.

"I mean you and Andy, naturally."

"I am thinking of what happened to us, to Erika and me . . . to all of us. That's how we were raised, with our parents' love, like some invisible dress which we felt was covering us. It covered us and protected us everywhere, always. They did not hug us all that much, because that's how it was then, and they were so busy—our father with the shop and earning a living, our mother with her never-ending work at home—and they didn't indulge us, but we still felt loved all the time and that they were looking after us. Not just for food . . . You are right, it's true."

She loved her children, but it was not easy with Naomi. Sometimes Naomi made her feel awkward. Maybe it was because she could see herself in her daughter, the way she had been as a girl and adolescent. Physically, too, they looked very much alike, "like two sisters," said the assistants, flatteringly, in clothes shops. Like Marta, Naomi was very independent, unruly, and liked being outdoors. Once the family moved to its own house, she wandered around the large plot, skirting its boundaries, strolled through the vegetable patch, climbed the olive trees, and tried to return fallen sparrow chicks to their nests. Marta observed her growing into a local girl.

Occasionally she let her do little jobs in the yard, like looking after the ducklings and taking them for a stroll or watering the fruit trees. At times, Naomi would disappear for hours, going on long hikes all by herself. A little girl walking through fields, in the hills, between stone fences and hedgerows made of cacti—Marta saw how it filled Naomi with inexplicable joy. Marta was so familiar with this pleasure of the outdoors. Now she was anxious and tried to find a way to tell Naomi it was dangerous.

"Why? What's so dangerous about a walk like that?" Naomi would ask innocently. "What could happen?"

"You could be bitten by a dog." Marta could not bring herself to talk about other dangers. She was aware this was wrong. She should warn her children, talk to them about threatening dangers, help them be alert, prepare them for reality. That was a parent's job. But she could not. Even the basic things any mother would say, like not talking to strangers, especially those who tried to tempt them with candy, she just did not know how to broach them. Marta was that wounded. She could not approach those areas, not even when it was only with words.

"What do your children know about what happened to you?"

"I'm not sure." She hesitated: "I've not told them anything." She moved her head. "They've never asked," she added as if to apologize because she knew it was not their fault.

"Nothing?" he asked. "Never? Not a word?"

We never told them anything, she thought, and felt guilty once more. For the first time, Marta could clearly see the abyss over which she and Andy had been raising Naomi and Michael. She was unable to do anything about it. It could not be different. She remembered one Holocaust Remembrance Day when Naomi told her about a school assignment they had been given, in which they were asked to look up local people who had survived the war, ask them for their recollections, and write them down. She had been unable to say to Naomi, "Look, your mother, I'm one of them, you need not find out at the neighbors. Come, let me tell you. Your mother was sent to Auschwitz on a goods train and her entire family was destroyed." All Marta told her was that she did not think it a good idea. Perhaps people did not want to remember. It was all she could say to Naomi. Still, the girl went on her mission that day with a friend and asked other people what they had experienced, and later they talked about it in their class. Marta looked at Dr. Neuman, and he seemed dismayed.

"But Marta," he said, his voice shaking a little, it seemed to her, "you have a number on your arm. Didn't she notice? Did she really not know her mother is a Holocaust survivor?"

She shrank in her seat, overcome by guilt again. "I don't think she knew. I never told her. When she was young, she asked me once about the number and I told her it was from the war. She never asked again, and I didn't say anything." She fell silent. "They don't know, but they understood—there's all these things in the schools . . . memorial ceremonies. They did not ask us, and we did not say anything."

"Not even now that the children have grown up?"

"Now it's more difficult. It's getting more and more difficult."

"Why?"

"So much time has passed that we are all afraid. They are afraid to know, and we are afraid to tell."

"You mean that you and Andy are afraid?"

"Yes."

"How do you know they are afraid to know?"

Marta had no answer. Perhaps *she* was afraid. It had been like that all through her life, between grief about silence and fear about talking. She was aware it had become absurd and that she must tell them, at least something. After all, she wanted to tell them about her family, but she could not . . .

"I feel I don't know anything anymore," she said in despair. "I wish I could write."

Dr. Neuman's expression grew serious. "We have discussed that already, right?"

"Yes," she said, greatly embarrassed, "thank you so much for the table and the chair and the new notebook. It touched me deeply that you took the trouble."

"I'm glad about that," Dr. Neuman said and smiled a little. "And I definitely think it can be a good thing for you, Marta, but also for the children. It all goes together." He paused briefly. "Writing won't be easy, but I believe you will succeed. It might be—what am I trying to say?—less difficult than talking."

"I don't know," said Marta and looked at Naomi's postcard which was still in her hand.

"So that's a postcard from Naomi?"

"Yes, she sent me a postcard from Eilat. It's lovely there." She smiled sadly. "You see, she escaped to the furthest possible place."

"She isn't running away from you, Marta. She is young, she wants to live her life, she wants freedom. That's how it is when you're young, surely you remember?" Seeing her ashen face, he was quiet. He leaned over to her and said: "I am sorry, Marta. I should not have said that."

Dr. Neuman reclined in his chair and suggested that the children might perhaps want to come and visit her. With or without Andy. Naomi could probably come on her own. He believed a visit might offer a good opportunity to start talking to them, to explain why she was so scared to tell them about the past. "We are here, you know. This is a safe place for you—and you may try." Marta was taken aback. Bringing her children here, to this place of sick souls, her sick soul? It was a scary idea.

"I don't know, I am not sure."

"I think it might help. Perhaps you could first ask Naomi for a visit. She is more mature than Michael, she is independent. It may be easier with her. Think about it. Invite her."

***

Dr. Neuman's suggestion troubled Marta's mind, but she grew used to the possibility. When she thought it over, she saw there was a point, yet having the children come to the hospital seemed unhealthy. She feared what a meeting like that would do to them, especially to Naomi. As the first child, Naomi must have experienced difficult things. Marta worried about her response and how she herself would be affected in turn. Why should they be involved with her illness? Bring them to such a place? The more she considered it, the more her doubts grew. Were she and Andy doing the right thing? What were parents supposed to do? Stand guard over the past and keep it hidden from the children's view—was that the right way? Did that really protect them? It had to be. They mustn't see it, they mustn't! Marta simply could not imagine telling the children what had happened, and certainly not now. Maybe at some point in the future. And yet she understood that the children would have to know one day. But it was frightening. How, then, was she to deal with it? Maybe close to Dr. Neuman it would be possible. She felt secure in the ward; if anything happened, the staff would be there immediately to help. Gradually a new thought took hold, though it vague as yet, that it was necessary to speak to the children.

After some days, Marta and Dr. Neuman talked about it again. He suggested again that the children might come for a visit. It was important for them to see her in hospital. She would find it easier to talk to them about what had happened. Which did not mean he thought it was going to be easy. "But let's say that in some way it suits the circumstances. You know you can trust me. This is the place and now is the time. And it will definitely support your treatment. And that's what we want, after all. We are treating people here, and we do have success. Didn't you see yourself that Dina improved and returned home?"

"Sometimes I don't believe I will get better, that I will learn to live in peace with all these things."

"It's a process and it takes time, Marta, a lot of time. But I believe there's a chance, because you have a wish to get there. The human mind is so intricate, and we don't know a lot. What is the soul? What is mental illness? What is it that heals the soul? It's more difficult than healing the body, but the mind and the body are closely tied. I believe a physician should apply his very being to any illness he treats, especially when it concerns mental illness. Medicine is important and helps, but without empathy, without listening to the patient with one's whole heart, it's hard to make the person well again—almost impossible. I believe that's the role of a doctor."

Marta observed him and was convinced that though he was again discussing her treatment, he was actually telling her something else too, which was maybe also about the two of them, their conversations.

"We are far from understanding what happens in the soul," he went on, "so how are we to understand mental illness? I don't mean its chemistry, which we are starting to learn more about. But it doesn't bring us any closer to knowing what disturbs the mind. There are so many nuances."

"Nuances, yes . . ." Marta grew alert, sat up straight. She looked at Dr. Neuman and seemed to simultaneously grasp his words and feel them slipping away.

"I am sure you appreciate what I'm trying to say. You are very well aware of the nuances."

She looked at Dr. Neuman and met up his gaze. For some seconds they just looked at each other. Some seconds which did not belong in the room, the meeting, the hospital.

"Marta," said Dr. Neuman, "your children might actually want to come and visit you here and listen to what you have to say. It might be an opportunity for your memories to emerge. To open the box. Maybe you are wrong when you think they avoid your past, that they are afraid and don't want to know. Your daughter went to the neighbors to hear from them, didn't she?

Marta actually thought that had been a disgrace. Naomi had even approached Erika and asked her about the family. "You can ask me," Marta had said, hurt. "I'll tell you whatever you want to know." But Naomi did not ask and her mother did not have the courage to tell. Maybe the time really was ripe. What had been very tightly locked inside for so many years, what had been weighing and interfering so much, no longer passed unnoticed.

"I . . ." she faltered. "I simply feel that I am afraid. There is a lot to what you say. But you see, it has been locked away for so many years. How can it be done? I feel lost."

"That's what we are here for." His eyes softened. "Let's talk about that fear. It's entirely understandable, but let's talk."

"It's fear tied up with more fear. A knot of fears."

"What if we tried to undo that a little? Take apart all those threads?"

"Right. So I am afraid of myself. I fear I won't be able to deal with all those memories, especially when I am facing them. I am afraid of what will happen to me when I air them—I fear my own reaction. I might collapse, cry, I don't know . . . That's one thing. The other thing that scares me is what will happen to the children when they have to hear it all and at the same time have to deal with my emotional state. I am sure I won't be able say anything without crying and crying. Why should they have to witness such a thing? Isn't it bad enough that I am like this?"

"You don't think that your silence does not cause them and you suffering? They know, even if they're not conscious of it, that there's a story that is being kept from them. Can you imagine how undermining that is? To know and not to know, not daring to ask. It's a difficult situation, don't you agree?"

"Yes," she sighed, "it is difficult. It hurts. Dear God, how does one get out of it? How does one even begin?"

"That's what we will try and figure out together. We will try to move ahead, maneuver between silence and speech. We are together. It is a step we can try and take. I believe that this is a moment when the door between their lives and yours can open, and—"

"I will ask Andy what he thinks, we will see," she interrupted. She was not sure she would discuss it with Andy. She was not convinced it was a good idea, but still . . . She shivered, worried, and was moved.

Later that week Marta spoke to Andy on the telephone. There was one pay phone in the ward's dining room, but on Dr. Neuman's advice Marta received her calls in the reception office. This was after she had told him she found it hard to talk with everybody eavesdropping. She told Andy about Dr. Neuman's idea and asked him what he thought. As usual Andy was practical. If the doctor believed a visit would be useful, there was no question in his mind about at all. He would talk to the children. Maybe it was best to start with Naomi. Michael was out on a field trip in the Negev desert with his class. They're picking potatoes, he told her, and she smiled. Andy knew how she loved simple food, potatoes, rakott krumpli, especially, with a lot of butter and sour cream.

The next day, Andy talked with Naomi and explained how important it was for her to visit her mother. He told Marta: "Naomi did not ask anything. All she said was that she would come by."

***

Marta waited for Naomi by the hospital entrance. The girl looked pale and tense and Marta experienced a wave of joy as well as worry. She hugged her daughter tightly. "Nomichka! So good of you to come. I have been missing you so. Let's first go to my room." They entered the department together and walked through the corridor. "Here it is, this is where I am staying now. Please come in."

Naomi looked distractedly at the room. "It's nice in here," she said, and sat down on the bed, sighing. Marta looked at her and asked her how the trip had been.

"It's a nightmare, with those buses. Those turns are killing me. I nearly threw up. But I took deep breaths, just the way you taught us." She smiled.

She is like me, thought Marta and asked, "Do you want to lie down for a bit?"

"No, no need. I'm already feeling a bit better," said Naomi, looking around and then at her mother. "And how are you, Mommy?" Again her eyes took in the room. "This is really nice. It makes me think a bit of our rooms in Eilat. Simple but pleasant. So how is it here?"

"When I first arrived, I shared with someone else. The painter who gave me that drawing of the Lake of Galilee. Now I live on my own and it is my place."

"Is that not sad? Wouldn't you like there to be another person so you won't be on your own?

"You won't believe it, Nomchik, but this is the first time in my life that I've had a room of my own . . . When we were children, we girls were in the same room, and later . . . no, yes, it makes me happy to be by myself. It suits me."

"That's lovely. And what is it like, generally, here?"

"Well, it's a hospital, you know, and hospitals are not the nicest places in the world." Marta slightly twisted her mouth. "But it's an good place, all in all. The doctor who is treating me an excellent physician and a nice person. And the staff is nice. But, you know, I want to get better, return home."

"Sure . . ."

"Nimi, it's so good of you to have come . . ." Marta whispered. "Shall I make you something to drink?"

"No, no, I am not thirsty."

Some furrows appeared on Naomi's forehead, causing Marta immediately to worry. She suddenly thought the visit might have been a mistake. Why burden the girl? I would've seen her the next time I went home. But when would that be? God only knew. And maybe Dr. Neuman too—she smiled to herself. She felt some relief.

"Come, let me show you around. You'll see it's not so bad, and there are some beautiful things here too." Marta got up, moved toward the door. "Come on, sweetheart"—and she realized that it had been a long time since she'd used the word "sweetheart."

They walked down the corridor, Naomi casting suspicious looks everywhere, which caused Marta to shrink. "Look. This is where you can do all kinds of crafts. People make very lovely things." There were some people in the room, and Naomi looked at them with apprehension. "This is my daughter," Marta announced. She smiled with pleasure when they said: "You look alike," "Welcome!," "You have a lovely mother!" Marta blushed a little and turned to her daughter. "Come, let's walk around a bit."

Marta showed Naomi her the colorful ceramics, sculptures, embroidery, and mosaics people had made.

"It's very nice." Naomi looked at her. "Is there anything that you made? I imagine you like working here, right?"

"I, um—right now I don't really participate, "Marta said, apologetically.

"Really? Why? You usually like it so much. And you know how to make such lovely things! The sweaters you knit for us are the prettiest."

"Really, do you think so? I am glad think so. Yes, I do love these things, you're right, but right now I find it a bit difficult to concentrate. Colors disturb me, I don't know why. Let's go out, I'll show you the garden."

Naomi stopped for a moment and looked at the patients who were immersed in their handiwork. Then she looked at her mother. "Come on," Marta urged her, and they went out into the garden. It was dotted with drying puddles, and it occurred to Marta that all of the rain that had fallen during the winter had not managed to make it green. A neglected place, she said to herself.

"Shall we sit on the bench?" she suggested, and Naomi nodded. They walked across the sparse grass towards the poinciana tree which already bore a green fuzz of budding leaves, and sat down wordlessly on the wooden bench.

"This is where I sit sometimes," she explained. "It's a good thing there's this garden. Just a pity it's so neglected. They could make it into something more pleasant. It's hard to be inside all the time, one has to be outside too, and now it's a little less cold and rainy. It will be spring soon. I wonder whether there will be flowers."

"In Eilat it's spring already. It will be getting hot soon, but it's very nice at the moment."

"And how is the work with the birds?"

"Oh, Mommy, it's just great. I'm so happy there. I love the work. It's just the right thing for me. Outside, in nature. Very, very close to nature."

"And what are they like, the people you work with?"

"Very sweet. They're from all kinds of places in the world. We speak English all the time. It's such fun. And this thing about bird migration, it's so interesting. Maybe one day I'll study zoology. Sometimes, you know, when we're in the field we lie down on a heap of straw and look at the sky through binoculars, and they just keep flying over, more and more of them."

"Who?"

"Flocks of birds," Naomi laughed, "endless birds, and you just lie down and watch them, like on film screen in the sky. When I think of it, the distances these birds cover, flying from the cold, and then back again, it's just mindboggling."

"Do you remember that winter when I showed you the little red-breasted bird in our yard? I was so excited. I remembered that bird from the garden at our home, during my childhood. When I was little, I always loved that round little bird."

"Of course I remember. You were so excited, you told me to quickly go to the window and look into the garden. Maybe in the end it is from you I inherited my love of birds."

Naomi smiled at her mother. Marta pointed at an open window and said, "That's where my doctor's office is." It seemed to her that Naomi's body grew more rigid. "I meet him every day. It's part of my treatment."

"What's that, this meeting? You talk?" Naomi turned towards her.

"We have a conversation. That's what you do when you meet a psychologist."

"What do you talk about?" Naomi quickly added: "Don't worry, Mommy, maybe it's not . . . You don't have to tell me . . ."

"The doctor actually thinks I should." Marta looked at her: "And so do I . . . It's something I would like to try. If not in speech, then maybe in writing. I think I will try to write it all down. So you know what happened."

"What happened," Naomi repeated, and Marta thought this was the moment she had to say something. Now. But she did not know what to say or how to say it. She looked straight ahead, and then heard someone coming.

"Hello," Dr. Neuman said, and walked up to them.

They both rose. Marta introduced Naomi.

"Very pleased to meet you." Dr. Neuman offered his hand. Naomi held it and immediately dropped her arm.

"I'm happy to meet you." Marta observed that Dr. Neuman saw their alikeness, and this made her happy. "And hello to you too, Marta," he said. "What a nice day. Just the kind of day to sit outside and enjoy the sunshine."

"A very nice day," said Marta.

It was the first time Marta had Dr. Neuman outside the unit. In full daylight he appeared shorter, a little boring and awkward. His awkwardness surprised her, and for a moment she wanted to make it easier for him.

"It's really a good thing that there's a garden here," she said.

"Yes." He addressed Naomi: "How are you?"

"All right."

"I heard from your mother that you are working on bird migration in Eilat. That must be interesting."

"Yes, I am working with a researcher. I am helping him."

"You're fortunate. That's something special indeed. I hope you'll have a good visit here with your mother. I'm happy we met." He held out his hand, and this time Naomi did not immediately withdraw hers. "Goodbye, Marta."

They watched Dr. Neuman disappear into the building.

"Nice doctor," said Naomi, "a bit old fashioned . . . I mean his clothes, but he is nice." That was exactly what I like about Dr. Neuman, Marta thought. His "oldness." There was something familiar in his presence, in his accent. She had noticed that from the first meeting. His clothes, the shoes with their laces, his gentle voice, his politeness. Yes, his politeness. It had always been important to her. There was nothing snobbish about it, though sometimes people held it against her. She was not a snob. She expected from others what she expected from herself: one should respect others, be polite, avoid vulgar behavior. She was repelled by coarseness, it even scared her. But in the hospital, it was everywhere.

***

"Come," said Marta to Naomi, "Dr. Neuman is right. Let's go out a little."

"Is that allowed? Can you go out?" Naomi asked.

"Yes. It's not a closed ward. We are not dangerous. We can go out in the afternoon. All we have to do is let the nurses know."

"Too bad," Naomi laughed, "I could have abducted you. Would be fun to escape. Can you imagine? Headlines in the papers: 'Mother and Daughter Escape Psychiatric Ward' or "Search Underway for Field School Worker Who Abducted Mother from Hospital. . ." Naomi halted.

"That is probably more appropriate for a film," said Marta gravely. "I am allowed to leave by myself, Shall we go?"

"Yes—where to?"

"The sea is very near and there's a nice promenade. I've heard there is a decent café. I've not been there yet. Let's get some cocoa or ice cream."

"I don't have a lot of time," said Naomi. "I have to be back in Eilat today, you know."

She's already planning how to leave, Marta thought. "Come on, let's go now, then. Wait here. I'll get my bag."

Marta went quickly into the corridor and to her room. Quite some time had passed since she had last been in a hurry. For two months now, ever since she returned from her break at home, she had been moving slowly, sticking close to the walls. Now she was in a rush, and the movement pleased her. She entered the room, took down the small leather bag which was hanging from a hook on the other side of the door, left, immediately returned, opened the cupboard, and facing the mirror she dragged a brush through her hair, looked at herself, and left the room. Naomi was waiting in the same place where Marta had left her, shifting her weight from one leg to the other, and said, smilingly: "You look nice, Mommy, come on, let's go." Marta, happy, blushed lightly.

Once through the hospital gates, they headed in the direction of the sea. A broad sidewalk took them alongside the beach. Passing by a sandy inlet, they observed some bathers, who put Marta in mind of the cold water of the river. As they walked the beach grew more and more rocky and wild, with small waves breaking on them and turning into a foam whose effervescence seemed audible. The café was in one of the stone houses that still survived along the old promenade. Stone steps led to a generous porch, and they chose the table in the middle. They sat opposite each other and when they moved their gaze a little it met the sea. "It's nice here," the two of them said, almost at once, and they laughed. Something about Naomi's presence made Marta happy and sad at the same time. It had been a long time since they'd last sat together like this, just the two of them. Though it felt good to have her daughter by her side, the intimacy aroused apprehensions again. What kind of mother am I? I should have talked to the children a long time ago about what happened, about my sadness, about me being sick and in hospital. Why am I not able to tell Naomi how much I love her? And why doesn't she tell me? We have been through a lot together. When Michael came around, he was born into a family . . . Naomi just had me—and I only had her. Andy was far away, in the army, and we stayed behind just the two of us, in the kibbutz. Something had become blocked.

"How is Daddy doing?" she asked.

"All right. It looks like he is managing really well. You should not worry, you know what he's like."

"How do you mean—what *is* he like?"

"Well, no, I am not saying he is all well. He is practical, you know. But he is missing you."

"I am missing all of you. Have you and he talked about it?"

"About what?"

"About me not being home, and about how he is coping. He hardly knows how to make an omelet, after all. Yes, he always manages."

"Well, for one thing, you should know he actually is able to make an omelet and also some other things." Naomi smiled at her.

"That's good news, then," said Marta. "I'm interested whether it will continue like that once I return home."

"What do you think?" Naomi laughed. "But you should not think. He may be coping somehow but he is having a hard time too, he's missing you. Even . . ." Naomi was not sure.

"What?" Marta tensed up. "Even what?"

"No, I think that you . . . I mean, you . . . . I don't think that . . . But yes, he does seem a little sad."

"Sad? I . . ." Marta fell silent.

"It will be all right. You will see. Now he's missing you . . . But you're so . . ."

"So what?" Now Marta smiled at her.

"Attached?" Naomi looked at her. "So connected."

It was Naomi's expression that struck her. It was true, she and Andy were very close. It comforted her to hear he missed her, that he was sad because of her.

"Nomichka sweetheart. "Marta collected herself. "Wouldn't you like to order cocoa? Hot or cold?"

"Cold," said Naomi, "and I am a little hungry too. With cake—can we?"

"Of course. Let's ask what cakes they have."

They sat across from each other. Between them, two tall glasses with cold cocoa and a straw, two plates with cakes. "Yours are nicer," said Naomi, prodding her fork into the cake, making it crumble on its plate. Marta tried a little of hers and put the fork down. Now I must say something, this is the time.

"I am really happy that you came, Nomichka," she said, "I . . . I hope it's not too difficult for you, sweetheart."

"Why would it be difficult? Stop it, Mommy . . ." Naomi went on digging in the cake. She looked at Marta and Marta shrunk even more, bent her head, and looked inside her bag for her handkerchief.

"Sorry, Mommy, I didn't mean, really . . . Don't worry. It's not hard on me. I hope you feel better soon. You will return home, and everything will go back to how it was."

"Yes," said Marta, and wondered whether that was what she wanted, for everything to go back to how it was. Noticing that Naomi did not answer, she decided not to insist. What was the use?

"Don't be sad, Mommy," said Naomi with surprising warmth, "you will recover. It will be soon. You'll see."

"I hope I can return soon and bake something for you." Marta smiled.

"But, Mommy, I'm not at home, did you forget? I am in Eilat."

"So we'll send you the cake in a parcel."

"That will be great!" Naomi exclaimed. "That would be such fun, getting a parcel with cakes from you! Your cakes are the best. But actually, Mommy, why won't you two come and visit me there and bring the cakes yourself? There's a lot to see there in Eilat. A wonderful place. I sometimes do some tourist guiding and I know the place quite well. Come and visit, you can stay over at my apartment, we will manage. We'll walk around a bit. I will show you this beautiful wadi in the desert, I'll take you on some hiking trails."

"Hiking . . . Naomi, we're not . . ."

"Stop it, Mommy! I'll take you to places that are easy for walking and beautiful as well. Trust me."

"And to the bird observatory?"

"Of course!" Naomi cried out in delight. "We can visit the bird observatory too. Why not? I'll show you what I do there, how we catch birds in nets, how we extricate them carefully and bind their legs. It's really interesting, you'll see. What do you say?"

Marta smiled sadly, surprised at Naomi's flow of words. She had not expected it.

"Maybe. But first I need to get better. Get out of here. Soon, I hope." She sighed and thought, maybe not too soon.

Naomi looked at her again and held out her two hands. "It will be fine, Mommy, you'll get out of this place." A breeze from the sea slightly ruffled her curls, and she quickly collected her hair and stuck a black pin into it. "It's nice here," she said. "Good we came."

Marta looked at Naomi's hands as they collected her abundant curls. A thin line of joy traveled along her spine. Remember this moment, this moment with Naomi gathering her disordered hair, the sweetness of the cocoa and the crumbling cake, the boulders heaped on the shore, and beyond that the blue expanse. It was a flash of possible happiness, unadulterated happiness. She would remember this moment.

"Oh, Mommy, I must be getting back," said Naomi, interrupting her thoughts, "The last bus to Eilat leaves Tel Aviv in two hours. I must catch it."

"And there's no direct bus from here?" Marta asked in alarm.

"No, I have to get to the central station in Tel Aviv. Let's go."

They walked back quickly along the promenade and went into the hospital.

"I'll accompany you to your room," said Naomi, "I have to get my bag anyway."

As usual, Marta hung her handbag on the hook on the other side of the door; Naomi got her rucksack and moved toward the door. Before leaving, she turned around once more, her eye catching the desk by the window, with the notebook on it. She looked at Marta questioningly and Marta nodded. Then she smiled at her daughter and hugged her tight. Again, Naomi's body was rigid. They stepped into the corridor and Marta watched Naomi walking away, her rucksack on her back. Saying goodbye was always hard, she said to herself, and it was especially horrible when it involved rucksacks. But her body still preserved the memory of a thin line of joy in her back, sitting on the café terrace with her daughter whose curls were slightly messed by the wind. But we will meet again. And Naomi's idea about a visit in Eilat, maybe that would be possible, in spite of everything?

By the time Marta went back into her room, sadness had already over-whelmed her. She sat on the bed. My poor little girl, it's hard on her. Her eyes. Nothing had worked out. Suddenly she felt defeated. Wasn't that why Dr. Neuman had said it was a good idea for Naomi to visit, to tell her something, one little thing, open a door. She had not managed it. Another failure. There was the desk; she took a long look at it. She had not been able to talk. Would she be able to write? She had everything here: a room, a table, an empty notebook, and time, plenty of time. And there was Dr. Neuman. But this is a hospital. She tried to resist. How can one write here? Wouldn't it be sick? She rose from the bed, walked toward the table, pulled out the chair, and sat down. The notebook was waiting, silent.

She raised her eyes to the window and looked at the garden, enclosed by its wall, its grey concrete pavement, and the broken furniture stacked in the corner. A flash of blue made her remember. "Maybe there?" she thought, "maybe there, why not? Why not there, actually?" And she already imagined herself sitting there, writing, on the café terrace. Like Hemingway in Paris. She smiled. Still, the café. A café in Haifa, by the Mediterranean—it sounded like something from a book. It would offer her inspiration. She would have to order something to drink or to eat, but they would probably allow her to sit there with her notebook and write. This image of herself, sitting there and writing by the seaside, thrilled her for a moment, like a childhood dream coming true. But what would they say in the unit? They would probably frown. But Dr. Neuman would not. He would have no objections.

Later that evening Andy phoned. It went very well, Marta said, but she was not really sure. Now that Naomi was gone and Andy was far away and Dr. Neuman had already left the hospital she felt overcome by loneliness. She lay down on the bed. Deep in her sleep she still sensed the uneven, rough surface of the bedcover, but it did not wake her. Her sleep was perturbed, troubled by dreams she did not remember the next morning.

***

During breakfast the next morning, a nurse approached Marta and told her Dr. Neuman would not be in today and their meeting was cancelled. Today of all days, she grumbled, after Naomi's visit. She was eager to see him, wanting to tell him about the café and maybe also hear something from him, though what it was she did not quite know. Disappointed, she asked herself what she should do for the day. She was close to giving up and returning to her room, her bed, the blanket in which she would wrap herself and forget about everything once sleep took over. Passing the activities room she stopped and looked inside. Some people had started to work already, and one of the instructors was busy preparing materials on the tables. She watched the instructor's hands moving things, shifting them, laying out, mixing. She observed the woman's fingers which buzzed with life, as it were. The instructor smiled at her and approached.

"It was nice to meet your daughter. She seems very nice."

"Thank you. She really is."

"What's her name?"

"Naomi."

"And how was her visit?"

"Good. We walked to the café. It was a beautiful day. We spent time together."

"That café on the promenade? I like to sit there too sometimes, when I have time." She smiled. "Are you joining us? There's lots of lovely things you can do here."

"Yes. But there's something important I have to do now." Marta smiled back at her as if she'd remembered something.

She turned around and left, and entering her room, she looked at the notebook on her desk, at the ballpoint next to it, and then sat down. She opened the notebook and her fingers lightly caressed the pages. Now? she asked herself. The paper, when she touched it, felt a little rough. She leafed through the pages trying to picture what they would look like filled with her handwriting, and remembered the diary she had written as a young girl. The thought that someone from their little town might have found it, read in it, discovering her deepest secrets, had troubled her for many years. Her infatuations, reflections about life, her parents, and siblings, things about Erika, notes on teachers and friends. Even after all she had been through, the thought of a stranger would reading these intimate things still worried her.

When she was an adolescent, she had pondered the idea of being a writer. It had been one of her dreams. There were many other things too that she had wanted to do. More than anything she wanted to study, leave the town for the big city to experience, see, discover things. She had a huge appetite for life. She read many books, some of which left her dreamy, yearning for love and passion, "just like in a story." She was sure her life would be different, that exciting adventures lay in store, amazing encounters; life was a wonderful promise. She had once had a taste of these riches when her family traveled to a spot in the mountains with a healing spring. Her father took the waters to alleviate his back aches, and they spent about two weeks at the resort. Though they were staying at a modest guesthouse, with her eyes she devoured the dance halls in the great hotels, the couples who moved along with the music or who raised their glasses filled with wine in the splendid restaurant. During those two weeks it was as if she'd been afloat in a sweet dream. It was their last happy summer, and they did not know it.

Marta closed the notebook, looked at the title she had written on its cover, "Haifa, Winter," and drew a line underneath it. Then she opened the notebook again and began to write:

I was born one and a half year after Öcsi, and I admired him no end from the moment I could think.

She wrote his name in the way they had spelled it there, not in Hebrew, and in the way they pronounced it. Öcsi, little brother.

I wanted to be like him come what may and it made me so happy when people mentioned any sort of similarity between us. He was my ideal, something unattainable. I was grateful for the merest crumb of his attention.

She raised her eyes and looked through the window. Again, the ugly yard presented itself, abandoned, brown and grey, the pile of broken and twisted furniture. The poppies which had emerged in the cracks of the exposed concrete had wilted and the radiance had left their redness which had been so reassuring when she had first sat at her writing table. Môj bože, it's so ugly. It's ugly and depressing, she said to herself, thinking of the blue view from the café terrace. I said I would write there, so maybe . . ? Why not? she thought and was taken aback. The plan appeared complicated, and she began to withdraw, give up. But the idea of writing in the café was powerful and gave her strength, made her rise from her chair, pushed her. She picked up the notebook and pen and put them in her handbag. Then she turned to the cupboard, took out a light jacket, wrapped a silk scarf round her neck, took her bag, and checked that her purse was inside. Today it will be hot cocoa, she said to herself, and felt a little more confident. Before leaving, she looked in the mirror and, shyly, smoothed her hair.

She walked close to the walls of the corridor. She had to pop into the office to let them know she was going out. It won't be easy, she worried. We are supposed to be in the unit at this time of the day. To her surprise, the nurse did not object. She knew that Marta's meeting with Dr. Neuman had been cancelled and asked her if she didn't want to go to the activities room. Marta answered that she preferred it this way. Her daughter had visited the day before and she would like . . . "All right," said the nurse, "But please be back in time for lunch." Marta headed to the exit, stopped, and took a deep breath. I am free, she said to herself, and continued walking. It was a pleasant day, and she felt the soft warmth of the air with each breath she took. She went to the promenade, along the coast, and looked at the sea, at the intense blue that shone in the sun, quiet and heavy. It's so good spring is coming, she thought, feeling the young, golden light entering her. From afar she saw the shadow of the large, abandoned building opposite the café.

When she go there, and had climbed the stone steps to the broad terrace, she was happy to see that the table at which she and Naomi had sat was unoccupied. Sitting down, she thought it was a good omen. Like returning to a familiar place. Then she got up, took off her coat and the silk scarf, and put them on the seat beside her. She took the notebook and pen from her bag, put them on the table, and sat down. The blue sea spread like a huge cloth before her. In the distance she saw cranes and some large ships that seemed to rest, waiting, on the water. Everything is waiting, I must take a deep breath. Between the sea and sky, small, white, downy clouds were floating, and a pleasant breeze stroked her face. It's so good I came, she said to herself and looked at the notebook and pen.

"What would you like to order?"

Turning her head, Marta saw the waitress, a woman about her age.

"Cocoa, please, hot cocoa." Marta smiled at her awkwardly.

"And would you like cake too?"

"Just cocoa, thank you," and she added quickly, "very hot please, I like it very hot."

Again, Marta looked at the notebook and pen, then raised her eyes to the blue line. Then she looked around. Most of the tables were empty. Not far from her, though, a man was reading a newspaper which was hiding his face, and from a table farther away the sound of giggling reached her. Turning her head, she saw two young, well put together women chatting with a kind of cheerfulness that pained her. She turned away and stared at the sea.

"There you are," said the waitress placing a cup of steaming cocoa before her. "Mind, it's very hot."

She stirred the drink vigorously. The steam coming from the cup produced a pleasant smell, familiar from her childhood. Cocoa mixed with hot milk. She took a careful sip, and even though the heat hurt her throat, she nodded in delight. Yes, that was the taste, that was the warmth. She went on taking slow sips so it would not grow cold, and before a skin formed. When she was done, she spooned up the leftover cocoa and sugar from the bottom of the cup and licked the spoon slowly; she then put the notebook in front of her and took up the pen. She stared at the faraway blue for a long moment and began to write.

The period of Marta's writing began in that café, with that motion of the pen. It continued until the end of the summer, when she was released from hospital. She asked Dr. Neuman's permission to leave the ward every morning and he, of course, agreed. All she told him was that her stroll along the promenade made her feel calm, and that she loved the movement of the sea, and sometimes, too, to sit in the café and read. She felt, she said, that that it was doing her good. She did not tell him yet that she was writing.

In the café she picked up the first sentences she had begun in her room, and memories which she had no idea how to capture in writing began to arrange themselves in sentences in her orderly handwriting, as if they had been waiting for years to be expressed. Writing excited her and made her happy, but it also roused fears. She was writing! Just as she had dreamt, in a café facing the sea, restoring to life what had vanished, things she had believed to have died inside her. Writing held out a promise of change. She didn't know how she would move on, where she was heading, when pain would halt her, how she would organize all these things. But for now, it flowed, this writing, and with it flowed the years of her childhood, when there the family, when there were parents who cared, when there were friends, when there was a world, and when there was sun. It was inconceivable what happened underneath that writing hand. Resurrection! Her parents, her brothers, sisters, uncles, and aunts, the house, the yard with the well at its center, the swing next to the vegetable patch, their father's cloth shop which faced the street, the river and the wooden bridge across it, the serpentine paths in the magical garden near the sugar factory, her girlfriends, the boys, infatuations . . . It was all there, intact, unblemished.

Writing restored order inside her. Lines, sentences, words, continuity. She was able to write and not die of grief. In the eye of the storm and amid chaos, inside her a small, stable kernel of order was forming, a space of sanity, an anchor that would hold amidst the furies of black waves. It was a vague feeling, like a sound reaching her from afar, barely registering.

Gradually more and more pictures from her childhood returned. These childhood memories were what reestablished her confidence in herself. She'd had a different life before she crashed. Writing led her ahead, opening stores of strength, reminding her of her mainstays, the supporting pillars that had enabled her to go on. Marta looked her past from afar. In spite of her arguments about her free time with her parents, especially with her mother who she thought preferred Erika, she'd had a happy childhood which had protected her and Erika when they found themselves alone, and which went on protecting her now.

Every so often she panicked about how she would write what happened after this period. About their expulsion, the camps, the violence, the humiliations, the fear, death . . . About the terrible sorrow that took hold when they discovered . . . Would she ever be able to write these things down? How could she write them and make sure they would not be too much for Naomi and Michael? How was she to soften them? Maybe it would be better not write about these things. She did not know how and in which direction to advance, but she was wholly immersed. As she went on, she realized that writing required her to be organized, and this, in turn, gave her peace of mind, stability, and strength. The flow of images started to take the shape of a story she managed to recount. There was movement here, forward in time, and sideways and backward, a complex texture of stories. Her childhood emerged. She wrote, of course, about her close family, her parents, brothers, and sisters, and she even attempted to write about her parents' childhood, stories upon stories that made up a family tree. Around this close family appeared the more remote relatives, friends, fellow towns-people, peddlers who came and went and who introduced them to the wonders of the big world, begging gypsies encamped on the town's out-skirts, the circus which visited, the acrobats, the guests her father invited to join Friday dinner, pale, intimidated yeshiva students, indigent strangers passing through, women farmers who arrived once a year and sat in the yard filling duvets with ducks' down, their nursemaids. An entire life; and gradually she managed to put these recollections into order, write them down. As she was writing she felt that something in her relationship with Naomi and Michael, and with herself was falling into place too. Even in her connection with Dr. Neuman something seemed to fit better. It had been, after all, his idea.

***

Spring filled the air with warmth and the smells of blossom reminding Marta of the Galilee. Good, she thought, I'm not there now that the olive trees are blossoming. She remembered her severe allergy, her red nose, her tearing eyes. Far away from the olive orchards, she had acquired a daily routine in the unit with which she lived in peace, a bit of near-normal life. She would quietly laugh at this, how she now lived there as though she had traveled abroad. There, of all places, and despite the distance from home, despite her home-sickness which sometimes got mixed up with a painful sense of guilt, there she was in a quiet spot. She was writing. In the mornings she would leave the hospital for the café where they now recognized her, and she felt all right about sitting there for long stretches, writing, gazing at the blue horizon, and back again to her notebook which was filling up. The waitress who served her cocoa would chat with her when there weren't too many customers, and she took an interest in her writing.

"Are you writing a book?"

"No," answered Marta, "I'm just writing down my recollections. Making order."

"I see," said the waitress and scratched her arm. "That's not easy and probably really meaningful."

"Well, yes, it does mean a lot to me," said Marta and looked at her, "one's recollections are always quite meaningful, at least to oneself!"

"Are you from around here?"

"Yes, I'm from really nearby . . . I'm staying in the hospital," and she pointed in that direction.

"Over there?" She pointed in the same direction. "You don't look ill . . . Anyway, I hope you feel well. I wish you good health."

"Thank you. You know, the illness does not always . . . how should I put it? It does not always show. One mainly feels it."

"Yes. That's it. Where are you from, though?"

"I live near Tsfat. And you?"

"I'm from the neighborhood. There are many immigrants here, you know. They brought us to this place and then we stayed."

"From where did you come?"

"From Greece, Saloniki. There were lots of Jews there, until . . . Well, I won't disturb you any longer. If you want anything, even a glass of water, just call me, ask for me. Don't feel shy."

Marta looked at her gratefully and with a smile. Recently she had been smiling more often and she was feeling better too. The change in the medication Dr. Neuman had prescribed had improved her sleep; it came more readily now, without flashes of painful images, and without memories. The nightmares had almost completely disappeared. She was eating regularly again and felt more awake during the day. She was glad that no other patient had taken Dina's place and that she had the room to herself. She mentioned this to Dr. Neuman, and it seemed that they were managing, or that there was no lack of place, or maybe there were fewer crazy people in the hospital. And nor did anyone else take Dina's place as her friend. There were "faces," as she put it. People she was fond of said hello to, and there were people she tried to avoid. Sometimes there were new faces, and being a senior patient now, she felt at ease with them. More than anything, though, she thought writing made her feel calmer.

She did not go back to the ward's activities. Writing had taken over and she made progress. About half the notebook was filled now with her dense and ornate handwriting. Almost everywhere she went, she took it along in her handbag, including her meetings with Dr. Neuman, but they did not discuss it. They discussed other subjects, and she found it easier to answer some of his questions. There were silences too, light ones, of the kind that had filled the room when she'd just started her treatment. Dr. Neuman, it seemed to her, enjoyed the silence; she felt that for him too the silence was healing. Occasionally they talked about things that had nothing to do with her illness, small talk, she called it. She felt something was happening between them, she was sure it was personal, not medical, not connected to the hospital.

Andy continued visiting at the weekends. Now that the rains had almost completely stopped, they went out sometimes for a stroll along the promenade, went down to the beach and stood on the rocks. One day she proposed that they go into the café.

"This is my husband," she said him to the waitress. And to Andy: "This is the waitress I told you about."

"Nice to meet you," the waitress said.

"Nice place, this café."

"Yes, especially now. After the winter, and before the summer heat. Good to meet you too. We see your wife here quite a bit."

"Really?" asked Andy, looking at Marta and then at the waitress again.

"Yes," said Marta, "I wrote you about it, don't you remember? This is where I sat with Naomi. And they have good cocoa. Do you want some?" She hurried to change the conversation.

They sat at one of the tables. Andy looked around, then toward the sea, and asked what she would like to drink.

"I don't know. What's is there?"

"There's cocoa. You just said yourself that it was good."

"No, no, not now," said Marta, thinking that cocoa went with her writing. "Tea. Tea with milk. And what would you like?"

"I'll have coffee and cake, naturally. I can't drink without eating something, you know that. What do they have here? Are the cakes any good? I'm sure they're not as good as yours. I miss them. And anyway, I am longing for you to come back . . ."

The waitress appeared, took their order, and looked at Marta. "You're not having cocoa?"

"Not now," she said and blushed lightly, "it's not right for now. We would like some cake, though."

"Yes," said Andy, "can you recommend some nice pastry. Do you have poppy seed cake, perhaps?"

"Of course. With so many Hungarian clients . . ." The waitress smiled and walked away.

"Let's see if that cake of theirs is worth anything," said Andy. "I have to come here on a weekday—I would like to talk with the doctor again."

"Why?" she asked, not sure whether she liked the idea.

"I want to talk to him, hear what progress you're making. Perhaps he wants to ask me something."

"I think there's some progress," she said, "I feel a little better, but . . ."

"I have noticed," said Andy putting his hand on hers, looking at her and smiling. "You will come back soon, I am sure." He paused and added, "I miss you, Martushkam. You're missed in the house. The house misses you."

"I feel I still need to stay. Dr. Neuman thinks so too. He says the treatment is not finished. I . . ."

Marta moved uneasily in her chair and smiled at the waitress who approached them. What they had ordered was placed on a round tray: coffee, tea, and poppy seed cake. Andy used his fork to cut the cake into small parts and began to eat, taking a sip of hot coffee between each bite.

"How is it?" Marta asked him and took a piece with her spoon.

"Tasty," said Andy and sipped coffee.

She ate and raised her eyebrows a little. It was not all that nice. A yearning to go back to baking suddenly flickered. Still, it was she rather than Erika who had inherited the gift for cooking and baking. She missed the kitchen. The smells, the mess of utensils on the table, on the work top, the dishes in the sink. Not yet, she said to herself, I have to stay here a little longer. Maybe Andy will learn to cook some more things. She watched him as he ate and drank. What happened to us? She asked herself remembering their grand love, full of passion. "My life," she used to call him, "my one darling, moja duša, my soul." She had totally given herself to their love, with all her might, as if her life depended on it, on him. Into what had that love transmuted? Did it still exist? Of course it did, she reassured herself, and looked at him lovingly.

"How are you coping?" she asked, "how about food? I heard you can cook."

"Where did you pick up that rumor?"

"Naomi told me."

"Well, I wouldn't exactly call it cooking. An omelet with a bit of salami. I know how to cut vegetables."

"I remember the meal you made when I came to visit. That was a long time ago. So you cope?"

"One gets by. During the day I eat at the restaurant near the office. Erika brought some soup over and I heat some up in the evening. Naomi is in Eilat, and Michael is out on another trip with his class, two weeks premilitary camp. I wonder when they actually study, those children."

"They're so lucky to be out in nature. We didn't have that. I miss everyone terribly. How is Erika?"

"All right, all right, don't worry—she'll will come to visit. Maybe we will all come together. We'll see."

"Do you feel sad, all alone?" She put her hand on top of his.

"I manage." His eyes blinked fast. "Nothing to worry about. Sometimes friends ask me over. And you will be back soon, anyway, right? Looking at you, like this, I'd say Dr. Neuman will decide soon."

"Who has invited you? Where have you had dinner? Friends from work?" Her voice sounded tense now.

"One evening I ate at Hanna's and Moshe's; he works with me. You know, very close to our place."

"That's all?"

"And I also ate with Tsofia and Meir."

"Did they invite you?" She felt a surge of envy. "Why would they?"

"Tsofia invited me. We bumped into each other. I told her what was going on and she said I had to come sometime."

"You bumped into her?"

"Martushkam, what's wrong with you? Of course. How else would I meet her? What business do we have?"

Tsofia was one of the women around whom Andy scattered his charm. In their village women smiled at him, beguiled. They were neighbors, but Tsofia, the daughter of the founders, was local aristocracy. She was loud, her short hair was dyed, and her lips and nails were red. They were not on visiting terms. She was not part of the immigrant community, but sometimes they met her in Tsfat where they did their major shopping. In their village there were no shops, only houses and agricultural land on the hillside. It was up on that slope that the founding families lived, and there they had their own grocery store. Down below among the olive orchards small homes for the immigrants had been constructed, and that population used Schwartz's grocery store—he was an immigrant like them. All the way down the hill in a black basalt house an old woman ran a restaurant; she cooked food for the truck drivers who passed by on the main road.

Marta removed her hand from Andy's and leaned back. She was jealous of these women who laughed at this Hungarian humor. She envied their laughter, unburdened by either the past or future. But she also felt contempt. To her their laughter was vulgar, and she was sure they didn't quite follow the subtleties of what Andy was saying, and were laughing at something else. She envied Andy his ability to laugh and make others laugh, be like others. Her sense of humor was different—ironic, subtle, and sharp. And yet these women in the village, like Tsofia, who were so confident of their place, they made her feel inferior. That was exactly it, thought Marta—her place.

***

It was in the evening, after Andy left, that Marta first realized. She felt good but different. She saw herself attached to him but at the same time somewhat removed. She wanted it to be more like that. She wanted to be more for herself. With Andy, but also with herself. She had given herself so completely that she had put herself into his hands. Life with him had seemed so promising! She had believed their love would save her. That she could truly exist with him. They were very close at the beginning: they had similar ideas, they sought the same spiritual life, one with meaning. A life in which they could express themselves, their unique personalities, their thoughts, their innermost feelings. In those days she felt she might perhaps be a poet. She'd had a tremendous longing for beauty: without beauty she could not live. The beauty of a book, of a forest, but always, always with Andy. She thought it was only with him she could experience beauty. That she could only live when with him. With him the prison gates had opened and she had been engulfed by happiness and freedom. She couldn't be without him. Even then she had wondered whether this was "real life." This urgent need she had of Andy, his proximity, his love for her, his respect—all this was like the air she needed to breathe; and it had made her wonder about her own sanity even then. Am I out of my mind? She'd asked herself. For sure. But it was a wonderful madness, the madness of infatuation, and a desperate desire to live in spite of everything. How wrong they had been, all of them. How wrong she had been.

The next day, at their Sunday meeting, she told Dr. Neuman about Andy's visit, about their walk, the café, and she mentioned that he had been sorry not to have been able to meet Dr. Neuman.

"Maybe we can arrange a meeting for another day. I would like to meet him too; I have really been meaning to talk to him. It's important."

"Yes . . ."

"And how was your meeting?"

"Good. I was happy he came to visit. We went to the café on the promenade. It was nice . . . yes . . . and later I thought . . ."

"About what?"

"Andy was my chance to get back to life. I think I've told you that several times. It's constantly on my mind, that thought. I don't know what would have happened if we had not met. I am not sure I would have been able to live without him. Yes, it's that profound."

"I understand. And it's a good thing you're here, alive. You managed . . ."

"I don't know. Anyhow, I managed not to die. You know, after the war, when Erika and I joined Andy in the movement, it was exciting. A real sense of euphoria. It's hard to understand."

"Tell me."

"You remember I told you about that summer project? And about the workforce in the mountains which we set up?"

"Of course."

"As I said, we were euphoric. Drunk on what we did and how we lived. It was . . . as though we had been hurled back into life, with all our might. And not any old life . . . It was so unlike what had been before. We felt that this was the real thing, and we were extremely close, in our group, with each other. We had heart-to-heart conversations far into the night."

"What did you talk about?"

"About everything. About the future, about how we would build a good and just world, about ourselves, only not about the war, not about what had happened to us and our families. We simply erased it. We sang a lot, linking arms, marching along the roads. We sang in Hungarian, songs about social justice, about hard-working laborers. We sang as though our future depended on it; and in Hebrew we sang about the movement and the Holy Land. We also sang in Yiddish, and sometimes we did not understand the words, but even so we sang with great enthusiasm."

"You were giving yourself psychological treatment . . . Without professionals. That's how powerful the force of life is. You seem to have known that this is what would pull you back into existence. I really think it's astonishing. It's interesting no one has studied it, so far . . ."

"I don't know. Maybe we should have done something about what still lingered in our souls. But nobody knew how. Today one might say that we had no choice, but it is absurd, really. The death that engulfed us was so total we could not mourn. No one sat shiva for their dead relatives. Actually, there was a hope, all the time, that they had not died."

"And the movement?"

"I never felt that what had happened to us interested anyone there. The Zionist youth movement, with all due respect, had its ideals and interests, I don't know . . . They did not think of us . . . and we weren't always in step with them."

"What do you mean?"

"People who were looking on from the side, or those who watched us from above, that's how we called them, they felt we were not quite keeping in line. Too much non-Hebrew literature and poetry—no Bialik, no Tchernichovsky, they did not mean all that much to us then. We read poets, rather, who were not Zionists. Andy introduced us to them, and we admired them. It's because of him that we identified with Endre Ady, the Hungarian poet."

"And with Jiří Wolker"

"You remember!" Her voice trembled a little.

"Of course . . . Very impressive. Andy was a well-educated young man."

"He's educated today too. He knows a great deal, but he rather let go of his ideals, like some other things . . . But in those days, I told you already, he was a kind of spiritual leader . . . That's how we saw him."

"And how did they take that in the movement?"

"Well, it wasn't long the criticism started. All of us were infected with 'Krausism'—that was the new crime."

"The companion piece of the 'holy family,' I would assume?" He smiled at her.

"Exactly. During our final years in the movement, and later in the kibbutz, we were so busy with our work, we didn't have time for discussions about the future or ideology. I remember I didn't have time to think. I often asked myself if this really was what they called life. I wanted to stop, understand what was happening to me, but it was not possible."

"What was your work in the group?"

"Childcare. That was what the women did. I had a 'class,' as they called it."

"And did you like it?"

"It was important for me to work, and when I felt weak and needed a rest, I looked forward to getting back. When a person works, they appreciate an hour's rest, but being idle for days on end, that's too much."

"Were you weak? Did you have to take breaks?"

"I wasn't strong. Every so often I had to stop because my body would grow very weak. And mentally too I was weak. And anyway, childcare is hard, physically, you know . . . and mentally."

Marta looked at him, half-smiling, and wondered whether he knew what it was like. Did he have children? Did he really know what it meant to look after young children? In the kibbutz they kept close watch over you. Things had to be done in a certain way. Around the raising of the children there was a whole ideology from which one wasn't supposed to stray, not an inch. They must not be indulged, and one must most certainly not allow oneself to indulge in them. And the most important thing was hygiene. The floors of the children's homes were washed over and over again, throughout the day: beds were moved out of the way, the tiny chairs were placed upside down on the tiny tables, the walls were wiped with wet cloths, and they used garden hoses to spray the children's playpens which were dragged from their shaded places to dry in the sun. Every day. The babies had a strict daily schedule in which nothing was to be changed.

"Did you like childcare?"

"Not really. I didn't like the way they went about things there. I wanted something more spiritual. For me it was important to read, to enlighten, that's what we called it with Andy. It was painful because I feared I was not going to manage to fill life with something more elevated and beautiful."

"More than what?"

"More than just work and sleep. That was very absent for me, and it always gave me a sense that it lacked perfection, I felt I didn't know anything, I wanted to learn. I think that feeling still remains with me. A feeling that I don't manage to reach a more spiritual place." Marta sank into her chair, sighing lightly, closed her eyes and went on: "For a long time I wanted to see myself beyond childcare. I hoped it would happen one day, but when you're in a group it doesn't always work out. I had a strong urge to fill my life with meaning, but that did not always suit the group's program. I wanted to arrange my own time so that I could work, rest, read, and also keep my things, my room, my clothes nice. Time, for me, was the most important thing, but my plans did not work out."

"Why was that?"

"Because there were more people, not just me. There was the group, the group meetings about important issues. There were intrigues between people. They really affected me badly. I felt I had no time to live, simply to live, without rushing around and worrying about all kinds of things. I constantly felt a serious lack, as though I had forgotten something, as though I had failed to do something important. As though my entire life was empty, air. It's a terrible feeling. Maybe it was my own fault, because I was pitying myself, maybe because . . . I don't know."

"Because of what?"

"Maybe because Andy was everything for me. I might have been more independent. But I really couldn't. Inside, I was broken, and every day I had to try and gather my strength, the strength I once had. But it didn't work out. I don't know . . . I was waiting for something to happen. It felt at the time that I was permanently waiting, as if all my life consisted of waiting. I woke up in the morning and was waiting for something to happen, surely it would, that day. During the day, I was expecting that by the time I returned home, definitely, something would happen. What was it about? It seems vague. A yearning for something sublime, something that would lift me, high . . . Perhaps to get ever further away from what was dragging me down."

"What was that about? What were you waiting for?"

"When Andy was in the army, I was waiting for him to return, come on furlough. I missed him terribly. It was like a wild stream of lava, flowing, on and on, all the time, and ever stronger, dragging everything along."

"And then?"

"Then? I don't know. I understood major things were going on inside me, huge things I couldn't explain. Didn't have to explain—couldn't. I thought everything might soon come to an end, it might not go on for much longer. But even just one day like that felt endless to me."

"Did you and Andy talk about it?"

"It was very hard. Often, I had bad moods. I knew the reason, I knew very well, but I couldn't talk about it with anyone. Not even Andy. I think we were scared to touch these problems. We feared looking too closely at things. It was like some kind of sin we were not allowed to speak about. Although we talked a lot. It was important for us to discuss the future, what our lives would be like, how we wanted to raise Naomi, what values we thought mattered. But about that, about the "sin," we did not talk. I was always hoping it would happen next time we talked, but it did not. And Andy too had a hard time, though he found it easier to close . . . to concentrate on our life, the future. I . . . I didn't really manage . . . inside me . . . the forces, in there, sometimes they simply tore me apart . . . and we couldn't talk about it."

"I understand," said Dr. Neuman, "I understand. It's so difficult."

He is a good man, thought Marta.

"Marta," Dr. Neuman continued, "I think you were demanding too much from yourself. With everything that happened . . . It was a terrible rupture, a huge catastrophe of the kind that transforms a person's life, destroys it. You did not give up, and still—how can I put it?—you're so sensitive, you get hurt . . . But you're stubborn as well, perhaps. You said yourself that you were as a girl."

Dr. Neuman halted and looked at her. That is a loving look, Marta thought, and she saw him in a different way, unlike his usual self. She saw herself differently and their conversation too. They were not talking like a doctor and patient.

"A stubborn girl and a dreamy girl. I had all kinds of dreams."

"Such as?"

"I wanted to be different, not like everybody else."

As a girl she wanted to be special somehow, her life not to be banal. When she got together with Andy she wanted everything in their shared life to be unique, true, absolute, uncompromising. She wanted for them to be close, soulmates. She was thirsting for intimate conversations. To talk about the higher things, beyond the plain and cruel humdrum. Deep talks like the ones she had with Erich . . . Poor Erich. What had become of him? She didn't know anything about what happened to him after they were violently separated on the train platform.

In the youth movement, immediately after the war, they had had soul-searching talks too, the comrades. After all they had been through, each in their own private nightmare, they simply had to touch something pure, make contact with realms of clarity. The need was almost uncontrollable: to find light inside themselves, to ensure that while their bodies had been ravaged, tortured, exploited, and their families murdered, some particle of purity inside them remained. She'd had such wonderful talks with Andy in Budapest, the kibbutz, in the letters they exchanged. It was a dream, a fantasy about attaining something sublime, which, over the years had become worn out.

"Now how does one get rid of that?" She smiled.

"Why get rid of it? You are special, Marta. And what about that dream of being a writer or poet?"

"I try." Her voice sounded suffocated; she wondered how he knew, and tried to remember whether they talked about it.

"That's good. I am glad to hear it. I believe writing will do you good. There must be a memory."

"Yes, there must be a memory. I think about that all the time. I try to remember the names—each of them, after all, had a name."

Dr. Neuman edged to the front of his chair, facing her. She looked at him, his brown corduroy trousers, his old woolen jacket, his shoes, his hands resting on his knees, his whole body leaning towards her as though he wanted to whisper something in her ear. And then he moved back and sank into his chair. Some minutes passed, and then he rose, still looking at her, and he stretched out his hand: "Let's finish for now. Tomorrow we meet as usual."

He accompanied her to the door and opened it. Passing close by him Marta walked into the corridor. Dr. Neuman sat down at his desk, took a bundle of white sheets out of the drawer, and began to write. For some time now he had been making his own notes about Marta, about Marta and himself, things that bore no relation to the therapy.

***

That morning, Dr. Neuman was in his office, working on the files of patients who were about to be released from hospital. Piles of paper accumulated on his desk while he prepared reports for the general practitioners to whose care the patients would return. Though it was morning, the room was dark. What's with this spring? he asked himself, annoyed, looking out through the window. It was not arriving, and he'd had enough of this gloom. He looked into the wet, desolate garden and raised his eyes to the sky. Thick heavy clouds were descending slowly. Soon there would be heavy rain. Winter is back, he said to himself, shivering. The ringing of the telephone shook him up.

"Hello, Dr. Neuman speaking."

"Good morning, Dr. Neuman. This is Shulamit from the office. The new patient has checked in and I think you should come over. There're some problems."

"I'm busy now. Could you please just finish registration, and I'll be ready for her later," he said, looking at the paperwork scattered over the desk.

"I really would like you to come now. I have a feeling that . . ."

"I am busy and don't want to be disturbed right now. Is it that urgent? What's going on?"

"Yes, it is urgent. I don't understand what's the matter, but when Marta passed by to check her mail, she saw this patient and they started shouting at each other."

"Marta? Is Marta there? Why didn't you tell me this immediately? I'll be there right away."

There was a small commotion near the office. Dr. Neuman was just in time to see Marta walking away hurriedly. "Marta!" he called, "Are you all right?"

She looked at him in a panic, her face as white as a sheet. "No, no! It can't be. I'm leaving! Goodbye! I can't stay here any longer. If she is here . . . I . . . no, no. Enough! I can't take it anymore, she always comes back. It's enough! How much more can I take?"

Dr. Neuman moved toward her, but she moved at a surprising pace. He stopped, not sure whether to follow her or to go into the office. He looked again in the direction of Marta, who was out of sight now, and entered the office. On a chair, near the wall, a large woman was seated, her head cast down, combs in her grey hair, her hands in her lap; she was lifeless, motionless, except for the heaving of her breath. Dr. Neuman looked at the nurse questioningly, and she raised her eyebrows.

"This is Mrs. Tennenbaum. She arrived this morning with a referral from a family doctor in Tiberias. Here's her file."

"Yes. But what's going on here? What's with all that yelling? What about Marta Kraus?" he asked while looking at the papers. He sat down and looked at the file more closely. Slowly, his head moved forward, his neck tensed, and he frowned. He closed the file and looked at the nurse.

"Good lord! How can it be? What happened here?"

"This lady arrived with her referral, and I started to register her . . ."

"Yes, and how did Marta come into the picture?"

"She just popped into the office to check if she had any mail. She has been receiving letters from time to time, recently, you probably know—"

"Yes, yes, go on."

"I think she gets letters from home, from her husband, and there are also postcards from Eilat. Anyway, this morning she came into the office and saw this new patient. They looked at each other and then Marta started yelling at her."

"Do you know what it was about?"

"There was all this shouting, but I couldn't get it because it was in Hungarian with some Polish, I think, or some other such language. I picked up the word "kapo." Marta was shouting at the lady, who got up, her back to the wall, and started shouting back. I suppose they know each other and that there's some bad blood between them."

Dr. Neuman raised his eyebrows and mumbled something under his breath. He looked into the file again and nodded, looked up again at the nurse and at the patient who was sitting there, slumped, and he sighed. He passed his hand over his forehead as if to wipe it clean. His face had turned grey. Shulamit offered him a drink of cold water. He told her to get some for the new patient, Mrs. Tennenbaum, too. Then he asked Shulamit to check on Marta and have another nurse sit after her, because what had happened was extremely worrying.

Mrs. Tennenbaum's file contained a special document—her personal history. She had been in charge of Jewish prisoners in Auschwitz in the summer of 1944, the year when hundreds of thousands Hungarian Jews arrived at the camp on uninterrupted transports. Tennenbaum reached Auschwitz with one of the first, in May, and became a guard—a kapo. In June 1944, she had been in charge of a group of young Jewish women who had come from the countryside with their families and were selected to do forced labor. She reached Israel after liberation, but had been identified by former Auschwitz inmates several times, which caused her to move several times. An official complaint against her was filed with the police and she was examined, but not prosecuted. She had begun to suffer increasingly from psychiatric symptoms. Her doctor referred her to the department and provided a detailed letter describing her case. Dr. Neuman read this letter attentively, closed the file, put it on Shulamit's table, and said that the woman could not stay here.

"We'll find somewhere," he said. "We'll find somewhere else for her. For now we will give her first aid, and then I will look into alternatives. Have you checked how Marta is?"

"Yes, Dr. Neuman, I phoned the clinic and asked the nurse, Rachel, to go and see. I haven't heard back from her, so we can assume Marta is all right."

"What? No, no! I don't want to assume anything," he said with unusual impatience. "I'm asking you again, please check with Rachel or whoever saw Marta. Right now! Is that clear?"

"Of course." The nurse shrank back in her chair. "I apologize. I'll phone immediately and get back to you."

Dr. Neuman thanked her and turned to Mrs. Tennenbaum.

The new patient sat frozen on her chair. "I am Dr. Neuman, the head of the department. How are you?"

The woman stayed lifeless; it was not clear if she'd heard. He lifted her heavily dangling arm and took her pulse. Then he raised her chin a little, but her eyes remained closed. "Mrs. Tennenbaum," he said, "Mrs. Tennenbaum, look at me. Can you hear me?" Gently, he shook her arm, and tried again: "I'm asking you to look at me. Do you hear me?" The woman looked at him with glazed eyes. "We will now transfer you to the clinic where you can lie down for a little and calm down. We'll give you something to help you feel a bit better. In the meantime, we will look for another hospital. You cannot stay here, you understand?" Mrs. Tennenbaum's gazed at the doctor. Her expression was empty and lifeless like her body, but she showed the slightest flicker of consent.

The nurse returned and busied herself with getting the new patient to the recovery room. Dr. Neuman got up from his chair, put the file back on the table, and headed for his office; but he turned around and began walking in the opposite direction, towards the therapists' offices and the patients' rooms. He stopped at Marta's door, knocked gently, and then, very carefully, opened the door. Marta lay on her bed, curled up, her face to the wall, covered in a blanket. He noticed her regular breathing and it seemed to him that she was quiet and calm. All of a sudden she turned her face to the door and opened her eyes. She looked at Dr. Neuman who stood motionless at the door—he caught his breath as their eyes met. Millions of charged particles flowed between them and then Marta closed her eyes and turned once more to the wall.

Summer

The encounter with the kapo was like an electric shock. Shock, short circuits, darkness, followed by a flashing light, on, off, and on again, as if the right connections were emerging and mental forces were recalibrated. It did not happen immediately. For three days Marta stayed in her room and slept. At night she sank into a deep bottomless pit, and in the mornings she awoke exhausted, as if she had done physical labor all night. Her body ached and she slept more and more. Three times a day, a nurse would bring her a tray with food and medication. Occasionally she would try to persuade her to get up and visit the dining room: "All right, all right, I'll get up. Leave me alone. I'm not hungry. I want to sleep. I am tired." She would eat a morsel sleep again.

I believe that Marta is now doing her own sleeping therapy, wrote Dr. Neuman in her file, we must keep an eye and wait. Patience is an important attribute of the psychologist.

On the morning of the fourth day something happened. Marta woke with a sudden wish to get out of bed, the room, and the unit, and into the open air. She stumbled to the small bathroom; moving mechanically, she took her pajamas off, turned on the shower, and waited for the water to get hot. She stood under the flow and let it wash over her body. She stayed like this for a long time. The movement of water on her skin, her hair, revived her. How good it was to feel clean. After the shower she put on the light summer dress she'd brought with her. She had known that the seasons would change while she was hospitalized. In front of the mirror, she pressed her wet hair close to her skull. That is how it was that morning when they shaved them. They did not recognize each other—bald little monkeys. She let go of the pressure, her hair came down in wet dark curls, and she brushed it. Drops of water fell onto her neck and she could feel the dress growing wet on her back.

On the table was a tray with yesterday's dried-up dinner. I am hungry, she said to herself—but not the dining room. I'm not setting foot in there now. She tried to nibble a little of the chewy food. It was not entirely inedible, but then it occurred to her that she might go to the café and have something small there. A lovely idea. It will be nice outside, she thought as she looked out the window. She left the room, taking the tray with her, placed it on the dirty dishes cart in the dining room, and continued towards the office.

"Good morning," said Marta to Shulamit.

The nurse said in surprise: "Marta! Good morning. Good to see you. Come and sit down. How do you feel? Aren't you cold in that dress? Winter isn't quite over yet, you know? Shouldn't you put on something warmer?"

"I'm all right, I'm not cold," she said and sat down. "I've slept so much these last few days. I did not do anything, I didn't go to my meetings with Dr. Neuman—all I did was sleep."

"You seemed need it. That's all right. You're in treatment when you sleep as well. We don't forget about you. Dr. Neuman went out to some meetings and asked me to let you know he can't see you today."

"That's all right. I didn't think we would be meeting," she said and wondered whether he knew that she would actually be well today.

"OK, excellent. So how about you? Have you had anything to eat? Have you taken your medicine this morning?"

"I haven't. I didn't go to the dining room."

"Naughty you," the nurse said, wagging her finger, telling her off, as it were, and smiling. "That's no good. I will phone the clinic right now so they can give you your medicine this morning; but we must have a little something to eat."

"Yes, fine," and she added under her breath, "here we go again—'we.'"

"Sorry?" asked the nurse, "I didn't hear you."

"Nothing. It doesn't matter."

"Wonderful. And then you'll go the activities room? That would be a good idea. Maybe you won't stay in your room today? It would be a good thing to get out a bit, talk to people. What do you say?"

"Yes, that's what I thought too. I feel like going out," she said, encouraged.

"Wonderful. So you'll go to the activities room?"

"I was thinking of going for a little stroll along the promenade. I want to be out in the fresh air for a while. Look what a beautiful day it is."

She had a feeling it was not a good idea to mention the café; she wasn't sure how the nurse would take it.

"What? Sorry, but what are you talking about?" She looked at Marta in alarm. "I do not think . . . Dr. Neuman did not leave any special instructions . . . But anyhow, that's impossible. You understand? After everything that's happened, all the excitement, we must be careful. You had better stay here under supervision."

"I really don't need supervision," said Marta angrily, "I am fine. I slept a lot. Sleep is the best tranquilizer. I feel a walk outside will do me good. I'll bring along something warm, don't worry."

"No. Impossible."

"Listen, I need time to think. Quietly. Don't worry. I really have to." Marta did her best to control herself.

"That's exactly why you should stay here. It's quiet and safe here. What if you suddenly feel unwell? You know how these things can happen. Who knows who you might meet out there? Today you must stay here. For your own good."

Marta's anger surged, she was so insulted. She could not bear this patronizing someone telling her what was best for her, as if she was a child. I know what's good for me, she said to herself, and she asked: "When is Dr. Neuman due back?"

"I don't know," said the nurse sourly. "You can imagine he's got a lot of things to do."

"Of course, but—"

"Now, you listen," the nurse was angry too, by now, "Dr. Neuman went out to the hospital on the Carmel. He managed to find a place there for that lady."

"What?" Marta asked, her voice shrill. "What are you talking about?"

"You need not worry. She's no longer here. Dr. Neuman had her transferred. But there's still a procedure."

Procedure. Marta sighed, remembering her own arrival—that too had been a procedure. Now, though, she had to get out, without any further procedure. Out into the air. To think in a quiet place about what had happened and what was happening now. Out of this madhouse.

"Well, I really must get out of here. Look," she said, trying to control her voice, to explain herself, "I'm really OK. It's all over. Please understand. Dr. Neuman would understand. I'm sure he would allow me. Can't you phone him?"

"It's not possible," the nurse decided, and began arranging papers on her desk.

Marta knew her anger was about to explode, that it would spout forth from her like a geyser. She was about to lose control. But no, no, she wouldn't give up. It was her right to leave the hospital; she would insist.

"I'm going to my room to get a sweater and my bag. I am going out," she announced.

"No, Marta, you can't do that. Definitely not before Dr. Neuman is back."

"What is this, a prison? I am a sane woman, and I can go out. I must go out. I'm suffocating in here. Don't you get it?"

"But Marta! You're not well, you're ill. Just a few days back we had a little drama here, and you—"

"Drama? What exactly are you telling me? What is this? Theater?" By now she was shouting. "You have no idea what you're saying. You haven't a clue. All of you, you don't have a clue—"

"Enough! Come on, calm down."

"I am calm. I don't want to calm down. Why don't *you* calm down? I want to go out for a bit—why is it so complicated? I need to breathe. Can't you see I have no air. I can't go on. I insist on my right to go out. This is not a closed ward."

"Why not go into the garden? There's fresh air there and—"

"You call that a garden, that miserable thing? It's a prison yard. I must go out, I don't know what will happen if I don't."

"Marta, calm down. What's the point of digging your heels in like this? Do you want something to drink?"

"Stop telling me to relax. I am absolutely fine. I don't want to calm down and I don't want to drink. I—"

"Marta, I am asking you, stop behaving like this. You cannot leave the hospital this morning, and that's that. And now I am asking you to go back to your room. You must take your morning medication. Let's go to the clinic together."

"I am not going anywhere."

"You have to take your medicine," the nurse yelled. "Stop it now or—"

"Or what? You'll send me to the gas chamber?" Marta yelled. "Stop what? What am I asking for? I'm not bothering anyone. I am asking for some fresh air, don't you get that?"

Now Marta was so excited she was no longer in control, waves crashed over her. She breathed rapidly, her face flushed, and a sweat broke out on her forehead. In her armpits too, sweat formed and began flowing down her spine. She could no longer hold back. Her anger and outrage had taken on a life of their own. They broke loose from her and dragged her along. I'm not giving in, she said to herself, I'm not giving in; but she felt terribly weak and had to sit down. The nurse tried to check her pulse, but Marta forcefully pulled back her arm: "Let go," she flashed, "let go of me."

She sat doubled over in the chair, breathing heavily, sweating. She tried to stand, pushing the nurse aside.

"Get out of my way. Look what you've done. I don't have the strength to move. Are you happy now?"

Marta looked at the nurse with unconcealed hatred and sat down again. The nurse asked if she wanted help, if she would like to return to her room in a wheelchair. But Marta just sat there, silent. The nurse left and came back with cup of tea, some dry cookies, and a little plate with medicine on it. She put the things on the table.

"Mind, the tea is boiling hot. Maybe better wait a till—"

"No matter" grumbled Marta, "no matter. I like my tea hot. Very hot. Very, very hot."

"Don't burn your tongue," the nurse tried.

"So what? What if it scalds, what do you care? Don't you think I can look after myself? At least when it comes to the temperature of my tea? You think I'm completely . . . Forget about it, it doesn't matter."

Marta drank her tea, swallowed her pills, but did not touch the cookies, which were the cheap and tasteless kind. She also wanted to punish the nurse.

When Dr. Neuman got back towards noon he was told what had happened. He inquired after Marta, and the nurse said she had gone back to her room. He asked her to check if everything was all right and went into his office. He'd had a busy morning. He made himself a cup of tea and, tired, sat down in the brown easy chair facing Marta's. He closed his eyes and sighed. He did not know that just then Marta was leaving the hospital with her handbag and an umbrella in case it rained.

***

It did not rain, and Marta stepped out into a nice spring day. She did not know how she managed to slip out without the nurse's noticing as she passed by reception. In the end it had turned out to be quite simple. What had been the point of all that fuss earlier? Anyway, she had not given in, she had insisted and managed to get out. She had won! She was still a bit hesitant and tense though. Someone might call after her: "Hey, missus, where do you think you're going?" but no one noticed, and it almost made her leap for joy. Briefly she felt like running across the hospital grounds, shouting, "I wanted, I got out, I won!," but that was not her way of doing things, and it would have been unwise. She only smiled at herself, pleased, and covered the distance to the gate with the largest possible strides.

The promenade was nearly empty. That suited her. Now she no longer meant to go far, not even to the café. She really only wanted a moment's peace, to sit down quietly, and enjoy the air, facing the sea. And such good air there was—just what she needed. She sat down on one of the wooden benches that dotted the length of the promenade, laid the folded umbrella next to her, rested her entire weight against the back of the bench, threw her head back, and took a deep breath. The pleasantness of the air entered, pouring into her, arranging itself like soft cushioning around her heart, lungs, the inside of her stomach. It like those first days of spring, after the long snowy winter, when she would again be able to go to school without her coat. How good, how good it was to want, to insist, and to succeed. It made you feel so strong. Like medicine. Better than medicine. That stupid nurse had not understood. She let her head fall back, looked at the sky, and smiled.

Marta relaxed her body as if to make space for the thoughts that began circling her like birds set free from their cages. Inside her they flew hither and thither, they flew up, vanished and returned. Her mind was working! She knew it would come now, the story about the German teacher. Of course. That memory always returned when her stubbornness came up again. Everybody had been talking about it.

It was some story. First she had insisted on going there, against her parents' will. (They said she was not strong enough to wake up so early every morning, catch the train for Nové Zámky. Her health was poor, and so on) Then, she managed, secretly, preparing herself for the entrance exams to the Nové Zámky Gymnasium. Her parents gave in. She felt that the world was about to open its doors to her. Her wish to study and leave the small town was going to materialize! But then, after what had happened with that German teacher, she insisted on not continuing. Nobody understood—why had she given up on everything? She had, after all, made a song and a dance to make her parents let her go to the gymnasium in the district center. But she could not forgive the German teacher's harassment, and she would not return to that school. It was her pride. Her dignity. Only her beloved and admired Öcsi had understood.

She shut her eyes and a sharp knife, as it were, cut loose a sigh of pain from inside. Öcsi. His name hurt. It was here, all the time, inside; she missed him all the time. He was not there, but he was. He could have stayed, returned. Where was he? It had all been so arbitrary. He could have remained and returned as much as he could have vanished and died. Where was he? She too could have disappeared had that kapo managed to drag her from the line-up, if the woman's commander had not reprimanded her for taking too long, had Erika not pulled her back with all her might. If, and if again. She too could have disappeared, it was sheer coincidence she'd found herself among those who remained, who returned. And the kapo had remained and returned too. And there they were, meeting over and over again. This time she did not lose consciousness out of sheer pain and shock. This time she shouted, she screamed at that wicked kapo. Anger restored her balance, pushed her into action: she lashed out. This anger reminded Marta that lava continued to boil, pushing outward, threatening to erupt and burn. Her anger made her aware of forces, folded away deep inside, a danger inside; it made her think of release from herself.

It was really strong and brave of me to have argued with that nurse. I dared to walk out, she said to herself, knowing it was a good sign. Öcsi would have been proud of me. Dr. Neuman too, perhaps. Unlike the nurse, he would have understood, she thought and remembered his office, their conversations. The lava inside her began to cool; she grew calmer. Thinking about Dr. Neuman made her feel calmer. Something about his personality shone out toward her, wanted the best for her, took her side. Sitting on the bench, with everything shining and going mad around her, she started to reflect, for the first time, about what was happening between the two of them. She was not familiar with therapeutic theories about the soul's movements between patient and therapist. She did not know they were a well-known and predictable part of the process. For her it was like a light appearing from the end of a tunnel, one that was growing stronger all the time. It was a miracle she was wholly unprepared for. She never imagined a stay in hospital could be like that, that she would meet a doctor who was so attentive to her, whom she could trust, who understood.

She tried to find the right words for what was happening between them, words that would express what he was passing on to her, the great closeness as well as the distance that reassured her. Yes, she felt Dr. Neuman was able to be very intimate with her and still, at the same time, maintain a distance. It allayed her anxieties, made her feel confident of her need for gentleness. Her suspiciousness and her fears, which kept her removed from her surroundings, locking her within herself, somewhat released their grip and enabled her to take in the good thoughts, the good stuff that strengthened her, like vitamins for the soul. And what was it that she passed back to him? What was he getting from her? What was it he saw in her, why had he chosen her? That was something for him to answer. She could only speak for herself. She felt good with Dr. Neuman, and that feeling accompanied her in the unit, its corridors, when she walked along the promenade, in the café.

What of this would stay with her? She worried. Because she couldn't stay forever. One day Dr. Neuman would tell her the treatment was done, that she could go back to her life. What would happen then? It surprised her, this troublesome question about returning home. She wanted to go back but she wanted to stay as well. She had been away for some time, and she was not dying of homesickness or fear. Why? How have I moved away so much? Is it part of the illness? Is it, on the contrary, a sign that I am getting better? And what will it be like to return? It was hard to imagine how things would be when she was better, when she got official permission to go back to ordinary life. What would it be like? She had grown accustomed to another life, she was writing . . . In hospital she was for herself. As though from deep inside an extinguished crater, lava was rising, fragments of passion which had once burned inside her. She must write. I'll finish what I have to write, here, what I've begun, and then I'll see.

And what about the children? The thought of them did not allow her to get away with it so easily—she told tell herself that she'd see later. She needed an answer now. What, really, should be done? She could not be away from them for a long stretch, under no circumstances! And Andy? He visited her every week, so faithfully! She saw him, he wrote her, it was convenient, possible—but Michael and Naomi? No, she would not. She had been without them for too long. Naomi had visited, and that had been wonderful. And Michael, how was her Michael doing? She was flooded by a sweet and warm wave of love, followed by ripples of bitter longing, infinite worry, as well as anger and insult. It was Andy who made the decisions, Andy who organized things, who was keeping the children away to protect them, a weak voice inside her was saying, but she rejected it impatiently. No! It wasn't right this way, she wouldn't go along with this. She would demand that Andy bring Michael next time. On this too she would insist. She wanted to see Michael; he needed her. He was an adolescent, it must be hard on him, this situation with its silences and cover-ups about such important things, and with a mother in a mental hospital. Suddenly, urgently, she felt that Michael should visit and that she should talk with him. Michael with his tender soul. She wanted to hug him from afar, in her thoughts. Good and caring thoughts would enfold Michael, protect him even when she was far away. She knew what she was talking about.

"Excuse me," someone said, "excuse me, can you tell me the time?"

Marta sat up and saw a man of about fifty wearing a long dark coat and a grey hat that cast shade over his eyes.

"Excuse me," she repeated, "what?"

"I was asking for the time," he said and smiled.

Marta looked at her wrist but there was no watch. She raised both hands and spread them, "Sorry, I don't have a watch."

"Nice day, isn't it? Would you mind if I joined you" he asked, and without waiting for an answer he moved aside her folded umbrella and sat down.

Picking up the umbrella, Marta shrank in her place, but that was a mistake, because it made him move closer. She shifted to the other edge of the bench and looked ahead.

"So, you are on a day off? Visiting from Haifa?" he asked, putting his arm along the backrest. Marta remained silent and went on looking at the horizon; her one thought was that she wanted him to go, but he stayed where he was, trying again to get her to talk.

"Can I invite you for a cup of coffee? There's a nice café nearby, a short walk from here."

Marta put her handbag and her umbrella between them, belatedly suggesting a boundary between them, a line that must not be crossed.

"So, you're not talking? What's wrong with you? It doesn't suit you?" Now he was trying his luck with a different approach.

Marta looked at him with contempt. "Thanks for asking. I want to sit here quietly on my own." She could not believe she was saying this. And returned to her argument with the nurse. "What's not to understand? I want to sit by myself."

"Ah, so you really think you're too good for this." He went on pestering her: "Look what a nice day it is. Let's watch the sea together. Have a drink, yes?" His arm approached, almost touching her shoulder.

Marta froze, she grew tense, and her gaze focused even more intently on the horizon.

"So, what do you want?" he asked.

The promenade was nearly abandoned, and here she was with this repulsive man. She decided not to react and went on staring ahead, rigid, ignoring his presence.

"You snobbish cow." The man rose, and she was startled, but she got herself together and went on ignoring him. "You think you're such a big deal, eh? Just go on sitting here on your bench. Who's even looking at you?"

He began to walk away, and she heard how he went on grumbling, cursing her probably, but she did not dare look at him, she went on gazing ahead at some nonexistent place. It took some a few before she allowed her body to relax and lean back. She felt dirty. The freedom men take to disturb and interfere with women. I should have yelled at him, she thought—but she still couldn't yell out loud. And certainly not when she was in psychiatric unit . . . She could see the other side of the bay in the distance. The air was clear and white houses, shining in the golden light, were clearly visible. She peered at the sun and then again in front of her. Soon the sun would descend and it would get chilly. I must start back, she thought. He might pass by again. She did not want another encounter. But going back to the ward wouldn't be easy either. Still, she managed to slip in without being noticed. Dr. Neuman would be gone by now, she thought sadly. He has a home too.

***

"Marta, I am happy you are back, happy we will be talking again," said Dr. Neuman the next day. "So much has happened since we last met."

"Yes," said Marta, smiling to herself, "a lot."

"What happened yesterday?" he asked. "Of course, the nurse told me. But I would like you to tell me what happened."

Marta smiled and said, yes, there had been a small scene, but the nurse was doing her job, after all.

"But what happened?" asked Dr. Neuman.

"I just had to get out a bit, breathe some air. The nurse did not agree, and then there was this scene.

"Did you go out in the end?"

"Yes, I did, and it was good."

"Where did you go?"

"I went for a stroll. I didn't do anything, I just sat on a bench and thought. Breathed some air. I felt good." She decided not to tell him about the man.

Dr. Neuman smiled. "What were you thinking about?"

"I thought about many things. I remembered things from my childhood."

"Really? What did you remember?"

"I remembered I was stubborn, I remembered how headstrong I was. And it made me happy to remember."

"Yes, you mentioned it before."

"Oh yes. Sometimes my parents did not know what to do with me. There were some serious behavior issues with me."

"Yes?"

"Yes, that's what they called it. I wasn't a good girl like my sister. I was 'problematic.'"

"How do you mean?"

"I wasn't really adjusting to their expectations. Anyway, I felt my parents would have preferred a son, a successful one like the other two, and then instead they had was me—and were disappointed."

"Do you really think so?"

"That's what I thought when I was a child. Maybe that was why I liked to be outside. I fled our home as much as possible."

"I recollect how you spoke about your attraction to the outside world. But why flee? You told me yourself about your home, your parents' love . . ."

"I was a kind of black sheep, or egocentric. There were chores to do, at home, all the time, there wasn't a moment's peace. Our mother did everything, even when we had helpers: she worked hard. And when Jews were no longer allowed to employ help, they expected that we, the girls, would pitch in. There were demands all the time. I felt it left me little space, that they were taking away my time. It suffocated me. I wanted to be outside. It's quite ironic, with all that happened, how things evolved."

"I don't exactly understand what you mean."

"You know—me of all people. You could say I really did not want to be at home, in the kitchen, I hated kitchen work, and I escaped time and again, to get out, even though they scolded me about not helping," she said and sighed. "I got stuck at home in the kibbutz, and later in our little commune . . . in the children's home, in the kitchen. Women's work, women's places. And nowadays too, as you know, I am at home a lot and I try to be outside as little as possible, I mean, in places with a lot of people. Don't you think that's strange? The irony of fate, isn't it?"

"I don't think so. There are reasons, you know. But tell me, where would you go when you went out? What would you do?"

"Oh my! It was simply joy! I was simply happy outside. I could act the way I liked. I was with friends, I had many friends, I was popular. We played outside all the time. We had plenty of ideas and we kept finding things.

We would discover a gap in the fence and sneak into the garden of the sugar factory. It was right by the river, a densely grown garden, full of trees, shrubs, and flowers. It was a magical place for our games, in all seasons. And all kinds of scary stories were doing the rounds about this garden."

"What kind of stories?"

"There were rumors that the wife of the keeper took sunbaths in the nude . . . And a story about a chopped-off hand with rings . . . We were scared but fascinated too. There was a guard at the entrance, but we knew how to avoid him . . . And we sneaked up on couples who made out in the garden. In the winter, the river froze, and we all went to skate on the ice. It was lovely. It was a biting cold, but inside we felt hot. It's a real shame that there's no ice for skating in the winters here." She gazed into the distance, as if she remembered.

"And how was it at home? In the end, after all, you'd go home."

"Yes, but I almost always came late. They would try and constrain me, tell me to be back by such a such a time; I didn't like these limits. I think it's a little in my nature. I'm not really good about times. Even now. But then I would return late, and my mother would be angry. I tried to find myself a corner, at home, to sit and read or dream, just so they'd let me be, not ask me to do things. My mother was annoyed because I really didn't help at home, and she was always presenting Erika as an example. Why did she help and I didn't? Erika was a good girl, she liked to help my mother, while I preferred to be in my own world. I wanted to be left alone. Yes, I was very stubborn. When I wanted something and my parents did not agree, I would stop eating."

"You'd go on hunger strike?"

"Exactly. I was a very difficult child. Hunger strikes were the most effective weapon against my parents. They would get so worried when we didn't eat . . . and that was before . . . Anyway, they worried when I didn't eat. They couldn't deal with my hunger strikes, so that was how I managed to get what I wanted so often. Can you imagine? Look at me today—it's hard to believe I was different. Even I find it hard to believe."

"I believe it, and I'm not surprised by what you're telling me about yourself. Interesting that you come back to it every time. Why do you make yourself appear less?" Dr. Neuman stopped and looked at her for a long moment. "I know you a bit by now"—he hesitated—"just look at what you did yesterday! You understand, right, that that's not easy. You decided to go out even though the nurse did not agree. And you managed." He paused. "What you did is against the rules here. Patients are expected to respect the decision of the medical staff, including the nurses! Don't tell anyone, but I'm proud of you."

"That's what I thought, that you'd be happy." She smiled at him.

"It's not about being happy. But, yes, it's a good thing you managed to get out. It's your small victory."

"Yes."

"And you managed to leave and come back without the nurse noticing. How did you do that? That takes some talent! I'm starting to worry," he said and tiny wrinkles of laughter formed around his eyes.

She looked at him and smiled back. "Yes, I was a little worried, but the return was really easy because it was during visiting time, with many people going in and out. Nobody paid attention. It didn't really take much talent."

"I think it did. I really do. Maybe talent isn't quite the word, but Marta, you wouldn't have acted like this a few weeks back."

"You're right. I don't think I would have dared."

"That's exactly the word. Thanks. Daring. That's what happened yesterday." He stopped briefly and smiled. "So maybe you're not that gifted after all."

"Dr. Neuman. That's no way to talk to your patient. You're lowering her morale." Marta tried to keep a straight face and then broke out into liberating laughter. It was the first time such a thing had happened to her in her therapy. They both fell silent, as though they wanted to hold onto the laughter. But they had to talk about the incident with the kapo. Dr. Neuman asked Marta if she felt she could talk about what had happened with the woman. So she told him about the kapo almost pulling her out of the line of women who stayed alive, and that Erika had saved her. She told him about her first encounter with the woman when she'd been waiting to see the doctor and what it had done to her—a breakdown, everything falling to pieces. It was because of her that Marta was now in hospital, and she'd met her again . . . The woman was the angel of death. A Jewish woman like the rest of them. How much evil does it take to send a miserable monkey who has managed to stay alive to her death? There were people who collaborated, but this one . . .

"You know," she suddenly said, "after everything that happened to us, Erika and me, we were simply unable to think about it. It was so terrible, physically. We couldn't."

"I understand."

"I know I am repeating myself. I've already talked about it, but I cannot control it. The thought doesn't stop gnawing."

"That's absolutely normal, Marta. It's a symptom of shock. One cannot understand, and yet one tries, one goes back to it, again and again . . ."

"That's it, that's what I feel. I don't understand what happened, so I think about it repeatedly—because in the end I will get it, perhaps."

"There's something positive about that, isn't there?"

"About me repeating things?"

"Yes. You talk! We are talking about that moment. It's not so long ago the you wouldn't dare to speak."

"I am trying to understand. Maybe if I manage to reconstruct every moment, one second after another . . . but it all happened so fast. All of a sudden, it was just the two of us. No father. No mother. No Eva. We were a family when we got off the train—and bang! Nothing left."

"Yes . . ."

"Later, we did not want to think about it; we just couldn't think about it."

"Of course you couldn't."

"You know, there was this one cousin who survived. The son of my father's brother. He survived and he wanted us to be in touch, but my sister and I just couldn't . . . It was terrible for him. We were the only relatives who'd stayed alive, and we wanted nothing to do with him. The two of us, at least, were together. It pains me that we treated him like that."

"You had no choice—that's what enabled you to live."

"Yes . . . I don't know . . . live . . . what sort of a life."

"Yes, a life. Look what you've done since then. It is a life . . ."

"I do wonder sometimes . . ."

"What?"

"I wonder about this life. What it might mean to be alive after what happened . . ."

"And how do you answer yourself?"

"Despair. I don't know. I need a lot of strength to steer clear of despair. The children. Their lives."

"Your life and their lives. And how was Naomi's visit?" he suddenly asked. "Did you talk about it?"

"No. I couldn't do it. I wanted to, but I couldn't . . ."

"What was it that you couldn't?"

"Talk to her. Tell her. I just couldn't. And nor could she."

"Maybe it will happen next time. I believe something will have been passed on to her. She did, after all, come to see you here. It might make it easier another time. Don't give up." He smiled, and added: "And then there is the option of writing, isn't there? Writing down your memories is another way of talking, telling them. Are you writing?"

She was not ready for that question. It was the first time Dr. Neuman had directly asked about her writing, and she was not sure whether to tell him.

"Yes, I am writing. I am writing, I am trying to write, I am making headway."

"I'm glad you're telling me."

"Glad I'm telling you or glad I'm writing?"

"Both, of course. And I'll be even gladder if you allow me . . ." He paused. "It's really wonderful you're writing, and thank you for telling me. It's important that I know, and not only from a medical point of view."

"I decided Andy should bring Michael along when he visits next," she said quickly, "I thought about it a lot yesterday."

"Really?" For a moment Dr. Neuman seemed surprised.

"Are you surprised?"

"It's a good surprise, Marta. It's an important decision and the right one. In all relationships, movements this way and that happen."

"Yes?"

"Yes, yes. You do tell Andy what to do, then, and I am sure it's not the first time."

"That's true."

"Even though everybody has their role, roles change."

"And between us?" she blurted out before she managed to stop herself.

Dr. Neuman smiled at her. "That's not quite the same, you can probably see that," he said and grew silent. Dear Marta, I cannot say everything that's on my mind." His eyes were laughing. "But what I can say is that your decision to tell Andy to bring along Michael is good for all involved. I am sure Michael misses you very much."

"I miss him too," she whispered.

"Just don't be surprised if he doesn't say much. You can probably imagine that it will be a little difficult for him."

"I must be prepared," she said, "I do understand, but . . ."

"It won't be simple," continued Dr. Neuman, "but you should know better than most that life isn't simple."

"I only realize now how simple my life was when I was a little girl. I had everything. But at the time it seemed complicated, there was a lot of conflict. But let's leave that for now."

"Indeed. Let's wrap up."

In the evening, in bed, under her blanket, Marta tried to recollect the moment of joy she'd experienced the previous day on the promenade. She wanted to remember herself, the way she had sat on the bench, her head thrown back, free; she wanted to remember how she breathed in the sky, how her thoughts flew free like birds every which way. She wanted to see it like an image projected on the ceiling. It reminded her of Andy's photographs. He had bought himself a camera, some years before, joined a photography club, and on Saturday mornings he would go out to take pictures of landscapes, people, objects. Often, he also took photographs of her. He developed them at home, in the dark room he improvised in their bathroom, where a wide wooden shelf served as his work table. On it stood brown glass bottles containing developing fluid, some large plastic containers, stored one inside the other, and an instrument that reminded her of a large microscope. When he was busy developing, the bathroom was forbidden territory. Red light escaped if the door opened a crack. He invited her in, sometimes, so she could witness the miraculous appearance of the image on the photographic paper submerged in the solution. Like a revelation, the picture would emerge, floating up from the container, from the void. A shimmering existence, gradually becoming clear, took shape on the paper. Like a memory. Each memory would hang drying on the long strings Andy fastened over the bathtub. Drops of solution left red stains on it, like blood.

Marta reflected on the images of her memory. Not one photograph of her family survived. She had to make them surface from the containers in her head. Looking at the dark ceiling, she hoped for a miracle, but no photograph appeared. The ceiling withdrew and she grew smaller and smaller. I will never manage, she said to herself, I will never get over what happened. She felt she was falling, and before she finally fell asleep, she recalled that Andy would come the next day.

***

Since she'd been hospitalized, Andy had visited her almost every weekend, and sometimes on a weekday too. Once a week she received a letter from him. In Hebrew, he wrote how he missed her, his dear, beloved, and faraway soulmate. He wrote about work, and about how he had realized it would be better if they moved nearer Haifa, so the hospital would be within easier reach if the need arose. He'd ask at work for a transfer to Haifa, he wrote, and she was not sure whether to be pleased with this or not. She looked forward to his letters, was glad when they came, and was excited to read them, the way one receives letters from someone close and dear, someone who was lost and then suddenly reappeared. But she also read them as though they were meant for another woman. Being away from Andy allowed her to see herself differently, free herself from him.

Her conversations with Dr. Neuman helped her to see things differently, especially in relation to Andy's decision to keep the children, Erika, and Yehoshua away from her breakdown and hospitalization. As if she only needed him, only he knew what was right for her. This was exactly how it had been when they first met and began to invent a new life. Andy, her Dušička, had been her new life. But now her life was something else. She knew he was trying to protect her, protect the children, but she was not convinced it was all for the better now. Dr. Neuman was saying other things. He said that the children would feel that they were being sheltered from their parents' past, that they registered the silence, and that they were bound to experience it as a threat. It was important to find a way to talk to them, reveal the secret. She knew he was right, there was no question; she just had no idea how to proceed.

Naomi's visit had been Dr. Neuman's idea. It had been an opportunity to touch upon the secret. Yet she had not brought it off, even though the visit was quite successful. Well, that was a good thing in its own right. She had been happy, and she thought Naomi, too had enjoyed it. Andy had not brought Michael, and at home he did not speak to him or Naomi. He had told Marta so himself. Nor had Erika and Yehoshua seen her yet. Andy was keeping things hidden from them too. He might have hoped that the matter would be sorted out quickly, but it hadn't. Later, when they heard, they were insulted. She is my sister, Erika told him, and Yehoshua said that it was no way to behave. But it was exactly how Andy behaved, most of the time. He was convinced his decisions were right and had complete faith in his analytic abilities. What had happened to her, what was still happening to her, troubled him too. He was protecting himself. He probably wasn't aware of it, she thought. And she hadn't understood it either, until now.

When Andy arrived that day, in the early hours of the afternoon, Marta had already made up her mind. She would not give in. She would be the one to decide. It did not even surprise her when Andy did not argue. He promised he would bring Michael with him the next time. And the following week Michael was with Andy, as well as Erika and Yehoshua. This had not been her plan. It was a huge, confusing surprise, and it was too much for her. She was quiet and tense throughout the visit. She wasn't happy or talkative, Michael was quiet and tense too; she did not even hug him the way she would have liked. The unexpected encounter with Erika and Yehoshua was strange. Facing them, she was lost for words.

Andy suggested they all go to the café on the promenade. He promised Michael cake and ice cream, but he wasn't particularly enthusiastic. On the promenade, he walked at some distance behind the four adults, kicking a stone he found on the sidewalk. Marta wanted to slow down to fall in with his pace, be near him, but Andy put his arm around her shoulder, embraced her, and Erika held her hand tight. That is how she walked on, embraced and loved from both sides, imprisoned, and her thoughts trailing behind with Michael, her child. She walked along with Andy and Erika, turning her head, looking for him, her heart wholly with him.

In the café, they sat around a table facing the sea. Marta had rushed to sit next to Michael, but when she tried to come close and hug him, she felt him holding back. He moved his head to the side and stayed frozen and remote in her arms. She let it be and consoled herself with the thought that he was still right here.

"Michi, how are you? You've grown a lot," she tried.

"He's a real big boy already," Andy inserted himself, "he's grown up and knows how to cope. You wouldn't recognize him."

But she recognized him very well. He might have grown, but she was familiar with his long and thin body, the eyes behind his glasses, his curly hair, which he had let grow long and which now looked wild and messy.

"Michush, I am so happy you're here. I've missed you so."

"Me too, I've missed you," he said—she hadn't expected it—and his eyes lit up, "I hope . . ."

He halted and Marta wondered what he intended to say and whether it was a script Andy had given him.

"I feel better. Much better," she said, turning to Erika as well, "I hope it will all be done soon so I can come home, and things will go back to how they were." She asked herself: How they were? When will I go home?

"Yes, Mommy," said Michael, his eyes fixed on the table, "I hope it'll be soon."

My Michi, she thought, and took his hand between hers, my Michael. Andy, Erika, and Yehoshua looked at them quietly, and Marta felt the strangeness between them.

"Well, there you are. Now you can see that I am all right. It's so good you came. Tell me a bit how things are with you," she said, "and let's order. You promised us coffee and cake, didn't you?" she said to Andy, "so please."

Andy called the waiter and they ordered.

"Martushkam," said Erika, "Martushkam, how are you? I am so . . ."

"All right, Erichkam, I'm all right."

"Martushkam." Erika stretched her arms toward Marta across the table, held her hands and pressed them hard. When the waiter arrived with their orders they let go of each other's hands. Four cups of steaming coffee and a tray with a choice of cakes were placed before them. "I'll bring the rest right away," said the waiter, returning some minutes later with a glass bowl containing three scoops of ice cream, a bottle of lemonade, and a glass. The arrival of the food released some of the tension, and a conversation unfolded. Michael remained silent and ate his ice cream intently. With each bite he left the spoon inside his mouth allowing the ice to melt there. Like me, thought Marta, when I scrape the cocoa from the bottom of the cup. And so they sat around the table, four adults talking and one adolescent who kept silent— an almost perfect picture of closeness. Marta looked on at all this from a distance. Something was eluding her. She was feeling remote. Voices were reaching her, at times she said something, answered some question, but the conversation went on without her, lively, even if she did not take part.

Michael's and Erika's very close proximity confused her like a buzzing that fell just short of being a distraction. There they were, finally they were there, but she could not reach them; it was as though they were separated by an invisible screen. She was with them, but far away. In another place. She looked at everyone—all of them dear to her. She loved them. She was with them, but did not belong. Nor did Michael. He left the table and walked down the steps, crossed the promenade, and descended to the beach. Marta observed him sitting on a boulder casting pebbles onto the waves. She rose and Andy looked up at her questioningly. "I'm going to sit with Michael," she said nodding her head in the boy's direction. "I want to be with him by myself for a bit." She walked down the promenade, approaching the bolder on which Michael was sitting.

Reaching Michael, she said, "Give me a hand. I don't want to get my shoes wet."

"Take them off," he said, stretching out his hand, "get your feet wet. it's really nice."

Marta took a big step and stood on the boulder, beside Michael. Supporting herself with her hands, she sat down and took off her shoes. She took off her socks and put them inside her empty shoes, looking around for a place to put them.

"Give them to me, Mommy," said Michael. "Don't worry, I'll make sure they don't get wet."

"Thank you my sweetheart, thanks."

"Put your feet into the water, it's so nice."

"Oh my God." Marta dipped one foot into the water: "*Brrrr* . . . it's cold. It gives me goosebumps."

"Nice goosebumps?"

"Give me some time, I'll get used. It will be nice."

"Now your other foot, Mommy. You'll see it's great."

Andy, Yehoshua, and Erika looked on from the café. Marta and Michael sat on the rocks, close, their feet in the water, looking at the horizon. It was impossible to see whether they were talking. Erika sighed and Yehoshua hugged her. Andy went on looking at Marta and Michael, and then he turned to the horizon. When they started back for the hospital, the sun was its way down toward the sea, behind the mountain, The ridge shone and the water turned deeply dark. The five of them walked quietly and closely together until they reached the hospital gate and stopped. Another goodbye.

"Will you come with me all the way to the ward?" asked Marta.

"Of course, Dušinka," said Andy, "we'll come with you all the way, won't we?" He turned to Michael, Erika, and Yehoshua.

"No question about it," said Yehoshua, looking at Erika, who was having a

hard time holding back her tears. She wiped her eyes with her hands and sniffled. "Take that," Yehoshua gave her a handkerchief, "you can see for yourself Martushkam is all right. She'll be released soon. Don't worry."

"I know," whispered Erika, "that's not why."

"All right," said Yehoshua and hugged her, "take it easy."

When they reached the door, Marta turned around and proposed they say goodbye there. It was difficult. She hugged Michael tight and felt his arms on her back. "Thank you for coming, Michi. It's made me so, so happy, even if we didn't have a chance to talk a lot. Next time will be easier."

"I'm also happy I came, Mommy. I hope you'll feel better and come home soon," he said from between her arms. "I love you."

"My sweetie. I love you too: very, very much."

Why couldn't it have been this simple with Naomi? she wondered, still holding Michael in her arms, until she felt his body signaling to be released. Then she hugged Erika very tight and wept with her. Yehoshua's embrace was brief and a little stiff. Andy held and pressed her so close that she couldn't breathe. "Dušička, my Martushkam," he whispered in her ear.

"Now just go," she said, "just go. Or else I'll really cry."

Marta went through the door. The others walked to the parking lot in silence, and Michael again kicked a stone along the ground.

***

Something happened to Marta following this visit. First there were episodes of minor short-circuits in her connection with the world. A light buzzing in her head, as if a stray insect had gotten lost inside, a passing blurring of her sight, like a milky screen descending momentarily over one eye, hiding the world and the lifting almost immediately. Her thoughts, from time to time, were carried away, she lost her orientation and context. She found it a little hard to focus during her conversations with Dr. Neuman, but they continued talking about the visit. In the evenings she felt tired, a tiredness which sometimes lasted into the mornings; and again and again visits to the café were postponed. On such mornings she wrote a little in her room, but often she fell asleep, her head slumped on her desk. Dr. Neuman did not ask her about her writing and nor did he mention her tiredness and distraction. In the hospital no one really paid attention to passing peculiarities of this kind. But it gradually became clear that Marta was just having more than just a blip. And again, Marta found herself in a crisis.

The next week, Andy's visit occurred towards the evening. As he walked past the office, the nurse told him that Marta was probably taking a nap in her room. Softly, Andy knocked on the door and entered. Marta was lying on her bed and looking at him. He approached her smiling and asked "How are you, Martushkam?" but she recoiled and moved close up to the wall, pulling the blanket with her.

"Marta," whispered Andy, "Martushkam, what is it? It's me, Andy, don't you recognize me? Come on, get dressed, we'll go out. It's a lovely day outside. Let's go and sit at the café on the promenade, we'll look at the sea. Get up, Martushkam."

He bent over her, and she looked at him suspiciously and in fear, shaking her head and mumbling: "No, no, that's not him." She recoiled from him and then sat on the edge of the bed, keeping her distance, holding fast onto her blanket. Andy stood there confused, not knowing what to do, while Marta took the opportunity to bolt towards the door, still clutching her blanket. She opened the door and slipped into the corridor. Andy went after her. With sure steps she strode towards reception, entered, and positioned herself opposite the nurse.

"Marta, what . . . what's happened? Why are you holding that blanket? What's going on—are you all right?"

"I'm fine. But some stranger just walked into my room. He stood by my bed."

"A stranger? Isn't that Andy? He was here just a moment ago and said he was on his way to your room to see you. I saw him."

"No. That wasn't Andy. That was someone dressing up like Andy. An imposter."

"Dressed up? What do you mean? I saw him myself, walking towards your room."

"The person in my room—it wasn't Andy. I know Andy very well. This man is pretending. I don't know how he did it, but he must have somehow gotten hold of Andy's clothes, and he's an imposter. Yes, an imposter" She was fully convinced.

"Are you sure? I think you are wrong, it's Andy."

"No," she yelled, "it's not true. It's somebody else. Could he have done something to Andy? We must tell the police. He's dangerous. I can't return to my room. He is there."

"Let me come with you. We'll see what's the matter, OK?"

Marta nodded, the two of them left the office, and immediately bumped into Andy, who was standing outside the door. Marta took a step back inside. "You see," she said to the nurse, "I told you. He's following me, he's an imposter. He's dangerous. Someone must call the police."

The nurse, approaching Andy, asked what exactly had happened.

"I have no idea," said Andy in despair, "no idea. I went into the room, and she simply bolted. All of a sudden she doesn't recognize me. She's scared of me. Now what do we do?"

"We will deal with it. These things happen."

"I really don't understand. I just don't understand what's happening to her. She's never failed to recognize me. On the contrary, she always asks for me when there's trouble. I'm the one who can restore her calm. Is her medication making her confused?"

"It's not related to her medication. Dr. Neuman has already left, but I will check who's available." The nurse made a face. "It's rather later for today. I'll phone the doctor who's on call and ask him to come in. She looks so scared."

"Yes, me too, I'm scared. Something like that . . ."

Andy's face had grown ashen and his eyes were blinking fast, as if to wipe away the tears that were trying to break out. He turned away, took a handkerchief from his pocket and put it to his eyes. The nurse put her hand on his shoulder which grew stiffer.

"It's scary but it will pass. We're familiar with these things. It's one of the processes. She must still be shocked by that encounter. The doctor will be here soon and then we'll see what we can do."

"What encounter? Why don't they tell me?"

"The best thing to do is to talk to the doctor. I think you'd better get some air, go to the promenade, to the café. We must allow her to regain her calm and wait for the doctor."

"Yes, all right. I am leaving. I don't understand. That she should be afraid of me. Unbelievable . . ."

Andy approached the entrance of the office and looked for Marta. She sat on a chair, huddled in the blanket, and when she saw him she covered her head. "Martushkam," whispered Andy, "I'll be back soon, don't you worry." He left the unit, his hands squeezing the grey woolly hat she had knitted for him. The nurse followed him with her eyes as he walked away, and then went back into the office and gently removed the blanket from Marta's head.

"Is he gone?" asked Marta, pale.

"Yes, he's left. Let's go to your room together."

"No, I'm not going there. I'm afraid he might return. We must notify the police. We must find Andy."

"Do you want to stay here? Don't you want to get dressed? Maybe we'll go to your room so you can dress, and then we'll come back? What do you say?"

"Will you stay with me?"

"Of course. Just let me make a phone call before we go."

"To the police?"

"No, I need to check a medical issue."

"But we also have to phone the police."

"Yes, yes, we'll do that later."

"Not later. We must do it now. There's no way of knowing what that imposter has done to Andy. It must be now."

"All right."

The nurse checked the list of doctors on call. It was Dr. Pasternak, a young intern. "Let's hope she'll be able to help," the nurse whispered, and dialed. She briefly explained what had happened, and the doctor said she could be there in about fifteen minutes and that Marta should be under supervision until then. The nurse said they would be waiting for her in the office. She turned to Marta, "Come on, let's go to your room."

"Did you have a word with the police?" asked Marta.

"Not yet. Let's first go to your room."

"First you talk to the police."

The nurse approached the phone, lifted the receiver, and dialed three numbers. Marta watched her.

"Hello? Is that the police? I am calling from the hospital. I want to report an imposter . . . Yes, an imposter. He's pretending to be the husband of one of our patients. His name is Andy Kraus . . . No, sorry, not the imposter. The husband . . . I would like you to check up on the husband . . . Yes, will you check and get back to us? . . . Yes. Thank you, goodbye . . . There you are," she said to Marta, "the police are on it."

"Did you explain everything?"

"You could hear for yourself. Now let's go to your room. Then we'll wait for news from the police."

Marta stood up unsteadily, and with the blanket trailing behind her, the two of them waked down the corridor. When they returned to the office, Dr. Pasternak was there. She was sitting at the desk, talking to Andy who still held the woolly hat in his hands. Marta drew back. "Come in," said the doctor, but Marta's eyes stared in Andy's direction. "Don't worry, it's all right, we are here. We will look after you," the doctor said, trying to reassure her and smiling brightly at Andy. "It will be all right."

Dr. Pasternak got up from her chair and approached Marta: "I am doctor Pasternak and I am on duty this weekend," she said. She held Marta's shoulders and invited her into the office. Marta allowed the doctor to guide her, all the while checking over to see where the imposter was, and sat down. Andy was seated at the other end of the room, his head cast down.

"Can you tell me your name, please?" asked the doctor.

"Marta."

"Pleased to meet you, Marta. Before you got here, I was talking to Andy ..."

"That's not him. I don't know where Andy is. This one here—he's a liar. He's pretending. He's dangerous."

"I see. You're telling me he only looks like Andy, but he isn't. How can that be?"

"He managed to steal Andy's clothes from the wardrobe, and he studied his body movements really well, and his voice. He's very clever."

"That's not easy, to do all that."

"Yes, I told you he was dangerous."

"If he looks so much like Andy, how could you identify the real Andy? Say he walked in here now, your Andy?"

"That's easy. I would check his scars. He has scars on his body. You can't copy them. That's the sign."

"You're right. They would prove it was him."

"It wouldn't be him if there weren't any."

"Right. So what would you say if we checked this man here. It'll be a test. This way we will know whether it's Andy or an imposter. What do you think?"

"You want me to touch him?" she asked in disgust.

"Yes, just in order to make sure it really isn't Andy. Just check whether he has scars. That way we can be sure."

"But I don't know this man. I cannot just examine his body."

"We can ask his permission," said the doctor and turned to Andy: "It'll be right," she whispered, then louder, she said: "Are you willing for this lady to check your scars?"

"Yes," said Andy and stood up. He took off his coat and sweater, undid the buttons of his flannel shirt, opened it, and stood in his white undershirt, his shoulders and arms bare. His skin was tanned below his neck and his arms were brown up to over his elbow. Marta's restless eyes roved between Andy and the doctor. The doctor smiled at her; Marta approached Andy. They were close to each other, heads and eyes cast down, bodies tense and alert. The room was silent. The doctor and the nurse stood motionless. A transparent screen seemed to surround Marta and Andy, separating them from their surroundings, two bodies that knew each other so well. She closed her eyes and stretched out her hands towards him, taking hold of his right arm. She turned his lower arm over a little and her fingers found the mark left by the burn. For a while she let them rest on the scar; then she let them slide down so they came to rest on Andy's hand. Her second hand moved up his body to find the birthmark below his left collarbone. The two of them stayed like this without uttering a word. Andy very slowly raised his arm and put it on Marta's shoulder, in a gentle, soft embrace. Then he bent his head towards her, and only then did she relax and let her head come to rest on his chest.

***

Dr. Neuman decided to present the incident during a staff meeting. What had happened since Marta Kraus's encounter with the kapo from Auschwitz, who then herself turned up for hospitalization in the unit, was a chain of typical post-traumatic responses, which they really should discuss. He gave a case description: "The patient's immediate response was a kind of loss of consciousness, deep sleep, three days of almost uninterrupted sleep. Then she woke up. A brief awakening, but an awakening all the same. Not just from sleep. Her strength now increases, she appears to have regained her balance. She can see things, make connections, she is reasonable. In meetings, the conversation flows, there's even some humor. Marta definitely has a sense of humor! In the wake of a family visit, which may have been premature or there were simply too many visitors, one can't tell, difficulties again arise. We observe lessened wakefulness, some anxiety, and eventually paranoia.

This paranoid development is interesting. Why? Because it may also be an encouraging sign. If I may put it like this: paranoia reveals an ability for logical thinking. Though from our perspective it is a crooked, sick logic, from the patient's point of view what's crooked, illogical, and sick—is exactly what happened to her—and that's trauma. Trauma is not logical, it cannot be grasped by human thought. It cannot be understood, neither when it actually happens, nor later, in hindsight—what we call post-trauma. Paranoia is one possible reaction to the insanity of the traumatic event. When the patient does not understand what's happening to her, when she's lost and finds herself in a world that makes no sense, paranoia is her way of making order in this chaos, organizing the world she no longer understands. I would even say," and here Dr. Neuman raised his voice, "that from the patient's point of view it might be a what I want to call creative reaction revealing strength and a will to live, to survive."

He was silent; he put his elbows on the table and rested his head between his hands, facing down. The room too was silent. He raised his head and said, "And there's one more important detail. Even more interesting,

I would say. Paranoia, here, occurred in relation to her husband. The patient had not shown any paranoid behaviors—this was a sudden manifestation. This is exactly how paranoia works, it is a response when everything becomes unsettled so badly that even the most familiar, which is usually a source of security and confidence, becomes scary."

One of the doctors asked whether, in treatment, Marta had showed signs of being afraid of her husband. "That's exactly it," explained Dr. Neuman, "and your question is important. Mrs. Kraus is not afraid of her husband. On the contrary, he is the one person with whom she feels safe. That was how it was until this incident. They grew up in the same little town and they have known each other from birth. Other than her sister, he is the only person she knows from way back then. Her husband, in fact, is her security. And this security crumbled, because what she sees is not really what things are like. Maybe this man only looks like her husband, maybe he is an imposter with bad intentions, maybe her real husband is in danger?"

He looked at his staff and began arranging some papers in the file he had before him. "That said," he resumed, "we may also want to investigate the possibility of there being some problem between them, in addition to the post-traumatic symptoms. It's not impossible. We must always look at symptoms from several directions. Mental issues are so complicated. Anything is possible." Overcome by a cough, he cast in his pocket for a handkerchief. The cough intensified, and someone handed him a glass of water. Dr. Neuman took a few sips and put the glass next to the file. "Yes, it's definitely possible. We will also take up that direction," he said once his cough subsided. "We will have to deal with that too, in the future. Mr. Andy Kraus is an impressive man. I'll invite him to join one or two meetings with his wife." He looked at the others around the table and said decisively: "Well. We are done with this case. Let's go to the other items on the agenda. What cases do we have? Who's presenting?"

After the meeting, Dr. Neuman returned to his room and made a call to the nurse. He asked her to send a message to Andy Kraus: "Can you let him know my office hours?" he asked. "And tell him to contact me as soon as possible."

A meeting with Andy was scheduled for the next Friday. Of course, this would need to be discussed with Marta. Since the beginning of the week, she had not been feeling very well and did not come in for their meetings. On the Wednesday, she knocked quietly on the door to Dr. Neuman's office, entered, and halted.

"Good morning, Marta." Dr. Neuman smiled and got up to receive her. "Please, come in."

"Thank you," whispered Marta and sat on the familiar easy chair. Dr. Neuman sat down opposite her, as usual, and the two of them were silent. It was a strange silence, uneasy, but not tense or threatening either. They simply sat in silence. Each of them alone and together. Then, suddenly, Marta grew tense, she leaned forward, and her face grew red: "I could not make it to the previous meetings," she said, "I am very sorry." Dr. Neuman said it was fine and that he could see she needed rest and time to calm down after what happened.

"So you already know what happened?"

"Yes, yes, they informed me."

"I don't understand. Who informed you? The Germans?"

Dr. Neuman looked at her in astonishment. "Don't worry," he said, "we can continue from where we left off the last time."

"I don't really remember where we were, having been where I was," said Marta.

"Yes, that must have been a harsh place—such an unexpected encounter."

"I did not have any encounter. They kidnapped me," and she reddened even more.

"What is it you are talking about, Marta?" Dr. Neuman asked hesitantly, "I am not sure I know . . . understand."

"Of course you don't know. I don't know who could have informed you. Nobody knows, because they kidnapped me and put me in a bunker three kilometers under the ground."

"Who kidnapped you?"

"The Germans," she whispered, "you know, the Nazis. They took me away and left me there. Nobody knew, and I couldn't get out."

"Three kilometers below the ground!" Dr. Neuman was appalled. "What happened to you there? And how did you get out?"

Marta had no answer. She really had no idea how it happened. She was sure of only two things: she had been in a German bunker, deep down in the earth, and now she was here again. She did not remember how she had been kidnapped and how she got out. Did she escape? Did they release her? She couldn't remember, but she was very sure of having been kidnapped, locked into an underground bunker. "I really don't know," she said, "it seems . . . I really can't remember . . ." and she looked at him in embarrassment.

"But now you are here, Marta, you're here and that's what counts. Can you tell me about what happened there? In the bunker, I mean."

"It was so frightening . . . I did not understand what's going on, and what was going to happen . . . Like then. Terrible."

"And how do you feel now?"

"Better," she said and looked up at him, "but it was very scary . . . I almost died of fear."

"I can imagine."

Marta looked at Dr. Neuman, trying to see whether he was serious, but he seemed very serious. He believes me, it's not a dream. Finally, someone who believes me, she thought. Dr. Neuman, as if reading her thoughts, leant forward a little in his chair: "Dear Marta, I am listening. Everything you tell me here, everything you say is important and relevant. As far as I am concerned. And I am not questioning anything of what you're telling me. Please remember that. We are together here, you and I. No matter how long it takes, we will move forward. We are already making progress." He bent further over the small table that stood between them, took her hand and pressed it. Marta let him and concentrated on the flow of warm and good feelings inside her. Dr. Neuman's voice reached her from afar.

"I spoke to Andy."

"You found him?" Marta sat up straight, pulling her hand away. "How is he?"

"He is well. He will be coming in on Friday morning."

They both leant back in their seats. Dr. Neuman asked Marta if she was happy for Andy to join their morning meeting. Marta did not reply immediately and looked thoughtful. Dr. Neuman said that he would like it if every so often someone close to her joined their meetings—a relative. It might help her therapy. Marta looked at him and smiled a little, remembering seeing Naomi and spending time with her in the café. And she had been there with Andy too. It would be nice to go back with him. She missed him, she longed for him.

"All right," she told Dr. Neuman, "yes. You know he was here last week?"

"Yes, of course I know. So let's invite him again. Excellent. Shall we meet again tomorrow, as usual?"

"Yes," answered Marta and got up. Dr. Neuman took note of her energetic movement and her measured and upright posture. He walked with her to the door and before she stepped out, he took her hand again and pressed it warmly. "See you tomorrow, Marta," he said, and followed her with his eyes as she walked away.

***

On Friday morning Andy arrived; the nurse in the reception office told him to go through to Dr. Neuman's office. After knocking on the door, he entered, and found Dr. Neuman seated behind his desk intently reading papers from the heap in front of him.

"Good morning, Mr. Kraus, I'm happy you're here. Please take a seat."

"Thank you," said Andy and made to sit down in the easy chair.

"I'm so sorry, please could you sit here," Dr. Neuman said and pointed at the chair on the other side of the desk. "That is where Marta usually sits, and perhaps . . . perhaps it will trouble her. It's hard to know, everything is so sensitive right now."

"I wanted to have a little chat with you before Marta arrives. I am not sure it won't happen again."

"What won't happen again?"

"Her not recognizing you, thinking you're an imposter, that you're not who you are."

Andy sighed and sank into the chair, his face growing grey. "This is something new. It's never happened before. Marta is so attached to me, she really depends on me. At times . . . how should I put it? . . . at times it isn't easy . . . But never mind. I don't understand why she wouldn't recognize me when she needs me so much. I don't know what to say . . . What do you think? It's not a good sign, is it?"

"It happens," said Dr. Neuman, "and when it happens there can be all kind of reasons. You know that Marta encountered one of the kapos from Auschwitz?—right here. It was very hard for her."

"No. No one informed me. Why wasn't I told?" Andy's voice was tense and cutting. "Why didn't someone tell me about this?"

"It's my fault. I apologize." He sounded tense. "Are you familiar with what happened with the kapo during the war?"

"Of course. She saw her when she was waiting in the clinic. That's the reason she's here in the first place . . ." Andy's voice rose and Dr. Neuman frowned.

"Yes, but what I wanted to ask is whether you know about any specific incidents with the kapo in Auschwitz? Do you know what happened there?" The lines on Dr. Neuman's forehead deepened.

"I know only one thing. They took people there to kill them. That's what they did there."

Dr. Neuman bit his lip: "When she saw the woman here, Marta responded very powerfully. I believe it's the cause for her recent symptoms, her paranoia. It's all part of an ongoing reaction. We will look into it."

"You will look into it?" Pale, Andy blinked rapidly.

"I don't think it's anything personal about you." Dr. Neuman regained his authoritative voice. "I am convinced that what happened here was an outcome of distress. As far as Marta is concerned, she was cast back into a situation of great danger?"

"Yes," sighed Andy.

"I can imagine how hard it is for you, but you must try to understand that it's not about you."

"It's very difficult." Andy bowed his head and seemed on the verge of tears. "You know," he raised his eyes to Dr. Neuman again, "I would like to tell you something I've been thinking recently, that is, since Marta's illness."

"That's exactly why I asked you come in. Marta's treatment touches on all her relationships, and with you especially."

"Yes, it worries me a great deal."

"It worries you?"

"That may not be the precise word. I find it hard to put . . . Since these things happened to Marta I . . ."

"You're afraid?"

"Yes . . . afraid . . . scared. I worry. In the end, someone has to go on functioning, right?"

"I understand. You're concerned about a snowball effect?"

"I cannot allow myself to collapse," Andy replied quickly. "It's just not possible. But I want to say that there is something to what Marta says. Her intuition is very good, she's clever woman."

"What do you have in mind?"

"I mean, maybe I'm not myself, maybe I am pretending, an imposter."

"I don't understand . . ."

Andy's voice trembled: "You really don't understand? I cannot really be myself and live with these terrible memories. There are no words for the mental anguish, the constant thoughts about what happened to my family. I pretend, try to forget, play a role. Otherwise I'll have a breakdown."

"I wasn't aware that you . . ."

"No, I wasn't there myself, I hid. It was just a matter of months, but my family, all of them—my mother and three sisters in Auschwitz. My father in the death march from Budapest. I cannot begin to think of them because I lose myself immediately . . . you understand? I cannot think about them . . ."

Dr. Neuman was silent. Andy shifted in his seat, pulled out a handkerchief from his trouser pocket, and blew his nose. The he used the handkerchief to wipe his forehead, and crumpling it, stuck it back in his pocket. His face had grown even greyer, and with the tips of his fingers he drummed on the wooden seat.

"My mother . . . I cannot think about her, because I don't know what will happen if I do. And she loved me so. I was her eldest. My father was very earnest, always busy with his teaching job and other things he took on to bring in more money. He was impatient, nervous at times, but my mother was exactly the opposite—she was soft, and kind, and she would hug you, she was warm. My sisters—I simply can't. Yes, Marta is right, I am a kind of imposter."

"You're absolutely not!" Dr. Neuman protested, "No! That's not pretense—it is how you cope. Sometimes there's no other way than to forget because remembering would be catastrophic. You know that yourself. You're not an imposter! You're the strong one in your family. The pillar of the family. You have strength. It takes strength, too, to repress, to stand up against memories. It's not pretense. It's absolutely not."

"I don't know. Sometimes I simply cannot take it anymore. I almost collapse."

"And then what happens? When you feel you cannot go on?"

"Nothing," said Andy, with frustrated irony. "Nothing happens. I go back to my role. It's about being or not being, really. Either I go on or everything goes to pieces. And Naomi and Michael must be looked after. They should not have to suffer because of what we went through. You see how much pretense it takes." He smiled sadly.

"You make it even harder on yourself when you call it pretense. And without any good reason." Dr. Neuman looked at his watch. "Marta will be coming in soon. Don't worry, it—"

There was a light knock, the door opened slowly, and Marta walked in. She stopped, looked at the two men, and hesitated. Her gaze moved from

Dr. Neuman to Andy. Dr. Neuman invited her to sit down. Andy looked at her with concern, which triggered her own concern.

"Good morning, Marta," said Dr. Neuman. "As we discussed, Andy is here for our meeting this morning—you remember?"

Marta nodded and went on looking at Andy. Then she looked at Dr. Neuman again. "It's not him."

"Who isn't?"

"That man," she said pointing at Andy, "he is an imposter. He is not Andy."

"Is he the same imposter as last time?"

"I don't know," said Marta, looking at Andy, "maybe."

"Do you think there are several people pretending to be Andy?"

"Could be," said Marta.

Andy's face was troubled. He approached Marta but she took a step back to the doorway.

"Marta," said Dr. Neuman, "can you check? I am not sure you're right. I had a chat with him this morning, he knows your entire history. Told me about Šurany, about the Jewish school, about his father, the teacher, and headmaster, about Öcsi your brother, who was his close friend. He knows all the stories. I am not sure he is an imposter."

He looked at Andy, who was now standing, his posture that of a man waiting to be sentenced. Though Marta was still by the door she no longer appeared braced to flee. Dr. Neuman invited her to sit in her usual place. She advanced a little, saying, "All right, let's check him." Andy shifted uneasily as Dr. Neuman asked her how she wanted to go about it. "If he claims he knows Šurany and everything about it, if he went to school there, then let him sing the Slovakian anthem."

Dr. Neuman looked surprised.

"You should ask her which of them she wants to hear," Andy said to Dr. Neuman.

"Marta," which anthem do you have in mind?"

"I mean the one we sang in school and in the synagogue whenever there was a national holiday."

"Until the Hungarians moved in," added Andy.

"Yes, that's right. Until the Hungarians moved in. Let him stand on the chair and sing that anthem."

"Why on a chair?" Dr. Neuman asked in surprise.

"Because that'll be more real. It's an anthem. It needs a sense of occasion."

Andy stood on his chair. He stood tall and smiling, looked into Marta's eyes, and put his hand on his heart:

> *Kde domov můj, kde domov můj,*
> *voda hučí po lučinách,*
> *bory šumí po skalinách,*
> *v sadě skví se jara květ,*
> *zemský ráj to na pohled!*
> *A to je ta krásná země,*
> *země česká domov můj,*
> *země česká domov můj!*[1]

Marta approached the chair, her eyes on Andy, until she came to a halt. Dr. Neuman, from the other side of the room, watched the them as, once more, the husband and wife found themselves as if enveloped in a bubble, separate from everything else, surrendering themselves to images known to them alone, places that had vanished from the face of the earth which, as if magically, returned to them briefly now, the house, garden, river, and the wide ranging fields surrounding their little town from all sides. "Go on," she told him, "there's more. Now the Slovak version." Andy raised his head, pressed his hand to his chest, and went on singing:

> *Nad Tatrou sa blýska, hromy divo bijú*
> *Nad Tatrou sa blýska, hromy divo bijú*
> *Zastavme ich, bratia, veď sa ony stratia,*
> *Slováci ožijú.*[2]

The Tatra mountains . . . she remembered. The town with the healing waters in the Tatra mountains, the vacation resort the family visited on occasion.

---

1 Where is my homeland, where is my homeland? / Waters murmur through the meadows,/forests rustle all over the rocky hills, / spring blossoms glitter in the orchards, / paradise on earth to look at! / This is a beautiful country, / the Czech country, my homeland, / the Czech country, my homeland!
  Translation: https://english.radio.cz/czech-national-anthem-170-years-old-8094024.
2 There is lightning over the Tatras, thunders wildly beat, / There is lightning over the Tatras, thunders wildly beat. / Let's stop them, brethren, after all they'll disappear / the Slovaks will revive.
  Translation: https://english.radio.cz/czech-national-anthem-170-years-old-8094024.

Mainly she remembered the vacation of that last happy summer of theirs, two weeks of bliss. She'd already been old enough to enjoy the atmosphere of the place and take in the pleasure awaiting in every corner, in the very air she breathed. It was like remembering a dream and experiencing again the pleasure after a dream slowly wanes . . .

Marta smiled at Andy. She turned to Dr. Neuman: "Yes," she told him, "yes, I was confused. It is him. It is my Andy. Andy climbed down from the chair and approached Marta. He took her head between his hands, kissed her forehead, and then wrapped his arms around her. Marta breathed in the familiar scent of his body. "Dušička," she whispered, "my Dušička, you remember?" Andy nodded and rested his head on hers.

"I remember," he said quietly, "the two of us remember."

Dr. Neuman went on standing there, looking at the two of them as they embraced.

***

The spring was drawing to an end. The air was light and pleasant and held good warmth even after the sun set. On some nights you could do without a scarf or jacket. The yellow dandelion flowers in the grass of the hospital garden turned into fluffy white spheres and a thicket of yellow chrysanthemums lit up its borders. The air teemed with the movement of tiny, transparent wings, humming insects creating a transparent cloud surrounding the jumble of flowers, and a weightless flight of yellow-weed seeds drifting like small strips of lace. Marta felt an ever-growing desire to go out, as she had as a girl. The recent meeting with her Andy had reminded her of other times. She wanted to move get away from the ward, the activities room, the dining room. She wanted to be elsewhere.

Since her encounter with the kapo Marta had hardly been to the café to write. Now she wanted to return to the balcony from which she had once looked out at the rocks piled on the beach that tumbled into the water; look far into the blue and at the soft white line of clouds above. She wanted to sit there again, write, lift her eyes every so often to the horizon, then to return to the page and continue her work, knowing the sea was right there, present and indifferent. She had a history in that place, memories—the times she had visited there with Naomi and with Andy, and the last visit with Michael, Erika, and Yehoshua, the waitress who had been nice her.

The walk from the hospital along the promenade was pleasing. On one side, the sea, so very close, and on the other, the neighborhood beyond which the green mountain ridge lay like a big hump, prone. There was something satisfying about the neighborhood. Low, simple apartment buildings and modest houses with gardens and fruit trees scattered between them; they reminded her of her home in the village. She felt reassured by the slight neglect of the gardens. And there was, of course, the sea. She had never lived near the sea. Her childhood had consisted of expansive agricultural flatlands lacking in surprises and rolling hills. Fields of sugar beets reached far into the horizon. And in both the kibbutz they helped to set up and the Galilean village where they settled down, the sea had been far away. There was the Lake of Galilee, which they visited on summery Saturdays, but they never went to the sea proper. In the bus to Haifa, on her way to the hairdresser in the Hadar quarter, she would have glimpses of the sea between the houses, flashes, like postcards from a faraway country. Here, though, it stretched out right before her. The promenade set it apart from the little houses. Behind the houses was the green slope of mount Carmel, on top of which were some large buildings she had never seen from close up; but from afar, they looked lovely.

A short walk along the promenade took her to the café. I am going back there, going back to write, she told herself. The walk became, again, part of her morning routine. Notebook pages filled once more with her orderly, regular, handwriting, and recollections, again, arranged themselves along the timeline which she followed. Usually she returned to the unit at noon, made a stop at the dining hall, and went to her room to rest before meeting Dr. Neuman. When progress was easy and she did not want to stop writing; she would order something light to eat from the waitress and continue. She went back to wearing the small round watch with the slim brown band that Andy had bought her years before, so she could stick to her times. She did not read back what she had written; that was hard.

The café became a friendly place. Though she did not make any friends there, it had some steady clients like herself. In time they began to greet her with a nod, and she would return a smile. Other than with the waitress, with whom she had a bit of conversation every so often, Marta kept her distance. She grew friendly with the spot, with the table close to the steps leading to the promenade, with the strip of beach below her, with the water line at the horizon of the sea's grey, blue, green surface. She also grew friendly with the movement of passersby. Unknown people walked in her direction and went by, maybe turning into one of the small streets leading into the neighborhood. The motion of the waves and of the passersby was soothing.

One morning, making out a familiar woman who was walking along the promenade, heading towards the café, she was alarmed. Her apprehension grew when she saw it was one of the occupational therapists who worked in the units activities room. The woman approached the steps, stopped, looked in the direction of Marta's table, and carried on. Shrunk in her chair, Marta observed the disappearing figure. What a scare! But why? It would have been insufferable she talked about me in the hospital. She could not bear it when people talked about her behind her back. Suddenly she thought of Dr. Neuman. What would happen if it had been him and he saw her writing? She let the images pass through her head like a film, a movie about an encounter. That's how it would be: Dr. Neuman would enter the café, they would share her table, order something to drink, look out at the sea together, talk. That's not very likely; she smiled to herself. He working during these hours. He didn't leave the unit to visit the café or take a walk on the promenade.

That day, the meeting with Dr. Neuman was longer than usual and Marta's words flowed. They came with an ease that surprised her. Dr. Neuman listened as she spoke, and when she fell silent, he too remained silent, without a question. She noticed his body was slightly inclined towards her,. She told him about the promenade, about the café and its view on the sea, about the waitress, the regulars, and about the fact that she was writing there. It had begun with the café. "I sit there and write, and at the same time, I see myself writing, feel that I am in an play. As if it isn't me. But it is me, it's real. I mean, I look at myself as if I were at the theater. Do you think I have a split personality? It's a strange feeling." Dr. Neuman did not respond, and she went on talking about the writing itself, the memories that surfaced, the way in which she arranged them. Yes, she was putting her memories into order, deciding what she could write and what she never could.

There was a quiet knock on the door, invading the space. Dr. Neuman looked at Marta, got up, and walked slowly towards the door, checking his watch and shaking his head. He opened the door a little and Marta heard a quiet exchange she could not follow. Dr. Neuman said: "Yes, I see. Something came up. I'll be there in ten minutes." He closed the door, sat down again, and resumed the same attentive position.

"It's time to end, yes?"

"Yes, we must stop now. I would have liked us to go on sitting here, with you telling me, and me listening, but one has commitments. But I simply have to get on with other things."

Marta saw how attuned he was to her. It filled the room, it filled her, this connection. She felt a burst of warmth inside her, inside her belly, her chest, her head—tiny capillaries of joy. She rose, her body supple, Dr. Neuman got up too, and they stood close to each other. He put his arms around her and gently held her to him. The tiny vessels inside her lengthened, intertwined, wrapped themselves around the two of them causing her put her own arms around him, for a closer embrace. Four armes softly held their two bodies together. They breathed together, quietly. She wanted to tell him, or was it herself, about this embrace, about Andy, but Dr. Neuman anticipated her: "We will meet tomorrow," he said softly and loosened his arms.

"Yes," she answered, stepping back. "Tomorrow."

They headed for the door and Dr. Neuman opened it. On the threshold, she looked into the hospital's bright corridor and turned her head once more towards Dr. Neuman. He took her hand in his two and pressed it hard.

"Goodbye, Marta. Have a good evening and a good night."

"See you tomorrow," she said, as if to herself, and left the room.

***

Like someone who has lost her direction, Marta remained standing in the corridor. Inside, happiness and fear swirled and the walls seemed to whirl around her. Someone called out her name.

"Marta, Marta, what's going on?" A nurse stood by her side, a file bursting with documents under her arm. "Marta? Is everything OK? Marta?" The nurse looked at her and at the door to Dr. Neuman's office.

"What?" Marta looked back in surprise. "Why?"

"What's going on? Do you need help?"

"No, no, I'm all right, I am perfectly all right."

"Are you sure?"

Marta stared at her and didn't answer.

"Maybe you should rest until dinner time." The nurse consulted her watch while trying to keep hold of the file whose papers were threatening to spill. "There's time."

"No, no. I don't want to go to my room now, I . . ."

"Well, I have to get all this paperwork to the office. It'll be all over the place in a moment. It's nice outside now, if you want to sit in the garden."

"Perhaps . . ."

The nurse strode away, fast, trying to keep the bundle of papers together, and Marta headed for the garden. It was empty. The poinciana was covered with generous green foliage and made a roof over the old bench which was more worn out than she remembered. She recalled the trees at the Scottish hostel in Tiberias, where she had given birth to Michael. Her breath had been taken away by the beauty of it, despite being racked with the pain of her contractions. She remembered: an avenue lined by poincianas led to the austere, black, basalt building—a thick, dark green from which flaming red blossoms pointed upwards, a glorious vision; the enormous green canopies cooled the heat from the Lake of Galilee and the dark basalt; the red flowers set the sky aglow. She cherished this beauty which confronted her when the rigid and serious nuns looked after her and the baby, or when she listened to other new mothers telling about the rats infesting the hospital and gnawing at the newborns' flesh.

The poinciana in the unit garden was not in full bloom yet, but already it cast its shade, wide and protective. Her gaze strayed, stopped briefly at a shuttered window, and returned to the wooden bench, which seemed even smaller now it was sheltered beneath the canopy. She sat down. The dense shadow calmed her. On waves of joy and happiness, an unclear sense of promise was borne. A promise of something good about to happen. Something that would keep the ground on which she trod steady so she would not fall, something that would let her grow and flourish. To blaze? It was a feeling of peace that Marta had not felt since she'd arrived at the unit. That night, though, was different.

She returned to her room after dinner. She had not been there since the morning, and she was happy to be back. Like coming home, she thought. So now this is my home? What about my real home, with Andy, Naomi, and Michael? It seemed very far away. Suddenly, a breathtaking yearning flooded her. She felt Andy, Naomi, and Michael watching her, and she wanted to rush and hold them tight and never let them go. It was still early, but she was exhausted. I must sleep, rest, she told herself.

In a sweat and scared to death, she woke from a nightmare in the middle of the night. She had been with a group of people who were on the run from something. They entered a cave to save themselves. Though the cave was dark and low-ceilinged they were able to walk. But the further they went, the more the cave's walls closed in and the ceiling got lower. On all fours, they made a long line. Her knees hit rocks protruding from the ground and her hands were cut. She could hear groans, but she gritted her teeth. Further ahead they were forced to get down on their bellies, the ceiling so low they couldn't raise their heads; and even though she kept her lips firmly closed, soil got into her mouth and nostrils. They continued like this until a rumor spread that there was light ahead. There's light—don't lose hope. But just then, they ground to a halt. It was impossible to go forwards or backwards. She was stuck between the walls of the cave, between the legs of the person who was crawling in front, and the head of the person behind. Her lungs were about to explode and anxiety shook her entire body. Trying to turn she hit on the person behind her, who was motionless. She began to scream, waking herself, in terror, wet with sweat and shaking. Her heart pounded, knocked at her temples, her breath was short, and she produced suffocated screams. She was alone, there was no one to soothe her, collect her, allay the storm, tell her it was just a dream. There was no one to bring her a glass of water.

She sat up in bed, drew her legs up to her chest, and hugging her knees tight put her head on them. In the darkness of the room, she looked like a parcel deposited on the bed. Gradually the shaking subsided and her breath grew more regular, slower, and longer. Still, the memory of certain death, the sense of no way out, was sharp and vivid. She had been going to die. She had almost died. Now she knew what it was like. She must calm down. Drink. She went to the little shower room, opened the tap, and drank. Then she wiped her wet lips with the sleeve of her nightgown. She looked around, took the bathrobe, which was hanging from a towel hook, stuck her arms into its wide sleeves, tightened the belt around her waist, and stepped into the corridor, heading for the office.

A spare light illuminated the desk. A folding bed was in the corner of the room and the nurse was asleep on it, covered with a speckled blanket bearing the name of the hospital. Marta knocked lightly on the door and the nurse leapt. "What's going on?" she almost yelled. "Who's that? Marta! God, what are you doing here in the middle of the night?"

"I had a nightmare," she whispered, "can you give me something to help me feel calmer?"

"Just a moment," the nurse straightened her clothes and put her disheveled hair in order, "let's first check what's the matter. Sit down here." she pointed at the chair by her desk: "Sit down and I'll take your blood pressure."

Marta sat down and sighed a little, her shoulders dropping forward, her back rounded and bent; only her head was slightly lifted with a movement that contracted her neck and shoulders.

Moving to the other side of the desk, the nurse took out the blood pressure cuff. "Just relax," said the nurse, as she wound the cuff around Marta's arm. The stethoscope's metal disk caused her to shiver. "Breathe deep." Marta felt the increasing pressure around her arm and her breath grew shorter. "It's very high. Let's try again, but this time really relax." Marta leant back, took a deep breath, and closed her eyes. After trying two more times, the nurse said: "OK, that's better."

"Could you give me something anyway? I want to sleep, but I can't."

"Yes, yes, of course." Opening a drawer, the nurse took out a box of medicines. "There we are. Not a very strong one. Now you'll sleep and wake up feeling refreshed." She filled a glass with water and, like a good girl, Marta put the pill on her tongue and took a small sip; she had a hard time swallowing. She tried again and then looked guiltily at the nurse.

"It's hard to swallow," she murmured, "sometimes I have difficulty swallowing." She tried once more, but the water burst from her mouth and dribbled down her chin, while the pill stayed on her tongue. She asked the nurse to crush it. "That's how I'll get it down," she explained, "sometimes it's the only way I can take medicine."

"Let's throw away this pill and I'll crush another." It seemed to Marta that the nurse was losing patience.

"I am sorry."

"It's all right, don't worry, I understand."

The nurse turned to the kitchen corner and got a little glass plate and a metal spoon. Putting the pill on the plate, she pressed on it with the back of the spoon, but the pill skidded away as if unwilling to accept its fate. "Let's cut it with a knife, that will be easier."

Marta put the spoon with the greyish powder into her mouth and took a quick sip of water. She grimaced and began sluicing the water round inside her mouth, her lips shut tight, trying to swallow little by little. Then she took some more sips of water, swallowing each slowly and with an effort.

"It's so bitter. Really bad. Why does medicine always taste so bad? It feels more like poison than medicine."

"Good question," laughed the nurse. "Maybe it's like with beauty—for health, too, one has to suffer. Look how beautiful you are. Now you will be healthy too. Come on, let's go back to your room; there are a good few hours till morning still."

"Thank you so much," Marta replied, got up from the chair, and pulled the gown tighter around her body. She now stood straighter. "I'll go back by myself, I am all right. Thank you again."

"I'll come some of the way, anyhow," said the nurse, and they walked into the dark corridor. Marta entered her room. In the window the night was beginning to grow pale. She lay down and slept until morning, waking up into a new day.

End of Summer

The summer grew hotter. The fans in the unit worked day and night, and it wasn't possible to go outside till evening. The sun beat down, the concrete surface emitted heat, and the sea shone and blinded. Haifa's summer came as a surprise. Marta was unfamiliar with the coastal climate, the salty, heavy humidity, the sweat running down her hairline, the wet touch of her clothes on her skin. The sky took on a steely grey hue. Lazily, smoke crept up from the chimneys of Haifa's oil refineries in the bay. Something got in the way of breathing, competing with the oxygen. Even so, her condition seemed to improve as the summer progressed. Her extreme mood fluctuations and the paranoia stopped; she had a better appetite, her sleep was undisturbed. She had grown visibly more beautiful, her face filling out, her hair growing longer; she collected it in a messy knot on her head. She spoke more easily to the people around her, laughed, sometimes she even made jokes. A slight grief remained, of course, from which she could not free herself, but it no longer got the better of her, she was able to live with it. Dr. Neuman still did not mention either full recovery or discharge. Her days continued in the same way, but only on the surface—because ever since they had embraced something inside her and between them had changed. Neither one of them spoke about it, but the very air in the room was different.

The powerful emotion and fear that had taken hold of her after the hug abated and Marta was able to come for their meetings, talk, touch his hand at times, and experience the intimacy between them without feeling awkward or guilty. What had happened was self-evident to them—and what did not happen too. Another reality, as it were, shared by the two of them, existed, but it did not clash with the reality outside the office. It unfolded in parallel, was understated, sufficient unto itself. She felt the world around her expanding, its inner movement altering direction. Generous breathing weakened the forces that had been closing in on her from outside, her ribs moved easily with the air's motion, her diaphragm supply rose and fell between her heart and lower belly.

In spite of the oppressive humidity, she noticed that she enjoyed breathing. The air brought something good from the world into her, undoing a heavy mass inside, yet not leaving her in a dark void, and without upsetting her equilibrium. She felt more secure. Her close relationship with Dr. Neuman did not worry her and she no longer asked herself what she would tell Andy and what might develop. She noticed that Dr. Neuman was relaxed and carried on being very attentive; she felt he was with her. And their conversations were freer. When they met outside his office in the unit he smiled at her, with open fondness, his face lighting up, and she reacted naturally and responded in kind.

When Andy visited at the weekends, Dr. Neuman was never around. Marta was happy to see her husband; they would walk along the promenade in the evening, looking for somewhere to watch the sunset. The concrete with which the promenade was covered still glowed, but once they sat facing the sea a light breeze came their way, carrying a reviving chill. When there was no haze, you could see the red globe of the sun sinking and vanishing behind the horizon, which itself turned red. This simultaneously slow and fast movement always surprised her. That was it: different things could happen at the same time. She loved the short minutes between day and night and longed for childhood's dilated time. Andy was familiar with this too and she felt it brought them closer together, but not as before, when she would call him "my life." Now when her head rested on his shoulder and he put his arm around her, she no longer huddled up against him for protection. They had separate bodies even when they walked close and arm in arm on the way back to the hospital.

On Thursday morning, the nurse walked into the dining room and Marta she had phone call that she could take office. Andy let her know he was planning to come on Saturday; she was going to have a surprise, he added, and laughed. She liked this excitement and enjoyed the surprise. He arrived and announced they were driving somewhere, and that it would be only a part of the surprise. Naomi and Michael were waiting beside the pickup truck. For a moment her heart nearly burst. They hugged and laughed, and Marta asked where they were going, unable to take her eyes off the children. "It's a secret," said Andy and winked at the children. She saw that the pickup was loaded with baskets, bags, and a large bundle of sheets; the big cooler was there too. A picnic, that was what it would be. "Let's get going," said Andy. Naomi and Michael climbed into the back and Marta sat in the front, turning around to look at the children, a shiver of pleasure running down her spine. Michael sat a little hunched up. He had grown since she'd last seem him, she thought—but he was so thin. A quiff grew abundantly over his forehead, and she thought of his full head of light curls when he was a baby. Naomi, opposite him, had her hair tightly tied back. Seeing them together after so long made Marta almost painfully happy.

"I didn't know Naomi'd come home," she said.

"I asked her to. I wanted us to go out together, the whole family," said Andy and looked at her, his eyes as it were taking hold of her. "A surprise, right?"

"Yes, yes. And what about Michael? He's grown. How is he? How did he feel after his visit? He was so quiet."

"Martushkam, he is fine. You shouldn't worry. He's a quiet one, that's all, he's playing his guitar a lot. He's all right."

Again she looked at the baskets and then back at Andy. He smiled at her.

It was lovely. Lovely to see them. She'd never suspected, and now look, such happiness. They left the city behind, and the sea stretched out to their right. She looked through the window at the blue expanse and saw large numbers of people frolicking in the waves, playing games, sitting on blankets spread on the sand, and sitting under shades.

"We're going to the seaside!"

"Martushkam!" He smiled back at her and put his hand on her knee. "Yes, we're going to the beach"

"But I didn't bring a swimsuit."

"I brought your swimsuit, towels, and a big blanket. And I prepared a picnic and a flask with tea even."

How did he find my swimsuit? He doesn't even know where his own shirts are in the wardrobe. Then she realized how long she'd been in hospital. God knows what the cupboards look like, she thought—but immediately stopped herself.

"Dušička, that's a wonderful idea, and we will be together for an entire day! I hope we will be together all the time, soon." Marta looked at him and then at the road that went rolling on in front of them. "I don't know when we were last at the beach. It's been so long."

She remembered the little bay, just about perfect, which they had visited on a movement outing. They had been five couples. Leaving their young children in the kibbutz's children's home, they'd set out on a three days' trip. They had to become a little more familiar with the country they had been dreaming of, and wanted to visit Jerusalem. They'd taken pictures of themselves here and there, a close-knit group of young people smiling happily as if nothing had happened. What she remembered especially was Jerusalem and

Mount Herzl. They took a nice photo there, exactly by the tomb. And she also recalled how on the way back they passed by a kibbutz near the sea. After having lunch there, they went to the beach and she fell in love with the place. They walked along a perfect inlet, and Andy and she went on, climbing a little hill which overlooked a carpet of lagunas. Sitting there, she'd said that maybe one day they would return, just the two of them.

The pickup took a right turn off the main road and onto a narrow road lined by shady eucalyptuses. The road curved a little; banana plantations and little white houses were visible through the trees. Then they took a bumpy road that led to a large dirt plot. There was a long, dense line of low tamarisks, between which a bent, iron gate opened wide to the glistening sea. Andy stopped the car. "We're here," he said, and opened the driver's door.

Jumping down from the pickup, Michael and Naomi ran through the gate. Marta couldn't identify the place. Michael and Naomi came running back, barefoot, shouting: "Mommy, Daddy, come and see, what a great beach. Come on. It's terrific!"

Andy put his hand on her shoulder, and they walked through the gate, past the wall of trees, and heading for the sea. "Dušička," she said to him, "what a surprise . . . you really . . . I . . ."

He held her more tightly. "Do you remember? We said we would come back. Now we can spend the entire day here, with the whole family." Marta took off her shoes and went barefoot to the edge of the water. Naomi hugged her. Andy and Michael stood watching them and Andy said: "Come on, Mikhush, let's get the things from the pickup. It's men's work!"

It was a wonderful day. Having found a shady spot not far from the water, they spread the blankets on the sand and found their towels. With some sticks and ropes he had brought, Andy built a little shade under which they could have their food, and they put down the baskets and the cooler. They then got into their swimwear in the changing rooms and spread their towels on the hot sand. Small clusters of people were scattered along the beach, each managing to set themselves up without bothering anyone else. The sea was smooth and quiet, and people were swimming all along the inlet. Marta could not swim, or rather, she swam only where she knew her feet could touch the bottom. If she went further out her breath grew shallow. She watched Andy and the children swim far out into the inlet, moving away from her, shouting and splashing, diving and coming up for air. They came out of the water covered by thousands of drops that sparkled like splinters, and lay down on their towels, surrendering themselves to the sun. Later, the four of them ate the picnic Andy and Naomi had prepared. "It's not up to your standard," said Naomi, but no one was hungry. They talked and laughed; they filled her in on news about neighbors, what was going on in their village. Then Naomi read a book, Michael built a big sandcastle, and Andy dozed off at her side.

I am happy, she said to herself; who needs more? She did not attempt an answer, knowing she was not going to think about anything now.

In the afternoon they had tea and cake, and when the sun began its way down and the heat was less ferocious, they took a walk along the waterline. Naomi took them to corners from which you could see white birds feeding in the shallow water. She showed them some unusual plants along the coast and pointed to archeological remnants on a hill. That's where an ancient settlement was, she explained. Michael was very quiet, and this troubled Marta a little. On their way back to their little spot, she walked with him. She felt that their shared silence brought them closer, and she remembered how he had said, simply, "Mommy, I love you."

"I love you Michi, and I also miss you."

"Don't worry, Mommy." Michael gave her a serious, grown-up look: "I manage."

"Yes, but I do miss you." She took his hand. "I miss you all, all of you."

"Of course." He surprised her with his restrained words. "We're missing you, but we must get over our longing."

When did he become like this? she asked herself. From being a shy boy, look what's happened to him. "Yes, we will get over it. I feel that once I am home, we . . ." She didn't know how to continue. What exactly did she want to say? "You are so quiet that sometimes I don't know . . ." She slightly shifted the conversation: "I know that's what you're like, but still . . ."

"Dear Mommy, don't worry, I'm fine."

She was not sure whether that was true. How could he be all right with his mother away in hospital for such a long time? She had to let it go. Not to spoil this wonderful day. There they were, all of them at the seaside spending a wonderful day together.

Towards the evening they began collecting up their things. As the beach grew emptier, Marta proposed they stay to watch the sunset. "I invite you for an ice cream at the kiosk," said Andy. "We can eat our ice cream while watching the sunset, what do you say?" They sat on a pile of rocks looking on as the sky turned red, the sea dark and obscure, crests of foam riding the waves and rushing onto the shore. The sun glowed on the water and colored it red;

then it sank heavily and disappeared. As the water turned even darker, the sky went on growing red, burning and blazing, until darkness descended.

They said goodbye, each convinced Marta would be home soon. Back in her room, after showering off the sand and salt, she said to herself: A gown, that's what I need, a dressing gown. And she found herself weeping bitterly.

***

One day, at noon, unannounced, Erika visited. Holding a large bag, she walked into the unit all sweaty and flushed and asked for her mother. It was noon, so Marta was at her usual place in the dining room, not far from the big window, having lunch. Next to her were two other people; they were all in silence. Erika walked up to her, positioned herself near the table, put her bag on the floor, and waited for Marta to notice her. Marta took a long look at her, as if wondering whether what she was seeing was real, and then an enormous smile spread across her face, as if a light had been switched on.

"Erichkam," she shouted as she leapt up. "Is it you, Erichkam, how did you get here? I had no idea you were coming. Did you come alone?"

"Yes," her sister replied. "I told myself I couldn't wait any longer. Last time we didn't manage to talk at all. I want to see what's going on with you. I want to spend some time with you. So I got on the bus. Just like that."

They fell into each other's arms. Erika wept for joy and Marta felt her heart leaping. "Come," said Marta: "Let's get out of here. I don't like the staring. But what about you, have you had anything to eat? You must eat."

"It's all right, Martushkam," said Erika through her tears. "I made myself sandwiches for on the way. I'm not hungry. I am all right. But how about you? You have to finish your meal."

"Nonsense," said Marta. "It's a charity to leave food like that untouched."

"Martushkam, it isn't right to leave food, to throw it away. You finish it, and then—"

"Come along, come." Marta took her arm. "Let's go to my room, first of all."

"Wait. My bag. I brought you some things." On their way to Marta's room they held hands, remembering the last time. They pressed hands until they went in. "It's a really nice room. I wouldn't have thought they had rooms like this in hospitals. You have this all to yourself?"

"Yes," Marta replied. "When I first arrived there was another woman. But she was released and since then I have been here on my own."

"That's good," said Erika. It's usually so crowded in hospitals."

"Not here," Marta said quickly. "Come and sit."

Erika sat on Dina's old bed. Marta felt a great joy and wondered why Erika was visiting only now, after such a long time. As if she guessed her sister's thoughts, Erika looked sighed.

"Martushkam, I have been wanting to come for such a long time . . . ever since Andy let us know. But Andy . . ." She looked at Marta, worried.

"What?" she asked, even though she knew what her sister meant.

"He kept telling us not to come, that it might not the right time, that it would be overstimulating for you . . . I reminded him that you're my sister and that I had to see you . . . but you know what he's like . . ."

"Yes," said Marta, as if to herself, "I know very well what he's like."

"Sometimes I wonder how it happened . . . that you . . . when we were girls, you were the star, weren't you . . . I don't understand . . . Maybe Andy's presence is rather strong . . . or too . . ." She looked at Marta, seemed alarmed. "Enough. Let's forget about it. I want to hear about you. How are you? It looks like you're getting better. Last time, Yehoshua and I were thinking you looked better. But now, Martush—tell me everything. I want to know what's going on with you." Erika paused. "Oh, I forgot. I brought you some things."

From her bag, Erika pulled a pair of clean and folded pajamas and a long robe. She held them out to Marta. Next, she produced some plastic boxes closed with rubber bands. "I baked you some roses," she said and placed the boxes on the desk. "And look," she added, showing Marta another box, "I made you some sajtos gombóc. Take one. We need a plate because they're so crumbly."

"Thank you, Erchikam! I have an idea. Let's take the box out into the garden and eat them there. There's a shady bench there. Come on."

They left the room. Erika followed Marta through the corridor until they reached the small, yellowing garden. The poinciana's bloom glowed like a fiery umbrella.

This is it," said Marta."

They sat on the bench and Erika put the box, which she opened, between them. Marta peeped inside and smiled. Poor Erika, she always tried so hard. Too-brown breadcrumbs covered the shapeless dumplings. She held one between two fingers; it was too soft. Sajtos gombóc had been their favorite dessert when they were children. Dumplings made out of sweet white cheese, rolled in breadcrumbs, and browned in butter—and with fruit jam on top. Round white shapes which kept their perfect form and exact texture when boiled in a large pot of water. The gombóc dumplings their mother used to make were unforgettable, and it had taken Marta several attempts to get them right.

"Delicious. Aren't these just what we need right now?"

"I know it's not the way Mom . . . the way you manage to do it. I'm not that good at cooking."

"Nonsense, Erichkam. They're really tasty. Andy told me you made him a large pan of really good soup. You cook very well."

"Not like you. You inherited that from Mama . . ." Erika looked at Marta. "I'm the not so good one, you . . ."

"Enough. Stop it, Erichkam. I'm really enjoying them. Why don't you eat some yourself? Why aren't you eating?" she said, feeling the faintest stirring of schadenfreude. Here was Erika, who had always been their mother's favorite: "You have some too, Erichkam, they're good."

"They're for you. I want them to be enough for you. Maybe I will try one." Some breadcrumbs fell to the ground and sparrows came to pick them up at their feet. The foliage of the poinciana made the heat bearable. With the plastic box between them, they sat some time in silence.

"Martushkam," said Erika, "what's the matter?"

Marta shrugged: "It's what happened to us . . ."

"Yes, but was there anything in particular? Suddenly you seemed to have a drop—"

"Erichkam, there was nothing sudden . . . It's going on all the time. It's here all the time. It doesn't go away."

"Yes, I know. It's the same for me."

"But apparently I can't deal with it."

"But Martushkam . . . You did such a lot . . . Something must've happened. What was it?"

Marta did not want to go over the story about the kapo. She did not only fear her own feelings, but Erika's response too. She did not think her sister would have a breakdown—obviously not—after all, she survived their catastrophe with less damage and better able to start a new life. Maybe Marta simply did not want to return to the subject. She had discussed it a great deal with Dr. Neuman and felt she could put an end to the story. For now at least. She was so happy to see Erika now she was in a good state and strong. She did not want to spoil things.

"Erika," she said suddenly, "I have a meeting with my doctor at three. Do you know what time it is? I left my watch in my room."

"It's almost two," she replied, "don't worry. I can return earlier or wait until you finish. What would you prefer?"

"Erichkam, of course I want to spend more time with you. I so much wanted you to come—and now you're here . . ." She hugged her warmly.

"Yes!" Erika hugged her back and laughed.

"Wonderful! I'll ask the nurse to tell the doctor I won't be coming today, then."

"Is that all right? Won't he be annoyed?" Erika worried.

"No, Erichkam. He won't mind at all," and thought to herself that he would probably be sorry; but that's how it was. Today I want to be with Erika.

"Are you sure?"

"Erichkam. Let's have a good time today, let's go out somewhere, what do you say?"

"Have a good time in this heat? And anyway, do they let you?"

"Yes. When it's a bit cooler we'll can the tram to the Carmel Center. There's a pleasant breeze and a lovely public garden; we'll find a nice café and have an ice cream. How about that?" She laughed: "Come on, let's go."

***

The journey to the Carmel Center was fun. The way the tramcars rose steeply surprised them and going through the dark tunnel was a refreshing adventure. They got off at the last stop, excited like two young girls. When they came out of the station, they were greeted by a lovely wind; it blew through the folds of their summer dresses and the tops of the tall pine trees on the avenue. They window-shopped. Mannequins, dressed in soft-hued cotton dresses, tiny handbags on their arms, stared back at them.

"Look," Marta pulled Erika's arm, "look at that dress. It's beautiful and simple. It wouldn't be difficult to sew. What do you think? I could make it, if you like. You can choose the fabric. When I am released, I will have plenty of time."

"Oh, Martushkam, you're so talented. Do you really think you could sew such a dress? I don't want you to tire yourself out."

"Stop that, Erichkam," said Marta, taking a closer look at the shape of the dress. "We must find some nice fabric. Pure cotton. There's a food shop in Hadar; we can check it out." She looked at Erika, remembering the dresses that were made for them when they were girls. They got new dresses twice a year. One winter dress, made from thick and warm material, and one light summer dress. The boys were given suits. The fabrics were of the highest quality, the best in their father's shop. Bales and bales which their father would unroll before his customers with a strong movement of his hand. He always knew what to show them, judging their taste precisely. Local farmers often paid with their own produce, like flour and bags full of vegetables. Everything was made to measure. Nobody bought ready-made apparel. The poor villagers, the bourgeoisie, and the directors of the sugar factory—they all wore bespoke clothes and handmade shoes. Twice a year their father would travel to the big city, Brno, to get the most up-to-date merchandise of flawless quality. She remembered how her father and the boys had brought the heavy bales all the way up to the attic. Our poor, good father, who always believed they'd return. When the two of them came back the bales of cloth were no longer there. "The Russians came in and took them," a neighbor said shamelessly without blinking an eyelid. Their father's best clients looked away when they returned hungry, wasted, and orphaned.

"We'll have to find good fabric," she repeated, and then she looked at Erika and said: "Let's go into the public garden and find the café."

They took the paved path that led into the park. Tall pines cast their shadows and on both sides of the path, dark and green grassy spaces opened up. Young mothers had spread colorful blankets on the grass for their babies, a small group of youngsters were beneath some trees, couples embraced, leaning against the tree trunks, and older people sat on the wooden benches. Erika and Marta walked towards the café terrace in the middle of the park; most of the tables were occupied. Marta immediately noticed how elegant the people were. In spite of the heat, transparent nylon stockings covered the legs of made-up women, while the men wore light summer hats and suits.

"Look, Erika," said Marta, "it's like in Budapest, remember?"

"Yes, it does look like it. A different world."

A not so young waiter approached them and asked whether they would like to sit, leading them to a table which had just become available. From the terrace, the park looked like an Impressionist painting, the play of light and shadow, the scattering of human shapes on the sun-dappled ground. It's pleasant here, thought Marta, you can feel it's up on the mountain, the sea breeze. It's so good here. She looked at Erika and took hold of her hands.

"Let's have ice cream!"

"Yes! It's amazing what kinds they have here."

Marta looked for the waiter. He gestured that he'd be with them, and she nodded charmingly. Because they could not make up their minds, they decided on different flavors, and the waiter returned carrying two goblets, each with a cloud of whipped cream and a crescent moon shaped thin waffle on top.

"Thank you," said Marta when he put the ices down. "Can we please have two glasses of water too?" She looked at him and he returned her smile.

"Mmm, it's so good. Want to try some?"

"Yes." Marta stretched her neck. "Let me have a try. And now you try mine." She held out a heaped spoon toward Erika.

"Just a moment. It's all dripping."

Marta looked in her bag for a clean handkerchief and gave it to Erika. "Take that. You can return it next time we meet." She stopped and added, "I hope that will be at home again."

"Yes, me too." Erika grew more serious: "Anyway, Martushkam, when I see you like that it's hard to imagine you . . . Well, you know. You're looking well. In a good mood, happy even. You're not just pretending, are you?"

"No. I'm not pretending. I really do feel well. Something happened. Something changed." She became reflective: "They do know what they're doing."

"Who?" asked Erika

"At the hospital." She looked at her. "Especially the chief doctor there, he's the one who treats me."

"The chief doctor is treating you? Why? Were you in such a bad state?"

"I was. And I don't think I'll ever manage to go back to how I was before. Before everything . . . I can't possibly recover fully, but Dr. Neu . . . This doctor, I don't know why, he decided I'd be his patient."

"And he's good?"

"Much more than that. He's a good person. We have . . . we have become very friendly. It began with therapy, but it has developed into a more personal relationship."

"A personal relationship? What do you mean?"

"I mean that we have a personal relationship. It's not just psychotherapy."

"What kind of relationship is it, then?" Erika sounded worried.

"It's a good relationship. I cannot explain . . ."

"Martushkam! What is this? I don't get it. Are you in . . . ?"

"We have a strong mental bond. A kind of understanding."

"And Andy?"

"What? Nothing. It's got nothing to do with Andy. It's between him and me," Marta responded quickly.

"But, Martushkam, what does that mean? You will be released soon, right? You'll return home."

"Yes. I really don't know how it will be. I will go back home. But . . . perhaps every so often I will return to the hospital. Once a month perhaps. I don't know what it will be. Something. Maybe . . ." Marta grew silent, gazing into the distance. There was a warm, golden hour light. "I'll have a very hard time leaving this doctor. I think I will have to meet him once in a while. I really don't know." Looking at Erika, she suddenly saw clearly how wide the gap was between her relationship with Dr. Neuman and her life with Andy and the children. It hadn't occurred to her until then. What would happen when she was released?

"But, Martush, Andy . . . Do you think he . . . ?"

"I don't know. Let's not talk about it now. I don't know how to. It's strange. This doctor, I feel safe with him. It's not just medical. There's something of the soul between us. I don't know how things will turn out."

"And what does he say about it?"

"Nothing. We haven't talked about it. We talk . . ." Erika looked at the empty bowl in front of her. She used her spoon to scoop out the melted leftovers at the bottom. "Don't worry. I'm feeling better, and that's what matters. I'll return home and go on with my life. Maybe do things I didn't dare to do before. I haven't told you, but I've started to write."

"Write? What are you writing?"

"I'm trying to put my memories into order. Ours. Recollections from home, about mother and father, Eva, Öcsi, Andy. I also want to write about what happened to our family and what happened to us."

"You're writing about that?" Erika sounded impressed.

Marta took Erika's hands in hers again. "It mustn't get lost, disappear. Our children must know."

"Martush, you will always be my big, clever sister." Erika squeezed her hands. "I'm such a little goose, what would I do without you . . . ? And what is it like, to be writing, I mean . . . Isn't it difficult?"

"It is and it isn't. I find it very hard to revisit our childhood. It really hurts. Life was good." She smiled at Erika.

"Yes, it was . . ."

"When I write I remember more and more. I didn't know all of those things were still inside me. But it's painful too. To see our home again, almost real, to recollect all those places . . ."

"Yes, but it's good you're doing it. I really want to read it."

"I want there to be some memory of our family. That's what gave me the strength to write. Dr. Neuman encouraged me. He thinks it will do me good, it . . ."

"That's that doctor?"

"Yes, I wish you could meet him . . . Shall we go back? You have to get home."

Erika looked at her watch and nodded. "Yes, I want to be at the bus station before dark. Let's go."

When they left, only the sky was still bright. The park had entirely fallen into shadow. The young mothers were leaving the park, pushing prams; on the wooden benches, young couples were embracing. Marta and Erika crossed the broad avenue and entered the tram station. All the way back, they sat side by side in silence.

When they got off the tram, Marta said: "Let's walk to the bus station from here. It's not far. And next time we meet I will give you back your bag; it can stay in my room. This way we'll be at the bus station in daylight and I will take a bus to the hospital from there." Erika nodded; they walked through narrow streets lined by stone houses and passed some small shops in front of which small groups of people were talking in Arabic.

"It's a shame it's over, Martushkam. I am so happy I came, to have seen you. I have been missing you so much."

"Me too," said Marta, "me too. There are so many things I would have liked to ask you, but I forgot. How are you, Erichkam? You didn't tell me anything about yourself."

"I . . . It's you who's important now, and I feel reassured now that I've seen you. I don't understand why Andy kept suggesting I shouldn't come alone."

"He didn't ask me. You know what he's like."

"I do!" Erika's eyes laughed.

The central bus station was crowded and dirty. Scores of people moving hither and thither, busses honking, the air thick and suffocating. At Erika's bus stop, people were already seated on the long benches waiting for the driver to open the doors.

"Here we are," said Erika. "Don't sit with me. You still have to catch your bus to the hospital. Go, before it's dark."

"All right, Erika, I'll go." She hesitated: "Erika . . . Andy doesn't need to know about . . . you know. . . I'll tell him myself. Perhaps."

Erika looked at her, and Marta did not understand what she meant. The doors of the bus opened and people crowded to get in.

"Go on," she told Erika, "so you don't have stand all the way."

Erika found a window seat. She opened the window and stuck her arm out, waved, and shouted: "Dovidenia Martushkam, zbohom!"[1] Marta looked at her in amazement. They had not spoken to each other in Slovakian for years.

She went to the window, stretched out her arm, and touched Erika's hand. "Yes," she said, "Goodbye, Erichkam, dovidenia. Soon." The door closed and the bus reversed.

Erika shouted again: "Martushkam, milujem ťa." And Marta managed to shout back: "Me too, Erichkam, milujem ťa."[2] The bus left the station in a cloud of black smoke.

***

When Marta reached the hospital, it was evening. She entered the wide door and walked to her room down the corridor. It was the first time since she arrived in hospital that she had been so far away on her own. It was nice to return to her small, familiar room. She wanted to remove the layers of that outside world that had got stuck to her skin and go back to belonging there, in the hospital. She went into the small shower room and let the water wash off the city. Then she put on the gown Erika had brought her. Erichkam, how good it was that she had visited. Images from the day came back. The two of them like real ladies of leisure in the café, window shopping, taking the tram. The thought of their ride through the dark tunnel took her back to the past. Their old home was there, far beyond black and dangerous terrain. One day she would have to cross it.

She had told Erika about Dr. Neuman! Poor Erichkam, she'd had a real shock, that much was clear. Taken aback and stunned by her passion, just like when they were girls. In those days, Erika had admired Marta's busy and exciting social life, the boys who courted her, the older girls who took her

---

1   Slovak: See you Martushkan, goodbye.
2   Slovak: I love you.

under their wings. She had been loved and popular. Erika's admiration had weighed on her and troubled her, but also flattered her. Now too she felt that admiration, but it was no longer the same thing, she realized. She would never be able to devour life as before. Dr. Neuman was a different story. She did not exactly know what it was, but Dr. Neuman was not just another suitor. He was not a suitor at all. What was happening between them was something entirely new. Maybe an encounter between two souls that understood each other. What would happen once she was out of hospital? She and Erika had not spoken about it, even though her sister had asked. No need to worry. Erika wouldn't talk. Marta felt unsettled. How would it be, life with Andy? Would Dr. Neuman remain part of her life and she of his? How would all this work out?

Marta remembered that she had not had dinner. It was too late now. Inside the bag Erika had left there was a large plastic box with the cookies she had baked, and in the other box some leftover cheese dumplings. Marta was not sure about the effect of the heat—she smelled them cautiously and wrinkled her nose. Well, she could have tea and eat some cookies; it reminded her of her first evening in hospital when Dina had offered her tea and biscuits from the kibbutz. It was winter, and the hot drink comforted her. Now it was midsummer, the tea made her sweat. She switched on the ceiling fan and thought that maybe, after all, she was closing a circle and would soon be packing her suitcase and returning home. But not before she finished her writing—no way. She had to get to the end while she was there, in the unit. It had to be there. It was clear to her that with Andy, at home, she would not be able to carry on with it, and she wouldn't want to either. Tomorrow morning, early, she promised herself, I will go to the café. What she had to write, she had to do here, close to Dr. Neuman. She might even show it him.

The next afternoon when she entered his room for their meeting, Dr. Neuman seemed more pale and tired than usual.

"You are tired," she said, "you look tired."

"Yes, a little. Tell me how it was yesterday, though. I understood you had an important visit." His eyes smiled.

"Erika, my sister, came. It was a surprise."

They sat down in the easy chairs. Marta sat up straight and Dr. Neuman sank back heavily. They looked at each other silently and attentively.

"Finally! What a surprise! How did she get here?"

"By bus," she replied. She leant back and was quiet for a moment. "It wasn't really all that complicated ... And yet ..."

"And yet—what?"

"She came because . . . Well, Andy asked them not to come on their own. That's what she told me. He believed it would be hard for me to see them without his support. That it would've distressed me, he thought." She seemed almost insulted.

"And what do you think?"

"I wouldn't have minded at all. She's my sister," she said and paused. "And I generally don't want Andy deciding things without talking to me first. But he's like that, he runs the show."

"He really thinks that what he decides and does is for your good," Dr. Neuman replied slowly, "but I understand it's not always easy on you, his deciding. It may be something that can change, you know? It depends on you too."

"Yes," she said, as if to herself, "I would like it to be different; but I'm pretty dependent"

"Of course," he responded, a little distracted.

Noticing he was troubled by something, Marta asked: "When will I be released? When can we say I'm all right?"

"You are all right, no matter what!" He gave her a weak smile. "As far I'm concerned, I think you can go home soon."

"I think about it a lot," she said, looking at him.

"What do you mean?"

"About going home. It should make me happy, but it also saddens me. I know that sounds totally . . . what's the word . . . ? Irrational. But that's how it is."

"Marta, you've grown stronger. There's no point staying in hospital when you can return to ordinary life. You'll go home stronger. You will be with your family, you will live your life. After all, that's what matters most—"

"I want to ask you something," Martha said, interrupting him. "I want to ask you something about what happens next."

"Please. I am listening."

"You're the only one who can help me with this."

"You know I'll do anything I can, don't you, Marta? What is it about?"

"As you know, I started writing. It hasn't been easy, but recently I have been progressing more or less steadily. That's why I go out in the mornings to the café on the promenade. That's where I write. I told you about it."

"And what happened with the desk in your room?" he asked and smiled.

"That desk pushed me to go out," she smiled in return. "It's the atmosphere in the café, you know, that's where I manage to write. Maybe it reminds me of Hemingway . . ."

"Yes, it's an inspiring place."

"Do you know the place?"

"I've seen it from the promenade."

"Have you ever sat there?" Her thoughts started racing.

"A long time ago . . . Now I'm not . . . So that's where you go. Nice. Very nice."

"Yes. I want to finish writing here, in that café, I mean, in hospital. It won't be like that at home. I don't think I would carry on there."

"I understand," he said. "That's very clear."

Marta observed him and thought that, like her, he was both happy and sad.

"So, do you think it is possible," she asked cautiously, "for me to stay here until I am done? It won't take much longer . . ."

"You should know, Marta, that the entire team here considers writing an integral part of therapy. I believe that your writing indicates the success of your treatment. You have succeeded in restoring your memory! That is extremely important. We think of that as very important."

"Thank you," she said and leant back again. "Thank you, I do feel it's important. You know, it's been easier and easier. I'm gradually managing to set things in order. It feels as though I am putting my life back on its feet."

"That's excellent, Marta. I can see that."

"How?"

"What I see is that you are here, Marta, you are here. Writing about what happened, your memories, is a relief. One day it'll be given a therapeutic name, this kind of writing, they'll recognize its value. Mark my words. But we have no need for confirmation, we know it."

"We?" Her eyes smiled.

"Yes," he returned her smile, "we. You were just saying that you feel less distressed, that there's less chaos. Sometimes I think that alongside our therapy here, you are also conducting your own: you write. That part does not depend on us, the unit. You and I don't discuss it, and I don't know what you are writing. It's something that belongs to you alone. Of course, I am aware you are writing down your memories. I know some of them because you've mention them. . . Yes, I know quite a bit already, but not everything, not the story you have been writing—your story."

No, she thought, no, not just mine. She felt that somehow it belonged to the two of them. Each time she sat down and wrote, he was there with her, even though they never discussed it. Sometimes, he felt so present that it seemed he was standing right behind her, reading along over her shoulder. She liked that feeling very much. She was writing for him too, and she wanted him to read it was complete.

"You write for yourself, and surely you will let the children read what you've written. You're writing for them as well as yourself."

"Yes, I think about that all the time."

"What do you think?"

"I think about how I am writing what I cannot say out loud, something that I want to tell them, that I must tell them. I owe it to myself, to my children." She stopped and her expression was one of grief. "I feel I owe it to my family. It is a rescue operation in every sense."

"That's it exactly. Rescue."

"Yes, but I don't seem to be brave enough." She smiled sadly. "I have the courage to write, but what about when I'm finished? When I consider giving my writing to the children I get scared."

"Why?"

"The pain. That weight. I cannot get rid of it. It's right here, like a stone around my neck. I am afraid it will be difficult for them to bear that weight. Or anyway that it won't be easy. These are sad memories. A sad story. So much pain. What are they supposed to do with it?" She took deep breaths. "You know, I'm not recording everything that happened. There are things that will stay unwritten. Because of me. Because of them . . ."

"I understand. Passing on that story, bringing it out into the open, is not simple. Writing it is one thing; passing it on is another. Especially when it comes to your own children."

"Yes, that's what's worrying me."

"Marta." He suddenly spoke up, as though he was sharing a secret. "I have something to propose—perhaps 'request' is a better word. Maybe it's even a personal request, but I really think it might help."

"What?" Her eyes opened wide.

"Well, I propose you stay here in the unit until you're finished writing."

"I thought we'd already agreed on that," she said, disappointed.

"Just a moment, I am not done . . . When you're finished writing, maybe it will be easier to hold off giving your writing to the children straightaway. Perhaps someone else, someone close, should read it first, before the children."

"You?" She smiled.

"I would be very glad to. What do you think?"

The question remained suspended in the room. His smile seemed sad to her. He is tired, she thought, he doesn't look well. His face was grey, and for the first time since she'd started her treatment with him, she felt a sense of her own power. For a moment she even felt healthy.

"Marta," he leant forward, "what do you think?" He leant back and gave her serious, intense look. "Of course, you're not obliged, but I want you to know it's important for me to tell you that I would very much like to read what you are writing, your memories. I'm interested, and not just as your doctor. You understand?"

"Yes," she said, as though she was talking to herself, "I understand, I understand completely. You know what? I would be happy if you read my memoir, and not just as a doctor."

The two of them fell silent, each in their own thoughts, and the sadness of their approaching separation stood between them. Towards the end of the meeting, before leaving the room, Marta observed Dr. Neuman's face again, and a dull sense of concern troubled her.

"Take a rest," she said. "I think you need some rest."

***

Marta stayed another two weeks or so in the unit and dedicated most of her time to writing. She wrote every day, mainly in the café, but in her room too, at the desk Dr. Neuman had sent her. The unattractive view from the window no longer disturbed her. She was writing urgently, in order to conclude. Her meetings with Dr. Neuman continued, and they too were marked by a desperate urgency to say what had somehow not been said. It was an attempt to hold onto something that was slipping away, to preserve a little of what there had been between them, in this room: it was like trying to keep something going that could never stay alive.

The silence that had dominated their meetings early on in therapy was replaced by talk, long conversations in low voices. Now they talked about her writing. One needs a story, said Dr. Neuman, that processes, communicates, and translates what can neither be voiced nor heard, a story that draws new lines along which one can then move. Marta thought that here she was, telling her story; she was writing down what she had not been able to say. And yet an apprehension persisted inside her, nagging. Would it also be possible for anyone to read the story, listen to it?

In these final meetings, Dr. Neuman also told Marta a little about himself. He recounted his medical studies, his late discovery of psychoanalysis, his great respect for it. It was such a shame that hospitals did not recognize the healing power of words. Nowadays, one had to be a doctor, write prescriptions. There were, it was true, some psychologists in the department, but their approach was still very medical. Dr. Neuman was convinced that in order to heal the psyche, one had to think differently about illness. He often had arguments about this with the hospital's managers. There was a note of frustration in his voice; she once more felt he was tired. She did not probe him about his accent and his private life. Nor did she want to.

"Are you all right?" she asked him directly.

"Excuse me?" he responded. "What sort of question is that?"

"A very simple one." She smiled. "I'm asking whether you are OK? Do you feel well?"

"Why are you asking?"

"Well, why does one ask such questions?"

"Tell me . . ."

"Because one is worried."

"You're worried about me?"

"Yes, you've been looking tired for a while. You're pale and there are dark rings under your eyes."

"Really? Is that how I look?"

"Yes, yes."

"I have been feeling a bit tired recently. I'm too busy. This tiredness—it has its reasons. I should get tested."

"You will?"

"Yes, of course."

"You promise?"

"Of course, Marta. I am a doctor, after all . . ."

"Look after yourself," she said, and her face grew serious.

"All right. We'll both look after ourselves. You promise too?"

"I promise," she said.

This conversation left her uncomfortable. There was something in the air, but she did not know what. Maybe it was simply that she was about to go home. Dr. Neuman had not told her about his life. What did she know about him? Nothing! Was he married? Did he have children? It suited her this way. The thought of a last meeting with Dr. Neuman pained her; but it was mixed with her excitement about returning home. She was already preparing her things in her room. She put the suitcase on the other bed, the one that had been Dina's, and filled it with clothes she knew she was not going to wear in the hospital.

While the recent meeting with Dr. Neuman left her sad, she also thought there was something magical about it too. The room was illuminated by a beautiful light she would never forget. It was late afternoon. On entering the office, the space presented itself in the same way it had struck her the first time. Again, she noticed the faded brown upholstery of the chairs, the old rug, the full bookshelves, the large brown desk. The late afternoon light slanted through the window and painted the room with glistening hues of orange. The upholstery looked like fertile brown soil, a freshly ploughed field. The dust on the large desk shone like the finest sheet of gold, while the piles of books on the shelves took on a sculptural quality. Through the window she saw the poinciana's final clusters of red blooms. This is the end, she thought.

"Come, Marta." Dr. Neuman gestured to her chair. "Sit down."

He sat down opposite her, and she noticed two cups on the low table between them and a small plate of cookies. The meeting was not long. Dr. Neuman tried to come up with something to mark the conclusion of her stay, but his voice broke. Marta too felt her throat contract. She was on the verge of tears.

"This is for you." He held out a parcel in wrapping paper: "I hope you like it."

She wiped the corner of her eye with her hand: "What is it, a present?"

"You could call it a present, yes."

"Thank you! Thank you so much! Can I open it now?"

"Please do. "

Marta opened the wrapping paper carefully without tearing it and took out a volume. She looked at the cover, at Dr. Neuman, and then at the cover again. She opened the book and glanced at the poems. Then she closed it.

"It's poetry," she said to him, serious and clear.

"Yes, I'm very fond of this book."

"I didn't know you liked poetry. You never mentioned it."

"Dear Marta, there are so many things I've not talked about. But yes, I like to read poetry on occasion."

She held the gift tight, studying its blue-green cover on which was embossed, in gold, the name of the poet: Leah Goldberg. She followed the movement of the letters. The letter *lamed*, ornate as though leaping up, the first *gimel* sending its roots down, while the final *gimel* ended in a confident line underscoring the name. Goldberg: Golden mountain.

"*Early and late*," said Dr. Neuman, "I remembered something you once said about poets, and I thought that . . . I hope you will enjoy her work."

"*Early and late*," she repeated the title, in thought, "*Early and late . . .*"

"Yes," he said and sighed.

"Marta." He suddenly sat up straight. "That's it. We're there. You're free. I will write a release letter and a report, and send it to your family doctor." His expression was downcast.

"I'm not good at saying goodbye," she said and tried to smile.

"I'm not much good at it either." He too tried to smile. "We . . . But I hope to hear from you every so often. Even if only through your family doctor, just to hear how you're doing, that you're OK." Fixing her with his gaze, he added: "You can always turn to me, you know. If you want to chat, you can just ring the hospital and ask for me. I'll always be there for you . . . I hope . . ." He smiled.

"Thank you, I hope so too." She smiled back. "Yes. And I would like to leave something with you too." She took two brown copybooks from her bag, "Here's what I wrote here."

Giving him the copybooks, she seemed unsure for a moment. Dr. Neuman took them in his hands and looked at the covers.

He raised his eyes to her. "We have really achieved something together, haven't we?"

"Yes, but I didn't do everything I wanted to. I mean . . . you'll see."

"What you mean?"

"I mean the memories are only up to when Erika and I returned. That's where I stopped then."

"So you are actually letting me read the first part of your memoir. 'To be continued,' as they say." For a moment this idea—*to be continued*—made her happy. Then she grew serious.

"Maybe. What's next is a different story altogether."

"But these stories are connected. They're your life . . ."

"Are they connected? I don't know. There's a hole between them, too. The first story ended . . . cut like . . ."

"That's the connection and that's your life. You might write more in the future. You can't tell."

"We will see. Right now I feel there is nothing inside me. A kind of emptiness."

"Until the next time. That's how it is when you create. Creativity makes a void but it also fills." Dr. Neuman looked at the notebooks again, opened one and turned its leaves, his eyes focused on the lines.

"Fantastic," he said to himself, "fantastic."

He raised his eye to her and their gazes met. He saw her sorrow.

"I am so happy you did it. That you wrote. Thank you, Marta, for giving me these. They're a gift I never dreamed of. I'm very touched."

"I'm the one who should be saying thank you."

"Both of us can."

"Yes," she said, and added with concern, "but there's something else. Something that worries me."

"Yes?"

"It's about what I have written. It doesn't worry me—that's not the right word. It's more like . . . I'm a bit embarrassed."

"Embarrassed?"

"I'd like to ask your forgiveness."

"I promise."

"You promise, just like that? You don't even know what I'm asking you to forgive?"

"I am sure you won't take advantage of my lack of responsibility." He smiled. "What are you asking me to forgive, then?"

"Forgive my spelling. And sometimes also my style. Don't laugh. I am aware my Hebrew is not perfect, I make mistakes; I don't understand how one is supposed to remember when it's an *alef* and when it's an *ayin*, when it's *tav* and when it's *tet*."

"But Marta, really . . ."

". . . And *khaf* or *kof*? How is one supposed to know? And those numbers . . . Yes, Dr. Neuman. I make mistakes—you know, grammar, spelling—and I have a hard time accepting it. One should observe the rules of grammar . . . Words have power. Yes, one must observe the rules, mistakes are . . ." She paused, annoyed. She raised her hand and let it fall back into her lap, giving up trying to explain: "Oh well, for now that's how it is. Not perfect."

"I promise. I forgive you already!" He smiled and then became serious. He Neuman took the two notebooks and looked at her. She took a deep breath and asked herself how she would get them back.

"Don't worry." He'd read her thoughts. "I'll give these back to you."

"You need not rush, there's plenty of time,"

"There is time, yes," he said, "I hope that . . ."

Marta was worried about him.

Dr. Neuman consulted his watch and got up. Marta stood too. They were close to each other. Dr. Neuman took hold of her hands and pressed them warmly.

"Look after yourself," she murmured.

"You too," he said back softly.

That same evening he began reading Marta's words; and he continued until very late into the night. He had an urge to read, as though there was no time and he had to race to the end.

Part Two

_____

THE NOTEBOOKS

_____

Šurany, Family, Childhood

I was number three in our lineup. Andy, my oldest brother was two and a half when I was born, and the next brother, Öcsi, one and a half. From the moment I could think, my admiration for Öcsi was boundless. More than anything I wanted to be like him and when people mentioned a similarity between us it would make me very happy. But we were not close. For me he was an example, the unattainable ideal, and I was grateful with the merest crumb of his attention. Even though I was born a girl, as was proper after two sons, I felt from when I was young that I was not meeting expectations. From bits of stories I understood that after two successful and beautiful boys I was kind of a disappointment to our parents. Even though it was never said directly, only through hints about my looks and shape, which did not agree with our parents' dreams.

About our parents we only knew very little, from stories. Our mother was eleven and a half when her mother fell ill and died of some bad illness (they did not say what and we did not ask). She was the first of five children and she was mostly the one who had to look after them. "Poor little bird of mine," the doctor who visited her mother called her, seeing her again and again working hard in the kitchen. According to the stories she was too small to reach the table and had to stand on a stool. Mother stayed home to care for the children after her mother's death until she married at age twenty-four. After marriage too she fulfilled the role of big sister in spite of geographic distance.

[Our] father, too, was not so fortunate. His father passed when he was eleven. On advice of relatives, he was sent to an uncle in Vienna to become an apprentice at a textile shop, and he stayed in Vienna until he was recruited to the army in the First World War, at age twenty-four. One could feel that his father, "our father" had "seen the world." He took in things and was influenced by the big city, for instance his German, sense of humor, his amazing generosity. He was more joyful than our mother, who did not smile a lot. About our father it was said that during his bachelor years, he had lived a merry life, lost his connection with religion, liked card games, etc. Before his marriage to our mother he promised to her father to stop those habits of his, keep the Jewish laws, not to touch cards. He fully kept this promise. By the time we got to know him he was a religious man visiting synagogue several times a

day, conducting the very complicated life of observant Jews. The one question is: did the promise to grandfather also make him believe with the whole of his heart? Or was he just keeping an obligation?

Andy was born prematurely. They kept him warm in a laundry basket lined with cotton wool and hot water bottles. Because mother had not enough milk they got a wet nurse, a goyish girl who had had a baby out of wedlock (what happened with her child?), stayed in our house for months, and her only job was to nurse Andy. He grew into a fragile boy, gentle of body and mind. From childhood he was like one of the 36 righteous. Always last in line, always ready to give up. I never heard him arguing with our parents, making demands. More than once he paid a price for his absolute considerateness to others. In fifth grade he had to decide where to go on studying: religious or general. Father was convinced by the rabbi's "request" and Andy was sent to "Talmud Torah" where general learning was only in the evening hours. He did not rebel but suffered all of his short life from this irrational decision. After he finished this, he was forced to go to a yeshiva for another year or two, he did this reluctantly because the place and its method caused him much suffering. Then finally he said he had enough and announced to our parents he was joining the Zionist youth movement, "Young Maccabeans," in Budapest. Only then, very late, he began to enjoy his life.

The midwife who helped with his delivery was a very old goyish woman called Novotny teta—aunt Novotny. She was very highly regarded in our home. It happened more than once that they turned to her after doctors had given up, and she, with her enormous experience, always helped out with some remedy. Her name was linked to many tales in our home. Here is one of them: tiny Andy was about three when he disappeared one day. They looked for him, but did not find him anywhere. He was discovered in a remote corner of the house, kneeling like a Christian, his hands clasped together, and wholly immersed in prayer. "What are you doing here, sweetheart?" and he announced solemnly: "I pray to God so he will protect Auntie Novotny and so she be healthy and live many years." That was his way, everything he did modestly, always thinking of others before thinking about himself. I loved his gentle sense of humor, a humor that does not try to impose. I loved his voice, he sang with precision and beautifully. On Friday nights, when only candles lit the room, the two of us stayed, sitting on the window sill and singing songs from the youth movement. It was Andy who made me join the movement.

After the war I got to know his friend from the movement and from him I learned about his fate, a fate foretold, given his character. When he was recruited by the workers' force he was in a large group of young men who were transported to the Russian front, from which there was almost no way back. They were put to use as live mine detectors and other such functions. At some point the friend and Andy had planned an escape from the train. Some of those around them heard about it. Then one of them approached and told about a regulation he pretended he knew about. If anyone escaped, the Hungarians would execute every tenth young men by way of punishment. When Andy heard this he immediately gave up on his plan to escape. "I am not willing to be saved in this way, when others pay with their lives instead of me." The friend ignored the moral question and went ahead on his own, and he was saved after many hardships and stayed alive. Later, this same friend told me, the young man who had "warned" them had fled the train at the first opportunity. Out of the goodness of his heart, Andy had already let go of at least one opportunity to escape. During their training period with the Zionist movement (before the German invasion, but times were already very hard) he was on a list of people legally granted to immigrate to Palestine. Shortly before traveling he heard about a girl, a refugee from Slovakia or Poland, who was in distress and could not stay in Budapest, and offered for her to go in his stead. Of course we heard about this not from him, and only after he was no longer alive.

One year exactly after Andy, Öcsi was born. His name was really Karol, after the uncle who was killed in the First World War. His Hebrew name was Shlomo, but everyone called him Öcsi, which, in Hungarian, means "little brother." He was the absolute antithesis of his older brother, Andy. Stronger, bigger than him, a rebel, fearless, mainly a nonconformist.

It was not for long that I stayed an ugly duckling, but I didn't turn into a beautiful swan either. The problem was rather one of character and conduct. Apparently I was an insufferable baby, who often angered everybody around. Among the few findings [sic] left behind from this period was a kind of little tin cup which came with a story: At around age two, when they were trying to wean me from drinking milk from a bottle and they gave me food in a ceramic cup I resisted and expressed my protest in an original way. I bit its sides until I managed to remove a piece. When this repeated itself another time, they replaced the cup with one made of tin. It was among the dairy utensils for years and whenever I saw it I felt embarrassed and it darkened my mood (why didn't I simply throw it away and that's it?).

Educational efforts were not successful, on the contrary. With my stubborn reaction I tried to show I had no intention to become a "good girl." And this is how I grew up introverted and a bit detached. Sometimes I escaped into bitter tears, for no matter what reason. It could be some dress I was not allowed to put on, or shoes

I wanted to wear at the wrong time, everything could cause a huge outbreak of crying which would go on until I was exhausted. I don't at all want to suggest that our parents did not love us enough, and me in particular. They loved us the way they thought right and educational. They never took a break from their endless concern for us.

I also had a "half-brother." I was born 23.II.26, and he five days later. From stories I learned that his mother saved me when it became clear my mother could not continue nursing (in those days none of those mother milk substitutes existed yet). She took me along with her son and apparently neither one of us stayed hungry. . . As usual, such juicy details don't stay secret for long, and the period of our nursing was mentioned from time to time even when we were already in school. Children, as is their wont, will take this type of material all the way. The two of us were the object of all kinds of jokes and giggles. For instance, they'd ask: Who knows why both of them have such a snub nose? The answer: Because when they were jointly fed, their noses got pressed against each other, and that's why they had this shape, etc. etc.

With his mother I had inter-relations [sic] consisting of dumb stares, smiling and well-intended. Not a word was said, nor was there a need for that. Quite often, when I started to grow up, I felt her caressing me with her warm look and I knew how much I owed her. He was the one child who everybody called by his family name, Pfeffer, and not many knew his first name, and that somehow signaled his social class. He was one of us, yet also an outsider. "A lone wolf," but informed of everything, knowing everything, and passing his stern judgment on everything. He had a clear gift for music and considered everyone who wasn't like him as somehow "second rate" and worse. Later, when the stranglehold around our necks was tightening, he said to me: "I have nothing to worry about. I will take the violin, I'll go to the villages, from village to village, I'll play on their parties, like the Gypsies, and no one will suspect me. I tell you, me and my violin, we will come through." They did not. . .

When we were young children our relations were mostly fond-and-hostile. But when we grew older we became closer and I felt he was kind to me, in spite of his judgmental attitude. In third or fourth grade, a rumor reached me that during "men's" talk, when they were trying to rate the girls in terms of beauty, he had expressed himself in praise of me: "I think Marta is the most beautiful girl in our class. All the other girls have crooked legs. One has O-shaped legs, another X legs. Marta is the only one with straight legs." Oh, poor boy! He did not know the trouble he caused me! The pet name "straight legs" pursued me for a long time and whenever some boy wanted to tease me he would use it. I tried to ignore it but it always embarrassed me.

*In time I got the main role in a school play, Queen Marianka.
We put a lot into the rehearsals and my mother ordered a private
seamstress to sew the magnificent dress of the Queen from pink
satin, including a crinoline and all kinds of sparkles. We performed
in the town's dancing hall on a real stage, two shows only: in the
afternoon for children and youth, and in the evening for the town's
adults. During the first act (before turning into a queen) I was a
village girl in traditional Slovak dress, with boys and girls in
the field. In the play, one of the boys expressed great praise of
Marianka (praise of me, that is to say). As he began to list all
my queenly qualities a sudden shout could be heard from the first
row: "And straight legs she has too!" That was a boy from a higher
grade who wanted to be clever and get attention at my expense. It's
very likely that not everyone heard his words, but I heard them very
well and was deeply hurt. I was confused for some moments, I lost my
lines, and I nearly broke into tears. Luckily it was the matinee,
which was considered a general rehearsal in which a small "glitch"
is permissible for anyone, me included. . .*

*When we became four (Erika, my sister, was born) caring for
us became a problem because mother was working in the shop most of
the time. They looked for a nursemaid and found one. Her name was
Juliška, she was a little over one meter tall, she had a hunchback
and a disproportionate head. She came from some place in the north,
with many recommendations, and she stayed with us for the next six
years. She conducted a terror regime of hygiene and discipline. We
were often punished, but often it was Öcsi, more than the rest of us,
who was found to be the culprit. One punishment was to kneel in the
corner of the room on a piece of wood for unlimited time. Sometimes
she would not let us enjoy all kinds of small pleasures like playing outside and so on. It is hard to tell whether our parents knew
what was really happening. They saw their children squeaky clean and
probably thought that satisfactory. When she took us out walking,
two girls facing each other in the pram, and the two boys at the
sides, we were an object of envy for plenty of parents: "How lucky
they are with Juliška!"*

*Once we were given a particularly grave punishment: not to par-
ticipate in the wedding of Uncle Gézco which was celebrated in the
yard shared by our two families. It was an unbearable punishment!
Our parents did not intervene, maybe they were afraid to annoy her.
As it was, she would announce her resignation every so many months,
which she would retract after her wages were raised. The wedding was
at its height, was joyful outside, and only we were locked behind
shuttered windows. Öcsi, who was about five at the time, suddenly
opened the window, stood there and before the assembled guests
shouted: "I d-o-n't w-a-n-t a h-u-n-ch-ba-ck! I d-o-n't w-a-n-t*

a h-u-n-ch-b-ack!" More than this I don't remember. I imagine he
did not escape without punishment. We remembered it as a case of
extraordinary bravery, for many years.

Erika was every parent's dream child. She was diligent, disciplined, and kind hearted. I knew I could not never compete with
her in making our parents happy. When we returned from school it
took Erika a few minutes only to appear in the kitchen, an apron
tied across her hips, wholly ready to begin helping. I sought out
the most remote corner of the garden, with a book, or just to hide
in the shrubs and dream. Often I ignored the calls of those who
were looking for me. Because it was impossible to collaborate [sic]
with Erika, I chose a way of undermining her, of irritating and
mocking her. Conflicts were frequent. I so much regret, from this
huge distance in time, that we never talked and tried to settle the
problems between us. All the walls between us fell only when we
found ourselves in those places. [Sic] There was unlimited sisterly
love and mutual support between us. Who knows, maybe that is why we
stayed alive.

I was six years old when little Eva was born on 31.XII.1931.
My parents were deeply sorry that she was not born one day later
because it would have enabled them to register her as one whole year
younger! I did not understand why this seemed so important. They
announced that her name would be Eva. Nobody objected, but only I
began screaming hysterically: "Don't want you to call her Eva! Don't
want, don't want!" Why? "Because when she grows up the children will
mock her and sing that song (not the most refined song), that rhymes
with Eva." When acquaintances or regular clients came in and asked
for the baby's name, I rushed in before all the others: "She's called
Lili, she's called Lili!" They left a little confused. It was a lost
struggle: I cried my heart out, I grew exhausted and then made my
peace with the name. Maybe it was because of the age differences that
we always saw her as a kind of baby, a fragile, beautiful girl, and
we did not really relate to her. Only Erika gave her attention and
you could see them together a lot, immersed in play. I am deeply sad
about how remote I was from her during her short life. It is something I cannot make good. She met her death aged twelve.

When Juliška finally left, after having harassed us for many
years, a young lady named Roszi arrived to be our nanny. Actually
she came to look after little Eva, a few months old. She was well
dressed. Today I would call her a "girl with style" or perhaps an
"elegant girl," the total antithesis to Juliška's monstrousness,
something which in itself made me very glad. From the start she chose
me as her special favorite. She would spoil me with little gifts, a
sweet, or sometimes plasticene, she would let me come along when she

went to the hairdresser or the seamstress, and gradually I became her confidante. I was also attached to her, whether because of those gifts or because of her personality, I was not sure. One night, when she was putting us to bed, mother came into the room. Maybe her peace of mind was troubled by our strange friendship. Mother approached to kiss and hug me, but I withdrew and refused to come near her. And then Roszi, with the smile of those who are secure in victory, approached me and I clung to her, I hugged and kissed her. Mother left the room without saying a word.

It was summer. Everybody who could went to the beautiful river Čierná Voda, whose literal translation is: Black Water. It was a magical place, surrounded by forests and natural lawns, and its own disadvantage was its big distance from town. Before lunch Roszi pulled me aside and whispered: "After the meal let's go to the river for a swim, you, me and little Eva. But it's a secret. Nobody is to know, you understand? I will prepare everything in the pram and we will go, like on a regular walk. Just don't mention it to anyone!" Little me, only six, being turned into an accomplice in such a daring action, and that of course flattered me no end. Immediately after the meal we set out. When we arrived, panting and sweating from our walk, it was a racket. Many young people were frolicking in the water, others were swimming down the stream while shouting gaily at each other. On the grass were bunches of people tanning themselves in the sun. "You sit by the pram for a bit, and I go into the water for a few minutes to refresh. Just make sure the pram does not move away," Roszi announced. I sat looking around, very interested, everything looked colorful and exciting, little Eva was asleep in the pram. During the first minutes I could not make out Roszi among the many people splashing in the water. Finally I saw her, surrounded by boys, it looked like she was having a pleasant time, as if they were all old acquaintances. I got so immersed in what was happening around me that for some moments I completely forgot about the pram's existence, let alone the task I had been given. I was adrift in the gay, colorful world around me. Who knows how long this daydream would have gone on if it had not suddenly been interrupted, there was a great commotion and I understood what happened: The heavy pram had become dislodged and started making its way, ever faster, straight for the river. Seeing this sad picture, I understood I had landed myself into big trouble. Fortunately for all, those who noticed what was happening stopped the pram before disaster struck.

The entire story reached my parents even before we returned. A relative who had witnessed the scene of course ran as fast as he could to report it to our parents. Our reception was difficult, and

I was considered responsible for the act no less than Roszi, and maybe more. They thought I should have told about the plan from the start and I had failed to do so. They did not understand the sensitivity of my situation. I could not be disloyal to Roszi, after all the good things with which she had showered me, all the kisses and hugs . . . My betrayal of my parents did, at that time, not seem so unequivocal. I suddenly felt sad because I understood that the "Black Water" incident was going to bring the day that Roszi would have to leave us much closer, and what I wanted more than anything was to run to some dark corner, where no one could see me, and cry until I was exhausted.

The house in which we lived belonged to father's Uncle Móric. They were a family with a great deal of property, property that constantly grew due to their excessive miserliness. They had a leather shop (the story was that our forefathers when first arriving in Šurany were tanners). In those days, people used to order their shoes from cobblers, "made to measure." A cobbler in those days had a more creative and a more respectable job than today. It was such cobblers who were their main clientele.

Uncle Móric was an old, small, and very ugly man, with a very Jewish nose but he also had his very own sense of humor. On Sundays, when the shop was closed, he was in the habit of wandering in the yard holding a big package of string in his hands, looking for a "victim." Sometimes he managed to tempt one of us, promising a sweet or some pennies, making us stand holding the end of the string, and he himself standing a few meters away, taking apart the string, dividing it into two and rolling each into a separate ball. With endless patience (children came and went but he stayed in place) taking apart ever more string, pursuing this sublime purpose: he would have plenty of string to tie his wares, almost for free.

Aunt Flora, his wife, was the true and undisputed ruler of the yard. She was the Tsarina, and everything happened at her command. Her stinginess could compete with that of her husband Móric, but unlike him she was evil and lacking the slightest sense of humor. When she noticed that the maid was putting sugar in her coffee, the latter immediately received instruction about the damage sugar causes to the skin of the face. "If you want a nice skin without wrinkles, then you must drink bitter coffee only." And the naïve and intimidated maid gave up on sugar without further question and had no words to express her gratitude to the "old lady" who saved her skin from extinction. She used a similar method to persuade the poor one to give up on ever more "harmful" things.

She was the one in charge of most business with the cobblers, even when her husband was still alive. In the eye of my mind I see her with a huge key opening the heavy iron door of the "magazine" where they stored hides in the yard, and I still smell the pungent hides. Noisy discussions could be heard far into the distance, but she always had the upper hand, and all the cobblers put together would not be able to budge her. Whispers in the yard had it that there, long ago, not entirely "businesslike" contacts had occurred in the "magazine" . . . Of course, those were assumptions only, and at the time we knew Aunt Flora, such a story was unimaginable and we categorized it from the start as unbelievable. In old age, her main activity—other than embittering the lives of everyone around her—was knitting socks. Huge quantities of socks, all of them grey, she knitted for her sons and sons in law. I never understood why a person would need such an amount of socks! She would sit inside a chair in the yard, her feet up on a little stool. Sometimes she would invite me, or rather, order me to sit with her, on the stool. I would be seated, my back turned to her, and from there I would hear her familiar, endless monolog. Everyone but every-one was trashed, and she had dirty names for all. Her name for Öcsi was "Weinreb the evil" (my mother's maiden name), Erika whose skin was darker was given the byname Černidlo" (a kind of black paste), etc. etc. Once she was done dealing with the yard's entire population (except for my father, whom she held in respect mixed with fear), it was the cobblers' turn. Not many escaped unscathed from her harsh criticism. "That one, that's no human being," she clamored, "He's hasn't got a bit of humanity, even less than in this knitting needle." And to make it clear how lacking in humanity the knitting needle was she used it to give me few wallops with it, directly on my head. Clearly, this seemed a doubtful way to pass my time and after a while I tried to free myself and get away from the stool, but she outwitted me and always managed to make me stay put. And when eventually I did get up, she made me come back with the eternal question: "Tell me, who do you love more, me or your grandmother?" There was nothing much to doubt, I knew there was only one answer possible, "I love you better." The truth was that of both of them equally I wasn't very fond.

On a rare occasion these two old women happened to meet in my grandfather's little shop. It was unfortunate that I did not consider the danger in time when I was sent to the post office opposite the shop. Aunt Flora came out of the shop and asked me to step in. I understood I had been caught and had fallen into the trap they had set. "Do come in! Now tell me who you love more?" I felt the ground opening up and leaving me afloat above a gaping abyss. If I chose Flora I would mortally insult grandmother, my father's mother. If I *chose grandmother, the big lie I had been telling all the time would be exposed. "I love grandmother more," the words escaped my mouth, almost against my own wish. Aunt Flora was left, her jaw dropping and pale, she was not used to losing. Grandmother was obviously celebrating her great victory, and I earned a cone of apricot ice cream. But how about tomorrow? How would I face Aunt Flora? I was perhaps the only soul who came close to her, even if under pressure and strangely, and now that was all over. . .*

In time, Uncle Móric and his wife had another floor added to their house. It was supposed to be the future house of their youngest son, Gézko, once he would reach marriageable age and get married. This program never materialized because when the time came they preferred, for reasons of prudence of course, to let the apartment to strangers who paid a lot. We, the children from the yard and the vicinity, exploited the house when it was in the final stages of construction, and in its beautiful, large rooms, with the abundant fantasy of our childhood, we organized exciting games and theater performances. But only as long as Aunt Flora was nowhere near. For this purpose we kept track of her daily schedule, and we were only completely at ease when she was on one of her outings to some spa in northern Slovakia. Then we behaved like those mice when the cat is away.

One day a young lady, fair haired, slim and pretty, appeared in the yard. It turned out she was future bride of cousin Gézko. It was hard to believe that Gézko, a short and fat man, no longer young but childish, whose life with his overbearing mother turned him into a wimp and lacking in any will of his own, was a proper husband for that fair haired young lady. She was from a really good family and came from a remote town in Carpatho-Russia. I thought, how could parents possibly allow for their daughter to be unprotected in such a place, to marry her off to such a groom, and in the presence of such a monstrous mother-in-law? Did they not feel they were abandoning their young daughter in an inappropriate place?

Within a few years that blossoming young girl changed into a frustrated woman lacking any joy of life. Very soon she understood that her new life was a kind of prison, with Aunt Flora in the role of the guard limiting her moves and imposing an oppressive regime of a kind she had never known and had no means to oppose. She missed her parents' home far away. Only at our place, in my mother's company, did she allow herself to express her feelings. We heard many stories and became experts on the lives of her sisters and brothers, her village, until we knew by heart entire portions of the stories she kept repeating over and over. Of course, we children, did not have the necessary patience, and we laughed often behind her back. Four sons, who she had at no more than one-year intervals, were usually seen holding on to the pockets of her home dress, two on each side. This because these pockets were always full of chocolates and other excellent sweets. She found an escape route from her hopeless life in the form of an addiction to sweets, and the children joined the party. This lovely, gifted woman proceeded with her self-destruction, her teeth decayed from eating so many sweets, and by age thirty she looked like an old woman.

Our summer vacations we would spend (other than two weeks with grandfather in Topolčany) in the garden of the sugar factory Fabriká Záhrada. It was a huge, wild garden, full of tangled trees and shrubs, a blend of light and shadow, and alongside it, the Nitra River. The garden once belonged to an aunt of my father, Aunt Kati, an old and slightly eccentric unmarried woman, who would allow herself, un-spied, to light an occasional cigar (!) while putting the blame of the smoke on some municipal official who had been on business. Apparently she was a feminist even before the name of that movement came into the world. She was fabulously rich. According to the stories we heard she owned much land, all kinds of buildings, as well as a brick factory. I never had the opportunity to see it, but in the conversations of this aunt's relatives, the subject of the factory was never omitted. The line of potential heirs was always growing and the pessimists among them calculated that by the time the aunt's final hour would come (after 120 years, they added) every heir would receive just one brick. I remember our family inherited only two items: Some makeup table with a mirror and a place for candles on each side, which for some reason reminded me of ghosts in a deserted castle. The other thing was an amazing desk, of enormous proportions, heavy and stunning, with many drawers which we shared. I was lucky to get the large middle drawer, of course with its own key, and this drawer safely kept all my secrets, including my diary. I made sure to keep the key always with me, and if it ever stayed home, I would not be lazy and return from no matter where to restore it to my control.

At some point in the past most of this garden was sold to the owners of the sugar factory, and hence its name. Entry to the garden was, in fact, forbidden, but we children would get in through a gap in the fence and we could always hide in the thick undergrowth when we felt the guard approaching. The guard was a tough and uncompromising man whom we suspected of being a child hater. Some believed that he chased children who broke into the garden because of his wife who suffered from tuberculosis, [and] who used to sunbathe in the nude on the lawn in front of their house. This discovery was circulated by some boys who had succeeded to sneak into that place. But they may also have invented the entire story. There was a ruin in the garden, steps led to a cellar underneath it, a place shrouded in mystery that made our skin creep. The story went that deep inside the cellar there was a table on top of which rested the chopped off hand of the late owner of the estate, a golden ring inlaid with precious stone on each of its fingers. We listened to these descriptions with pale faces and pounding hearts, but we never met anyone who had seen it with their own eyes. Hearsay was enough to convince us the story was true.

In the big vacation we would get up early and not to lose precious time, we would drink our cocoa at the dairy table (as opposed to the meat table which stood in the kitchen too), and we ate our roll on the way to the garden. The garden had a magnetic pull to which we gave in willingly. Most of our regular company would already be there and we would pick up our game where we had left off when it grew dark the previous evening. We were immersed and the thing electrified us completely. Only when the church bells rang at midday, did we feel hunger arising suddenly. We ran home to eat and immediately after the meal we returned to the garden. The same schedule every day. (Where were all those activities nowadays, the summer camps, theater plays and films to satisfy our children's hunger for entertainment, and then still to hear that "I'm bored"?) If you had some secret you wanted to share with a friend, there was no better place to do it than in the garden. There you got encouragement during the crises that announced a new phase, full of anxieties, that of the onset of adolescence. In the garden of the factory, undoubtedly, we spent the most beautiful hours of our childhood.

I was strongly attracted by the outdoors, where I felt free, without the usual criticism. Whenever I could I spent time with my friends or at the neighbors', places where I was warmly received. Often I forgot about the existence of the clock, arriving home at late hours, and not as I had promised. The mood would become troubled and I acted "angry" . . . Sometimes it happened that on my return I had to hear the hated sentence: "Again you are behaving like Aunt Margit, yes, that's exactly how she behaved when she was young." This would always hurt me, it would get straight at me. This aunt, my father's sister, was the black sheep of the family. A widow who lived with her two children and her mother—our grandmother. Her character was disturbed, her family lived in poverty, and no help or support availed to relieve their desperate condition. I heard, usually from my mother, talk about an inability on their part to organize their lives differently, to be more responsible and sensible about how

*they dealt with money. Mother who was exceptionally thrifty and cre-
ative could not understand this method of splurging today when there
was cash at home, and [then] to weep and complain tomorrow when the
money box was empty. Father, whose generosity knew no limit in general, and even more so when it came to relatives, went on giving,
also when he no longer had a regular income.*

*Sometimes when they thought they were not being overheard, my
parents argued about this sensitive issue. Mother tried to curb
father's good-heartedness. Times were hard. She tried to remind him
of their five children when the future was threatening all of us. I
felt that this was why most of his support was given secretly. Not
seldom, an envelope was sent via one of us children to grandmother
and the aunt. For many years, my mother was not in touch with this
branch of the family and we children, too, were not eager to frequent them, and we mainly felt embarrassment and shame towards them.
In spite of all this we would join father on his Shabat visits, a
visit which always caused me grief. I remember the dark, unaired
apartment, the two pictures of prints by Abel Pann above the bed.
One showed the Pharaoh's daughter pulling Moses from the Nile, the
second I don't remember but I am sure it was a similar subject. On
each such visit I focused my gaze on the figures in the picture and
prayed we wouldn't be offered anything to eat. They were wretched,
not just because of their difficult material situation. I think
about the loneliness in which they lived, the lack of hope to change
their lives even a little. Their daughter Magda, a girl my age, and
son Zoli, were born with a stigma that accompanied them throughout
their lives.*

*I was very insulted that mother observed a resemblance between
me and Aunt Margit. I knew I was different from her and that I was
being done an injustice. I quietly swallowed the insult and did not
react. And so, again and again, whenever I did something thought-
less, the familiar accusation returned. What annoyed me and height-
ened the sense of insult was that Erika (who was an extraordinarily
disciplined and obedient child) was compared, whenever the occasion
arose, to Aunt Jolly, my mother's sister, the young, charming aunt
whom we all loved. "She resembles her in her appearance and on top
of that she received her pleasant nature too" they explained. And I
wanted to climb the walls for sheer jealousy and despair. And she,
the little girl, her sole crime was her good heartedness and her
constant willingness to help at home (without pretexts, like I did).
But I found it hard to get along with her, exactly because of those
positive characteristics. Sometimes I feel the residues from our
childhood still play a part in our relationship now, and I hear hints
of bitterness: she also suffered, because of me . . .*

We are getting ready for the wedding of our beloved young aunt, Jolly. Erika and I are given new dresses, silk "creations," something very festive with frills and little satin flowers, mine pale blue and Erika's pink. We were promised we would be the bridesmaids carrying the bride's veil. On the Saturday before the wedding we asked to wear the dresses. "Just this once," we begged, "We will be really really careful." Till mother eventually gave in: "Just please be careful so nothing happens and so they stay clean and all right till the wedding."

I had planned to make a walk with a friend in the afternoon. My parents asked me (as usual) to take along Erika. "Don't want to. I don't need a tail." This did not convince them in the least, and so, after a rather vocal negotiation, Erika was made to join us. Let no one envy Erika's vulnerable situation after I was forced to take her with us. Most of the way I made sure she was quite aware how unwelcome she was. My friend and I were big already, almost eight, and she no more than a baby aged six and a half. What cheek to even think of asking to join us! But after a short walk, we calmed down and changed our arrogant attitude, and we continued as a united group. We walked all the way to the quarters of the sugar factory workers and continued beyond. We reached a piece of land, apparently a dried-up swamp. The soil looked dry and entangled, and it was lined with wild cherry trees. It was early summer and the trees were heavy with ripe fruit which there was no chance of reaching because the trees were tall. Here and there we saw a cherry on the ground. It was very tempting to walk to a part of the terrain where more cherries could be seen. But there was also a sense of fear of the unexpected and a wish to give up the entire adventure and return home. In the end we stayed. We started to collect fruit, one more, and another one and it seemed we were successful. We were filled with a kind of excitement and we dared to go even further in. Erika was the more daring one between us. She shone each time she reached another cherry. We were deep into this picking when suddenly we heard a weak cry, more like a wail. Erika was calling out for help. We saw her a little further away, sinking down to her ankles into the mud. The ground which had appeared dry, turned out to be a trap. I don't know how we managed, in the nick of time, before disaster struck, to pull Erika out without getting ourselves into a mess too. Only once we had moved away from the swamp, we discovered the real disaster, Erika's pink dress sewn especially for Aunt Jolly's wedding was all covered in muddy stains, not to mention the shoes and white socks! The sky collapsed! We were in a panic. Erika wept and begged: "Let's go to one of the houses, any one, we have to find good people, and ask them to help *us clean the dress." Well done Erika! Even at critical moments she did not lose her practical sense.*

We started to walk, a strange funeral procession. Erika had to make a big effort, her shoes full of mud, her dress wet. We entered the first yard. Only after some moments we discovered it was the house of the seamstress who had made those party dresses for the wedding. She received us with a forgiving smile, reassured us, and promised everything would be all right. She took the dress off Erika, took off her shoes, and told her again not to worry. Then she set to work. With impressive skill, and not even taking a very long time, she restored everything to its original condition, clean and ironed, and Erika herself too was clean and combed. We couldn't find words to thank her, we only asked her not to tell our parents. "No, of course I won't tell. This will be our secret forever," she promised.

It was evening by the time we came home. We tried hard to behave nicely, we hung the dresses in the wardrobe, and the ceremony of going to bed was shorter than usual, without the usual debates about it being too early, etc. Only when we were in bed, covered up to our heads, we could breathe quietly again. Thank God, it was all behind us, no one suspected anything. In the morning we continued on good behavior. In a few moments we would be on our way to school. Mother was combing my hair when I suddenly noticed a woman's face pressed to the kitchen window. A familiar face, smiling a broad smile, and winking meaningfully at me and Erika. Woe on us! That was not at all what we planned! It was none other than the seamstress who had come all the way to be there before we escaped from home, and to tell mother the story with a smile of victory! Such a disappointment, such a blow to our faith in humanity! Hadn't she promised she would not tell and keep the secret forever . . .

Weiss Báči, Uncle Weiss, was a big strong Jew, a kind of hulk (I pictured the Prague Golem exactly like this). He had introduced himself to our family via something to do with my parents' shop, a relationship that developed into a strong and naturally warm attachment to this naïve and wonderful old man. Two or three times a year he would do his rounds among the villages peddling his wares. He walked, a big wooden box strapped to his back, full of all kinds of notions, little things the villagers needed, like little napkins for embroidery (produced in our shop, which we would print in the evenings, after the shop closed), with the appropriate thread. The box held a whole department store of products, from shoe laces, to candles and matches, indispensable things. And all this was tied to his back as he walked from village to village. The villagers couldn't believe their eyes that a Jew was actually capable of this huge effort. I think they treated him with respect and affection.

We feared these trips of his had another reason, namely, to get away from his nasty wife who marred his life in different ways. When he returned after some weeks, the wooden box empty, and him looking healthy, suntanned, happy, he would resume his work as a lumberman. Sometimes he found refuge in our home, we would invite him on Saturday afternoons. There was a steady ritual when he arrived: We children ran towards him, yelling "Uncle Weiss, what a guest!" He made light of himself with a rhyme: the same reply to our call. It remained amusing even when we no longer took it seriously. He'd sit down in the corner by the hearth, saying little, and dozed off for some hours after coffee and cake. He never complained or expressed grievances about the difficult conditions of his life. Only after the death of his nasty wife did he experience a kind of rejuvenation. Suddenly he looked as if he had grown wings, free as a bird, eating to his heart's delight. He discovered life could be a party. Small pleasures like making a soup filled him with excitement. He told us enthusiastically how he would pick his vegetables, with each having its role in this important composition: carrot for color, parsley for flavor, noodles for substance, etc. Clearly he had suffered starvation during most of the years of his married life because of the woman's meanness and evil nature.

Father had other despondents [sic] of various kinds whom he took under his wing. All kinds of people on the run from the authorities, homeless people, whose families had stayed far away somewhere in Romania or Poland or God knows where. I remember one, an orthodox Jew with a red beard, who had dinner with us every Wednesday. We knew nothing about him, where he slept, what happened with his family and why he was here and they there. He appeared at the same time, regular like a Swiss clockwork, for years. Throughout that time I heard him say no more than two sentences, and those, too, in Yiddish. He was one of the most taciturn people I ever met. Once, while we were eating, father noticed a couple of policemen (those with the notorious rooster's feathers, who always moved in pairs) approaching our house. Father got him up from his chair quickly and pushed him with some force toward the door trying to explain the situation. They ran in the direction of the garden where father helped him climb over the fence and instructed him how to leap into the garden of Benda—the Christian inn owner—and to escape into the faraway street in order to save his skin. These policemen would sniff around after types without documents, mostly Jews, and whoever was caught was doomed.

They were expelled to a camp on the border with Poland from which no one returned.

Father did not believe in thriftiness, he was devoid of all materialism and willing to take off his winter coat (and did so, for real) to give it to a refugee or destitute foreigner. He did not ask anything for himself, he was satisfied with the minimum, but he did want to bring some progress, some "modernity" to our home, for the family's comfort. That's how it came to pass that Uncle Gézko could come to our house every single day in order to read the Prager Tagblatt—a daily newspaper in the German language - and to hear the news on our radio (among the first ones locally). We were years ahead of them with quite a bit of modern equipment. He would come in, day after day, with the same question, every day the question repeated itself: "Julinko (a pet name for my father which only he used), has Haman perished already?" That was the heart's desire of many Jews during the first years after the Nazi rise to power in Germany. Gézko asked this question at the top of his voice, [and] many Jews asked themselves the same waiting for a miracle, for Haman to really expire one day . . .

Father believed in quality. Everything they bought for the house, the clothes that were made for us, the shoes, etc., had to be of the best quality. "We are too poor to buy cheap" was the motto. We wore the same boy coats with their velvet lapels and gold buttons for years. They were indestructible and we often rebelled being fed up with those quality clothes. One day father saw an announcement in the Hungarian newspaper: "Dear Lady, throw away your knitting needles! With our new knitting machine you will knit your and your family's clothes in just a few hours!" Father was enthusiastic about the idea, and mother, who knitted everything herself, no less. It only took a short discussion, and from their next trip to Budapest they returned with a large parcel: the knitting machine! There was just one problem with the machine, and for us: its pace. It could hardly compete with the speed of mother's good old needles. We did not give in and tried all kinds of methods, but no sign of improvement. We understood the machine was not going to knit sweaters and hats within hours. When my parents complained at the shop in Budapest it turned out that in order to acquire the necessary skills, mother would have to follow a course in far-away Budapest, which was impossible, and that put an end to that dream. There was no choice but to put the machine back into its box, which was stored away on top of the wardrobe in our parents' bedroom.

Most of the things we needed for our daily existence were homemade. The rules were quite rigid. We did not get pocket money, and

I wonder how we managed. My parents did not even consider giving us pocket money, not because they were stingy but theirs was a simple educational method, namely, to teach us to treat money with respect. Money for which people have worked hard and honestly should not be wasted on nonsense. Sometimes I was envious when my friends at the Gymnasium spent money with insufferable casualness on sweets and me pretending I couldn't care less. I was eight or nine when while I was hanging out with two friends, who were a year older than me, we stopped at a Valina sweetshop. We had a look at the shop window and our eyes fell on something that took our breath away: a little dwarf made out of chocolate, a golden coin stuck in his bottom. We were hypnotized. We had to have one like that, there was no question about it. From sheer excitement I forgot I did not have the fantastic capital (!) of one and a half crown, the price of this dream. My friends had no such problem, they could even offer me a loan which I could return in a few days. I was ashamed to admit I would not be able to return the money, but I accepted the offer. "Everything will be OK!" as they say today. Everything was wonderful! Drunk with joy we returned home, each with her dwarf. Soon enough I understood I had gotten myself into trouble. Where would I get the money? How would I pay back the loan?

An opportunity to get out of this pinch offered: The next day our teacher asked the students to buy a prayer book (siddur) at the cost of seven crowns. Now I planned a complex move which would not embarrass any banker. First, I convinced my parents (which, as said, was not always easy) that we were obliged to buy the book and I got the full sum. Next I had to take things up with Mr. Fuchs so he would agree to accept a payment of five crowns only with the rest owing as a debt. Surprised with this novelty (we always paid everything in time) he nevertheless agreed. I left the shop with the prayer book and two crowns (it was a coincidence that my cheating involved a holy book of all things, but I didn't think of that at the time). I would pay my debt to the girls and even be left with half a crown, great!

Disaster struck when my cousin, with whom I never had a good relationship, and who didn't mind to cause me some trouble, saw the chocolate dwarf among my possessions. Her next step was to run off to my parents to reveal to them, her face all innocence, what was supposed to remain my secret. The entire brilliant plan collapsed. An investigation began: Where did you get the money? Though the pressure on me mounted, I did not reveal anything. The mood grew more intense and I kept a stubborn silence. I found myself in a very complicated situation: If I didn't tell the truth, I would be branded a thief, as simple as that. Still, I didn't tell them the truth. Today

I try to understand, why? Why did I accept being branded a thief when I hadn't actually stolen? I walked around with that stigma for a long time. And even when everyone had forgotten the incident, I still felt shame and remorse. And the story about the debt to Mr. Fuchs burdened me and there was no chance of clearing it. Several times he inquired after my debt. I learned to slip by his shop without him noticing. More than anything I was afraid he would eventually turn to father. Whether that actually happened, and father paid, I never learned. Or maybe he understood my great distress and decided to let it go and cancel the debt?

This story is just one example of the relations at home. We were always protected and looked after, but still . . . Some distance was observed between us and [our] parents, and also among the siblings. I didn't know how it was in other homes, but there was a kind of unwritten law to keep feelings and thoughts to yourself, to keep "secrets" thoroughly wrapped. Nor were there all kinds of expressions of intimacy, no kisses, no hugs, almost. My parents were also strict about not showing physical closeness, as though there was some barrier that must not be passed. Only on Friday nights or religious holidays we would approach father, after he returned from synagogue, after kiddush, each in turn, in order of age, and he would put his hands on our head, bless us, and kiss us. Or those evening when father sat next to the girls' bed (we were very little then) saying the evening prayer "The Angel of Redemption"—hamalakh hagoel—repeating every word of his. The final sentence was: "God is with me, and I will not fear." I knew what the words meant, and when I was afraid at night, I tried to use them to feel stronger: God watches over me, there's nothing to be afraid of! These moments of intimacy, mostly, were somehow connected with religion . . .

Winter, the end of the Shabbat. Father and the boys were still in the synagogue. We, the girls, were hanging around near the steps to the synagogue, our eyes on the sky, waiting for the first three stars to appear, the sign that the Shabbat had ended. Then we could run home and switch on the lights even though the men hadn't finished prayers yet. Because we could not even spot one single star, we gave up and went home. The living room was shrouded in a dusk, it was not completely dark yet. The stove in the corner was scalding hot, the chimney flue glowing red, providing most of the lighting. Mother and little Eva sad huddled, close by the stove and mother was singing in her quiet gentle voice. It was a moment of rare intimacy, Erika and I sat on low stools, very near. Mother sang a Hungarian love song. These songs usually had a tragic undertone, disappointed love, separation forever, death of the beloved, and so on and so forth. Maybe the dusk in the room made mother feel free of the usual holds and inhibitions. One of these beautiful songs I remember to this very day, words and tune: "If you had come to the café today, my fair boy, I would have talked to you, I would have told you all was over between us, my fair boy" . . . We sit in silence, holding our breath so the spell won't suddenly break, and I think, if only the three stars wouldn't appear, so we could all go on sitting like this huddled in the dusk with mama singing in her beautiful, delicate voice.

On winter evenings our kitchen would suddenly change its appearance. A big table was added, in the middle of which a pile of feathers collected from countless geese throughout the year. Around the table sat five or six old farmers' wives (maybe that's only how they appeared to us) and they were dealing with the feathers. This is how it went: Each woman around the table had to take a handful of feathers, put it down in the space made by their apron in their lap and remove each and every feather from its vane, to build a soft heap on the table in front of them. These soft feathers would be used to fill a new duvet. A bystander might have considered it a punishment inflicted by Cinderella's stepmother, or a kind of pointless drudgery, but this was not so. These were thrilling nights, full of excitement, with the actual work of plucking wholly secondary. The "senior" farmer would get up every so often to shove the feathers into a sack which eventually turned into the long-awaited duvet. These feathers however were only part of the goose feathers used in our household. There was also the soft, delicate down from the belly area which needed no treatment. There was only a tiny quantity of it, but its quality . . . ! Unfathomable softness. It took some years of collecting to make a down duvet. And there were the large, coarse feathers which were passed on to experts: their vanes were woven into brushes used for spreading things on cakes and cookies before baking. And finally the wings, which were turned into small brushes for cleaning the corners of the house, hidden spots below wardrobes and so on. No feather, in fact, was wasted. This work with and processing of feathers became, over the years, a symbol of the good housewife. I remember this saying: A good housewife will jump across the fence to get hold one fly-away feather. There were times like that, really!

All these women were dressed in several layers of skirts, they were always dark (due to their age), shirts of a similar color, kerchiefs tied under their chin, faces ploughed through with creases, callused hands, women who from their earliest childhood had worked hard in home, field and farm. They looked joyless and lacking any expectations from life. Sometimes I saw them, sitting like that around the table, like huge chickens perching on their bar in the coop as night was falling. Earlier in the evening the women gossiped: stories about a lazy daughter in law or about a son in law who spent too much time at the inn. Sometimes the husband—"that old beast"—was the culprit. How he had burnt his new shirt on Sunday when he lay down for a rest and fell asleep with a cigar in his mouth. Or the fashion doll granddaughter who was only fourteen and already putting all kinds of creams on her face and plucking her eyebrows. We were not all that interested in this part of the evening but we knew the mood would change after tea and the apples that were baking in the oven. As the hands of the clock moved on, there would be the horror stories and fairy tales, which even if you had heard them more than once would always give us goosebumps. About cursed princesses, about the cruel king who jailed his only son in a pit full of snakes and rats, and one of them sung the saddest ballads in the world.

We girls were seated at the end of the table, afraid to breathe for sheer terror but also of the moment we would be sent off to bed. My gaze strayed to the kitchen window: it was pitch dark outside. Walking up closer to the window I must still have been lingering in a fantasy world. What I saw was not our usual yard. It had turned into a mysterious forest and I saw the shining eyes of Viktorka, the beautiful girl who went mad with disappointed love, as if she has just come out of Božena Nemcová's story. There she was running, her dress torn and her feet dripping blood, her tangled hair loose in the wind, and no one could ever save her. . .

The feast continued evening upon evening, but once the sack was filled, it would all come to an end. A kind of party was held on the last evening, cake or cookies were served, and the women received a glass of sweet rum or liqueur in addition to their tea. Wishes for health and happiness were expressed, and after getting their very small payment, they were swallowed by the darkness in the yard . . .

A group of jugglers arrived in town. They set up all the equipment, a thicket of poles, they fastened ropes, trapezes, etc. A real circus! In the evenings they performed breathtaking shows, and we children followed their each and every movement with pleasure and mortal fear. But we were especially mesmerized by a girl our age, a beauty of about ten or eleven who appeared in a tightrope act at enormous height. She sparked my and my friends' imagination as we stood down below in the crowd. She seemed a fairy tale figure, a princess from other worlds. And yet, in spite of all the difference and remoteness, I felt that underneath her heavy makeup and her sparkling costume, she was a girl like us, hungry for the company of her peers. The question was, who would make the first move. We sent her looks full of curiosity, invitation and encouragement for her to come and approach. Gradually, the barriers fell, and initially hesitant, we became friends. After the show she would join our group of girls. That's how we stood, for hours, on the illuminated, feasting square. The hoarse loudspeaker sounded a Czech march: "Come and walk with us, golden girl, maybe you will have a wonderful experience . . ." and I could not take my eyes off her as she hummed the refrain and moved with indescribable grace to the rhythm of the tune while never stopping the conversation with us. Fascinated like this we stayed every evening until when they would pass with their hats, through the audience who would throw in their pennies. Our parents' implorations went unanswered, about how we would be sure to be late getting up in the morning if we didn't go to sleep immediately. But we were far out in a world without schools, no need to get up early, a world all fantasy and dream, a dream that only vanished when the lights went out, and we had to go home. After some days, they dismantled their structures, everything vanished into the wagons, [and] they too vanished as suddenly as they had appeared. In the morning we found an empty square, and we never had an opportunity to say goodbye, not even to our little "princess" . . .

Weeks and months passed and I entertained myself with the illusion that one day I would wake up and the troupe would be there again on the square. Sometime later a rumor reached our town. Someone had read it in the newspaper, another had heard it on the radio. I did not want to listen to this talk, and whatever did reach my ears, I did not believe. It was a mistake, a lie! But it was the truth: "Our" troupe had broken up following a disaster; the little tightrope walker was killed, she fell and was killed. . .From the distance of years I think of her death and I see how it was the first to penetrate my small and protected world. Sometime later I got to witness my two Christian friends, who suffered from tuberculosis, dressed up like brides, in their coffins and their faces yellow like wax, their hands folded together and on their chest some forget-me-nots . . . and the smell of incense hit and blurred my senses in the darkened room.

On the outskirts of the town lived the gypsies of my childhood, "the music-makers." A type of nation nearly all of whose sons were born with a natural gift for music. Without studies, without being able to read notes, they played their instrument (mainly string instruments) from earliest childhood till grand old age. Some, especially in the big cities, grew famous and reached the top. They managed to play on the radio or in luxury restaurants, and sometimes they attained wealth. The gypsies in Šurany were very far from [having attained] such a position. They stayed in a kind of *place that was actually a ghetto, no stranger ever entered or even approached their area. We were scared of them, but at the same time we were attracted by the air of foreignness and mystique surrounding them. When we went out, second or third grade girls, for a walk on Saturdays, we sometimes went all the way over there. We stopped at a safe distance and found a spot for observation. It was like watching some film about people who were lost, exiled to some island for lepers, disconnected from the world. Men, women and children were moving as if in their sleep, mongrel dogs wandered between poor clay huts. The place was wrapped in sadness and a strange monotony which we felt distinctly from where we observing them. There was a contradiction here which I found hard to understand: How could people, who had music in their soul, look so depressed and lacking in vitality. Their settlement looked lifeless, the square at the center was covered in quicksand during the winter, and in the summer everything was covered in clouds of dust. We stood hypnotized and could not take our eyes off this. We were forced to leave the place only when the dogs noticed us and began to bark.*

On Fridays, when begging was allowed, some of them, mainly those with obvious physical disabilities or some form of retardation, came and begged at the doors of shops and houses. I especially remember a couple, man and wife probably, who were a really grotesque spectacle. Each had some eye defect, which caused the woman to look only upward holding her head raised, while the man was able only to lower his gaze to the ground. Two people whose eyes would never meet. He wore the same type of brown, rough and worn-out suit as most of the men there, more or less, and the same brown felt hat whose shape is undefinable. The woman wore a regular dress, one that surely had seen better days when still in the wardrobe of some lady in Šurany.

Another type entirely were the "Romanian" [Roma] gypsies who drifted across the whole of Europe and whose homes were nowhere. They were colorful figures who got about on wagons carrying their "property," with many children and a dog chained below the wagon, something that always again broke our heart. Rumor around them was rife and no one knew how much of those stories was true and how much invention: they stole children, hid them in faraway places in dark caves where they trained them to become thieves.

When such a group visited the town we were on high alert. They would park on some empty lot and from there they headed in all directions. Traders had to be more than doubly sharp about protecting their wares, and the same went for housewives when it came to the laundry drying on the line, chickens and geese in the coops . . . There was an old woman among them by the name of Boriška who was very well known throughout town. Her face was the color of a nut, and it was grooved like a nut too. Her dress, consisting of a type of wide colorful tunics, was many-layered and the vegetable vendors on the market could not find out how she managed to pilfer the best fruit and vegetables and conceal them between the layers of her useful costume. My father reached the logical conclusion that he would close the shop as soon he saw her coming down the street on her way to "buy" something in our shop. He did not believe he would be able to protect his merchandise—not even with our joint support—when Boriška came to sample things. The shop would close until things blew over. Acting more hospitably would have been too costly . . .

Christmas Eve. I went out with a small group of friends into the clear, enchanted night. We walked a long way, towards the Christian quarters. The streets were deserted, windows lit up, everybody sitting down for their holiday dinner before midnight mass. I envied them so much, that night! Why didn't our festivals have that sacred feel? We walked in silence, not to interfere with the magic of the moment. It was a clear, moonlit night with lots and lots of stars. The snow on the path was dry and crisp, glittering in the moonlight. All you could hear were our footsteps. I vividly recall the snow squeaking underfoot, a sound that filled me with unspeakable joy. I was in high spirits and an unusual optimism came over me. All of a sudden, the world seemed so beautiful, so full of promise, as if there were no wars, the future no longer threatening, and nothing existed but this hush and this wonderful crunching of the snow under our shoes. How many such moments happen in a lifetime? How many of them does the future hold?

Student

At the Jewish school we went to there were five classes, distributed over two rooms: one of them held the first and second grades with Mrs. Weiler, the teacher, and in the other, were the third, fourth, and fifth grades with Mr. Samuel K. (yes, Andy's father), who also was the principal. As soon as I started first grade, I understood there were expectations of me, and I would have to prove myself—simply because my two brothers had come before me. They had made themselves a name as brilliant pupils. I remember a girl who was studying with the bigger children approaching me during break time, eyeing me curiously, and asking: "Are you a good pupil, too, like your brothers?" I did not know what to say, but I took note when another girl, a class mate of mine, answered on my behalf: "No, she's not so good at all." Which was the truth. I never matched their level even though I was considered a good pupil in those years.

At school in Šurany we celebrated the two most important national holidays of the Republic: Independence Day on 28 October, and the birthday of our beloved president Tomáš Garrigue Masaryk on 7 March. The tricolor, white, blue and red, hung from every house. On such an occasion, father received a big order from the municipality to sew a new supply of flags for public buildings. A sewing machine was brought into the shop and a hired seamstress worked round the clock in order to make it in time for the holiday. I loved the fresh smell of cotton in the shop which always meant the approach of the holiday.

On these holidays our school too was covered in decorations from top to bottom. Some students were chosen to recite, there was communal singing. On these festive occasions all five classes assembled in the big children's classroom, with three or four children squeezing together in each two-person bench. All along the walls stood the invited guests and some parents. I was in second grade. I had a fixed place, on such celebrations, in Nadja Izakovič's bench, a fifth grader who had taken me under her wing from when I started school. She fostered me, she served as a kind of older sister. Nadja was half-Jewish and her Jewish father had died. She lived far from most of us, so that I only met her in school. She belonged with the fortunate high-ranking staff of the sugar factory whose living standard was the envy of most of the town. Nadja had a boyish look, she was full of beans, gifted at sports. I felt lucky that of all girls, I was chosen to be her protégé.

The party begins. Dressed in our finest clothes, full of expectations, we all crowd together. I too was chosen to recite (by heart!) a poem dedicated to Masaryk's birthday [which] I managed, despite feeling very shaky in my legs, to recite without mistakes, I was no disappointment. During the party, a bit late, Mrs. (Pani) Sklenárová arrived, the mother of two students, Milan and Rudo. She was not just any other mother. She belonged to a Czech Protestant family and preferred to send her children to a Jewish school. The father was a former legionnaire (enlisted in Masaryk's legion during World War I). They were an extraordinary and well-loved family. The lady took a very active role in the school's cultural and artistic activities, contributing her talents and her inexhaustible energy. So it came as no surprise that they called me onto the stage once again, so as not to, God forbid, leave out Mrs. Sklenárová. By this point I was already flushed and sweaty, due to both the crowding and the great honor that had come my way. But that wasn't the end of the story. At the end of the evening, my father also joined. Mr. K., the teacher, thought it would be inappropriate if the popular recitation was not presented to him as well, and as a token of respect I was called onto the stage a third time where, with what was left of my strength, I managed [once more] to recite the celebratory poem. I don't remember having reaped such artistic success ever since . . . Later all students and guests went to the synagogue for a prayer dedicated to the president. The local dignitaries, [and] our rabbi attended, the atmosphere was festive. We sang the national anthem under the direction of Mr. K., [and] the rabbi gave a sermon, at the end of which we left quietly and in perfect order, as was our wont.

In third grade I moved to the big ones' classroom. There three classes[,] third, fourth, and fifth grade, studied together. Here things already were a lot more complicated and sophisticated. Teaching was done in rotation: When Mr. K. (who must have been a true virtuoso) was teaching the lower grade (us), he would make the two higher grades do individual work, and the other way around. When our group was doing individual work, I was always listening in to what was being said there, among the older ones, and on certain occasions I was insolent enough to raise my hand and offer the right answer. Of course that was [during] a language lesson.

I reached the final class [of elementary school] and decided to take the exams and study the following year at the Gymnasium in the nearby town, Nové Zámky. This was a bold and rather pretentious decision. As was to be expected, my parents were strongly opposed, for various different reasons, starting with "You can study here in Šurany at Meštianská škola," which was a kind of local secondary school, of a much lower level than the prestigious Gymnasium, "just *like everybody else." And: "You are too weak for such a strenuous physical effort, to get up so early in the winter, in the snow, when it's still dark outside, and get to the train station and travel every day, you won't cope." But they left me some kind of hope, "Let's see. If you do well here you can take the test in another two years when you'll be stronger and then switch." I understood I was not going to gain the upper hand in this discussion and I stopped mentioning the subject, and I continued my actions secretly. Our teacher, Mr. K. ran a preparatory course—on a voluntary basis of course—after school hours for children who wanted to try the Gymnasium's admission exam. Graduates from our school had a high level in spite of difficult physical conditions, but our teacher, averse of taking the risk, gave the children some additional, thorough preparation. You mainly studied language and arithmetic. I registered (my parents did not know), and toward the end of the course we took a mock test. Having passed that test successfully, I turned to my parents again, facing them with a fait accompli. In view of my determination and steadfastness, as they say, my parents gave up. I felt no one could be happier than me. The world was about to open its doors to me, my obsessive, inborn pull "outward" was going to materialize. I would try new, exciting things, I would leave the small town's confines.*

The day of the exam arrived. I traveled with father, and we took along my good friend Helenka Seidlová, whose father had been faraway in Palestine for some years, and she, together with her sister Mariška and a little brother lived with their mother and grandmother. I was happy that Helenka was going to be with us and that my father was going to look after her as he looked after me. We were also joined by my cousin Ady, whose decision to take the exam surprised us because he was known to be an average, or even lower than average, student . . .

When we arrived at the Gymnasium's front yard, a large group of boys and girls had already gathered. We joined the others who were waiting. It seemed to me that the majority were girls and their mature looks surprised me, their fashionable dress, their professional haircuts. They did not look excited or worried by the occasion. Suddenly I felt all my self-confidence dwindling, my heart filling up with doubts and fears. How had I even dared to think of this idea? What chances did I have to compete with these girls, girls from the "big world"? (For some reason, I felt nothing at all about the boys.) But when the gate opened and we were put into a classroom, I grew calmer again. Someone explained the exam procedure and distributed sheets. We took an oral and written exam in language and an exam in arithmetic. About two hours later we went out again into the open air of the yard to wait for the results. After an eternity, someone appeared in a window on the first floor and read out the list of the lucky ones who had passed the exam. Many foreign sounding names could be heard, and I also clearly heard Helenka's name. And what about my name? Panic struck and things looked bleak, I had failed! One moment I felt optimistic, the next I despaired. I looked at father, but there was no encouragement to be found there either, his face looked tense too. Thoughts were racing through my head, What if I had not passed, how would I cope with my shame? I was so immersed that I did not notice when my name was finally read out too, and it was only father's hug that brought me back to reality: I had passed! In September I would start at the "Czech Gymnasium for Secondary Education, the Hungarian Branch, Nové Zámky"—that was the long, respectable name of my new school. Until this very day I am convinced that this was the most important and dramatic event of my childhood.

Our way back to the train station felt like floating on clouds. I looked at father who did not even try to hide how pleased he was, and I was proud I had not disappointed him. And something else: This was one of the rare occasions when I felt the intimacy of our closeness. That day he was my father. The one less pleasant thing was that my cousin Ady was not among the successful ones who passed the exam (his fateful mistake had been to write the name of Jesus—Kristus—with a small k, and this was unforgivable, poor boy.)

At the station, father invited us all to celebrate the event in a kind of restaurant with a raspberry drink. No, this was not the same kind of raspberry drink we had at home almost every day. This was raspberry juice in a real café, in which, until that day, I had never set foot. I felt this was a due reward for all our tension and effort. I can still see the bright red color of the drink, with sparkling bubbles dancing inside, and the dew drops on the tall, cold glass. What a moment of joy!

At home we were received as the heroes of the day. Mother made my favorite meal which included, of course, garden pea soup, which still remains my best loved soup. But I knew the party would not last forever, and that I was only "queen for a day." But one fact did not change: I had become our family's one representative at the Gymnasium (until Öcsi joined one year later).

So I left the security of our school in Šurany where the teachers were like family. I knew them in their everyday lives, their children were my good friends, and I could always trust their good will and their pure intentions. What was awaiting me in that alien place, a place in which I would probably be no more than a tiny, unimportant crumb.

Now I was in a different place. It took me time to get used to the unfamiliar, Christian surroundings, to start the day with "Our Father Who Art in Heaven," and the unfamiliar smell every morning on entering the building. Here, there was a teacher for each subject and you turned to them with "Mr. Professor," and they addressed us, little girls, in the third person singular, with a kind of fathomless seriousness and politeness. Everything was done in an unfamiliar style, and the senior students in the background left me with my jaw dropping. Such unhurried elegance, everybody seemed to know their place and stick to unwritten rules. Tradition gave the place its aristocratic countenance.

14.IX.1937. It was only two weeks after I began my studies at the Nové Zámky Gymnasium. In the middle of a class the principal walked into the classroom and asked the teacher permission to make an announcement: "Studies will stop now. Please collect your satchels and return home quietly. Our dear president Tomas Garrigue Masaryk has died today." The class burst into hysterical tears. Today it is hard to understand how I loved Masaryk, the first president of the Republic, was. I adored him, for me he was the perfect man incarnate. The perfect leader. He was educated, a philosopher, a great humanist, spoke many languages, and was a champion of justice and truth. But there were two more things I admired in Masaryk. First, his unusual beauty. He was beautiful in his younger years, and in old age his beauty was stunning. Into his eighties he sat astride his beloved horse Hector, straight backed, in his legionnaire's costume, looking like a fairy tale prince. Even though he was part of a larger group of kings and princes, all eyes were on him. "He's a born prince. The way he moves his body, his noble gait, his perfect manner, and yet his almost childlike simplicity and innocence. Something like that is not learned, one has to be born a prince for that," people said.

Masaryk was perhaps the first (and last) feminist man I heard of. Women never forgot his exceptional act when he adopted his wife's family name—Garrigue—to precede his own, Masaryk—for short: T. G. M. and they considered it proof of his respect for all women. Yet regardless of Masaryk's great sensitivity, Mrs. Charlotte Garrigue Masaryk was not spared the fate of many of the wives of ideologues and national liberators throughout the history of mankind, and of women on the whole.

As I write this I realize how he influenced me, in the values that guided me, by which I wanted to live my own life. I don't want to say that I did not receive values at home. On the contrary, Masaryk, for me, confirmed that the values we were taught at home were universal and victorious. For me, Masaryk's motto, "Truth will prevail," was not an empty slogan but a signpost pointing into the right direction for one's personal life, for the family and the life of the entire Republic. Masaryk, for me, symbolized the human spirit, the spirit's desire to develop, learn, become educated. I believed, then, that nothing could stop this desire. If Masaryk could, so could I. He was, after all, not born a "prince," his parents had been poor sharecroppers lacking any human rights. His father was a coachman on a landowner's estate and his mother a cook in the castle. His parents sent him off, aged eleven, to become a blacksmith so he could add to the family's income. An accidental encounter with a former teacher enabled him to continue his studies, first at secondary school and then university. I felt, at the time, that I, a student at the Gymnasium, could go on studying, I believed nothing could prevent me.

I studied in a girls' class, one that was not at all homogeneous. There was the first circle, the "flashy circle" made up by the town's girls, daughters of dignitaries and famous people. This included the daughter of the Gymnasium's principal, the daughter of the mayor, Éva Bielická, with whom I actually became friends, the daughters of the high-ranking officials in important institutions. They were largely Czechs. It was hard to get into this circle, if it all, but there were other circles and after a short time I found my place. I learned that it was not difficult for me to become part of a Christian environment and make friends.

No one supervised us at home when we did our homework, and this was for several reasons: my parents' lack of time, [and] their lack of command of the language and the study material. So everything was up to us. I used to postpone my homework from the afternoon to the evening, and come evening, being tired, I would fool myself that I would manage to look over the material in the waiting room at the train station, in the morning, and if worse came to worst, on the train. I don't remember this working out even once. Often I did not manage to open a book before the school bell. I was lucky they were subjects that required no review.

The teachers, predominantly Czechs, treated me fairly (excepting one teacher to whom I will return). There were the Procházkas, the husband a geography teacher, and the wife teaching natural science. I remember her desk full of plants, and how I'd feel sick at the thought of being called in front of the blackboard to name them. And when, eventually, I was called, unprepared as usual, she herself offered the pretext for my failure, reminding me that I had been absent a few times, recently, due to illness. "You will have to make up for what you missed," she said and did not grade me.

Our math teacher was an old bachelor who looked like a bear (to us at least), a peculiar man whose name was Šir. As he paced between the benches he would stop by my side, glance into my copybook and stroke my hair, or open and close the zippers of the pockets in my sweater, amused at that wondrous invention which he had never seen before.

The music and choir teacher mainly focused on the "flashy circle," girls who were his private piano students. His explanations were addressed exclusively to them, they were asked to reply to his questions, etc. He took no interest at all in the other girls, did not know their names, and certainly did not test them. We, the "anonymous girls," collectively and automatically were graded two (good). Only his piano pupils were awarded a one (very good). It was a convenient arrangement for all parties. Too bad, only, that I did not enrich my poor knowledge of the world of music during that year.

I had a serious problem with my Slovakian language teacher, Kettner, who was known as a Slovakian nationalist and no great lover of Jews and Czechs. I had a real opportunity to learn about this at the very start of the year. Once a month one had to write a paper, it was called "monthly assignment" or "composition," and was very important, constituting a major part of the final grade. Copybooks for this particular purpose were handed out at the start of the lesson. The atmosphere was very tense and it was unusually quiet in the classroom as the teacher wrote the topic for the assignment on the blackboard and sat down in order to make sure there were no improper behaviors, that no one would, God forbid, peep into her neighbor's copybook and similar tricks. The copybooks were returned about a week later, corrected and graded. This teacher had an offensive habit. Before returning the copybooks he would read aloud a list of the grades from high to low. The elite group who received a grade one, which never was long, followed by all the others, down to the miserable last ones who received a five (unsatisfactory). This was a very dramatic moment, but I sat unperturbed and self- confident. What was there to worry, this was, after all, "my" subject in which I always did effortlessly well. To my astonishment, my name appeared neither in the first group nor in the second, only somewhere in the middle with a grade 3 or 3-(sufficient). I was dumbfounded. This could not be! It must be a mistake. When I received the copybook back I looked for a "Red Sea" of corrections, but to my great astonishment or confusion, there was no such thing, other than a comma or a period here or there. Why did I get a "sufficient" grade? I was on the verge of tears.

This spectacle was repeated month after month. Why didn't I ask? Why didn't I turn to the teacher for an explanation of the low marks while my compositions were almost flawless? I was familiar with the hatred of Jews from the past and in the present, we heard rascals in Šurany cursing and yelling at us: "Jews to Palestine," or sometimes for a change, "Jews to Madagascar." We took these expressions as no more than bothersome flies with which we had somehow learned to live. They were "punks" from whom we could not expect a fair attitude. But this respectable professor, the Gymnasium's vice-principal? How come he descended to this level? He fought me and the other Jewish students with the weapon he had at his disposal, by giving unfair marks. In time I learned that the blind hatred of Jews exists in all [social] layers and that neither "punks" nor professors mind hounding a little Jewish girl . . .

A miracle happened towards mid-term. Kettner was transferred to another function and we got a new, Czech teacher, a woman with the rather strange name Cebecauerová and I started to observe a change in my marks for the monthly assignments. I asked myself one question only: What does she think to herself when she sees my earlier marks?

I continued my studies at the Nové Zámky Gymnasium. Every so often I would suffer pangs of conscience for having imposed my will on my parents without any thought of how much it cost, these studies. They were expensive for everyone, but for us, Jewish children, they cost even more. First, there was the Shabbat. Studies went on as usual on Saturdays, but because we were forbidden to travel, we were obliged to find somewhere to stay during weekends and this cost our parents a lot of money. When I could set aside this unpleasant fact, I could enjoy the interest and novelty this added to our lives. First, [there was the] absolute autonomy. We were a group of six girls and one boy and we fully exploited our freedom. We would wander about town, getting up to all sorts of mischief which often ended badly.

Usually I went hungry all through the Shabbat because I did not like the meals we were given at the Bribram family, who ran the pension. From the moment I set foot into the building my nose was hit by the unbearable smell of "laundered duck," and my appetite did not improve at the sight of the pile of parts of this disgusting bird. I refused to eat and the one dish that crossed my lips was some slices of yeast cake I exchanged with the other girls for meat, fish and side dishes. This was a good arrangement for all parties for some months, until it all blew up unexpectedly when one of the girls betrayed me and told my parents everything. There was great dismay. How could I do something like this? Their good money was being thrown away, and how could I behave so irresponsibly? Such things and the like were what I was accused of. I was ashamed and no matter what I said in my defense—the laundered duck, the fish served cold and not as I was used at home—none of this was admissible. Things were dramatically clarified with the owner who, by the way, was deeply insulted by the affair. And the result? My independence of choice in matters of menu came to an end, I was under surveillance from all directions, and more specifically, my uncle Heni, who lived in town, was appointed supervisor.

Another additional expenditure was our private religious lessons. Like all students who were not Catholics (the country's official religion) we were required to receive instruction in our own religion, Judaism. We went to our ancient teacher, Mr. Graf. I still see him before my eyes very vividly. He was so fat he could hardly move from his spot at the head of the table. Seated in his sitting room, we would read chapters from the Bible, and there were lots of giggles each time we came across some juicy sentence, which sorely annoyed the old teacher. These religious lessons were mainly a source of entertainment. His wife, who was many years his junior, usually stayed in the back of the apartment from which you heard the dull noises of her doing her chores. Sometimes when the teacher nevertheless left for a moment, she would appear on tiptoes in order to inform us about some details of their joint lives. This is how we learned that she was his second (or third?) wife and thirty years younger than him.

One day, in the middle of a lesson, there was a knock on the door and a beggar woman appeared. Our presence made him feel uneasy, he knew he could not ignore the poor woman. He cast a fearful look towards the rooms, rose heavily, moved over to the sideboard, took out a sugar cube and headed for the door. But suddenly, as though remembering something, he turned back, broke the sugar cube into two and went over to the beggar woman. We saw his face, the satisfied expression, he felt he had done a great good deed.

These extra expenditures troubled my conscience quite a bit. Some solace came at the end of the year when my name appeared in bold print in the school's magazine. This meant that I was among the excellent students and entitled to a big reduction in school fees. How this came about, I still don't understand.

The year came to an end, and I was looking ahead full of optimism. It was a summer of happiness and I did not know this was to be our last happy summer. We traveled with father, for the first time in my life, to a real resort. Neither to relatives, nor to grandfather in Topolčany, but to a beautiful resort. We rented a room for three unforgettable weeks. Father took us there because of his rheumatism which required hot baths. But, as usual, since his conscience would not allow him to leave mother with the shop and the five of us, he took Andy, Erika, and me along. It was a wonderful place, surrounded by mountains and forests. There was an ancient, picturesque castle and a swimming pool. I spent hours listening to the saccharine music from the balcony, looking at the lovers sunbathing on the lawn or, towards evening, dancing on the parquet to music produced by a real orchestra, dressed beautifully and radiating happiness and romance. I had never come into such close contact with the "sweet life" about which I read in Krásny roman, love stories. The world appeared a place in which it was worth growing up, a world holding plenty of happiness and excitement.

That was the summer, also, during which I had my first period, a subject that had never been mentioned directly at home. I would pick up a word or two from conversations between my mother and aunt Katinka, Gézko's wife, or the maid who would confide to me that her friend did not get "her thing," the poor one, and was in great danger. Some girls in class were at times excused from sports. We all knew what was the matter, but nothing was said about it.

The festival of Shavuot was approaching. It was decided that I would go directly from school to Aunt Jolly, her husband Uncle Miklos and their beloved little daughter Žužika in Párkány. I felt so big and independent for being allowed to make the journey on my own. On the eve of the festival we had a good time and went to sleep late. When I woke I understood it was late. It was totally silent in the house[,] they must have left with the girl according to plan to swim on the Hungarian side of the Danube (the river formed the international border between the two countries). I could not have joined anyway because I did not have a passport and they decided to let me sleep.

I felt strange, I had never felt this way. I felt I was lying in a kind of puddle and I did not dare to look what it was, yet I also knew I couldn't postpone looking for too long, and when I saw that the strange puddle was blood, I became panicky. My first thought was to hide the evidence quickly. I took down the sheets and tried to clean them in the shower. As far as I could—the reader can form their own idea. In the face of this failure, another thought occurred: To escape, run away and never return. But where could I go, I was, after all, in a town I didn't know. I remembered some girls I got to know on earlier visits. Two of them, sisters, and the daughters of a cantor or a butcher, who lived in the yard of a synagogue, somehow seemed to be the right partners for this plan. My aunt's house was in a suburb, not so near the center, but even though my movements were a bit awkward it didn't take me all that long. I joined in their games, but I wasn't focused because my thoughts were distracted. I felt totally exhausted, I had not had a meal in the morning and I wasn't invited for lunch either. I had to tell them about my plans to run away, I was just waiting for the right moment to let them know. "I want to run away, do you want to come with me?" Only one of them showed willingness to join the adventure. Our plan was that we would first go by my aunt's house, take provisions for on the way—I hoped my family had not returned yet—and then set out . . . And indeed, in the empty house we only found the maid who had just returned from her holiday. I remembered a big cream cake in the larder from that morning. It still was there but had miraculously changed shape since then. Now it looked black and was abuzz with frenzied motion. From closer up you could see hundreds of ants creeping over the cake. We did not want to tarry, we went out and began to head for the unknown. We walked and walked until it was totally dark and we were quite a long way from the town whose distant lights did not encourage us to go on. This must have been what eventually caused the, already weak, wind in our sails to die down completely. We stopped and sat by a mile stone on the roadside. We stared into the dark and were scared. Clearly our escape had failed. We turned around and with hesitant steps that grew ever faster until we nearly broke into a run, we returned to the town. When I entered the house and my worried aunt saw me (I must have looked awful), she did not even mention my bizarre disappearance, and only said gently: "You are a big girl now," and kissed me. Oh how grateful I was! The next day she traveled with me to my home to deliver the "big girl" to her parents.

After the summer vacation I returned to the Gymnasium. This year Öcsi too would study there. Though he passed the entry exam, he didn't know any Latin, so he had to start in third grade rather than fourth, as suited his age. It was a great victory to have resisted the heavy pressure the rabbis had put on father for years, not to send their son to a "goyish school." The two of us, together with another girl from Šurany, found rooms with a Jewish family to spend the weekends. Magda and I shared the room, and Öcsi was given a sofa in the nursery school which the aging daughter of the family ran at home. No more Bribram pension! I was cheered by the change and looked forward not having to cope with laundered duck on my plate. But there was no dearth of shortcomings in the new place either.

Fate had it that we did not spend many Saturdays in our new premises. The year seemed to have started off on a bad footing. There was a restlessness in the air, the German minority in the Sudetenland rose up, and in south Slovakia Hungarians began to demand annexation to their "motherland." Feverish international activities were underway concerning the problems of the various nationalities. All of these were hankering after various parts of the Republic, which *was forced to mobilize its reservists. We felt that a period of calm and security was coming to an end, and that the future was likely to bring something bad, very bad. Debates between students of the two ethnic groups were intense. They started with verbal collisions, a lot of shouting which escalated into physical violence. What shocked and scared me was the Czechs' massive departure from the town. They had come to Slovakia in the early years of the Republic to take up official functions the Slovakians themselves were not yet trained to undertake. This caused great animosity and an explicit striving, on the part of the Slovakians, to separate and declare independence, and in time they realized this goal. The "flashy circle," the envy of the entire class, packed their suitcases and returned to their faraway homeland. There was something sad and heart rending about the rush in which they left, as though the ground was burning under their feet. (Not so many years later I witnessed departures that were incomparably more rushed and tragic, but at this point my poor imagination could not fathom such a possibility.) The admired Czech teachers, too, disappeared. Nobody at this point knew what would be, there were all kinds of rumors. We tried to remain optimistic in spite of the daily worsening crisis. One student in my class said to me: "You Jews will probably be happy for the Hungarians to move in here, haven't you always supported the Hungarians?" (After the invasion she and her parents were among those who were welcoming the "liberating" Hungarian army most loudly.) Proper teaching had stopped. Our minds, those of the teachers who stayed behind as well as of the students, were somewhere else.*

Persecuted

---

*1938, Yom Kippur. It's the first time I fast through the day,
like the adults. I feel important, I belong . . . But the day, so
bright, full of promise and happy feelings, ended badly. The family
returns home from synagogue, we set the table, there are the bless-
ings marking the end of the holiday. I can smell the food, soon
we will break the fast . . . These are days of instability, full
of doom, especially here in the Republic of Czechoslovakia. Father
switches on the radio. Even before I manage to swallow my first
bite of meatball, I hear the voice of the news reader from Prague,
a dramatic, ill-boding voice, announcing a speech by the president
Eduard Beneš, and next he's already speaking, his voice trembles,
and here and there fails him completely. Addressing the people, he
announces his resignation and his intention to leave the country.
Three words he spoke are engraved in my memory: "Ja mám plan"—I have
a plan. Three words which became history and were quoted for many
years. He bade farewell to the people and asked their forgiveness,
saying that he was unable to collaborate with people whose intention
it was to tear the country apart, give away large parts to Germany
and Hungary (the Munich pact). All he could do was leave to England,
from where he would try to save what was possible. He had a plan!
Within moments, the mood in the room changed. The adults, pale and
appalled. [Sic] That was it. It had begun! Something bad, very bad,
was about to happen! The meat stuck in my throat, I couldn't swallow. My body started to tremble uncontrollably. The meal was done,
as far as I was concerned at least. Things would never be the same
again, I felt, the future looked scary. Still trembling all over,
I found myself in bed, unable to calm down. Afraid and trembling.
Father went to the shop and we could hear him for the next hours
moving the more expensive bales of cloth to our apartment in order
to save what was possible, in case there was looting—a new concept
for me. Head of the family and father of five, he looked beyond the
riots and his present concern was the family's livelihood. But the
expected riots never materialized (the rabble apparently did not get
the authorities' go-ahead) and there were no attacks on Jewish businesses. Worries still gnawed, nevertheless. The main question was
whether we would be annexed to Hungary or remain part of Slovakia
which had received autonomy. The grown-ups were in favor of annexation. They still remembered the Hungarians from before 1918 when*

they lived in relative peace under the Austro-Hungarian monarchy. They trusted the Hungarians, partly because they were familiar with the culture, as opposed to their serious fears of the uncultivated Slovaks. The Slovaks' hate of the Jews, their coarse nationalism, these were well known.

We did not have much time to mull these fateful questions. The die was cast, we were to be annexed to Hungary. Everything was decided, the borders were drawn, the entry of the "liberating forces" scheduled, to us they looked ridiculous, worn and torn, like plucked roosters. Öcsi my brother and Andy K. were so bold as to move ahead to see them coming. They walked some kilometers until they witnessed them before everyone else. On their return I heard Öcsi say: "We saw them and as far as I am concerned they can go back to where they came from! Frankly, they don't impress us, the Hungarian army!"

All this happened early in the day. The evening was still awaiting with a great, unknown upheaval . . .Thursday evening. The traditional bath, a kind of huge wooden tub (there was no running water in the house), washed hair [sic], clean pyjamas and bedsheets. It was a moment of real indulgence! But even before we managed to get into our beds, there was a tremendous "boom." And again. And again. One stone after another hit the window. All kinds of noises could be heard from the street and they were getting louder every moment. Something terrible was happening! The crowd seemed to be answering a call: "Go run and attack the Jews' shops, now, this moment, everything goes, the street is yours!" And that's precisely what they did—with a free hand. People who were neighbors, decent clients, workers, acquaintances even, only yesterday, had turned, at the blink of an eye into savage vandals and looters. We were struck by great anxiety. The first thing my parents did was to bring us, the three girls, to a family who lived in the back of the yard. Mr. Weiss, the head of the family, was a metal worker, a very poor man who made a living from hard labor. Clearly no one would do any harm to this family and their home seemed safe shelter. We woke them and they made space for the three of us in their very small apartment.

Obviously sleep was out of the question. Even though the apartment was further away from the streets we still heard dull noises, the thundering mob, shrieking. The mob was ecstatic[,] and later we also heard a single gunshot. My parents and "big" brothers stayed in our home, we were very worried about them. I buried my head in a pillow in order not to hear the threatening noise from the street. If only morning would already come!

Come morning we returned to our apartment and heard a little about what had happened at night. The main square, where all Jewish businesses were situated, looked like after a natural disaster.

*I cannot say "like after a pogrom" because it really was a pogrom
. . . Raided shops, almost emptied, quantities of goods they had
not been able to carry along left in the mud, and some few looters
still at it, rummaging. Our shop and Gézko's, next door, were left
unharmed and we heard why: Father, who had served in the army for
four years during the First World War had Christian friends from
that period. One of them was Bartovič who would later become head
of the local council. Our families were on friendly terms. We often
visited their house, very far from the center. When first rumors
about what was going on began to circulate, this man appeared at
our home, armed with a gun, and took position in front of the shop.
When the mob approached he shouted: "I'll shoot anyone who tries to
come near!" and to prove he was in earnest he fired his gun, once,
into the air[:] the gunshot we had heard at night. He also protected
uncle Gézko's shop. Only one simple thing slightly marred this ideal
picture: because [sic] after things had settled down, the wife of
the head of the local council paid a series of visits to our shop,
from which she always returned with plenty of parcels but for which,
with tacit agreement, nothing was paid. That said, he saved us from
big trouble and this was not forgotten.*

*Calm returned during the day, but toward evening the populace
began to gather on the square again. The Jews turned to the authorities with a request for protection. Yes, they could increase polic-
ing but only if they received the necessary financial support. The
Jews paid, they had to come up with such sums every so often, but
nothing much changed on the ground. We continued to go to the Weiss
family and Bartovič appeared again with his gun standing in front
of the shop. I passed these days trembling, my jaws clenched. I
couldn't relax and even when peace finally was restored, I stayed
anxious.*

*This is how the new government began. It took quite sometime
until we understood what was going on and how our lives would look
from now on. First of all, we were disconnected from part of the
family. Grandfather, uncles and aunts, including our beloved Aunt
Jolly and her two lovely girls, stayed on the Slovakian side. Now we
were separated by a border, and not a friendly one, and if we wanted
to see them we would need to use a passport, with all the difficulties and constraints that involved. When longing mounted (especially
mother's), we traveled, Eva and I, together with mother, to grandfather's home where we used to spend the summer vacation every year.
But this visit was different, nothing was left of the cheerfulness
of those summers . . . The mood in town was heavy, like before
impending disaster. In the mornings announcements with new decrees
and prohibitions appeared on the walls and the Jew's living space*

became more and more limited. At grandfather's house, of course, the mood reflected this. And even so we were very happy to see each other, though the happiness was only partial. Some days later we left them with a heavy heart and a sense of foreboding. Who knew whether we would see them again and when? Later it turned out this had indeed been our last encounter. The terrible news reached us in grandfather's final letter. He wrote that all of them, all Slovakian Jews, were to be rounded up and transported to the east. Even though we did not know then what the notion of "being sent to the east" meant, it was a fatal blow on [sic] us, and especially mother, whose entire family had vanished and we had no idea of their fate. At first we tried sending food parcels to some doubtful address, but we never received confirmation that they were received.

We tried to get used to the new situation and the changes it brought in its wake. One important change for me was that the Slovakian Gymnasium in Nové Zámky (Érsekujvár) where I was studying was going to be transferred to Šurany (Nagysurány), my home town. It was an exceptional act for the Hungarians to allow a minority such a privilege. Šurany was on the whole intensely nationalist-Slovakian, and the Hungarians had to make some gesture of good will to keep the peace. I was planning to continue my studies there, but the place made it very difficult for us, Jewish students, to fit in. The teachers' level was lower than we had ever known. Discrimination sometimes bordered on the absurd. I continued, gnashing my teeth, until I couldn't and left, before the end of the year. I looked for alternative solutions. I tried to study at places which were still open to us, but I saw that my dream about "studying," "succeeding," "making it," was coming to an end.

Öcsi was the only one not to give up, as though this reality had nothing to do with him. He did not lose his self-confidence and did everything he could to make it known. It happened that he entered political discussions with his teachers in class, some-times consciously putting himself at risk. The war had started and people who cared about their freedom kept their mouths shut. But my brother Öcsi was exempt from this rule. He was never willing to adjust himself to existing frameworks. He was unable to live in such structures.

And so the war really broke out, as we know, on September 1, 1939. Events seemed to unfold rapidly, as though the world had lost its brakes. War was something new, and yet it felt familiar as though we had been through it long ago. We had been raised on stories about the horrors of the First World War. "Four years the World War raged," we read in our textbooks from the moment we learned to read in the lower grades. Stories about the trenches in France and Italy, a yellowing photograph of Uncle Karol, father's brother, who was killed in the war, father's stories about the Italian front, which always included some funny part. I remember an image (it may have been on a Sunday afternoon when the shop was closed), all of us in the living room, father lying on the couch, reading the paper or napping, but sometimes he would sing. Songs from the war. The room grew so silent that all you could hear was the ticking of the clock. And then father broke into a song which always gave me goosebumps and scared me: "megjött a level a fekete pecséttel, megjött az orosz százezer emberrel"—"the letter with the black stamp arrived, the Russian with a hundred thousand men arrived." And the song ends on [sic] one poor guy who has not died yet but is nevertheless buried . . . Father sang in a pleasant and touching voice. Then silence fell, leaving everyone to their thoughts and fears.

From the outbreak of war the amount of rules against the Jews had multiplied. By now we were considered a state enemy, more or less. Jews were not allowed to work except in certain professions. A period of retraining began: lawyers and other people in the free professions retrained to become shoemakers, tailors, etc. Some took this with a degree of black humor entertaining hopes that it would be temporary. The war would end quickly with the collapse of the Axis states, which included Hungary. This was a wholly unwarranted optimism. The permits of father and the other Jewish shop owners were withdrawn. The shop was closed and sealed by the authorities. Sometime later, a Christian family materialized and the shop and all its contents passed into their hands, probably at a bargain price. Our source of income was blocked. What made things a little easier was the fact that father had made sure, before the new legislation, to put part of the stocks into (another) hiding place and so we could, from time to time, sell to old, faithful customers, taking extreme caution, until nothing remained in store. This was illegal and very risky, especially under the scrutiny of the new owners. Only in the weekends, when the shop closed and they returned to their village, we felt freer. For sometime we made ends meet in this way, with the help of certain moneys we received from people who still owed us.

Suddenly father had a lot of time on his hands. It was sad to see him trying to kill all that time. I didn't know anyone more diligent, most of his time went to the shop or to related travel, it was really hard work at times, but it was always done with great concentration and with an enthusiasm we couldn't understand. Mother took a serious role in the work too, and during busy hours, we, the children, were appointed "observers," especially on market days, Mondays and Thursdays, when the farmers brought their produce from the village and did their own shopping. The shop would fill up then, but not as much as during county fairs when the town swarmed with hundreds of traders from all the corners of the country. One can picture the colorful choice of things for sale! Christian religious articles, meat and sausages fried on the spot, utensils, fabrics, shoes, sweets, toys, etc. etc. On such special occasions we were given a bit of money to "waste." We wandered around a long time before deciding to part with the "property" in our pockets. We always ended buying the same, good, familiar "Turkish honey" which I am still looking for today, wherever I go. On days like that the shop was practically "exploding."

During a lull in business father would use the time to make things easier on mother: He would prepare our afternoon snack, bring coal and wood from the shed, or offer some small services to customers who came from the villages, like for instance filling out all kinds of forms, or listening to their physical complaints and giving them some of the medicinal tea a doctor in Budapest recently prescribed to him. When we went to elementary school we would be taken aback at the sight of father appearing, during break time, with huge slices of bread, covered in butter or goose fat. It was very embarrassing and sometimes I wanted to die of shame. He was always involved in looking after us. On Sunday afternoons, when the shop was closed, he took us on long walks, far out along the road that encircled the sugar factory, during the winter to the frozen river for skating, in the summer for a swim. The objective was two-fold: to give us a good time and to allow mother sometime off. It was sad to see him unemployed now (we had grown too big to need his care).

Seeing him in the room trying to focus on a book, my heart broke. Father was not into books. All the rest of us, including mother, were "bookworms," [but] father just read the daily newspaper, Prager Tagblatt, and later a Hungarian paper whose name I forget. Our radio, one of the few in town, of course played an important role. News, sports, etc. Father liked to have political debates with his friends but he never tried to read a novel.

Mother spent her evenings listening to the radio, but her hands went on working. Any handicraft, knitting, embroidery, darning socks (a boring activity which devolved on me when I grew a little older). Mother had hands of gold, she had the rare gift of "spinning straw into gold." That we managed reasonably well was not to a small extent thanks to her talent. Everything was put to use brilliantly, nothing went lost. In the summer, the house turned into a fruit preserve factory, jams, vegetable preserves, tomato paste, all manner *of pickles, in quantities that lasted through the year. Sometimes father stayed up all night to keep an eye on the powidl or plum jam, as it was cooking in a huge cauldron in the yard. Father made wine, sometimes from unusual fruits, his exclusive patent. Work, work, work . . . Not a moment, not a penny, were wasted. Sometimes I wonder whether my parents also had other times, times of entertainment and pleasure, lack of worry and mischief? How had it been before the four of us started arriving, year upon year (only little Eva was born after a longer break). Did they go to films, a play, a party? There was this one item in our home, a ceramic figurine of a village girl carrying a basket with flowers and on her head a broad-rimmed hat. We knew that they got this figurine one day in a lottery at a party. The figurine sparked my imagination, I saw my parents young, dancing, laughing, mother wearing a jolly flowery dress. I very much liked to see them like this, young and happy . . .*

I would like to expand a little about the Gymnasium in Šurany. They brought in teachers from God knows where, teachers who had not been part of the system at the time of the Republic due to either lack of skills or subversive ideas. This was a big step back. What happened with the graceful atmosphere, the elegant manners? Most students were extreme nationalists. It was these provocative braggarts who now set the tone in our classrooms. The girls were more moderate and friendlier, but still absurd situations sometimes occurred. The common greeting, for instance was the fascist arm salute accompanied by the Slovak Nazis' Na stráž. I had no choice but to answer with this Na stráž (on guard), which made me feel tense and unbearably ashamed. I tried to find ways to avoid meeting these friends after school.

This was only a small part of the grotesque and embarrassing phenomena we had to cope with. It was an inner struggle each morning to get up and go to school. Something else that added to our already troubled existence originated on our own, Jewish religious, side. This was the prohibition on writing on the Shabbat. This prohibition allowed some vengeful teachers to humiliate us, something in which they were eagerly joined by the students. Subjects like drawing, algebra, geometry, etc. were transferred to Saturdays on purpose, and this completely paralyzed us. All we could do was to sit quietly and wait till the end of the hour. I wonder how I agreed to accept such a paralyzing constraint. How come I didn't rebel against this unreasonable rule which galled my life and interfered so much with my studies? Maybe I was afraid my parents would be told, because I did no longer fear God. I suspected that Öcsi had released himself from this idiotic limitation right from the start of his studies, but I never asked him.

In Nové Zámky I had had a problem with Prof. Kettner, the anti-semite. Now, I had more serious problems with most of the teachers. Eventually my fate was sealed—maybe this sounds exaggerated—changing the whole of my life, by the German teacher. He mocked me—as if in good spirit—saying it was no big deal for me being good at German "because you speak a lot of German at home." Here too we were assigned monthly compositions. A student who sat near me regularly let me help her with German by often copying me shamelessly. I had finished writing, my copybook lay, as it should, closed at the edge of my table. When I leaned over to quickly answer some question from my neighbor, I saw the teacher jumping up and telling me furiously to pass him my copybook. When I commented that my copybook was already closed, he reacted angrily.

Due to some illness I was not present in class when the corrected copybooks were returned. A student, the son of our family doctor, brought me mine. My grade was "insufficient" with a comment— "You copied most of the task." I was outraged by the injustice. My spontaneous reaction was that I would never again set foot in that terrible place. It was a decision that seemed to put an end to any possibility to gain an education, something for which I had struggled so hard.

As usual I hardly reported anything about this incident at home. From the next morning, all kinds of aches made their appearance—whether real or invented (somatization, they call it today). Days passed and I stayed at home. Headaches, bellyaches, diarrhea, etc. Even though there were not many weeks to go before the summer vacation I could not overcome my powerful repulsion. My parents, at their wits end, turned to a doctor, but he couldn't help either. Until one morning, my father got up and said: "Now you and I will go to the principal and we shall once and for all find out what's the matter with you. This is completely over the top." Apparently they had started to see that it was something other than illness that kept me away from school. Well, there was no way out of this. We went to the principal. I felt as if I was taken to the slaughter. First father went into the principal's office and I stayed in the corridor, waiting for what would follow. I dreaded the moment they would call me in. After a seemingly very long time, I decided to bail out. I left the building and began to walk until I reached the farthest outskirts of town. I wandered for hours looking for some idea that would get me out of this embarrassing situation but nothing useful came up.

Arriving home I announced to my worried, and also quite furi-ous parents that I would no longer study at Šurany's Slovakian

Gymnasium, and that my decision was final. They tried to explain how unreasonable this was, as the end of the year was approaching and they might not give me my certificate (How ironic! Our roles had switched! Only two years ago I had fought them hard to be allowed to go to the Gymnasium.) Nothing availed. I was not willing to hear one more word on the issue.

I was at home, depressed and bored, feeling thoroughly on the side of the losers. Sometimes in the afternoon, when Gymnasium students walked past on their way from school, I'd stand by the window, hiding behind the curtain, looking at them longingly. I felt like an exile who, in pain and rage, witnesses those who have set foot in the promised land. When I saw that girl, the one who was indirectly responsible for my situation, walking by happy as if nothing had ever happened, I felt my heart contracting even more. But I was also annoyed with myself for having given up.

After the summer vacation I registered, gnashing my teeth, and having no choice, for eighth grade at the Jewish elementary school. On the one hand I was happy to return to the warm and secure embrace of a Jewish institution, but at the same time I realized studies could not be very serious if six classes had to squeeze into one hall. In the course of the year I saw I had been wrong because the teacher, Mr. K. acquitted himself wonderfully and we managed to end the year having learned more in most subjects, and with an improved morale, as far as that was possible.

To go on from here, I had to do entry exams, once more, and at the same "civic secondary school" which I had rejected in the past as unsuitable. Now one had to take what one could and be quiet. My only thought was: No matter where I go, I must be the best, because that is the only way to survive in a hostile atmosphere. Though I could have taken the entry test for the fourth, final, grade, I preferred to be examined for [the] third grade so that I would be older by a year than the other pupils, something that gave me some advantage and boosted my self-confidence. The level was reasonable and I knew I would easily get to the top of the class.

It was an all-girls class. On the first day I found myself seated in a back bench next to a blond girl, reddish and freckled, who was called Bernardina and she was from Komjatiče, a place notorious for its extreme antisemitism and nationalism. She reviewed the classroom with a sour expression and said: "Look how many Jewish girls there are this year, it's really awful!" Not knowing how to respond I remained silent. Of course the fact of my belonging to that same awful group did not stay hidden for long, but miraculously, we became best friends and we shared the same bench in the back of the class for two years. She was the only one to whom I told my greatest secrets. She knew about my great love for Ivan, and we occasionally skipped school in order to patrol near his home in hopes to glimpse him from our hiding place. I was friendly with the other girls as well, even just because my copybooks were available to all. My social status was never so good. Most teachers treated me and the other Jewish girls, including Erika, decently.

I only had a rough ride with a math teacher whose German-sounding name disclosed his origins and opinions. He was out to break my spirit come what may. But I developed a self-defense method, and managed to outwit him more than once. This is how it worked: Since he ignored it when I raised my hand in answer to a question, I would raise my hand whenever I did not know the answer, trusting he "would not see me." And the other way around, when I had the correct answer, I would make myself scarce and almost invisible. Then he would jump up, and his eyes spewing hatred, shout: Wollner! I rose and recited the answer as though I just now remembered it.

The Slovakian language teacher organized a "club for self-enhancement" which convened after school. Usually the program included readings from students' compositions or immature creations. The teacher intended to appoint me as the president, but that did not materialize because of his fears of the school management. Who, in the years '41-'42, would even consider putting a Jewish girl in this illustrious function? The compromise in the end was that I became secretary, a totally meaningless role, but still a daring act on the part of this teacher. I planned to write a composition and read it on the next meeting. I wanted to write something really good, maybe because of the great trust they had in me, but I had no inspiration and confidence. So I turned to Öcsi and told him to choose a subject. The next morning I received a profound philosophical essay. I was slightly troubled that the audience might not understand. The title of the essay was: "Only those who are forgotten are dead." For years I wondered how he came to choose this topic. Did his essay contain a prophecy, or is it only me, after all that happened, who thinks so?

The school year came to an end, quietly without any traumas and, you could say that I even enjoyed it most of the time. The second year too was coming to an end and now questions and musings began about what was to be next. From time to time we stayed on after our classroom teacher's hour to approach the question from all possible perspectives. She gave us information, advice and discussed the options with us. "And as far as you're concerned," she turned to the Jewish girls, "You also have a whole range of options. You can learn some interesting profession like portrait photography or dental hygiene or sewing." I felt insulted and hurt by these comments. All those girls who had been copying from me shamelessly for two years, *and on whose behalf, mostly, I had been doing the thinking, they were free to choose any future they fancied. And what about me, the "star" of the class? I could be a wedding photographer, dental hygienist or seamstress—at best. I understood that all doors had slammed shut— while all I had wanted to do was study.*

Once the jolly graduation parties were over, [and] a dance like out of a fable, a period of emptiness and total lack of interest set in. I sat at home, getting up, once every so often, with blatant lack of motivation, to help with the chores (the "Jewish law" strictly forbade Jewish families to employ Christian maids). Some of my older friends had already opened a dressmakers' "salon" and were earning, only I was loitering, doing nothing. My parents tried carefully, enumerating all the advantages of learning to sew, but the more they insisted, the more I refused, and my final answer was a resounding no. I devoured huge amounts of books, anything that came my way, but most of the time I was just dying of boredom. My parents went on imploring and finally they stopped.

The war goes on, bad news from the front, the Jews try secretly to listen to the BBC to counterbalance Hungarian announcements about victories, and to keep up their morale. News reaches us about Polish refugees who tell unbelievable things about what's going on with the Jews in Poland. We hear about camps, about Jews who are hiding out in the forests, the underground bunkers that are being constructed in various places. The information was rather vague and all we understood was that their lives were in immediate danger. One Jewish refugee from Poland, an engineer, brought along plans for the construction of bunkers, both under and over ground. He gave these to the Zionist organizations and that's how they reached us long before the danger caught up with us. All this dramatically changed our way of thinking, among the young people. It was not as if reality left us any room for illusions, but this is when we first saw fully how serious it was. Blacker than black! Though it hadn't caught up with us yet, sooner or later, a similar fate was awaiting us, and we had better be prepared. At the youth movement, we talked about it a lot. And when, at the end of the day, we returned home through the dark streets, the mood was downcast, we felt disaster impending, as though we were returning from a funeral.

In that period I had a dream: We, some friends from the move- ment, are in some foreign place, far away from home, a place unlike any we know. Barbed wire and long, gloomy-looking buildings, some- thing like wooden barracks. Not a plant, not a tree. Everything is grey and monotonous. It turns out we are all captives or prisoners. Quietly, in hushed voices, we are making plans, how can we escape. [Sic] We must act fast or it will be too late. Only one boy, standing apart, does not join the conversation. It's Edgar who is a few years younger than us, he has a distinctly Jewish appearance, a clever boy with a good sense of humor. The next morning it transpires Edgar is gone. Under the cover of darkness he has escaped on his own. I woke from this strange dream all shivering. It was the weirdest dream I ever had and even now it's still a riddle to me. A year later when we arrived in Auschwitz, I saw that scene from my dream, I recognized the fences and the barracks. When we, a handful of survivors, returned, I heard about Edgar: He and a friend had escaped from the camp, they were caught and put to death.

It's not easy for me to continue after Edgar's story, but I cannot stop. I return to the subject of the Slovakian Gymnasium. At some point, a group of boys, mostly twelfth graders, appeared so as to end their school year here [sic] and take their final exams. They were from a northern part of Yugoslavia (which had been annexed to Hungary), but they actually belonged to a Slovakian colony which had settled in that area in the remote past. While the Hungarians closed the Slovakian school, they allowed for the students in the higher grades to complete their studies with us in Šurany. The distance between the two locations was about 430 km. Their very arrival caused a stir in town. Öcsi immediately became friends with them and spent most of his time in their company. They went about things differently, they were unfamiliar, and that alone entranced us and stirred our curiosity. Among them was a Jewish boy, Ivan. I fell in love with him even before I met him. I chose him because he came from afar, he simply had to be different and strange, and also because he was Jewish. (I understood my parents would object to any relationship with a non-Jew.) When I first met him, I saw he was totally unlike the image that had already taken root in my imagination. He did not look different or strange in the least. He looked like a very average Jewish boy, rather dull, kind of a proper boy. But it was too late for me and I would not let any fact spoil my illusion. I loved him desperately throughout that year and went on suffering even after he left. He was the only boy I actually reached out for, I even sent him an anonymous letter, but the relationship remained quite one-sided. After the final exams (he was the only one who sailed through the exam and did not have to return after the vacation, to my great chagrin!) he said goodbye and returned to his home, hundreds of kilometers away. My world fell apart. After a while, our family received a letter from him thanking them for having hosted him so often during the past year, and I was deeply hurt, to begin with. How could he not have written to me personally, had he not felt how much I loved him? I answered him and told him, without further ado, about my entire love story, and this is how we started a correspondence that went on for two years. These letters became the very water, food, and air of my life. I would wait by the gate for the postman and when I saw him my heart went crazy and my breath stopped. These letters were only about everyday issues, not a word about love, nothing. And yet they were precious to me. A sixteen-year-old girl's love, a love that's all illusion, spiritual and special.

It was through his connection with this group of Yugoslavians that Öcsi learned about the partisan activities there, and he grew more and more interested. It was in his nature to be forging his personal plans, part of which somehow reached us (not our parents, of course!). He tried to get into touch with people who might help him cross the border and join Tito's units. This possibility scared me greatly. My main worry was that Öcsi's disappearance would land my parents in "unpleasant" situations, like cross examinations, etc. I knew that there was no convincing him but I asked to talk with him anyway. We stepped out onto the sidewalk in front of the house for some privacy. It was a dark night, there was no one about other than us. I tried to convey my worries, my concern for our parents and for him. He listened to me quietly, I perceived his distress, and he said: "I have to, I must go. I cannot go on doing nothing. I will simply go mad if I stay here." My heart broke for him, my heart broke for our parents! And then I decided to take action: I asked one of the young men there for the phone number of the contact person, I went to the post office and rang my brother Andy (whom I informed about the plan) and I asked the contact person to prevent Öcsi from going. In the end, he sent Öcsi a message that the route was not clear right now . . . I acted in a great panic. Now I know I did not have the right to interfere in his life and act behind his back. Deep grief I regret it. [Sic] Shortly afterwards Öcsi left school. He began spending his evenings at the card games, smoked a lot, and got up late in the afternoon. His physical condition deteriorated a lot. He was a strict vegetarian from age 15 and his nutrition was quite inadequate. This combination of his new life style + [sic] physical weakness, worried us.

Here I am, one summer afternoon, all of my family are taking a nap, it is their Schlafstunde, when I suddenly conceive of an idea to do something. I left the house and started my way to Mariška Seidlová's "dress-making salon," the sister of my good friend Helenka. Now that the pressure had abated, my reluctance too grew less, and I wanted to find out about the possibility to learn how to sew. I was received with open arms and immediately employed as an apprentice—or in fact, another pair of hands. By the time I returned home they were already having dinner. "Where have you been? It's very late." "I'm learning how to sew," I answered laconically.

This was the beginning of a new period. Mariška's salon was about a kilometer away from home. They lived near the train station, a typically Christian area. I became acquainted with a new type of people who came and went. Neighbors, a variety of clients, women who just popped in to gossip, Helenka's boyfriend Lipu, and of course, the admirers of the well-dressed and feminine Mariška. The mood was permanently cheerful, a lightheartedness I did not know from home. Helenka's and Mariška's mother was a relatively young woman with a very liberal attitude to her daughters. She was abandoned by her husband who had been wandering about somewhere in Palestine for some years now, but this was not obvious in the way she conducted herself. She was like one of us, a friend, we laughed at the same juicy jokes and we exchanged details of the most recent gossip. Her daughters were free to meet with their partners with hardly any constraints and did not owe her an explanation. She was a wise and good woman. And in the background, there was the grandmother, who only rarely made herself heard, and when she did, it wasn't always clear what she meant to say. In the mornings she would serve us potatoes boiled in their skin and onion rings with salt, a classic dish of the poor about which we were crazy. In short, I really enjoyed this new and refreshing environment.

As the seasons changed, or before holidays, when there was more work, we had to come in on Sundays as well, the day we would go to the river, either for a swim in the summer, or to skate in the winter. We did not like the idea of working on Sunday and tried to wriggle out of it whenever possible. This is when Mariška's mother decided to act. She went about it in a piecemeal way, extending a personal treatment to each and every reluctant apprentice. I often heard her, when she could be sure I was within earshot: "I don't know who will or will not come this Sunday, but if there's one thing I do know it is that Marta will be there. I know her very well and I am sure she will not leave us in the lurch. Here is someone I'm sure who can be trusted." That did it—I needed no more. After such a statement, how could I disappoint her? And this is how she gently imposed her will on me.

31.XII, New Year's Eve, but winter had not yet come. There had been no snow fall yet. To mark the end of the year, Öcsi invited me and my friend Erich to the movies. We saw a sad film, called "Sentenced to Death." It is about a beautiful girl who suffers from heart disease or tuberculosis, who meets, on a ship, a young man, who is sentenced to death. Needless to say, they fall in love, a love without hope and with a tragic end. We left the cinema in a low mood. It was late but we did not want to return home yet. We walked a little in the empty street, [and] in the end we sat on a little bridge by the side of the road, opposite our house. We sat in silence, no one tried to start a conversation. Suddenly I was flooded by the thought that it was we who were sentenced to death and [that] this was our last year. Where would each of us find themselves cast away? What would happen to our home? Our parents? I felt clearly that this newly beginning year would bring us catastrophe. No one would escape. We sat for a while longer. I knew the two boys had similar thought on their minds. Wordless, Öcsi and I went into our home and Erich into his. And we did not wish each other a "happy new year."

I celebrated my eighteenth birthday in Mariška's salon on February 23, 1944, and it spelled the end of my youthful innocence. There were only twenty-four days left before the earthquake of March 9th. The ground has not stopped shaking under my feet ever since.

Deportation

March 20, 1944. I wake up to sounds from the boys' room. So early—what can it be? What are they talking about? I thought I heard Andy K.'s voice. No, that couldn't be. It's the middle of the academic year and Andy must be at teachers' college in Budapest. There's no vacation now. I got dressed, somehow, and went to check what was going on. The boys were still in bed, and Andy K., in a blue suit, was standing in the middle of the room, very pale. "What's going on, why aren't you at school?" I understood something bad had happened. "I brought you the tickets for the Opera," and he took a bunch of tickets from his back pocket. Yes, a few of us, girls, had asked him to get us tickets, because he had been telling us exciting stories about the wonders of the opera he attended in the big city. And then he added this short sentence: "Yesterday the Germans entered Budapest." One short sentence. We were in total shock. And then Andy told us how it had happened. How the Germans captured, early on, his school building and how they had managed to organize themselves and escape in a few minutes, reaching the station before they'd start rounding up Jews in the streets and especially at the station. Towards noon rumors reached us about Jews who had been caught on the run and locked up in prisoners' camps. We were all paralyzed by the force of the blow we received. I felt this was the last act of a tragedy which had begun at the end of that Yom Kippur when the Prague radio announcer had announced the resignation of Edvard Beneš. At that critical moment that thought had obviously not occurred to me. It took some more days until the brain could think a little.

About an hour later we saw Öcsi was getting ready, seemingly for travel, preparing a small bag, hastily throwing in a few things. Yes, he had decided to travel to Budapest, yes, today. It wasn't clear for how many days, maybe for a day, maybe longer. He had to be there and see what was going on, maybe he could help somehow. My poor parents! What did they feel at that moment? Totally broken, they did not even try to intervene. Where would he be staying? Would we see him again? He was traveling into the lion's den—from which every sane person flees. At the same time we knew that that was Öcsi, and no one was going to change him. There were very few telephones where we lived. We waited about two days (or was it two years?) and then Öcsi returned. He didn't speak and nobody asked anything.

Some days later, when air was reaching our lungs again and our heart went back to beating at an almost regular rate, we, the young people, started planning. What would we do? It was time to take our rescue plan out of the drawer. We decided to build a bunker in the cellar of our family's house. To continue digging beyond the existing cellar and construct a wall behind which the shelter would be. We acted under cover. Every night two boys would come and dig. The girls would start preparing preserves and other dry food. Öcsi and Andy K. were the first to dig. The family were asleep when Andy arrived and they went down into the cellar with their digging equipment. I stayed awake, sitting in the boys' room and trying to gather courage from Bible verses that seemed very relevant to our reality.

Sadly, the first night of digging turned out to be the last as well. There was a scene in the yard the next morning. Neighbors expressed various opinions about the source of the terrible noise that night. In the end we were forced to tell our parents everything and we saw that our plan was totally unrealistic. My father explained that the place was dump [sic] and dangerous to spend even two days, it would not hold the number of persons we were planning, where would we get fresh air, etc. etc. And, on top of all that, didn't we know that the place was regularly flooded by rising ground water, every spring?

The next route we tried was different: We would move to a farm, live and work there like laborers and vanish from the Germans' sight. Like certain animals who try to blend in with their surroundings when danger threatens, taking the form of a stone or leaf or branch. We would be there like all the other workers, we wouldn't stand out. We found such a farm and they took us in for work. It was at some distance from our little town. We left, a group of six or seven boys and a smaller number of girls. In regular times our parents would not have allowed us to go like that, together with boys, for who knew what could happen in such a "summer camp" situation? Boys were commonly allowed to participate in any activity, including weeks away from home. But girls, at least in our family, were kept safely in the home. We were allowed to go out with boys, also for a swim, but we had to be at home overnight. No begging or arguments could change that. My poor parents! Now they resigned themselves to the new situation and did not utter a comment or warning. They had, in fact, nothing to worry about because we had very clear boundaries at that time which did not extend beyond kissing, if at all . . . We began to get ourselves ready at the farm. The girls got a kind of room that also functioned as a kitchen. We slept on straw sacks and the boys in the stable. It took sometime to get used to the work.

It was then that we saw a hoe for the first time, but we were in high spirits. The "real" workers taught us how to do our job without killing ourselves, investing a lot less effort—that was the trick! At night we sat outside with the workers, men and women, and we sang with them and the boys played their instruments. These were spontaneous gatherings, barriers fell, and we were admitted as equals. "You are so nice, it's as though you weren't Jewish at all!" that's what they said, it was a great compliment in their view.

But not all nights were like this. Nights we spent in the room, seated on our straw sacks and giving vent to the many anxieties we [kept inside] during the day. We sang sad songs, or somebody recited poems by Ady, the tragic poet, or other heart-rending texts. Did that soothe us? Yes, we found brothers in fate, people we respected and loved, who had suffered a lot in life. We were not the only ones . . .

Sometimes father visited the farm, and each time he was the bearer of bad tidings. My brother Andy was called up to join the Hungarian work forces. Because Jews were not drafted to the army, harshly disciplined workforces, adjunct to the army, had been set up especially for them and they were deployed on the Russian front. Andy had to join up within days. This was the first sign that here, too, we wouldn't last, and that they would get at us. In spite of our ability to blend in with our surroundings, they would get at us no matter where. The next time, the news was even worse. We were all told to return to our homes and await orders. Jews from the entire district were assembled in Šurany, interned in the homes of local Jews, and the place was transformed into a ghetto. Each family was given a room, and so our apartment filled up with families we did not know at all. This is why we preferred to move in with Uncle Gézko where we would at least be among our relatives. Because we stayed in our familiar surroundings our situation was quite tolerable (though crowded). For those who came from the surrounding villages it was more difficult, with all their luggage and mess they couldn't make themselves comfortable. And they had been forced to leave most of their property behind. The future frightened us all, an unclear future, or perhaps rather: an all too clear future? There was no reason for optimism. There was not even the tiniest light, a small spark in the dark! Days and days went by. But we knew they had no intention to leave us here, thousands of Jews in the middle of the town.

Öcsi was drafted. In spite of the heartbreak this caused him, I hoped Öcsi would oblige. Again, the same fear I had already experienced in the past. What would happen to our parents if Öcsi decided to disappear? But no, he began to get ready to enlist. Andy K. came in to say goodbye. It was sad, sad . . . Sometime after the boys joined the army, Shosha Steiner (now Barzel), a member of the Zionist youth movement from Budapest, turned up. She took the train all the way to us, even though Jews were strictly prohibited to travel. I admired her courage and self-confidence very much. She brought us, Erika and me, Christian papers, and suggested we come to Budapest where we could manage and weather this period with the help of the pioneers' underground. She had a long conversation with my father at the end of which I heard him say: "The girls will stay with us. Whatever happens to us as a family will happen to them." And Shosha stopped trying to convince him, realizing, it seems, that he was not going to change his mind, and she said goodbye.

It's not clear how long we've been on this transport train, and it's not clear where the train is heading. When did we leave home? How did all this happen?

It was Sunday afternoon. Even though it was only the middle of May it was very hot and hazy, there was something strange in the air, strange and ill-boding. I was walking in the street, alone, aimlessly, when I saw father approaching. He was different, not the father I knew. His face was pale, nearly grey, his expression fearful. Initially I thought he had not seen me, but he approached and exclaimed in a rush: "Don't be out in the street, get into the house." Something awful was happening. I understood father had reliable information which had just reached him. A few hours later everything was clear, the order had been given: Each of us was to make a small parcel with necessities and to stay home. Did we go to sleep? I am sure nobody managed to close an eye. I was tensely listening to the smallest stirring of the night. At daybreak, loud voices could be heard and a loud knocking on the door. Mother said, her voice weak: "Oy, it's Monday, baking day, we have no bread to take with us on our way." I remember Erika crying because of her dearly beloved dog Akim. What would become of him now? Who would look after him? And I realized that in spite of all the searches after jewelry they had not noticed my golden earrings. Only after breaking them (they had been soldered shut so I wouldn't lose them) I was able to throw them down in the yard.

Our parents are together with most adults, deep inside the train wagon. We, the young people, sit on the floor of the wagon, in a corner, underneath a hatch. I don't remember everyone who was there with us. The fact that Erich was sitting next to me made it a lot easier and gave me strength. In low voices we talked about escape but no one really believed we could. We arrived in the late evening or

night. Doors opened, orders in German were shouted, "Get off! Off!"
The light of many flood lights, shock . . . Many German soldiers as
well as ghostly figures holding batons who to me, for some reason,
appeared to be faceless. These were Jewish prisoners who acted as
guards, trying to impose order, and starting the job of separating
men from women. Before the two clusters have fully formed, father
is suddenly next to me and stuffs a little bag full of nuts into my
hand. Yes, at home they had some sort of idea that when the need
arose nuts could save people from starvation. They don't occupy much
space and are very nourishing and reinforcing. They were on the list
of necessities we took with us. And father, even now in the middle
of this chaos and terror, father's concern even now was for us to
have food.

We felt we were in a place beyond which there was no worse.

When the men and women were standing in separate blocs, I sud-
denly saw Erich, wearing the green canvas coat I knew so well from
our walks in the rain, and he walked directly towards me, almost in
a run, as though he had forgotten the last, most important word, or
to ask a question that broached no delay. He approaches and I think
he says something but I don't understand. At that moment one of those
ghostly presences materialized, his baton landed on Erich's back and
he was pushed back to join the other men. I never saw him again . . .

Everything happens at a frantic pace. Already we find ourselves
facing a man, maybe an officer, who's looking at us from some higher
up place, Erika and I on one side, Mama and Eva on the other. I don't
know how it happened, I did not notice who told us, and when, to do
these things. All of a sudden, he stops our mother, as if he changed
his mind, like someone who wants to check one more detail, and asks:
"Wie alt bist du?"—"How old are you?"—I feel unbearably insulted.
It is the first time I experience personal insult. Insult aimed at
me alone. How dare he address our mother like this, in the second
person? Where does he take the cheek? It hurt me so badly, seeing
my mother humiliated, that I wanted to cry. And I hear my mother:
"Sieben und fünfzig," "fifty-seven." What happened to Mama, I didn't
understand. Could it be she forgot her age? Or did she add ten years
for some other purpose? Maybe her maternal instinct told her this
was the way not to be separated from little Eva and continue together
into the unknown . . . And the man, over there, already making that
gesture with his hand, and they were out of our sight. Everything
unfolded like in some nightmare, and after all these years I still
cannot see it in any other way: a nightmare . . .

I am surrounded by many girls, in some huge hall, we are wait-
ing. I'm trying my utmost to swallow the nut I have in my mouth.
I also try to persuade Erika to eat. It doesn't work . . . In the

morning, after a night of terror, we all look alike, with our hair
shorn off, bald. Dresses that are not ours cover our bodies, there
is no underwear at all, and [we wear] Dutch clogs. That's our gear.
All around, ghostly sights, electrified fences, chimneys bellow-
ing smoke in the background and flames surging from somewhere. Some
Jewish girls, who were here for a longer time, came along, they must
have had some function, and spoke to us to reassure us. Yes, we would
see our relatives in a few days' time. They were here, not far away,
being looked after. It was their task to pacify us with these prom-
ises. There were postcards, too, which we were free to send wherever
we wanted. The words were already printed, all you needed to do was
add your signature. The sender's address was some invented place in
Germany. Everything aimed to cover the traces. I had no one to send
a post card to, and anyway I felt it was a ruse.

They trained us to stand in groups of five, ready to be counted,
several times a day, and this was our main activity. On the first
morning we stood, waiting to be surveyed by the German officers who
were followed by a trail of Jewish functionaries. One of these went
ahead asking us if there were any girls amongst us who were younger
than fourteen. They probably did not trust the preceding night's
selection and wanted to check us again by daylight. Since no answers
were forthcoming, she moved between the rows to find any young
"offender" who was trying to slip between the mazes. She pointed
at me: "You, there. Step forward. You are not fourteen yet!" I was
eighteen and always appeared younger, but now, without my big head
of hair, I really looked like a kid. I tried to tell her my birth
date, but she grabbed my arm and pulled me out of the line. I knew
she meant ill and I resisted with all my might. She could easily have
overcome my resistance, were it not for the officers with their dogs
who just then appeared on the scene, and one of them called her away
on some very important business. She let go of me and rushed in their
direction. While we were in this camp we went through quite a few
selections and there was [always] the danger that in the blink of an
eye, if one of us moved away too much, the other might find herself
en route to another barracks. We learned to maintain eye contact and
stay sharp and ready for any sudden change.

For some unclear reason a very large group of girls (following
yet another selection) was transferred to a remote ghostly place
called Plašow. This place was even worse than where we came from.
In deep despair, we only asked ourselves: How long would it take
until we would rot away here, alive? We had to move stone boulders
from one place to another. The next day we were told to move them
back, over and over again. The overseers were Jews, and they outdid
the Germans in cruelty. We did not completely break down because we

began to hear the sounds of war approaching. We heard the roar of canons growing louder by the day. The front was coming near, the Russians were approaching, our liberation was at hand! We took care not to show our joy, but a spark returned to our eyes. There was one work leader, a political prisoner, a German liberal whom we all liked, who shared our joy, encouraged us to keep going, it wouldn't take much longer, one more day, another . . .

But things did not unfold as we hoped. Some days passed and then we were told they were about to move us from here. Where? This, of course, they would not tell us. We saw the trains, ready for us to board. They did not apparently want, or indeed they did not have the capacity, to move all of us out at this stage. They put us into the carriages in "regular" numbers but the train stayed stationary for a long time. The blessed idea to bring along a container, some sort of container, with water, had proven itself earlier. But we waited so long that our water ran out and thirst began to trouble us. The military situation kept changing by the hour and they had to change plans. Hours passed and then the doors opened and another group was added, and then we waited again. By now overcrowding had become extreme and it grew hotter. We could not have imagined that they'd add about another twenty girls. We heard orders, doors were being shut, the train moved. I don't want to mention numbers, they were not clear to anyone present. The space allotted per person sufficed [only] to stand. It was a ghost journey. In the middle of the summer, water almost completely run out, and not enough air to breathe.

Erika had been suffering from lesions on her feet for some-time. She had contracted a festering infection [sic] and [her feet were] very swollen and made it impossible for her to wear shoes. I begged those who stood near us to look out, but again and again someone would step on her feet. Even if they meant to spare her, it was impossible. And this is how we continued, parched with thirst, half-fainting, but still on our feet. It's not clear how long we were on our way, but for me this was the longest and most traumatic journey of my life. Stopping every so often, the train continued and eventually we arrived. As transpired, later, back to Auschwitz. We had been dreaming about freedom just some days ago, we felt it with body and soul, and here we were in this terrible, frightening place.

Still dazed by thirst, exhausted, we were put into a huge hall, thousands of girls. We waited longingly for our turn to get to the faucet. Jewish guards brandishing whips were maintaining order. We were in the back of this space. It would take forever to get to that faucet! The floor there was strewn with broken glass. Suddenly I grew aware that Erika was acting strangely, talking nonsense, sitting down naked [sic] on the broken glass. "That one there, that's Lila," she pointed at one of the guards, "That's our cousin Lila, she will give us water." I took great fright, I understood that something very bad was happening to Erika. I tried to move ahead to somehow get closer to the faucet, which was in a cordoned off area. I didn't manage to make headway because the women with the whips were using them and the crowding was huge. When I returned I saw that Erika was in the same, strange condition, mumbling unintelligibly, and still amid the broken glass. What could I do? How was I to cope with this new situation? I would have to keep all this secret. We had already learned what happened to anyone who acted in an unusual way! How could I keep Erika's condition hidden from their all-seeing eye? And for how long, if at all, could we go on like this? Pressing questions for which I had no answer. The fear of losing Erika paralyzed me.

After an eternity we found ourselves in front of the faucet and we were able to drink, drink, drink. Lots of water. Gradually Erika showed signs of recovery and suddenly everything was wonderful, I even forgot, momentarily, where we were. All I knew was that Erika was given [back] to me.

Again we underwent the usual "treatment." Our hair, which had grown back a little, was shorn off again, etc. We were among the "lucky" ones to have this experience twice over. But an abyss gaped between the girl who had first arrived to this place, and the beaten, hardly human looking creature, now. Just a few months had passed but we had been through lightyears. We started the routines of the place for which, until this very day, I cannot find the right words. One may say, perhaps, that in that place we never raised our eyes to look at the sky, and hence I am not sure at all whether there was such a thing, a sky. We spent time in this place, time whose duration I don't recollect. We all lost our sense of time, days, weeks, months, everything flowed together. We stood on roll call, again and again, and this is how, in the early morning hours, shivering with cold, we gathered that fall had come.

Forced Labor

We must be close to being transferred to another place. There is no way of knowing whether this is for better or for worse. When this happens, there is a lot of fear, rumors circulate, nobody knows where they come from. But when you take the shower and come out of it, you can breathe quietly again. One lines up to receive a dress after the old one has been taken away before the shower. A refreshing novelty: another line for underpants, something about whose existence we have forgotten. Here Erika, who was a lot more astute than I and in the possession of a more healthy resourcefulness, took an initiative that led to us having three pairs of underpants between us! Once each of us already received a pair of underpants, Erika pushed hers into my hands and re-joined the line. That was criminal conspiracy! It's horrifying to think what would have happened if they had found out. In any case, Erika returned with another pair of underpants, an unimaginable improvement in the quality of our lives.

After a rather humane, long journey—if one can call it that—we arrived in the Sudetenland. This was the territory, once part of the Republic, which was inhabited by Germans who had for a long time striven to become annexed to their motherland, Germany. The camp was on the outskirts of a town called Oberaltstadt. As we stood, once again, in the familiar five-person formations, the director of the local factory, a civilian, appeared and selected a few girls whom he wanted. Passing among the rows he pointed at about one hundred girls who seemed appropriate. Here we really were fortunate: we were among the chosen. We only learned after the war how harsh life had been in the nearby camp to which the remaining girls were transferred.

We immediately noticed the big difference from everything we had come to know. The place, originally constructed for Yugoslav and Russian forced laborers, was empty for some reason. Showers, a dining hall, rooms for twenty girls. This was a different standard, meant for Aryan workers. We felt as though we had risen from the depths of the underworld to a place with air in which you could lift your eyes and see the sky. A place for humans! We had been promoted to the level of regular prisoners. The place was no worse than a prison, not too bad.

We started to work in a factory for cotton thread. A very big place in which British and French prisoners of war were working, as well as East European forced laborers, free Germans, and we, the

Jewish girls. Other than us, the new arrivals, there was another camp with Polish Jewish women who had been here for some years. Erika and I worked on a team that started at two o'clock in the afternoon until two in the morning. It was a difficult shift which included half an hour's break for dinner. It was hard to stay awake in the critical evening hours. The machine required constant attention and it happened more than once, that, my eyes closing for just a few seconds, the machine went spinning, threads snapped, and it was very hard to catch up with the delay. And sometimes, if you were out of luck, the German guard happened to be looking in at just such a critical moment.

But there were also moving human experiences while we operated the machine. It just so happened that I had an overlap of a few hours with an old German worker, who did a daytime shift ending at four o'clock. She was small, thin, and bent like a paragraph sign(§). She looked as if she was about to give up the ghost any minute. She was a poor woman who had spent the whole of her life at the machine working hard, a real proletarian. Between us we spoke about matters of work only, but we felt, Ženka [her Polish friend in the camp—T. K.] and I, that she was fond of us in her quiet and introverted way. She would bring along lunch which consisted of a small jug with vegetable soup. After she moved behind the machine in order to eat, she would call one of us to eat the remains she kept for us.

It was a modest soup whose taste was paradise for me. The same vegetable soup I still treat with respect today, it remains the symbol of real life. After the war, Ženka and I went to visit her at her home. She lived in some dingy hole, together with her ancient mother. I also met Dora from the Polish women's camp when I was there. Those girls looked unlike us, they had a civilian, almost regular appearance, they had hair, they were dressed normally, and only their pallor was striking. Hard labor and insufficient nutrition left its traces. Even though she was a Pole, Dora's Czech was fluent. She came from a town on the border with Czechoslovakia and knew both languages. She was a Czech character, this was probably what attracted me to her. She was the middle one of three daughters. Dora worked in our department and we very quickly developed a wonderful friendship. Though she was only one year older than me she felt like my big sister. There was no need for long conversations. Feeling her right there, beside me, added color to my life.

One day I came down with food poisoning, the one person among hundreds of girls who ate that food. Pains started during work and grew worse. It was Dora who turned to the Germans asking permission for me to stop working. [Her request] was answered, and I sat in a corner while the pains grew worse and worse. She brought warm water so I could put my feet in it, in hopes that would help. In the end the Germans decided to have me put in the camp's sickroom which was about one kilometer away. And then Dora was bold enough to ask if she might accompany me to the sickroom. It was not so easy or common to ask for something like this! It could have been interpreted as cheek and impertinence, and there was no telling how they'd react. Miraculously, they agreed, and Dora supported me all the way. I stayed there for twenty-four hours and then I returned to the usual routine. This may sound like a banal story, but it still moves me and warms my heart. And I am overcome with longing and sadness for a friendship I once had and which is no longer.

Ženka was a twenty-year-old Polish girl who was born in Auschwitz. She was very experienced and responsible for the machine on which we both worked. She was serious and diligent. The kind of girl who is the "best student" in her class. We felt a lot of sympathy for each other and worked together well, but we never reached the level of enchanting friendship that I had with Dora. And then there was that beautiful, blond Polish girl whose romantic association with an English POW was discovered by the Germans. I cannot imagine there was much more to it than gazes and secretly exchanged letters, because we were being closely watched. They searched her tools and found letters in English. What happened next was heart rending: They took her, sheared off her lovely blonde hair and sent her away to another, much harsher camp. They staged this as a great show, to warn off others.

Winter was approaching. Though they gave us some extra bit of clothing, it was not enough. To cope with the intense cold of Sudetenland, we began, on the advice of the more experienced Polish girls, to filch cotton thread from the factory as well as, from different departments, thin metal sticks that could double as knitting needles. A trade developed: I'll steal thread for you, if you steal needles for me. To begin with they carried out searches, impounded materials, [and] we were punished, but in time they learned to turn a blind eye and ignore us. They realized that freezing workers can't be productive and they wanted us to work. We began to knit in earnest. Returning from work, at three o'clock [in the morning], rather than go to sleep, we sat on our beds and knitted. We'd knit until, spent, we collapsed on our mattress and slept. We knitted socks, shawls, shirts, everything, and this is how we managed to get through that winter.

Sudetenland spring was changeable, rainy and very cold with some very few fine days. We were so immersed in our daily problems that we knew little about what was happening in the war, except, of course, the frequent sirens that allowed us to leave work and go into the shelters. We did not know, however, how near the front was. It was only after they told us that the factory was closing and that we would be digging [sic] around the town, when we realized the situation was not bad at all. Every morning we went out in an endless line, along a very long road. As said, the weather was unstable so it happened more than once that we were soaking wet by the time we reached the spot. One day there was such a terrible storm, rain, snow, hail and tearing winds, that the officer announced to the guards that he wouldn't allow them to set out in such weather. Only he himself and the Ukrainians left with the Jewish workers. Nobody of course felt sorry for us and they did not let us off the hook that day. We marched through a forest, struggling against the wind and wet to the bone. The scenery on both sides of the road was stunning. But who had eyes for the landscape? We marched through heavy fog, clouds actually covering our heads, we walked through the near dark.

Suddenly we see a little house by the roadside. A young woman sits by the window, working on her sewing machine. She does not even lift her gaze as the strange procession passes by. I was hypnotized by this young woman. How had we never noticed this house before, it must have been standing there for a very long time? [Sic] To me the house appeared like a castle, and the woman, a fairy tale princess. I was flooded by despair. I felt humiliated and despised. I felt the chasm between us, unicellular [sic] beings, and proper humans. We were covered in mud, freezing. The woman by the window looked so clean and happy, remote and unattainable, even after we passed by and the little house vanished from our sight. [Sic] And this was the thought that passed through my mind: If ever I am granted to be a free person again I will not ask more from life: only a small house, a small hut, with a window and a sewing machine next to it. And on rainy and stormy days I will sit and look at the rain.

Days are passing, there is a feeling of things happening around us. We continue with our digging work, but the belt of severe discipline is loosening a bit. They don't care so much anymore if, on our way back, we collect twigs to heat the room, something which not so long ago could earn us a blow from the Ukrainian guard's rifle-grip. An abandoned store of potatoes also appears from which we can take some to cook in our room.

The front, it seems, is coming nearer. Everyone is holding their breath. One morning, when we stood on roll call, the director of the factory faced us, strange and solemn: "The war is over, Hitler is dead. You are free now!" Though he said more, those words no longer entered my mind.

We had dreamt so much of this moment! Now there was absolute silence. It took some moments until what he had said reached our consciousness. I don't remember outbreaks of joy. The rows in which we stood dispersed, we were free. What did that mean? What would we do tomorrow morning? Would we return home? Return to where we started? Where was home? Where was our family?

We understood we would have to deal with reality from now on, however grim it proved to be.

Some girls gave vent to feelings of revenge and there were assaults on the German women soldiers, those who did not manage to flee in time. There were also raids on German civilian homes, and food was confiscated, etc. There was anarchy everywhere. Very soon units from the Russian army, our liberators, appeared, who contrary to expectations did not always behave like gentlemen. They were supposed to protect us, but it was dangerous, especially at night, with the camp breached and soldiers, mostly drunk, roaming the place. Only some of them maintained their humanity following six years of war and the inferno they had been through.

Return

———————————

We wanted to get away from there as soon as possible but we had no definite plans. After sometime (days? weeks?) some buses arrived to take citizens of the Republic to Prague. We left, Erika, me and Magda, a girl from Šurany who had been close to us throughout this period at Oberaltstadt, and had become a kind of third sister. Though she was about four years older than me, she depended on us for everything and never had any suggestions of her own. She had been raised as the one daughter of her parents, with two unmarried aunts who lived with the family. We always knew that "Magda has three mothers." Maybe this was why she lacked independence to an extreme degree. We reached Prague on the bus, and from there we would have to make our own way, many hundreds of kilometers.

We started a journey that took weeks. We took every form of transportation that came our way. Freight trains, trucks, peasants' carts and a lot of walking. The roads were full of people. It seemed all of Europe was afoot, as if a huge ant heap was upturned and now millions of ants were running hither and tither, a surreal spectacle. Different ethnic populations, a great mixture of languages, women, men, forced laborers, prisoners of war, German soldiers in civilian dress—whom we identified because of their fearful look, like hounded animals, including, probably, not a few war criminals—as well as camp survivors like us. Every so often we reached stations run by volunteers or maybe it was the Red Cross, where we were handed out soup and bread, and then we would resume our journey. Sometimes we reached farms, we asked—and sometimes were offered—to stay overnight in a loft over the cows' stable. This is how we traveled through part of Bohemia, [and] Moravia (two Czech-speaking regions). Now I wonder how three young girls like us managed, with never a thought of all the dangers on the way. It simply did not trouble us at all. Our aim was to move on, burning one kilometer after another . . . How did we know which way to go? It seems we had a kind of sixth sense, like blind people. Perhaps we covered many superfluous kilometers but we made headway.

We arrived to Northern Slovakia, a beautiful scenery, whose legendary mountains I had dreamed of visiting all through my childhood. We passed by these amazing places in utter indifference, taking not the merest notice of the views. There was nothing else: all we did

was move ahead. It was only when we approached the southern plains
of our "fatherland" that anxiety crept into our hearts. Without mentioning it, we instinctively slowed our pace. To delay the end, not
to face reality, drag it out one more day, keep time from moving. We
felt that scorched earth was awaiting us—no home, no living soul of
all the people we had once had there, thousands of years ago.

Finally we reached the outskirts of Šurany on a farmer's cart. We
asked to get off, to take sometime to reflect before we entered the
town. Maybe we thought about that spectacle, a year earlier, when we
walked, hundreds of Jews, young, old, aged. Women and babies, [car-
rying] their bundles on their way to the railway station, closely
guarded by infamous Hungarian policemen. And the villagers, in their
droves, stood by, watching the spectacle with indifference, and at
times, with unconcealed satisfaction. And now we return, almost on
all fours, beaten and plucked. No, here there is no danger of anyone
receiving us with good wishes, a smile or a word of commiseration.
There isn't the smallest part in either our bodies or our souls that
wishes to return to this place, but it is the one place to which we
can return.

We entered the yard of our parents' house. It was busy inside
the house, strangers were living there. We stood there for some minutes, looking at the house, but we did not even go in. A neighbor
came out and told us that the things we left in her keeping had,
unfortunately, been discovered by the Russian army in their hiding
place, and she was very sorry. Germans hadn't found them, but the
Russians had taken everything. She talked a lot about how sorry she
was and what a shame. It was very clear that all this was a staged
performance but it left us cold. We didn't see the need for any
objects, and we were not interested to hear more of her. We went away
and did not try to approach the area again. Many years passed until
once again I had a place I could call my home. That was in 1953 when
we arrived, already as a family with a little girl, to the Galilee.
Something very similar happened to Erika as well.

The few people who came back assembled in one of the houses and we
joined the collective. There I saw a letter, in Andy K.'s handwriting, in which he announced that he had survived and asked for anyone
who knew anything [sic] about his relatives to inform him at the
address mentioned. I decided to reply to the letter. Andy was a good
friend of my brother Öcsi, they had been in the same class in school
and he was a good friend of ours too. I wrote to him that I had
spent sometime in some camps with his sister Zorka[,] we helped each
other and were very close until we were separated. When I returned
to Šurany I heard that Zorka had survived. After writing and sending

the letter, it turned out, to my great sorrow, that the rumor of her survival originated in an error.

Sometime later we—Erika and I—were traced by Heni, our uncle from Nové Zámky. It transpired he had spent the entire period in hiding, together with his wife and baby. He invited us to live with them. Even though we had never been on the same wavelength, we accepted the offer. We had a roof over our heads, food, and something to wear, yet it was not easy for us to be with them. Their excessive "normalcy" disturbed us, their return to "business as usual." I did not understand how one could go on living as if nothing had happened. Even though he tried to show empathy and make life as pleasant as possible for us, the difficulties in communication with our uncle were palpable. We knew we were not going to stay there for a long time. We found a way to connect with friends from the movement, old ones and others. We discussed moving to Hungary where most of the movement's members were concentrated, to join one of their training camps and [then] move to Eretz.[1]

One evening when we returned home, Uncle Heni received us with unusual excitement. We immediately understood something very important had happened. "Some guy from Šurany, a goy, came here, he served with Öcsi in a partisan unit in Yugoslavia. He claims that Öcsi is alive in the city of Kiev, in Ukraine." It is hard to describe how I received this news. It was a type of feeling I had never experienced. Like a blind person whose eyesight is suddenly restored, or to wake up [sic] from a terrifying dream then to realize it was only a dream and not reality. That night Erika and I didn't sleep at all, we wept for sheer happiness. We had never been so close as on that night. This miracle brought us close together, we held each other tight until day rise.

In the morning I traveled with a friend from the movement to meet this young man. We sat with him in his room, talking about Öcsi. He told us about his great courage and how he always volunteered and was the first to get going when they had to go out on a particularly hazardous action. He did not repeat the story he had told my uncle. He made absolutely no mention of his being alive in Kiev. But what took hold of me? Why did I not shower him with questions to confirm yesterday's story? What was I thinking when I chose to remain silent, bringing upon myself decades of torturous uncertainty? Even as I am writing this, uncertainty still has me in its grip. Because

---

1   Before 1948, when Israel was founded, many Jews used the biblical-historical name Eretz Yisrael—the Land of Israel—for what was generally known as Palestine. Marta, here, is still using that old name.

I never had another opportunity than this one, an opportunity I let slip at that time.

For years, out in the street, in Budapest and also in Eretz, I'd imagine spotting him here or there, once in a bus driving by, another time on television. It occurred to me that he might be wandering about seen but unseeing, maybe he had lost his memory after getting badly injured in the war, remaining a man without identity, and it was my obligation to find him. In another thought I pictured him in Russia, having become a major Party figure after being brainwashed, and other fantasies like that which drove me crazy.

Later I tried all kinds of ways to find out what happened to him, all of them doomed to fail. In despair I even tried to trace this young man from Šurany, to shake him up and force him to remember. But decades passed and I did not even have his name!

When I was in Budapest, I knew a member of the movement by the name of Leah Neuman. When she understood who I was, she gave me two letters in Öcsi's handwriting. One was sent to a group of movement members in Slovakia, and one personally to her and it included two poems he had written at the front. From her I learned he escaped from a Hungarian labor camp, crossed the border with Slovakia in order to join a partisan group once the revolt broke out. In the meantime he found shelter in Leah's parental home, in northern Slovakia. Her father was among the very few who were included [sic] as crucial to the military effort, due to his rare professional expertise. Still, the family had made sure to prepare a hide-out because they had no trust in the Slovakians who could change this policy any moment when the need arose. And when the threat grew palpable, the family moved into their bunker. Öcsi was with them in hiding for sometime. When first rumors about the start of fighting reached them, he left the secure hiding place (the entire family survived and was liberated). His tempestuous nature did not allow him to stay inactive. He had to take part in the war against the Germans.

He had always lived as though the entire burden of the world was on his shoulders. All social injustice, [and] discrimination alarmed him and with all of his youthful enthusiasm he would go out to oppose it. There were debates in the movement, where Öcsi argued that as long as there were injustice, oppression, and exploitation of the weak, we could not fence ourselves off and deal with our own problem, no matter how pressing. Though it was true that we were suffering from antisemitism, and that we had no national home, we must not remain indifferent to the rest of suffering humanity. Not everyone agreed with these opinions of his, and they branded him a Communist. From the letter he wrote to Leah, I understood that all the starry-eyed ideas of his youth had crashed in the face of his harsh experience. I read his letter so many times. I remember exactly what he wrote to Leah:

> *Ever since I left all of you, I have been through a great deal. Most of my time I spent in battles. I think a lot about you. And I want to believe that you at least will stay alive. Today this is how I see things: This is not our struggle. If you manage to get through this, please, go to Eretz Israel. Be a pioneer and fight our struggle in that way, because there is where it begins and ends. Look, I'm still scribbling rhymes, and this is more or less how my mood looks:*

> > *Yesterday was the Great Fast,*
> > *My Father went to the house of prayer,*
> > *A cape covering his shoulders, soaked with his blood*
> > *And in his eyes dark and horrid the dream*
> > *That it is a Great Day.*
> > *And I will tell him, the first time,*
> > *That he's dreaming his dream here, and lives his day here,*
> > > *now,*
> > *The same hour rests on him and me,*
> > *Dying.*
> > *Oh, mother's last hour,*
> > > *And all of you fasted that Day of Awe,*
> > *Those who are good when thing go well and when they go bad,*
> > > *too,*
> > *These are our last holidays,*
> > *All of us [judged] to die.*
> > *Let us pray, say after me:*
> > *"God, we were as in a dream,*
> > *I to a canon model 30*
> > *And you there who run [?]*
> > *Let us pray . . ."*
> > *(at the front, Yom Kippur [Day of Atonement])*

Summer '45

We're on our way from Budapest to Balaton to join a summer colony, the first after the war. "We" are Andy and the four girls: Zippi, Leah, Erika, and I. We reached the place after many wanderings and not a few adventures. From the distance we already heard young people shouting, a mix of yells and song from where the tents were pitched. My first reaction was unease: Everything sounded free and normal, as if . . . As if nothing had ever happened! As if we had arrived at a place that wasn't ours. How would we be able to fit into this cheerful place, we who were still living [in] the [very] smell of those places? This question lingered throughout those summer days.

In the morning we met a group of young people, some of them familiar, others not. Among them one boy caught my attention. He radiated something fresh and clean, as though he had just taken a warm bath, something we did not usually encounter in those days. He was wearing a white, knitted, "turtleneck" sweater, and he appeared amused and curious at the same time. Andy said: "That's Yehoshua, my friend. We were together in the bunker." Memory is unreliable, and there are several versions of our first encounter, but I insist on mine. The image is clear, engraved in my memory and it has not worn off. That morning in the colony, I did not imagine we would become family, a "holy family" even.

When the colony came to an end, we drifted aimlessly for a while. Every so often we got lucky and had a hot meal, made by Yehoshua's mother, Mimi néni [Grandma Mimi—T. K.], whose good heart did not remain indifferent to us. We were waiting to hear what the "big ones" would decide about what next. Eventually the decision was to start a work force in Csillebérc mountains, based on a small core of senior movement members, and new people. Finally we had reached our destination. We saw the place and were amazed! It was a wonderful place! An abandoned summer cottage in a peach orchard, I'd never seen anything like it. And the season was early fall, the fruit was ripe in huge quantities. All this was surrounded by wooded hills in ravishing fall colors. The feeling was that the gates of paradise had opened before us. We did not need any more than that. We could not have dreamed of a place like this.

Work added an element of euphoria and romance. Our job was to thin out trees that were growing too densely. The forester marked trees for felling. Our pay was in the form of a few of those trees we

had felled. The mood was like in a children's tale. Mornings we left
with our tools and spent the entire day in the woods. This wasn't the
same when we did chores, but those too we accepted with innocent joy.

We were dizzy with the beautiful new world we were going to
build. We were sure no one was as good as us. Only we had a great
goal in life. Most of humanity had not seen the light yet. In this
atmosphere, people who had their two feet on the ground were sorely
needed, people who had not lost their sense of reality and were doing
the grey everyday work, which was also the most important. Yehoshua
was someone like that!

And there were philosophical conversations deep into the night
and early rises at first daylight so we'd manage to read some poetry
before setting out to work. We sang a lot. In a row, linking arms,
along the roads. We sang songs in Hungarian about social justice,
about the poor workers, we sang as if our lives depended on it.
And in Hebrew we sang songs of the movement and the homeland. We
sang in Yiddish even though we did not always understand the words.
There was great enthusiasm. Those who observed us from the side,
or from "above" might have thought that we were slightly losing
our way. Too much foreign literature and poetry. Neither Bialik
nor Tchernichovsky[1] they did not mean so much to us. We identified,
rather, with Ady, and we admired the poets Kosztolanyl and Josef
Atilla. Arrows of criticism did not take long to reach us. "All of
you here are infected with Andy-ism!" was the new reproach.

Then the day came when, to our sadness, the woods no longer
offered us work. We had felled all the trees that needed felling
and we had to move on. We moved to a new place but the miracle did
not repeat itself. And now our work conditions were already linked
with the political reality. We had to pretend we were members of
the Communist Party to get work and housing. It didn't take long
before we left, or rather, escaped in the middle of the night after
a small "misunderstanding" with some representatives of the liberation forces, the Russians. Again we were refugees. Maybe not exactly
homeless, we were taken in by existing [Zionist] groups in the city,
but we were only being "tolerated."

It was in this grey reality that they began talking about the
entire work force immigrating to Eretz Israel. This faced me with a
difficult dilemma. What was I to do? Go with my friends, or stay with
the friend I loved? Did I have a right to personal happiness? The
general mood was that one was more or less obliged to forego personal
interests. Society came before anything else. On the evening before,

1   The Zionist preference was for the "national" poets Bialik and Tchernichovsky.

I talked with Yehoshua. The two of us stayed up late into the night. Yehoshua tried to convince me to stay with Andy come what may. He quieted my "social" conscience, took part of the responsibility on himself, and released me from guilt, removing the stain of betrayal.

Sometimes I wonder what my fate would have been had Yehoshua not stayed up that night? How would things have developed then?

Part Three

DR. NEUMAN

When he finished reading, Dr. Neuman's body hurt from the long hours he had spent sitting, and he felt exhausted and lonely. He closed the two note-books and rested his elbows on his desk, his head between his hands. This had been the first time he had suggested writing as a part of therapy. It was good it had been Marta. She knew how to write! He believed writing could assist therapy. Wasn't that, in the end, what psychoanalysis was all about? What had he been doing all those years on the couch if not telling the story of his life? Here, before him, were Marta's notebooks which held all those stories together—and they had power, narrative consistency. These brown books were a story in their own right, about the pains and fears, the appre-hensions and hesitations that had accompanied the composition. She had literally written with all her heart.

Dr. Neuman read through the notebooks several times, but his first reading, that night, was especially emotional. Marta's presence shone from the pages—and he wasn't looking for anything more. Neither to analyze, nor to interpret—just to feel, just to dwell with the memories as they resonated. In later readings came the insights he would formulate and record in Marta's therapy notes, some of which were to do with the therapeutic aspect of the text and some of which weren't. From a medical perspective, the notebooks testified to the success of her treatment. Writing had proved a healing activ-ity, the therapy was complete, and the patient was home again. But for both patient and therapist, the it meant much more than that.

Marta's notebooks were a subtle work of recollection. Rather than a heap of memories, a black hole, or a stew cooked up from mere scraps of life, they were an orderly progression along a timeline. That was a good sign. Dr. Neuman was somewhat surprised, because in their conversations he'd observed that Marta was quite distracted. But here! Such order! Memory arranged. The restoration of memory to consciousness. "Restoration" was the term that came to mind—archeology. That was what Rafi, his son, was doing with ancient fragments from digs. He sat in the basement of the Department of Archeology at the university and restored broken vessels, healed them, gluing shards into parts of a whole that had forever vanished, filling gaps. Dr. Neuman sensed a similarity. The names, for instance: the way Marta recovered names: her close and remote relatives, her teachers, friends, and neighbors, even passers-by; the names of newspapers, books she had read. They felt to him like the surviving fragments of a trampled, broken existence, which her writing had somehow reassembled. And the language!

Healing and saving. The salvaging of a buried life. Indeed, he thought, life restored. Not reconstructed. It was a return of life as it had been, down to the smallest details, stories that brought together everything she could remember. And there was so much she remembered! Life at home, in the town and nearby, life around the river, the garden, the fields, the life of the sugar factory, the gymnasium in the center of the district. From all this wealth her life emerged, until catastrophe struck, until the crash fully unfolded. And from this point onwards she was unable to put the pieces together. Her writing reflected that so clearly, he thought. These fragments of life didn't connect to anything; the life could not be brought back. And, he feared, there probably was no way to heal it. Her writing choked. Marta wrote in an almost radically spare manner about the period of expulsion and forced labor; it was cautious, minimalist writing, held back, remote, a writing of silence. The pages also reflected a before and after. She did not put down the worst of it, he was sure about that. Nor had she told him anything more. As she approached that moment in her story, it was as though she walked on tiptoes, moving gently, looking after herself and those for whom she was writing. In his heart, Dr. Neuman thanked her for everything she had managed to write. He knew how much pain it had caused, and how much pain was in store. Something is still bound to happen—the thought passed through his mind—this is not her last word. It would not be the last word of her story. Though he was no expert on literature, he knew, as a physician, that it was impossible to write after Auschwitz. Some philosopher had said something important about that. But it was equally impossible to keep silent. In the long term.

Reading the pages for the first time, it seemed to Dr. Neuman that Marta had written just the way she was. This was her. Not a bit of melodrama, not a trace of exaggeration or excess. Subtle precision. She had a gift. She could have been a writer. May still become one . . . She had only exaggerated about one thing: there weren't many mistakes. Tomorrow she would be leaving the department, but these notebooks would stay with him for a while longer.

***

Marta finished packing the next morning. She collected her possessions from the wardrobe shelves and the shower room and cleaned the shelves with a wet hospital towel. It would not enter her mind to leave behind anything dirty. She also got her things from the desk, passed over it with the same towel, and checked whether she had forgotten anything in the drawers. Everything was packed, except for the notebooks which stayed with Dr. Neuman. She was ready. Andy arrived towards noon, she took a last glance at the shower room, opened the cupboard, and took her handbag as well as her coat, which had been hanging there since winter, off the hook behind the door. Andy approached her bed and moved it a little away from the wall. "We won't leave that lamp here," he said, pulling out the plug. He took the lamp in one hand and the suitcase in the other, Marta opened the door, and they left. That's the first part, she said to herself, not looking back at her room or wondering about who would live there next, what sadness would once more reside between its walls.

They walked along the empty corridor to the reception office. The nurse invited them to take a seat. Andy put down the suitcase and the lamp, its electricity cord dangling onto the floor. The release procedure was simple. The documents were ready, and Marta signed in the places the nurse pointed out.

"Well, that's it. We're done," said the nurse. "You're going back home! Good luck."

"I'd like to shake hands with the doctor. Can I just look into his office?" asked Andy.

"Dr. Neuman is not here. He's had to go out for some meetings," said the nurse.

"Ah, too bad," said Andy, "I would have liked to thank him personally." Looking at Marta, he asked: "You already said goodbye, right?"

Marta nodded and felt her cheeks burning.

"Please can you tell him thank you from me? A special thank you."

"Of course I will. All right, so here are your documents—you give them to your doctor." She held out a white envelope bearing the stamp of the mental health clinic.

Andy took the envelope and rose. "Thank you," he said streching out his hand and the nurse shook it fondly.

"Thank you too," she said with a broad smile. She then held out her hand to Marta: "Good luck." Marta wondered what luck the nurse meant. Luck staying well? Going on living?

Andy lifted the suitcase and tried to hold the lamp in his other hand.

"Give me the envelope," said Marta and took it from him, "you only have two hands."

She looked at the nurse, who was observing them with amused curiosity, and held the envelope, trying to feel its weight.

"Come on," said Andy, heading for the door, "we are leaving."

"Goodbye," the nurse called after them.

With the suitcase between them, Marta and Andy walked toward the entrance door. A flow of cool air came in when they opened it. Winter had arrived—soon the rains will start, she thought. Andy stopped on the entrance porch, put down suitcase and lamp, and hugged her with both arms.

"Dušička," the two of them said simultaneously, and Andy added: "Moja duša."[1] Then they walked in the direction of the parking lot and vanished between the cars.

Dr. Neuman knew that when she left the department, Marta might disappear from his life. The thought that they'd never meet and talk again made him sad to the point of pain, real physical pain. He was grateful that Marta had left the notebooks with him; she had written them for him too, and had chosen him to be her first reader. He went on reading them until she came in for the follow-up meeting which had been arranged. He felt a little embarrassed whenever he read in her notebooks. Maybe it was the embarrassment of an infatuated man, but it still was a pleasant thing to do: it removed him a little from his professional position as a psychiatrist, allowing him to feel a more regular connection. He had no intention of denying his feelings for Marta, repressing them, or making sense of them, even if his job required him to. When it happened, Dr. Neuman was even a little amused by the situation. He enjoyed this small personal triumph over the theory and practice of relations between therapist and patient. There was a terminology for the infatuation that often arose in the therapeutic process: transference and countertransference. They were common, but there were of course clear instructions concerning appropriate professional conduct. Without guilt or awkwardness, Dr. Neuman felt these clinical definitions and instructions were irrelevant in his case. This was nothing to do with either arrogance or disagreement, nothing to do with contempt, a need to cross boundaries, or a desire to let himself off the hook. What had happened between them was and would remain a matter of the soul, and this made him happy. Nothing but some grains of happiness. There was no point in asking how such a thing could occur, or why it had been her. It had simply happened when they sat in that room, close, talking or in silence. He had never considered where it would lead. It also never crossed

---

1   Slovak: My soul.

his mind that he should tell Zelda about it. He knew the relationship with Marta would not develop. And yet, it had been love.

From their first meeting, Marta had moved him. Her sadness had touched the very tissue of his heart. In the course of her therapy, a living, present, pulsing feeling had grown inside him. His decision to stray from the procedure he himself had determined and be her therapist was not medically indicated. Dr. Neuman, who was usually seen as rather formal, prudent, and reserved, both at work and in his private life, surprised himself. Their meetings were therapeutic and only took place in the unit—nowhere else. He loved talking to her, listening to what she said; he loved her wisdom and intuition, her gentle, quick humor. She was unconditionally decent and carried inside an ever-present sadness which only grew stronger. He knew that he could do nothing more about it.

When Marta began to improve and felt his love, she responded. Was it perhaps his love that helped her heal? He'd felt her response very clearly, but they'd never talked about it. Except for that one long embrace at the end of that meeting. Nor did not mention it with their bodies. And yet, as they sat so closely, love shone from their bodies and their hearts spoke. They had a tacit agreement that what was happening only concerned the two of them. It was no secret, but it wasn't the business of any of their relations either. Not Andy, not Zelda, Rafi's mother, with whom he had been living for twenty-five years.

When she came in for her appointment, Dr. Neuman awaited her like a man in love. During the meeting he gave her back the notebooks and felt that something precious had been taken from him. It was their last meeting.

***

Marta saw Dr. Neuman about one month after she left hospital. As far as therapy was concerned, nothing remarkable happened. But it was not a therapy session. The air felt heavy, the clouds in the sky were normal for late fall, but the summer heat was not yielding so easily. In Dr. Neuman's office the fan stirred the warm air that the window, open to the garden, let in. Light and joy came with her as she entered the room. Dr. Neuman rose and pressed her two hands between his, saying how happy he was to see her.

"I am happy to see you too," she laughed. How beautiful she had become, he thought.

"Can we sit?" She laughed again.

"Of course, come in and sit down," he said and put an arm around her shoulder. He felt her shiver.

They sat in the easy chairs, just as they had during the long months of her hospitalization. Dr. Neuman could not stop looking at her. Her eyes shone and her skin was soft.

"It's good to see you again, Marta," he said emotionally.

"Yes," she said, "it is good to meet again."

"Tell me how you are. How do you feel?"

There were so many things he wanted to ask her, know about her, but he restrained himself, waiting for her, allowing her to speak. She was relaxed as she spoke, telling him about her return home, her return to life. It hadn't happened overnight, but there was progress every day; gradually she was finding her way back to her life. What a difference, he thought, she speaks about herself with such ease now.

"Excellent," said Dr. Neuman, "rapid changes always worry me. It's better this way, and healthier."

"I really feel it happening." She grew more serious.

"What do you mean?"

"I feel healthier inside." She pondered for a moment: "A little healthier. And that little extra helps to keep me afloat. Do you see what I mean?"

"Yes, yes, of course . . . And it makes me very happy."

"Maybe you will also be happy to know that we plan to visit Naomi in Eilat. You remember her, don't you?"

"Naomi your daughter. Absolutely! We met for a moment in the garden." Dr. Neuman grew silent, noticing this "we," which came so naturally it ached, and then he went on: "I am very pleased for you. I know how important it is for you, and for Naomi too. You mentioned her a lot."

"I talk to her all the time now. And Michael," she said seriously, but laughing too. "Only in my heart, naturally. Only in my heart for the time being."

"For the time being. It will get to them anyway. You can be sure of that."

"Yes, I know that hearts can talk . . . It's true."

The two of them grew silent. Suddenly Dr. Neuman felt a sharp pain in his chest. He hadn't done anything about it, although he had promised Marta to look after himself shortly before she left. Seeing him still looking tired and weak, she was certain that he was still neglecting his health. He knew he must have some thorough checks—that it was urgent.

"And you?" Marta asked, picking up his thoughts. "How are you? How do you feel? Have you been to a doctor?"

"Not yet, as you can see," he said, feeling scolded.

"You promised me," she said seriously, "or have you forgotten?"

"I haven't forgotten, Marta, but I've been so busy I haven't found the time. I promise you I will go for that check-up. Do you want me to sign a statement?" he asked, pretending to be serious.

"Yes," she answered, laughing.

He looked at her and knew he couldn't continue talking like this—he had to do something.

"I have some forms we need to fill out . . ." He took some sheets from a folder with her name printed on it and began to write. "I think we can start reducing the medicine gradually," he said.

"Do you think so?" she asked, with some alarm.

"I definitely do. We will not stop everything, it will be slowly, of course . . . We'll lower the dose a little, and maybe in the future we can stop the medicine altogether. We'll see. But doing it gradually is important."

"Ok," she said, "thank you."

"Thank you for what?" he asked in surprise.

"For everything," she said, not smiling now, "thanks for everything."

Dr. Neuman completed the forms, signed them, and set them aside. Then he bent over his briefcase, took out the notebooks, put them on the low table between them, and looked at her.

"It's me who should be thanking you, Marta. For leaving the notebooks with me, letting me read what you wrote." His voice trembled a little and his face contracted as if he was in pain. "I want to talk a little about them."

"Yes . . ." Marta grew tense in her chair.

"So, I read what you wrote."

"Yes? I am happy you did—it's important to me," she said mechanically.

"First of all . . . how can I put it? . . . it's hard . . ."

"Hard?" Her voice expressed concern.

"It's hard for me to say anything, Marta, your writing moved me very much. It is so alive. Really . . . I read it all through in one go."

She had never seen him so enthusiastic. "What do you mean?"

"Everything you described, I could see it before my eyes. It's excellent!"

"Really? You think?"

"Yes, I really think so. You've done something very significant. You managed to arrange your recollections and capture them in language. That's very important for you—and your children when they read it."

"I'm not sure they will read it . . . I hope . . ."

"Of course they will. But for that to happen you will have to actually give them it! You will do that, won't you?"

"Yes, yes. I just have to find the opportunity, the right moment."

"You will. I trust you."

"I need the courage . . ."

"I am sure you already have the courage." Dr. Neuman paused: "I want to tell you something else important. It's not just the question of writing these memories. How you wrote them—that's an important too . . ."

"Yes? . . . What do you mean?"

"Your write beautifully, Marta. I couldn't stop reading. It was so touching. You managed to express things so . . . it's . . . you really write well."

"Do I?" she asked in a shy voice, "do you really think so?"

"Marta dear, you know I do. I told you so a moment ago."

"What did you tell me?"

"That what I am telling you now is what I genuinely think. We do go some way back in that matter, don't we? We have some shared history, don't we?"

"Yes. But I wanted to hear you say it again."

"And I want to tell you something else."

"Oh dear, you sound serious—what is it?"

"You really overdid it, that thing about your mistakes. There are some here and there, but nothing terrible. I think it even adds . . ."

"It adds? What could it possibly add? I wish my Hebrew was flawless . . ."

"You know, if you should decide, one day, to turn it into a book . . . those mistakes can always be corrected; but when the writing itself is no good, nothing can be done."

"A book?!"

"Why not? I believe . . ."

Dr. Neuman stopped and thought about everything he hadn't told her, everything he felt and hadn't said—and he wished the meeting would end. Nothing of her would remain with him, no concrete part of Marta, now that he was returning the notebooks. Just a memory. He could not hope to see her in his office again. He hoped she wouldn't sink again. Meetings outside the hospital were out of the question. And anyway, now I must really get myself examined, he reminded himself. I'm not in good shape, my chest is always hurting. The meeting was sad, and their farewell even sadder. Marta left the office with her notebooks, went out of Dr. Neuman's life, and the sadness that took hold of him was heavy.

Marta decided to walk to the central bus station. The air weighed her down, but she preferred to walk rather than get another bus there. Wandering through the busy street, pressing the notebooks close to her, she was holding onto something from the office, from Dr. Neuman. At the sooty station, she boarded her bus and sat down by a window; she clutched the notebooks even tighter to herself and watched the traffic go by.

Part Four

NAOMI

Some weeks after my mother left hospital in Haifa, she and my father came to visit me in Eilat. I had suggested the idea when I visited her in hospital. Just as I was rushing to catch the last bus, I invited them, without giving it any thought. They accepted my offer and told me they wanted to see me and make a real trip of it. I had forgotten all about the invitation, and I was completely overwhelmed when they reminded me. Already? So soon after her time in hospital? And what if something goes wrong? I was worried about spending several days with my parents, but it made me happy too. Although I needed distance from them as much as I needed air to breathe, they were also, at the same time, the center of my life, the very thing that allowed me to breathe. And anyway, what better sign that my mother was recovering, finally, after such a long, desperate time in hospital?

I have never managed to understand how our mother's hospitaliza-tion, such a dramatic event in our lives, went by with me and Michael hardly noticing. When our mother went to hospital we were not aware she had suffered a breakdown, that she was suffering from deep depression; and we didn't know she was on a psychiatric ward. What did we make of it, her being gone for so long? It was erased from our memories. And when she returned home for a short break, and she told us a little about the hospital, we still didn't know what was going on and didn't ask about it, even though she was clearly unwell. We were used to not asking. Nothing. When I was little we once had this conversation:

"Where are your mommy and your daddy?"

"They died in the war."

"What's that blue number on your arm?"

"That's from the war."

And then I stopped asking. That's how it continued, in silence. Our par-ents did not tell, and we did not ask. We were afraid to ask. We didn't know. Nothing. And we lived as if that was all right, as if there was nothing to know. That was how it was in our family. And we were, actually, really all right as a family. A mom, dad, and two children who were loved and cared for. We had a little house and a yard and a garden, and we had some chicks until they were devoured, and on the other side of the wall lived a family with two daughters: there was a lot of yelling at them in a language we didn't understand, and sometimes they were beaten with a belt. But we were loved. Mom and Dad didn't beat us; we were not aware that they, and we along with them, were suspended in the air. Dull sounds, blurs, figures moving behind a screen all around us, but everybody was trying their best to only see ordinary life. Over the years, the figures behind the screen grew into a black, lumpy mass. We knew without knowing that it was there; we just acted as though it wasn't. There was a tacit agreement at home to ignore it: we weren't looking behind the screen, even though we were aware, by now, of its presence all the time.

With hindsight I think that our mother's hospitalization could have been an opportunity to start undoing that black mass, dislodge some threads. Michael and I were rather grown-up already and we knew something wasn't right. Mother and Father could've told us something. It had to come from them, though. I remember a moment when it nearly happened. Mommy and I almost began talking. Almost. It was when I visited her in Haifa. Hospital is a good place to talk about illness, it stands to reason. My mother is sick, I visit her in hospital—and we talk about her illness. But talking about this illness wasn't obvious. Nothing related to that black lump was obvious in our family—other than silence. Even my visit was not self-evident. Because, after all, I hadn't been told, until then, that she was there. My dad wrote and asked me to drop by there.

"What? What hospital? What's happened?" I said into the phone, alarmed.

"Don't worry. But she is really asking for you to visit. It's important. I am asking you." His phone voice was different.

"Where is it?"

"In Haifa, in the psychiatric wing of the hospital."

"The psychiatric wing?" Now I was even more taken aback.

My father explained where I was supposed to go, but added nothing else. Deep in the back of my mind shadows and blurs were on the move, but he didn't say anything else. I remember getting to the hospital and being very tense; I didn't know what to expect. Psychiatric departments are scary places, very scary, and they're even scarier with a black, lumpy mass in the background. And yet, the visit was surprisingly good. The department consisted of some shacks in the corner of the hospital grounds, not part of the main building. From outside, it looked a bit like a small kibbutz. Nothing extraordinary happened and my mother actually looked quite OK. Better than she had when she'd stayed that weekend. She seemed calm, she laughed a little, spoke with ease. Totally normal, you could say. I asked myself why she was there, and why it was so important that I come, but all in all I was happy I'd visited. I have a good memory of it.

My mom showed me around, invited me to see her room, and that was really fine too, for a hospital. She had a room of her own. She showed me the activities room and the things the patients made. There were some really nice crafts, colorful; I wouldn't have guessed they were made by people who were mentally ill. My mother introduced me to some nice instructors, and the atmosphere in the room seemed peaceful. People were sitting there, focused on their work. That surprised me. I'm not sure what I had expected, but it was not what I imagined. Then we went to some sort of inner yard which included a small garden. There, we met the doctor who was treating her. Dr. Neuman.

It was strange meeting him. I don't think his sudden appearance was a coincidence. He walked up to us, he was very polite, kind of European, a bit Old World. My mom introduced us, and he was friendly, shook hands. He asked me about Eilat, what it was like working with the birds, what I was going to do afterwards, what my plans were, etc. I wasn't very forthcoming— I felt sort of reluctant to be nice to him, as if it was his fault my mom was there.

After we said goodbye to the doctor, we left the hospital. It wasn't a closed unit. My mother took me for a stroll along the promenade that began near the hospital and stretched the length of the coast. Waves were crashing on the rocks that lay scattered on the beach and salty splinters of water reached all the way up to us. There was a small café at the end of the promenade, and we sat outside on the terrace, very near the water. We drank cocoa—we really love that, both of us. Hot in the winter, cold in the summer. We were drinking cold cocoa and eating cake, and then I sensed that it was there, about to happen. That my mom was about to say something about why she was in hospital; she'd want us to talk, any minute now. She probably noticed I was waiting for something, or maybe she herself was worried she might not be able to go through with it. We didn't speak for a while, and then we just talked about the birds and Eilat, about how Daddy was managing at home. Nothing about her illness, and we certainly didn't mention the psychiatric ward.

Once my mother was released and returned home, it stayed that way. She came back in a good mood, as if she'd never been to hospital. She seemed to have recovered, but we were cautious when we talked, we walked on egg-shells and maintained the silence. Life seemed to go back to normal, and the silence simply continued. I'm trying to understand why. I think it was fear that kept us silent. Their fear to talk about what happened, about things that are impossible to talk about, perhaps. I think they kind of infected Michael and me with that fear, so we too, we too are afraid. They never tried to talk with us, and we did not try to talk with them.

But it wasn't fear alone. I am convinced they maintained the silence because they loved us so much and were concerned. They did not want us to be hurt. That must have been what they thought. Fear and love continuously fed into this silence, which grew deeper and developed into a bunker, three kilometers below the ground. But even though everything was buried so thoroughly, there was no way of getting rid of it. These things somehow surrounded us, and I felt me and Michael had to keep a distance from Mom and Dad—if we got too close it would be dangerous for both them and us. I loved them from a safe distance, and Eilat was quite a long way away. From there, I could love my parents without having to be constantly on guard, without having to worry about the fear, especially my mother's fear. My father was always stronger than her. I don't remember any cracks, anxiety, or any other type of weakness in there. His bunker was more hermetic.

Still, it was my mother who was the one who found the way out of this bunker of silence. She filled two entire notebooks during her time in hospital, and she gave them to me when they visited in Eilat.

Mom and Dad were in high spirits, and I got carried along too. As soon as they arrived I stopped worrying. I was happy they had come and that they could see my life in Eilat. I was a research assistant at the bird station and I also conducted tours at the field school; I walked barefoot and wore shorts, was suntanned like a desert dweller. It was kind of exotic, this existence, wild and free, close to nature, healthy. I wanted to impress them, for them to be happy I was like that, free of the black mass, the bunker—that my life was different. I was healthy. They came for four days, and everything seemed to go well. My roommate, Hagit, had left on a vacation and that enabled me to host them. The cheap appartement was a bit spartan, but Hagit and I had made it nice. Before they arrived I gave the place a thorough cleaning, so it would be pleasant and comfortable for my mom. She had all kinds of sensitivities about cleanliness. And I wanted to show her I was independent, that I knew how to run a home, and didn't just hike in the mountains.

"What a nice apartment," they couldn't stop telling me.

"It's so clean here," said my mom, "everything's sparkling. It reminds me a bit of our room in the kibbutz," she said to my father, who smiled at her.

She especially took to the small wooden book case Hagit and I had built in the sitting room. She said she was happy we read too. Having shelves at home was important, there must be books. I wasn't surprised to hear this—she loved books and read a lot. They had a couple of books subscriptions through my father's job—Sifria La'am (the People's Library) and Am Oved (Working People). Every so often, I remember, a new book arrived and we would all read it. Sometimes Mom and would discuss it.

"What do you think about that one?" she asked when I put Hemingway's *The Sun Also Rises* back on the shelf.

"The plot just drags on and on, the hero plods from one café to the next, they drink, get drunk—what's it all about? Nothing."

"But that's the point!" I could hear her disappointment. "It's literature. The writer makes you feel what it's like to be the hero, doesn't he?" She really was disappointed in me. "That's how one describes a life without meaning, inner emptiness."

"Really? I don't know . . ." I was surprised. I hadn't thought like that about novels.

The weather, too, was favorable. Late fall is a lovely time to visit the desert. The great heat abates, and large flights of migratory birds pass overhead. The schedule I made for them was busy. I wanted them to see as much as possible; I wanted the days to be full and for them to have a special and interesting time. It was not going to be any ordinary touristy trip to Eilat! In the mornings we would go out on a hike. My mother had grown stronger and walked without difficulty. It was my dad, actually, who found it harder and lagged behind, but basically they kept up with me pretty well. I showed them the desert as if it were my kingdom. I was the queen of the desert. We went down a steep trail to Ein Netafim, we took my father's pickup to cross the plane of Moon Valley, and the highlight was a walk in the Red Canyon. We passed through all the crevices, we went down ropes and ladders, real hikers' stuff. In the evenings, we went home covered in dust, our faces red from the sun, our legs tired and our eyes shining. We were happy.

One morning we drove along the fields and date plantations of a neighboring kibbutz to my bird station. The nets were distributed in the surrounding fields, and by this time in the morning, some birds were already caught in them. My job at the station was to disentangle birds from the nets and bring them to the hut, which was where Steve, the American researcher, was working. I wanted them to see everything from close up: how I would free a bird from the string very gently, holding it in my hand with two fingers clasping its head, and then put it in a cloth bag where it would become calm. I wanted them to see the pounding of the startled heart in the small bird's body. "This tiny, tiny bird covers thousands of kilometers in its short lifetime," I explained. "For such journeys it needs a strong heart."

The American researcher would identify the bird, attach a numbered ring to its delicate leg, and then examine it thoroughly while recording its weight, the condition of its feathers, its fat reserves. He even identified the parasites that migrated along with the bird, and put them in a small jar of formalin. (I was appalled to learn years later that the entire project was part of a secret US military study into the use of bird migration in biological warfare) The best moment, for me, occurred at the end of the process when you released the confused little bird, which dizzily took off into the sky. I observed my parents as they watched spellbound, and suddenly they seemed so foreign in this setting, among the fields, the birds, the desert. I felt I had managed to surprise them with all these special things I was now doing, impress them with how far I had come. My attempt to lead a healthy, free life had been successful. They were proud of me.

On the eve of their departure, my dad festively announced we were having dinner in a restaurant on the north beach. As we walked down the avenue lined with date palms towards the beach, my father put his arm around my mother's shoulder and pulled her close. I thought it had been years, many years, since I'd seen them like this. I remembered the glances they exchanged when I was little, communicating without words. Something would pass between them then, something that was theirs alone. Sometimes, my mom would ask Dad to zip or unzip a dress, turning her head at him as he stood behind her. Sometimes she'd asked him to hook her bra, and then he would put his hands on her exposed shoulders. Mommy was very different in those years. They walked like this all the way to the restaurant and on the way back too. Eilat made them romantic. Before bed, we had tea in the sitting room and ate cookies my mother had brought from home. I saw her looking at the bookshelves. Then she got up, got a book, and opened it.

"Does this one belong to you?" she asked.

"What is it?" I asked.

"You like Leah Goldberg?" she asked without answering me.

"Show me?" I asked. "I can't see what book you're talking about."

My mother raised it a little and I immediately recognized the blue-green cover.

"Sure, *Early and Late*. I like her poems." I hoped she would not look at the dedication. "You know her?" I asked. My mom did not reply, but smiled mysteriously.

The next morning, when we'd had our coffee and my father had begun taking their bags down to the pickup, my mother approached me and handed me a brown envelope.

"Here's something for you," she said. "Read it when you have time. There's no rush."

"What is it? A book?" I opened the envelope and looked inside.

"No, it isn't a book," she whispered. "It's . . . something I've written. You'll understand when you read it."

I peeped inside and saw two brown notebooks. I took them out. On the cover of one of them, it said, in handwriting: "Haifa, Winter." It was her writing. I knew those slanting, slightly strangely formed letters. As a girl I used to love watching her hand when she wrote. It really fascinated me. She seemed to write each letter from the wrong direction.

"It's for you," said my mother quietly. "These notebooks are for you. Read them later, when we've left. Leave them for now."

"But what is it, Mommy? Just tell me. What have you written?"

"They're my memories. I wrote them down when I was in hospital."

"Ah . . . yes . . . the desk . . . . Thank you, Mommy, thank you. I will read it," I promised, but didn't know how I could bear to.

I saw that she was embarrassed; she seemed to be searching for something. "Later," she said. "There's no hurry." Again I promised I'd read the notebooks, still unsure if I could.

My father had already put the bags in the pickup, as well as the big cooler box which arrived full of food my mother had made. She brought a lot, to make sure there would be some left when they went home. Hagit and I would be eating Mom's food for days. My mother went into the yard and I stood with the envelope in one hand and the notebooks in the other, not knowing what to do. I put them on the bed and followed her outside. My father's pickup was parked near the gate and my mom was just getting into the passenger seat. My father walked over to hug me tight. I walked up to the window on my mother's side and gave her a kiss.

"Thanks for coming," I said, "it was lovely. I hope you enjoyed it too."

"Of course, it was wonderful," said my father. "If you need anything, any help, let me know."

"It was wonderful," my mother added. "My darling. You have no idea how I enjoyed it. It's unbelievable here."

"I'll let you know, Dad. Goodbye, then."

My father started the pickup, they waved again, and were off.

"Safe journey," I shouted, "mind the desert road!"

I stood there for a while. The moment when they drive off, leaving me behind, always opens a black hole; I get lost inside myself, in the world; the earth swallows me and I disappear. It always takes some time. Then I get myself together, tell myself that I'm not a baby anymore, desperate in the kibbutz baby home; but I know it's not just that. The monster is always just below the surface, biding its time, waiting to leap and strangle. I stood there wondering what my mother meant when she'd used the word "unbelievable." I wondered if she was puzzled about the word too and was just thinking about it herself. Mommy seemed to have truly recovered.

When I got back inside the apartment and closed the door behind me, my eye fell on the envelope and the two brown notebooks next to it on the bed. They were the same as the ones we had used in school when we were children. I quickly leafed through one: pages and pages filled with her hand-writing—dense lines. On the first page, I read:

> I was number three in our lineup. Andy, my oldest brother was two and a half when I was born, and the next brother, Öcsi, one and a half. From the moment I could think, my admiration for Öcsi was boundless. More than anything I wanted to be like him and when people mentioned a similarity between us it would make me very happy. But we were not close. For me he was an example, the unattainable ideal, and I was grateful with the merest crumb of his attention.

I felt like I could hear her say it: Öcsi. Suddenly, there was a name. The radio presenter on those programs my mom listened to tensely every day mentioned so many names. Names and more names—of people, places, and anyone who might have any information on their whereabouts.

I was just a little girl, but I remember it really well. My mother would tune in every afternoon to listen to the *Program for the Search after Relatives.* It was like a ritual, and it could not be interrupted. The presenter read and our mother listened, sucked in by the broadcaster's voice; she listened to the names, more and more and ever more names. She listened with all of her being, desperate, swept away on the stream of names, vanishing into her fierce listening: maybe the next name, maybe the next program. Sometimes she listened while looking at me playing by her side, looking right through me as though I was transparent, not there. That's the way I grew up, it was part of what went on at home when I was little. At the time it did not seem strange or unusual that Mommy became wholly absorbed, every day, as she listened to a radio program with foreign names.

Öcsi, I thought. Now there's a name. So it was this name for whom my mom was waiting all of those years? When did she stop waiting? When did she give up? Or has she never given up, never stopped waiting? A strong wind started up outside, and through the window I saw clouds of dust and bits of paper being swept up. Fall in Eilat. In my stomach too, something began to move. These were my mother's memories. This was what she had written in hospital. I could picture the table in her room, an old desk with some drawers on the side. I tried to imagine her there, in the room that reminded me of a nun's cell, sitting at that desk and writing. It was as though I was watching a movie about someone. I remembered she used to make spelling mistakes, funny ones. She and daddy too. Sometimes it was amusing how it changed the words and turned them strange. When she wrote a *tet* instead of a *tav* or the other way around. I put the notebooks back into their envelope and placed it on *Early and Late*, which my mother hadn't put back on the shelf. I put them both on top of a pile of books on the shelf, and pushed the whole pile until it touched the wall.

A year later, towards the end of the fall, my work in Eilat came to an end and I moved to Jerusalem. I started to study biology at the university. It was the first time in my life that I'd moved and taken things with me to the new apartment. I had accumulated all kinds of thing during my time in Eilat—property, you'd call it, I suppose. Books, kitchen utensils, a red bedcover, stones I had collected on hikes in the Negev and Sinai deserts, a large green one a geologist at the ancient Timna copper mine gave me, and various odds and ends. I packed everything into two big boxes which I mailed to my new address in the Greek colony in Jerusalem. Two friends and I rented an apartment in an old stone house. On my first weekend there my parents came over to lend me a hand. My father found me an old desk that reminded me of the one in the hospital, and my mother brought plastic boxes with food to tide us over during our first few days. She had also knitted me a long, yellow, woolen scarf. "It's important to keep your neck warm, down in the back," she explained. "I am familiar with cold weather: Jerusalem is not Eilat."

I noticed the two of them were very excited about me studying at the university. My mother even teared up a bit. She said something about how she had always wanted to go to university, but hadn't gone because of what happened, and how proud she was of me. After they left, they also sent me a telegram wishing me good luck with my studies in natural sciences. My degree would enable me to do research on bird migration, that mysterious flight across continents and oceans. In my first year, I found myself doing chemistry, physics, and mathematics. It was very hard work and completely took over my life. Birds, the desert, and Eilat were far in the past.

Some weeks later I received a large envelope from Hagit in the mail. "It seems you forgot these things in the flat, so here they are," she wrote. Inside the envelope were Leah Goldberg's *Early and Late* and my mother's brown notebooks. I hadn't even noticed they were missing. The notebooks had caught up with me, come back into my life, and were demanding to be read. I decided I would read them soon. I put the envelope on my desk so that I'd see it every day and not forget. At the weekend, I'll read, I would remind myself every week. I'll read it during the next vacation, when the semester ends. And when the semester break did arrive, it was impossible to delay any longer.

I got into bed, wrapped myself in a blanket and started to read. I held my nose and swallowed my mom's writing as fast as I could, trying to avoid the bitter taste of this pill: don't bite, don't chew, just get it down without noticing. The story had to be administered somehow, once and for all. I read uninterruptedly. It took a few hours—and then I must have fallen asleep. I remembered nothing the next morning. I had read without understanding, read words and sentences without taking them in, the masses of names of people and places unremembered. I read the story without following the narrative, the order of things, the events, the plot. Many years later, when I was finally able to read my mother's memories properly, when she was no longer alive, I could see the order, the timeline she had shaped. But on this first reading, I was too taken aback by the words, the names, too scared of the story. All I wanted was to get to the end, close the notebooks, and put them back in the envelope.

"I read your recollections," I wrote to my mother. "Thank you very much for letting me read them. Let's talk about it next time I visit. I'll bring them with me so you can give them to Michael too." I didn't want to be alone with those memories.

It was a long journey from Jerusalem to home. I liked to catch the Friday midday train to Haifa and from there take the bus north. Though the trip took more time it involved fewer transfers at bus stations which always reeked of urine and the sticky filth that was on the floors, walls, railings, and benches. The journey home began under a grey sky and the humid chill went right into my bones. By the time I reached Haifa the sky was black and it was pouring. The rain came down in sheets to form huge, dark puddles on the side of the road. Cars sped by, spraying pedestrians with the muddy water, and by the time I got onto the bus my legs were soaking. The bus left the station and through the window I gazed at the wet streets and the people rushing along them on their way somewhere. I fell asleep.

When I got off the bus, the rain was still coming down hard and I reached home completely drenched. Situations like this, when a cold or some other illness loomed, always worried my mother. She immediately told me to get a hot shower and put on warm, dry clothes. When I came out of the bathroom, a cup of hot cocoa was already waiting on the kitchen table. The house was cozy, but I felt an oncoming temperature and shivered. I spent that entire weekend in bed with a high fever. My mom nursed me the way only she knew. I slept most of the time. She came in every so often to check how I was doing, bringing me freshly squeezed orange juice or chamomile tea with honey. She also wanted me to get up and gargle lemon juice, her ultimate treatment for any kind of cold and flu, which she'd learned from Dr. Netzach, her herbalist. But all I wanted was sleep. I stayed at home a few more days until I was well again, and then I returned to Jerusalem without the notebooks.

On the morning of my departure, my mother made me a "sustaining" breakfast—that's what she called it. "Breakfast is the most important meal of the day," she would say. Another thing that Dr. Netzach put into her head, but there was something to it. It was lovely to eat salad, an omelet, white cheese (she made it herself), and bread (also her own) with butter and jam (home-made). My father had left for work and Michael was at school, so it was just the two of us. When I finished eating, we had coffee and ate a slice of pastry left over from the weekend. Mommy had prepared a few boxes with food for me to take to Jerusalem.

"Look after yourself," she said.

"I will," I promised.

I returned to Jerusalem; we had not talked about her memoir. Not a word. Nor did I mention that I'd left the notebooks in the room. I had put them on my bed so she would see them when she came in. I was afraid. It seemed that she did not know how to discuss them either. Neither of us was able to do anything about the silence that had settled between us, a new silence, unlike that of the bunker, but related to it and one that would continue many years.

I took up my student life at the Faculty of Natural Sciences again. I managed to cope with the work got quite good results, but I decided to stop at the end of my first year. Much as I loved biology, I did not want to become a researcher. What I loved about nature was nothing to do with science. A war broke out that fall and disrupted the academic year, and in the general mess I managed at the last moment, and despite of having no training, to get accepted at the Academy of Dance and Movement. My parents, I think, were somewhat disappointed with this decision, but they didn't say anything and only asked: "So you will be a dance teacher?" I was not planning to be a teacher at all—all I wanted was to dance, overcome gravity, fly.

Though the academy was exhausting, there was something fascinating and addictive about the physical effort, in the sheer movement, the ability to master space. It put me in mind of the kind of effort you had to make on desert hikes, the grueling trails in the Eilat mountains. In the same way that the steep climbs and descents had challenged my body and balance, I now enjoyed the labor dance demanded, to feel the life pounding under my skin, the strength and flexibility of my muscles.

I studied dance for three years, years of immense exhaustion and joy which took me to the limit, years of enormous discipline, of utter awareness and unrestrained embodiedness, of tempestuous intimacy and injury. Dance took me upwards, away from the ground which was always there, mysterious and heavy. I loved arriving at the academy in the mornings, its modern, well-balanced architecture. I loved the white, rising presence of the nearby Terra Sancta building. I preferred those places to the ever-developing campus on Mount Scopus, a windswept and dusty construction site in those years.

My mother's notebooks sank like stones into deep water, along with the hope of ever talking about them, talking about the writing and what it meant. When I returned home for weekends, my mom never mentioned or even hinted at anything, never demanded a response. I don't know whether I should be grateful or not. Had she said something or asked me, things might have opened up. But I know that it was me who should have said something, told her what I thought about her memoir. Hadn't she written this for us, for me and Michael? I wondered whether Michael had read the notebooks, and whether they had talked about them together. But Mom and I observed a silence. There are things which, if not mentioned at the right point in time, cannot be said later. Words turn into stones. One may write, instead of talking, but it doesn't repair a lack of speech. There's something sad about it, a sadness that doesn't go away. And that's what happened to us.

During those years it our mother seemed to continue to recover. The joy she had shown in Eilat, and her subtle humor, did not subside. The meals she cooked were wonderful. She experimented with new recipes, and surprising flavors appeared on the table. In the evenings, when we sat together, she was again knitting colorful sweaters. On spring weekends we would sometimes go for a picnic. They had their own special taste, over and above the food itself. In nature, all of us together, we were a happy family. There was a sense of freedom when we got away from home. After eating, we would lounge on the blankets and read the books and papers we'd brought with is. We'd indulge in our joint amusement: reading the lonely hearts advertisements. There was something about the occasionally desperate loneliness of the people in the adverts that held us together by the subtlest threads of happiness. Not all happy families are alike.

My time at the academy drew to a close. I had no plans to look for work or to settle down. I had no plans at all other than to travel, move to even more distant places. Michael was also finding his own ways to gain distance. We both detached ourselves. We were not particularly close at that time. I planned an open-ended trip. To get the money together for it, I worked as a guide at the Eilat field school again. They paid quite well, and I liked the job, and Eilat, of course, was remote. I worked a lot. I guided school classes during the week and amateur hikers at the weekends. I hardly visited home, and when spring approached, I left.

It was my first trip abroad, the first time I had left Israel. A bird station in the south of France was the first stop I had arranged. I did what I had learned to do in Eilat—and a thousand windows opened. I grew used to drinking my morning coffee in a soup bowl while dipping my croissant; to having wine with dinner (water was for the ducks, they explained); eating totally unfamiliar cheeses, whose sharp taste made me forget the sourness of yoghurt and the blandness of Tsfatit cheese.

At the station there were some good-looking, men who had not been in the army and fought in wars. At the weekends we'd go out to watch birds, pitch a tent on an empty beach, and pop to the nearest village for breakfast. A bigger distance than this I could not imagine. I sent photographs home, and my mom and dad didn't recognize me. I let my hair grow long and tied it up with a colorful scarf. My face filled out, I grew rounder, but at the same time lighter and lighter. I didn't stop dancing. When my contract at the bird station came to an end, I continued the same way. I went from one place to another, taking all kinds of jobs on the way. I met people, got to know new places, and then left again. On occasions, I travelled with another person. Some loved me generously, while others broke my heart. I'd move on again, putting more distance between myself and the notebooks, the black mass, the bunker.

I stopped in Paris. At first with Philippe, whom I had met at the bird station. He returned to the city and his studies, and he lived in a servant's room on the seventh floor of a rather grand building on the Place Boucicault near

Sèvres-Babylone metro station. A grubby service elevator took us as far up as the fifth floor, and then we climbed two flights of stairs.

The room was at the end of a corridor, and it contained a large mattress, which lay on the bare concrete floor, a desk, and a chair. A narrow window, which could only be reached if you stood on the mattress, opened westward. From this window we witnessed glorious sunsets over the roof of the impressive Art Deco building of the Le Bon Marché department store. On the other side of the square stood Hotel Lutetia, the first luxury hotel I'd ever seen. A uniformed doorman stood by the heavy revolving door. Every so often a Jaguar, Bentley, or Rolls Royce drove up, dropping off well-dressed passengers who entered the lobby with the quiet confidence of the rich. Philippe told me that famous artists had stayed there at the beginning of the century— people like Pablo Picasso, Charles de Gaulle, and Josephine Baker. James Joyce wrote part of *Ulysses* at the hotel. Hemingway stayed there too, and I remembered *The Sun Also Rises* and the dilapidated café its depressed protagonist frequented. During the occupation the building had served as Nazi headquarters, and later it was put to use as temporary accommodation for the refugees who had flooded the city after the war. A kind of short-term luxury residence for the survivors who returned from the camps. Distance, at one blow, shrank.

I left Philippe and the window with its red sunsets on the sky's screen, but I stayed in the Paris. I stayed for many years. I wasn't just the distance I liked, but life as a stranger, an outsider, someone who doesn't belong. It was a mode of existence that suited me. But I didn't cut all ties or burn all my bridges. There are piles of letters that I received from my parents and friends. Once a year, during the summer vacation, I visited home and met up with everyone. At first I returned on my own, and later I was joined by Dan, an Israeli I got to know in Paris; and then our two children joined us—two little French kids. And there were many visits from Israel too. In my small apartment I hosted friends, and Michael came to stay a few times. He had changed, my little brother, I felt. I remembered him as quiet and shy; now he was a real Don Juan who brought a different girlfriend with him on each visit.

My parents visited several times too, and my mother came on her own once. I was amazed to see how confident she was in a foreign country, without knowing the language, curious and happy. Maybe this was the kind of life she had dreamed about when she was a young girl. I took a few days off work and we spent quite a bit of time together. We sat in the Tuileries and had hot cocoa, "to remember the cocoa on the promenade," I said, and she smiled. We sat on the metal chairs at the round pool in the Luxembourg Gardens, watching the wooden sail boats on the water; we had lunch in small market restaurants on the Rue Mouffetard. We visited some museums too: my mother loved the Impressionists most of all. We even made a day trip to Giverny, Monet's house and garden, where he painted his wonderful water lilies.

We were surrounded by masses of tourists speaking a jumble of languages. There, in that Tower of Babel, we could have talked in our own language about what we needed to talk about. And yet, we didn't. Maybe the distance had already grown too great, or maybe neither of us dared to begin, or both of us feared to use the wrong words. Or, perhaps, we chose to keep the magic of our time, just the two of us, in Paris intact, rather than spoil it with that black lumpy mass. About a week later I accompanied my mother to the station where she took the night train to London. She continued her trip to London! Alone! Without my father being with her all the time. Even now I find it hard to believe, but she did it. She traveled in Europe on her own. When the train moved away I saw her waving a handkerchief from the window, and then the train left the station and vanished. I was alone on the platform, alone in the world once more, abandoned, sinking, and disappearing; the monster had raised its head again, as if nothing had changed. My fear remained, across all the distance.

Dan, the kids, and I returned to Israel after some years. We didn't want our children to grow up in France. But the transition was difficult for all of us. The children at school; Dan at his new office; and I had to get used to things too. Everything had changed. The open landscape had filled up with buildings and new neighborhoods, and the Galilee was now strewn with villages consisting of monotonously designed white houses with red roofs. Something in the general mood had become harsher, even the language had changed and included some jarring, unfamiliar expressions.

My parents helped a lot with the children. They were wonderful grandparents, present and warm. We didn't live far from them and saw them all the time. My mother hosted Friday evening meals, and on Saturdays we went on joint outings. The family picnics were reinstated. Michael would come from Tel Aviv, bringing his girlfriend, and we spent the time together in a nature which had changed too. We were no longer alone, and it often took time to find a quiet spot, the kind of nature we liked. One might have assumed there was no more point in mentioning the notebooks, that the whole business with that black lump had evaporated or dwindled of its own accord. But that's not how it was.

Something was stirring at home. My parents were following events anxiously: What would happen with Mikhail Gorbachev's reforms and glasnost? Then things started to come down like dominoes. It couldn't be stopped. They read the papers, watched TV, and my father scanned shortwave radio for more news. There was Lech Walesa and Solidarity in Poland; Hungary was changing into a democratic republic; and then Berlin wall fell. People did not know what to do with themselves for sheer joy. And with careful steps, my parents' republic joined in too and liberated itself: Dubcek returned. I saw how happy they were. They even started speaking some Slovakian, mentioning the names of places, people, and more places. I gradually understood they were thinking of a visit there. Soon it would be possible, and they'd be able to go to their town, Šurany. They wanted to see their homes again, finally close that circle, finish that chapter.

Once they'd made up their minds, they couldn't stop talking about it. My father sat poring over the map and sketched an itinerary. He worked on where they could stay overnight, sites to visit when in Prague, and, of course, how to get to Šurany. I wasn't sure what to think about their plans. I wondered whether everything would be easier when they got back to Israel. They could take photographs and bring them home, pictures of their old homes and streets—and their stories. Once there were pictures, it might well be better. Finally they would talk to us. The trip might release them from a longing that would not let them be. Yes, it might be a good sign. They felt strong enough to go encounter the past. But would they be able to take it? Would they bring it off without more heartbreak? And how would my own heart cope? I sensed danger, but did not know how serious it was.

Erika did not go with them. They asked her and Yehoshua to join them, but she decided against it. She may have understood immediately how impossible it was, that it would only cause pain. I've always felt she was better at protecting herself than my mother. And she was right. The trip was devastating, and afterwards my mother lost all hope. As soon as they stepped through the door, Michael and I saw that it had not been what they'd expected. They were somber and didn't say anything; they showed us no photographs, told us no stories. Something inside our mother, it was obvious, had been crushed. It was the beginning of a very difficult period, the end of which was even more difficult. Our mother went back to being withdrawn and silent. Her eyes were red as though she was weeping a lot. She grew weaker, she faded.

The change in her condition developed so fast that we couldn't help her. We didn't know how. I visited her every day and saw how she was growing more withdrawn, how pain was taking hold of her body. I wanted to do something, relieve her, say the right words. I just wanted to tell her about my work, the children, show her that I still had the yellow scarf she'd given me in Jerusalem, and how it went on warming my throat and neck during Galilean winters. But I couldn't. Fear suffocated me, fear that once I started to talk with Mommy, I would begin crying and never stop. So I sat there, at her side. I'd prepare her a drink, sometimes eat with her in silence, and sometimes, when she lay on the sofa, I'd read to her from a book I knew she loved: *Wild Animals I Have Known*, *My Family and Other Animals*, or *My Travels with Charley*. Sometimes she asked me to read her poems by Haim Gouri.

"Maybe Mommy should go back to the hospital in Haifa" I said to my father. "The treatment she got there was so good. That doctor really helped her."

That's how we learned that the doctor died some years earlier.

"He died?" I contracted in pain. "Why? How come? What happened?"

"It was his heart. They told me he'd had heart trouble."

"His heart? Who told you?"

"The secretary."

"So maybe . . ." Michael tried to come up with something.

"No. Impossible." Our father's voice was sad. "It won't work."

"Mommy had a special relationship with that doctor," Father explained, "he took her on as his only patient. Just her. He was the head of the department, but Mommy was his patient. Just her. It was a very special relationship."

"What do you mean?"

"Like I said: a very special relationship."

"And you . . ."

"I don't want to talk about it." He stopped me. "Don't say anything it: Mommy mustn't know. It will kill her. She cannot know."

I reflected on the good years she had had after her time in Haifa, how she had been able to pick up her life again. Mommy and her doctor? And how Daddy . . . I never could have imagined. And how everything had been destroyed by that trip of theirs . . . But no, she didn't know that her doctor had died—something would have happened when she'd found out.

While our mother was fading away with grief, our father was as strong as ever. Daddy was strong. For as long as I could remember, he'd been the strong link in the family. In his walls not one crack appeared. This was the first time I'd seen him cry. Just like that, in the presence of everyone, his whole body shaking. After we finished my mother's shiva, he showed me a letter she'd written two months after their return from Šurany. It was to her doctor. She'd never sent it—she knew he was no longer alive.

My dear Hermann,
I am writing to you because I want to tell you what has been happening to me recently. You are the only person to whom I can speak about these things, even though I know you have not been alive for many years now. Yes, years ago, when I still felt well and I thought I was healing, I wrote to you. When, some months later, I heard from the hospital, I thought I would die too, but I saved myself. I closed both the letter and what it announced. I knew that I could not cope with a reality in which you no longer existed, so I silenced it, the same way I knew how to silence other pains and continue with my re-found life. I really did find it.

It was like a dominoes effect, when things started moving in the Communist bloc. In our republic, the revolu-tion was beautiful, the velvet revolution, they called it. When Vaclav Havel was elected, Andy and I started thinking about a visit, and eventually the two of us decided it was time to close the circle and free ourselves from all that longing for where we grew up. We felt we could do it now. That's what we thought. There was such excitement. I wanted Erika to join us, the three of us to go together, but she wasn't sure and in the end she did not come. She had always been better at protecting herself. First we went to Prague and spent some days there. We were so excited to go there, because despite the traces of Communism, Prague, for us, had stayed, as ever, the capital of the republic and the city of Kafka. The most moving thing of all was the language—to be surrounded by the language, where everybody speaks it, not just a few immi-grants like here. But what happened after that simply wiped out our elation, and our pleasure turned into one big depres-sion. We haven't recovered from it.

Some months have passed now since we returned from that "journey to our roots." We returned sad and exhausted. I go on waking before sunrise, returning there, and a flood of tears I could not find then starts and goes on and on . . . I did not close any circle and I did not free myself from years of longing for that place, as I had hoped; and most of the burden I brought back home with me will stay with me till the end of my days. Now there is no more hope.

On our visit there we found a horror town. We wandered like sleepwalkers, like survivors after a flood, searching for signs of the life of that past. Everything was surreal, like out of some nightmare. I was scared to death of encountering the past, but I did not imagine that I would face nothingness. Scorched earth. Most difficult of all was discovering that our house was gone. I hear myself asking in a child's voice: "But where did our house go?" Images keep inundating me. I imagine the house being torn down, how the heavy machines attack the walls, clouds of dust covering everything as they collapse. I see people standing there, watching the destruction, as if it was a play, and I see how the rooms in which we lived the most important years of our lives as a family, are turning into dust. I see my home as it comes down and the same goes for the shop, the place into which my father put all his energy, enthusiasm, and love.

With these images, these images of my home's demolition, everything comes back. I look at the people who are watching the demolition and ask myself whether anyone there is thinking about the human beings who lived in that house once upon a time, struggled for their daily existence, always honest, people who never hurt a living creature, who were good through good times and bad. I remember the crowd, the whole town, in fact, lining the road as we were marched to the train station. We were a long procession of people condemned to death, and they were standing there, their faces indifferent. And some didn't even try to hide their satisfaction. Was there anyone who wiped away a tear or felt a tiny pang in that spot where there should have been a conscience? Just one even? We lived together, after all, as neighbors; they bought cloth in my father's shop, they respected him. He was an honest man. Maybe when they saw us walking towards our deaths, they were thinking about the riches that would land in their laps like ripe fruit. You just had to make sure to be quick and be among the first to break into the recently abandoned homes. Help yourself. Now they could be happy forever after.

But when the two of us walked through the town's streets it seemed like a ghost town. We did not see happy people there. We saw people stealing away along a wall, casting suspicious looks at us, or avoiding our eyes. The paint on the houses is peeling, the entrance gates are rusty, everything is neglected, and I know that the people in such a place cannot be happy. And for a moment I thought, "Maybe God does exist." A moment later I changed my mind . . . God may exist, but He doesn't care.

The gate to the yard in which our house once stood was open. We went in. Other people now live in the house opposite—our uncle Gézko's house—the house whose construction we followed as children, one stage after another, with such interest. A husband and wife, more or less our age, who live there now, noticed us and came down into the yard. They bent over backwards in their effort to create "a friendly atmosphere." "Please come upstairs with us for a moment. Please join us for a drink." But I could not let go of the question: How did they get the beautiful apartment Gézko's parents built for him, to live in when he got married? I found it difficult to feel anything, not even hatred—all I felt was endless exhaustion and nausea and a wish to get out of there . . .

Another blow was seeing the synagogue, the splendid building stands in ruins, like a wounded giant, bleeding. It's true that we, the young ones, never agreed with what was going on inside there, the religious establishment was alien to us, hostile. But the synagogue building itself meant a great deal to us. We were deeply attached to it. The most exciting meetings of our childhood took place by its entrance stairs. The entrance square, which had been so splendid in our childhood, is uncared-for now, the steps are crumbling—it's terrible, desolate.

I woke up from a nightmare this morning. In my dream, my sister and I entered the empty yard, just the two of us. It was silent, everything seemed to have frozen, no sign of a living thing. As we walked toward the entrance door, I saw a figure lying near the wall. At first, I couldn't tell if it was a person or a huge animal, but suddenly I realized that it was a huge shark devouring a sea lion. I felt that I'd seen this spectacle before, and I remembered that it had been on the television the day before.

Despite of our fear, we carried on towards the door, which was a few steps away—and that's when I saw the serial killer. Although he was following us, I believed we had enough time to reach the door, slip in, and close the latch. But once there, in the locked kitchen, I did not feel safe, which is why we went into the boys' room, to the left of the kitchen. I saw a key stuck in the door, and despite my shaking hands, I managed to turn it.

There were noises outside; I knew that the serial killer was at the entrance door; and I also knew that we were lost, that he would also find the boys' room. It was a matter of minutes, and nothing was preventing him from discovering us. My eyes fell on one of the windows. Maybe we could save ourselves that way. I tried to open the window's wing [sic], but it refused to budge. This seemed natural because the windows had been closed for many years . . . I made another, last effort, and the window gave. The yard was wholly empty, not a living soul in sight. So I climbed up the window sill and yelled at the top of my voice: "Segítség!" Help! I understood that nobody could hear me and that we would meet our end here, my sister and I . . . [sic]

I felt a light touch on my shoulder. My shouting had woken up Andy and he tried to reassure me. But I could not calm down. I felt my heart pounding through my entire body. I shook with fear, not only from the dream, but because there was also the possibility of another series of nightmares which would not let me be from now till the end of all my days . . .

I think about our visit there. There was no solace there. We were naïve. The visit opened wounds that had healed a little, and flooded me again with the most terrible grief of all, the memory of the home and the family I'd once had. The grief does not go away—on the contrary, it grows. Time dulls the memory of physical suffering, the humiliations and fears we endured, but the sorrow for our beloved family, the grief about them, about me, about us, only grows.

One day I will not be able to take anymore. That day approaches. I feel it. Only to you I can write this. I think about you a lot. Maybe we will meet again sometime soon. Marta.

Our mother could no longer live. Everything passes to me. What will become of me now? What will I do with it? I cried again. Ever since our mother's funeral, it doesn't stop. During the funeral I cried so much that I couldn't read out what I had written. The evening before I'd sat with a sheet of paper and the words had come unbidden. Something like that had never happened to me. Words, sentences, fragments of stories poured out; I didn't even think about what I was writing. It was all there, ready, all the words had just been waiting to come out. Suddenly there was so much I had to say about her, without fear. Words of love for a mother who was defeated by grief. Words about her love for us, Michael and me, infinite love, which keeps going round and round, inside us, around us. I began to weep when I stood before her coffin, ready to read. I felt a comforting hand on my shoulder and knew it was Michael. He stood close by me, but it didn't help.

"Her Hungarian friends called her 'Martushkam,'" I began . . .